KIMBERLY SULLIVAN

Dark Blue Waves

First paperback edition May 2022

Book design by Maxtudio

ISBN 978-1-7377293-4-1 (paperback)
ISBN 978-1-7377293-5-8 Digital Edition (Kindle)
ISBN 978-1-7377293-6-5 Digital Edition (ePub)

www.kimberlysullivanauthor.com

To Alessandro and Nicolò

*For accompanying me on that long-ago Jane Austen walking tour
in Bath that sparked my imagination to write this story.
Thank goodness you were too little to protest ...*

Also by Kimberly Sullivan

Three Coins

Chapter 1

Janet pressed her forehead against the cool glass of the train window. The sun shimmered on the River Avon, creating a glimmering ribbon snaking lazily between lush green fields. In the distance, fairytale grey spires stood their guard like sentinels up a gentle hill.

The weather forecasts had predicted rain. This morning, she'd repeated to herself that the skies would most probably be grey, her new city blanketed by thick sheets of unceasing rain.

And yet, blazing sun and blue skies welcomed her.

"We're here. Why we couldn't have rested first and taken a later train is still beyond me." The grating voice beside her shook Janet out of her reveries.

Malcolm.

So excited to have been allowed this semester abroad, she hadn't even fought her father's insistence that dreadful Malcolm accompany her. Malcolm, the son her father never had, was ostensibly sent to London to meet with partners on a recent project he and her father had taken on. She'd kept her thoughts to herself when her father insisted his assistant travel with her. Little did her father know, she would have accepted

Jack the Ripper himself as her chaperone if it would get her to Bath.

"Yes," Janet fought to keep agitation from creeping into her voice. "We're here. Let's be the first out."

Jumping up, she scooped up her bags before fussy Malcolm could insist. With a sense of freedom, she leaped onto the platform. Tomorrow Malcolm would be gone, and she'd remain alone in Bath. Eight glorious months.

Her first exhilarating moments were cut short as Malcolm huffed up beside her. "Janet, don't race off like that again."

Janet bit her tongue. Better to be quiet. In a little more than twenty-four hours, Malcolm would be safely dispatched on the train to London, followed by a long flight back to Boston.

Janet attempted a smile that only Malcolm, so well informed about architecture and so ignorant of the human heart, could ever interpret as sincere. "My enthusiasm got the better of me. It won't happen again." She gazed beyond his shoulders at the bustle around her. "Let's find our hotel."

"Let me help you."

He made a strange grimace Janet felt certain was intended as a smile. She thanked him sweetly, passing her bag to shoulders far less sturdy than her own.

What had her father been thinking with his heir apparent? Yes, Malcolm was a wildly talented young architect and an extraordinary sycophant, but how could her father imagine she could ever be attracted to him? Then again, her father was simply used to getting what he wanted. If she wasn't allowed to choose her own profession, why should she select her own spouse?

As they made their way down the broad Manvers Street, her heart soared. For years, she'd longed to visit this city, had dreamt of this very moment. Okay, none of her daydreams factored in Malcolm lugging her suitcases behind her like a hired man-servant. Still, she could hardly believe her good luck. A whole summer, followed by a full fall semester taking part in a seminar on Jane Austen, in Austen's very own Bath.

Of course, she'd only managed to sway her father by agreeing to also take part in an internship at the architectural firm of one of his former colleagues. Once again, she'd embark on the delicate balancing act: her passion for English literature tempered by the architecture studies he insisted upon.

She wondered—if she married the architectural Wunderkind, could she give up her architectural degree and pursue her doctorate in English literature? Probably not. With her luck, she'd still be forced to become an architect, married to the dullest man alive to boot. *Eight months of freedom*, she repeated like a mantra.

They paused at the eighteenth-century Pulteney Bridge, watching the Avon flow underneath its arches. "Palladian," she whispered.

They continued, veering through a series of narrow streets, until Malcolm stopped short in front of a small guesthouse.

"Here we are."

Janet looked around her, eager to check in and slip back out to explore the town, preferably ditching Malcolm for a few hours of blessed solitude.

A young woman greeted them from a desk in an exquisitely furnished nineteenth-century drawing room.

"Welcome to Bath. You must be Ms. Roberts and Mr. Nowak. We've been expecting you. Please, follow me. I'll show you to your rooms."

Rooms, at least. With her father, you could never tell. He probably imagined the romantic setting bringing Janet and Malcolm together.

"Mr. Roberts stipulated you'd want adjoining rooms." The woman opened the first door.

Janet surveyed her room, with its soaring ceilings, plush carpets, fireplace, and canopied bed. Inviting pillows surrounded a reading nook nestled against large windows framed by thick velvet drapes. It was perfect. She could even forgive her father his transparent romantic intentions.

"This is for Ms. Roberts. Mr. Nowak, if you'll follow me, your room is through there."

Malcolm glanced at Janet. To his credit, a faint blush passed over his cheeks before he ducked into his room.

Janet sank into the thick, padded benches of the window nook, gazing down at the Georgian architecture, and the world passing by. If only she had an inkwell and some writing paper, she could transform herself into the heroine of one of her beloved Jane Austen novels, observing the world and writing letters about it in the witty manner all Austen heroines seemed to possess.

As she watched the tourists snapping photos and the mothers leading their children through the crowds, she heard Malcolm cough. He stood at the adjoining door, his blush a deep scarlet.

"Uh ... Janet. I want to apologize and to let you know that your father made the reservation. I would never have presumed to request adjoining rooms. I didn't want you to think this was my doing."

"It's okay. I know my father's handiwork when I see it. Anyway, I think we can lock this adjoining door and knock from the hall."

"Of course, of course," stammered Malcolm, relief washing over his face as he stepped back. "That was my intention all along."

Janet locked the door, unpacked a few items and brushed her teeth. The next day she'd move into the student housing in the late eighteenth-century Crescent itself. Her internship at

Mr. Perry's architectural firm would be only a short walk away at The Circus.

She slipped a brochure out from her purse before going to knock on Malcolm's door. He opened it immediately. Had he been waiting behind his door, ready to pounce as soon as she knocked? Or perhaps he was listening furtively for her footsteps in case she tried to sneak away?

He motioned her in. His room was handsome, too, with masculine fabrics and solid leather furniture. Hunting scenes graced the walls. She knew from her years working with her father's studio that this was the favored decorating scheme for the offices or libraries of all their nouveau riche clients.

Malcolm observed her, and his face broke into a smile, a real one this time. "I know. It looks like the offices we did recently, doesn't it? So many of our clients think leather furniture and paintings of red-coat-clad fox hunters provide the veneer of inherited wealth."

"Ah, so you see the ridiculous side to our work as well. You're always so serious, I never can tell." She sat down in one of the leather chairs.

"I'm sorry to give that impression. You know how much my work means to me. But I'm not ashamed to admit to my working-class background. If you ever catch me trying to hide that with my collection of hunting prints and polo mallets, feel free to give me a good pounding with one of my collectibles."

Janet smiled despite herself. "I will." She walked to the window, looking briefly at the crowds milling below before turning back. "Malcolm, you know how long I've been dying to come here. I want to join a Jane Austen walking tour. It will bore you. Why don't I go alone and we can meet up in three hours?"

If threats of a Jane Austen tour weren't a surefire way to send a man packing, Janet didn't know what was.

"A Jane Austen walking tour? I had no idea. That's brilliant!"

Had she imagined the pleading tone in his voice? Had he misunderstood something? Malcolm, worryingly pale from days holed away in his office running CAD, was a closet Austen fan? Or was he so desperate to please her father that he was willing to do anything to stick by her side?

"Um ... " She struggled. "Are you sure? Touring Bath for Jane Austen sites? You won't be bored?"

"Not at all. Let me grab my camera and backpack. I'll join you in the lobby."

Janet went downstairs, stunned. How had she managed to fumble this one?

They walked the short distance to the Bath Abbey Church Yards and the Roman baths, the same buildings she'd seen depicted countless times in BBC adaptations. They bought their tickets and joined a small group gathering on the square.

Not surprisingly, the group consisted entirely of eager women. Their guide was an energetic, elderly lady with wisps of white hair escaping her top knot. Belying her age, the guide kept up a frenetic pace in her sturdy walking shoes.

She concentrated on the town's Golden Age and glittering Bath society, which had already begun to fade by the time of Jane Austen's arrival during her first Bath sojourn in 1801. She described Austen's love-hate relationship with Bath and pointed out scenes from her two Bath novels, *Northanger Abbey* and *Persuasion*.

They visited the Pump Room, where nineteenth-century new arrivals registered. Here they would sign the registry announcing their arrival to town, then return almost daily to take the waters and to see and be seen. They walked through the so-called common parts of town, which looked quite impressive by modern standards, and the best addresses the town had to offer in Jane Austen's time. In the Assembly Hall, they saw where the dastardly William Elliott tried to come between Anne and Captain Wentworth.

"Those who've read *Persuasion* will recognize this gravel path," said the guide, as they walked along it on their way to The Circus and The Crescent, the beautiful structure Janet would soon call home.

Malcolm asked the guide insightful questions about Jane Austen and her references to Bath, questions that made Janet realize he'd actually read the novels and hadn't simply faked his enthusiasm. Perhaps she'd been too hard on him. The tour ended at The Crescent, where she and Malcolm stayed. Sitting on the vast green lawn, he showed her his photos.

"Can you believe I'm going to live here?" Janet's voice sounded breathy to her own ears as she admired the building before her, bathed in a honey light. "Apparently some wealthy Oxford professor, the last member of an old, noble family, willed his property to this study program."

"I hope you'll still want to come back to Boston after your time here." He squinted into the bright sunlight.

"With my dad, do you think I have a choice? So, what's up with this hidden Austen knowledge? You had our guide wrapped around your finger, especially when you started feeding her all the Georgian architectural background. You surprised me."

"Favorably, I hope."

In the past five years he'd been working with her father, Janet swore she'd seen him smile once or twice. He was usually so stuffy, nodding seriously at everything her father said, racing off at the drop of a hat to do his bidding. Anticipating his every need.

"I know your father pushing me on you hasn't helped. But I'd like it if we could start over, become friends. I think we have a lot in common—like books."

"I didn't know you liked English literature."

"I do. I've always loved to read, even if no one else in my family did. My father was a fisherman, like all our neighbors in Gloucester. We didn't have much, but late at night I always had my nose in a book, whatever I could get at the public library. Hawthorne, Hardy, Melville, Austen—I devoured it all."

He looked up at The Crescent, the sunlight glinting on copper highlights in his thick hair. He had good features, if only he'd lose that pallor of someone who lives by the light of his computer. When he smiled, he even looked handsome.

"I love Austen's books, and I'm not saying that to impress you. I know what it is to be passionate about something, even if no one else understands. Like my love of architecture. My father thought I was insane. But I was determined. I begged a local architect to take me on as an unpaid intern." He was silent for a few moments. "At first I was a charity case, but the architect quickly discovered I had potential, and he nurtured it. He helped get me into Carnegie Mellon on scholarship, and he introduced me to your father."

"I remember when you started. Dad always talked about your promise."

Malcolm's whole face lit up. "Your father changed my life. He believed in me. Maybe he saw something of himself in me, understood what it was like to pull himself up by his bootstraps. I admit, I never cared if others considered me dull. Until I met you. I'm not trying to encourage your father's attempts to set us up." He leaned back, propping himself by his elbows. "I'm only sorry we might've gotten off on the wrong foot. I'd like to be friends."

Janet looked up at The Crescent. Her dislike of Malcolm—if she were honest, her jealousy—had been a constant over the years. She spoke slowly at first. "I'd like that, too. I can be very critical with my father, but I know he and I are alike in many ways. I definitely inherited his stubbornness. When he started pushing you on me, my first reaction was to reject you out of hand. Even as a friend. I'm sorry."

Malcolm turned to her, happiness so evident in his eyes that it caused her pangs of guilt.

"Let's start over. You can send me news about your Austen studies." The sun shone down on the pensive lines of his face, adding a golden glow to his pallor. "Reading Austen was a lot like my afternoons in the architect's office. When I first started there, I thought it was a parallel universe. When I think back, I realize Austen's books first got me thinking about reaching beyond my world."

"So you're telling me your stellar career is all thanks to Jane. As an Austen fan, you know that *Pride and Prejudice* was originally entitled *First Impressions*. I see my first impressions were entirely wrong. My silly prejudices weren't even against you, but against my father." She took a last look at The Crescent. "What do you say to a walk around Bath?"

"Sure. I should warn you, your father reserved some romantic, candlelit restaurant. Dinner's on him."

"I'd be honored to dine with you on my first evening here." She smiled. "Especially if Dad's paying."

They made their way back to The Circus, before following the map through the older streets of town. Janet had studied her guidebook so many times that the street names—Queen, Brock, Gay—sounded like old friends. They headed over to Milsom to see the grand houses.

Janet enjoyed their discussion. When Malcolm saw a building he particularly liked, he sat down on a bench and pulled a sketchpad and pencils out of his backpack. She sat beside him and pulled her own from her bag.

"Uh, oh. You, too?"

"Occupational hazard."

They sketched for a while in silence.

"May I see some of your sketches?"

Janet blushed as she handed the pad over. "I've seen so much of your work. I'm nowhere near as good as you are."

Malcolm studied the drawings. She'd copied her favorites from numerous trips with her father into this notebook.

"These are really good." Malcolm flipped through the pages. "You have a lot of talent. You only need to decide where to apply it."

She wasn't sure what he meant. As they started down the hill, the comment nagged at her.

Her father often said she lacked ambition, that hers was the classic problem of someone brought up having too much, someone who didn't feel she had to earn her place in the world. Janet knew that was one of the reasons her father treated Malcolm like the son he'd never had. He recognized Malcolm's talent and raw ambition, his hunger to make it in his profession. The very characteristics his daughter so sorely lacked, and which kept him from loving her as much as a father should. He'd simply transferred that love to someone he felt was more deserving. It was easier to laugh it off when Malcolm was the simple, sycophantic buffoon. A mere Mister Collins ingratiating himself with Lady Catherine DeBourgh.

But Malcolm probably *was* more deserving of her father's affection than she. He was more talented, and he was certain about what he wanted out of life. Where did that leave her? Was she really cut out for the academic career she longed for? Her English advisor always told her she had potential, but was that enough?

Bath was supposed to resolve her confusion, not leave her more muddled than before.

She rubbed her throbbing temples. The familiar signs of a headache. "I'm tired. Do you mind if I go rest before dinner?"

"Of course not. I'll accompany you."

In her room, Janet sat at the window seat, watching the people wandering the narrow streets. She read a few pages of her book before giving in to her exhaustion and crawling into bed. After setting the alarm, she drifted off to a troubled sleep.

A piano played in the distance. Mozart. *Voi che sapete*. Janet struggled to breathe. Something constricted her chest and waist, yet her feet still carried her forward at a brisk pace, through candle-filled hallways she didn't recognize. Full-length portraits lined the walls. Thick velvet brushed against her legs as she walked.

An inexplicable sense of relief washed over her when she reached a room. Her hand clasped the doorknob and turned. She slipped inside, closing the door behind her.

Darkness enveloped her. Her heartbeat slowed as she looked up to something familiar. Individual, disjointed images captured her gaze. A billowing pink cloth. An alabaster face, slightly turned. Arms reaching up to the sky. A splattering of green. These flashes seemed to calm her, but she struggled in vain to see the single parts in their entirety.

A movement under the soothing images caught her attention. A chair was positioned before a fireplace. Someone stood. A man, his back toward her. He was tall, dressed in fine, old-fashioned clothes. There was something so familiar about him. Now he was turning and taking long strides across the room to where she stood. Her heart beat faster.

Janet tried in vain to make out his features but quickly gave up. It was as if she were glimpsing him through a fog. She longed to retreat, but her feet remained firmly rooted in place as his confident gait narrowed the distance between them.

Although he was mere inches from her, she could still not distinguish the features of his face. Only the depths of his blue eyes were distinct. As she gazed into them, she felt an unfamiliar fluttering in her stomach. The man slipped a book into her hand. She opened to see shadow words scrawled in thick, black ink. Squinting did not help bring them into focus. He began to speak. She watched his lips move. She heard his voice as if she were under water, not comprehending the individual words. Oddly soothing, but indecipherable.

He reached up and stroked her face before enveloping her in an embrace. Who was this stranger who was overly familiar with her? She knew she should scream and flee, but her thoughts did not control her body. Her legs made no attempt to move from this unknown man. Inexplicably, she felt safe in his arms, with his heart beating solidly beside hers. Now he was pulling back, stroking her hair, searching her face.

Janet still only saw the shadow version of him, soft and out of focus. She gave up trying to reconstruct his face. His gaze mesmerized her. It seemed so familiar, made her knees feel weak. Those piercing blue eyes kept coming closer and closer to her own face until firm lips brushed against her own. A warmth spread throughout her body. High-pitched yells rang out. Her knees buckled.

A burst of pain exploded at her temple, and she woke with a panicked start. Her eyes flickered around the room in confusion. Deep breaths.

It was nothing. Her hotel room in Bath. A dream. Only a dream.

As her heartbeat slowed and her breathing calmed, she realized it was most likely the jet lag or all the silly talk of romantic literature. Her head throbbed. Willing the pain to stop, she closed her eyes and drifted back to sleep.

Chapter 2

Later that evening, Malcolm knocked on Janet's door. She picked up her purse and met him in the hallway.

"You look beautiful."

She appraised his trim suit and the wash of color on his previously pale face. "You look pretty good yourself. You're tanned. It suits you."

He offered her his arm and they made their way to dinner.

The restaurant was indeed romantic, and ridiculously expensive. She could see the guilt etched all over Malcolm's face as he examined the menu. "Your father certainly went all out tonight."

"Let's take it as a generous welcome to Bath. I don't want to see that pained look on your face for the rest of dinner."

Malcolm smiled sheepishly.

After ordering, they discussed first impressions of Bath until Malcolm abruptly changed topics. "I know you may not feel comfortable talking to me. You know how close I am to your father. But I wonder if you'd prefer a career in academia to working in the firm."

Janet observed the eager glint in his eyes. Her first reaction was to evade the question, but she also longed to speak with someone who could understand. Until that afternoon, she would never have imagined that person to be Malcolm.

"I wish I knew. I'm so confused." She swirled the wine in her glass, trying to organize her thoughts. "I'm hoping this semester will help me think things through. But even here, there are strings attached. Part of the deal to come here was the internship in Mr. Perry's office."

"I know. I tried to talk him out of that."

"Since when is it your job to defend me to my father?" she snapped. "You're taking the role of heir apparent quite seriously."

Malcolm reeled as if he'd been slapped. He seemed to weigh his words carefully before responding. "You have every right to be angry. That came out wrong. Look, I always knew what I wanted to do after that Gloucester architect's studio, but you have more options. I know you could be a wonderful architect, too. But only you can decide if you have the passion for it."

His gentle eyes were filled with concern. Their meals arrived, and they began to eat in silence.

When Janet spoke, her voice was calm and measured. "Look, I know I have to decide. I do love many aspects of architecture. I grew up with it. My dad dragging me around with him on his projects. He didn't want me to miss out on the culture and contacts he lacked as a young architect. You know we used to live in France? Then I studied for a year in Italy before I started college. He wanted me to have a broad experience before I began my studies, to move easily among his clients, my future clients." She twisted a lock of hair. "Unfortunately, in all these careful calculations, he never considered what I might enjoy."

"Are you sure? Your father talks about you all the time. He's so proud of you."

"I do admire my father for what he achieved, but at what cost? I'm not sure we've ever had a heartfelt conversation about anything not involving architecture. I don't think he takes any particular interest in me as a person." She concentrated hard on her plate, not trusting herself to meet Malcolm's eyes. Not wanting to see pity there.

A waiter arrived to fill their water glasses. A welcome interruption. When he moved to the next table, she continued.

"It's never been easy between us. I know he took things hard." She adjusted her watch, still not daring to meet Malcolm's gaze. "When my mother died, he never comforted me or spoke to me about it. It was as if it had never happened, like she'd never even existed. He concentrated all his energies on his work. I was eleven." She breathed deeply through her nose, willing the tears not to well up. "So yes, it's true I haven't always had the best rapport with my father's profession. I wonder if a clean break might be better. Maybe it's time to decide my own path, make my own decisions."

"I'm sorry. I didn't want to open up old wounds." He fidgeted with his napkin. "I know this is forward, but I'm leaving tomorrow and I won't have another chance to say this otherwise." He reached for his wine glass, taking a big gulp. "I've liked you from the day I met you. I was flattered your father could see us together, even if I didn't dare hope so myself." He looked into the flickering candlelight before meeting her surprised eyes again. He swallowed hard. "If you could ever consider me in that way, I'd do everything to deserve you. I know you think I'm only obsessed with work, but I'd never let that get in the way of a relationship. I know what's important. I think we could work well together, but I would also support you if you wanted to do something else. We could complement one another. I'd seek out your advice on architecture, and be the first reader of your Jane Austen papers."

He lay his hand over hers as she sat in stunned silence.

Eventually she found her voice. "Malcolm, I hardly know what to say. I'm flattered, but I'm so confused about what I want right now. It doesn't make sense to add any romantic entanglements into the mix. I need some time alone to think and to gather my thoughts. I think that's one of the reasons I've been clinging to this time in Bath as a kind of lifeline." She fidgeted with her water glass with her free hand. "It's time I start acting like an adult, decide what I want out of life."

It seemed odd to say these words to Malcolm, the same man who was so odious to her up until a few hours ago. But oddly, as someone who was so close to her father, he was one of the few people in her life who could truly understand her predicament.

Malcolm smiled faintly, keeping his hand over hers as the candlelight flickered, casting shadows over their faces. "I told you I needed to say everything, otherwise I would have tortured myself on the flight home. You know how I feel. That won't change. I can be patient and see if you could eventually feel the same. If not, I would still value your friendship." He took a deep breath. "I know that your father has plans, but you can't force someone to love you. I wouldn't want anything on those terms. But I do hope you'll think about it."

"I will." She smiled. "I grew so used to disliking you that this has rather taken me by surprise."

He looked relieved. The waiter arrived and Malcolm withdrew his hand, indicating her plate. "I don't want to keep you from your dessert. Now I have to do everything to stay on your good side."

Later, they walked back to the hotel, climbing the stairs up to their rooms. On the landing, Malcolm gave her a gentle kiss on the cheek. "Goodnight, Janet. Tomorrow you'll start your new life, and I'm happy for you."

She wished him goodnight, closing the door behind her as confused thoughts swirled in her mind. Already on her first day, nothing was turning out as she'd imagined.

Chapter 3

The next morning, Janet and Malcolm walked to The Circus to meet Mr. Perry.

She noticed how striking Malcolm was in a light cashmere sweater over a crisply ironed shirt, and casual, but elegant shoes. Malcolm had always been invisible to her, a drab lackey of her father's. How had she never noticed his good taste in clothes or his elegant features before?

When they arrived, the receptionist showed them into a grand parlor. They were soon joined by a trim, energetic man wearing a tweed jacket. His grey curls were slightly disheveled; eyeglasses hung from a slim cord around his neck.

Malcolm rose. "Mr. Perry, what a pleasure to see you again."

"Malcolm, my boy. How are you?" He turned to Janet. "And what an honor to welcome Richard's daughter. How lovely to finally meet you in person. Your father has told me so much about you over the years."

"The pleasure's all mine, Mr. Perry. I've grown up hearing all about you and your time at college with my father. "

He motioned for Janet and Malcolm to be seated and settled himself into an ornate armchair. It was arranged that Janet would spend her first week getting settled into the program before beginning at Mr. Perry's studio. They spent a pleasant hour chatting with him before taking their leave.

Later that afternoon, they arrived at The Crescent and carefully checked the number against the registration material.

"This must be it." Janet rang the doorbell.

A stern, middle-aged woman opened the door, her impossibly black hair pulled into a severe bun. Her black wool dress looked out of place for the warm spring day.

Janet smiled reflexively at the rigid face before her. "Good afternoon. I'm Janet Roberts. This is my friend, Malcolm. He's settling me in. I'm here for the Austen seminar."

The woman nodded curtly and introduced herself as Miss Smith. She motioned them into the house. Despite the day's warmth, a fire burned in the parlor fireplace. The room was elaborately furnished in the style of grand homes of the early nineteenth century.

"Please follow me to your room." Miss Smith led them under an enormous crystal chandelier and up a dramatic mahogany staircase.

Janet's eyes grew large. How would she ever return to her dorms after this brief experience of opulent living? As they walked up two flights of steep steps, she observed all the full-length portraits of the generations of noblemen and noblewomen who once occupied this house.

"This'll be your room," said Miss Smith, with the bored air of someone reciting a prepared speech. "Your roommate is expected later today. The welcoming cocktail is downstairs at seven sharp. Punctuality will be carefully observed during your time here."

Not a suggestion, but a command.

"I'll allow you to unpack." Miss Smith shut the door behind her.

Frescoes brightened the room's ceilings. Another spectacular crystal chandelier reflected vivid colors on its multiple glass surfaces. Janet found herself wondering who climbed up to such vertiginous heights to dust the numerous shards of luminous crystal. She hoped the temporary residents weren't expected to do so.

A fireplace dominated one nook of the room, with an oil painting over the mantle. She stood before the painting, observing the details. The artist's hand skillfully captured Apollo and Daphne, when the love-struck god catches up to the beautiful nymph. Daphne's arms were raised to the sky. Her face turned slightly towards her pursuer, while her rose-colored garments billowed dramatically around her. The artist depicted the exact moment the first branches sprouted from Daphne's fingertips, capturing her transformation into a laurel tree.

Definitely Italian School. But who was the artist? Or was it a copy?

Janet squinted and noted the blur of colors and images. There was something oddly familiar about the painting, a strange sensation that she knew it already. Perhaps she'd seen this image in one of her art history classes. Still, she couldn't shake the peculiar feeling that washed over her as she studied the composition.

She turned away to concentrate on the room. Two single beds were on one side, while two small dressers and one wardrobe were positioned along the back wall. Two large windows—they had to be almost four meters tall—looked out onto the Crescent lawn, the same spot where she and Malcolm sat yesterday speaking after their Jane Austen tour.

She turned from the window to Malcolm. "I feel like Marie Antoinette. Can you believe this place?"

KIMBERLY SULLIVAN | 20

He smiled and glanced at his watch. "Why don't you claim a bed and unpack some of your things? I'll take a walk and be back in a half hour. You'll have time to see me off before your cocktail."

Janet set about unpacking her clothes, placing them in the drawers and in half of the wardrobe. *Wait until my Boston roommates get a load of this place.*

"Malcolm, take a picture of me here under the fireplace, with the painting in the background," she said when he returned to pick her up. "I'll never live this well again—might as well immortalize it."

Malcolm snapped the photo.

Thirty minutes later, Janet and Malcolm left the building and set off across the green expanse of The Crescent. They stopped at a tea shop on Milsom Street and sipped their tea from delicate china cups.

"I'll report to your father that you're well settled in. I'm afraid you'll never want to come back after this."

"It's true. I could definitely start getting used to this. When I start donning corsets and ribbons, you'll all have to worry. Let my father know I'm fine. I'll email him with updates."

"Will you email me, too?" asked Malcolm, his eyes soft.

"I've enjoyed our talks. To be honest, I resented my father's foisting you on me. It's been nice finally getting to know you after all the years I thought I already did. I'll keep in touch, especially now that I know what a closet Austen fan you are."

Malcolm paid the bill and they continued on to the Bath station. Pausing on the platform next to his wagon, he stroked her tenderly on the cheek. "Take care of yourself, Janet. I envy you your seminar in Bath. Take advantage of your time here, and do write me." With that, he climbed onboard and waved as the train pulled away from the station.

A little over twenty-four hours ago, Janet had eagerly anticipated Malcolm's departure. Now she was almost sorry to see him go. Could it be that her father wasn't completely wrong and she'd simply misjudged Malcolm all this time? The idea was too absurd to consider.

When the departing train disappeared around the bend, she retraced her steps back to The Crescent.

Chapter 4

Intent on heeding Miss Smith's advice about punctuality, she raced to her room. Items had been placed on the unclaimed bed and the other half of the wardrobe had been filled.

Eager to meet her new roommate and the others, Janet changed quickly, feeling like a *grande dame* as she walked down the ornate staircase in her simple dress and heels. How could people have once lived like this?

Portraits lined the staircase. Corpulent, ruddy-faced men in uniforms, women squeezed by their corsets into elegant, yet uncomfortable-looking gowns. Rich jewels dripped from their necks, their glittering stones captured by the artists' expert brushstrokes. Children stood frozen for eternity, looking like miniature adults. With their jarringly blasé expressions, they stared boldly out from the canvases. All these generations of long-deceased lords and ladies who had once called this elegant address home now appraised Janet as she made her way to the reception.

Janet paused, catching her breath before a full-length portrait of a slim, beautiful young lady wearing a white empire-waisted dress. The woman's golden-blonde hair coiled high on her head, delicate tendrils breaking free to frame her lovely face. Her large blue eyes were luminous, smiling at the viewer. Inviting him or her into her long-ago world. Long, elegant fingers clasped a dewy white rose. Behind her, in the distance, stood a grand manor—definitely Palladian.

A portrait of a young man hung beside the woman. Her husband? He was strikingly handsome, tall and well-built, with strong, chiseled features. Positioned in his study, surrounded by all the classic symbols of learnedness and virtue—books, instruments, a globe, a dog, a scale of justice—he looked assured, haughty even. But it was his gaze, that piercing blue stare, which kept her frozen in place. Why did he seem so familiar? A famous British statesman from a long-forgotten history class? She blinked several times, searching her memory in vain.

Music from a harpsichord wafted up from a distant room, disrupting her thoughts. Following the music, she passed through the library and the formal dining hall. She emerged into the drawing room, from which she immediately longed to flee.

Janet blushed as she looked down at the simple summer dress she'd mistaken for sophisticated. The two men present wore white tie and gloves. Women in floor-length evening gowns sipped wine. How had she missed the information in the orientation packet asking them to dress like invitees to a royal wedding? No name tags were required. Absolutely no one would fail to identify her as the hapless American colleague.

A gloved waiter proffered a silver tray. She gratefully accepted a glass of wine. As she sipped it and attempted to hide her discomfort, an older gentleman materialized at her side.

"Welcome. You must be Janet. What a pleasure to meet you in person after reading your charming essays. I'm Professor Williams."

Janet shook his hand. "A pleasure, Professor Williams. I've been so excited about this semester, but I had no idea we'd be living in such luxury."

"My dear, don't get too used to it. We try to make a grand impression at our opening cocktail, but from tomorrow on things are more relaxed. If you'll allow me, I would like to introduce you to your new roommate."

He led her across the room to an elegant woman with long, black hair and dark eyes. She wore an intricately beaded, blue sari.

"Amrita, may I introduce you to your new roommate, Janet? Amrita joins us from Oxford. Janet is our American student, here from Harvard, where I understand she's studying both English literature and architecture."

Janet shook Amrita's hand. "I'm excited to focus fully on literature these next months. Although in this stunning house, I'm sure architecture will never be far from my mind."

"I know. We're so lucky."

Professor Williams took his leave. A moment later, a spoon clinking against a wine glass captured everyone's attention. Professor Williams surveyed the students.

"Good evening, ladies and gentlemen. My name is Professor Williams, and it is my great pleasure to welcome you here this evening to Huntington House. For the next eight months, I hope you will consider us family. We will eat together, read together, study together, and take full advantage of our beautiful surroundings. Since we will be studying Miss Austen's nineteenth-century England, nothing gives me greater pleasure than teaching in this atmosphere, in Jane Austen's very own Bath."

There was a round of applause. When the room quieted, Professor Williams resumed.

"This house belonged to the Huntington family, prominent among the nobility from the seventeenth to the late nineteenth centuries. The family maintained several properties, but the crown jewel of their holdings is an extensive seventeenth-century estate, not far from here. We shall visit the palace and grounds later this week."

Janet and Amrita exchanged smiles.

"Huntington House was, if you can believe it, one of their more modest properties. Work on The Crescent began after completion of The Circus, in 1766. The Huntingtons were one of the first families to purchase a home here. This served as their town retreat when they came to Bath for the season, and to enjoy the curative waters."

Janet looked out the windows. The streetlamps were aglow.

"Since the Huntingtons were a prominent family in town, I like to think that they and Miss Austen may have crossed paths during her sojourns in Bath, although we have no written documentation of any such meetings. Still, I do always ask my students to carefully examine their rooms in case any love letters from Miss Austen to the dashing, young Lord Edward Huntington have been lying around unnoticed these past two hundred years. Hope springs eternal for Austen scholars."

Smiles broke out across the room.

"Nevertheless, with or without the discovery of illicit letters, this is the perfect environment in which to study Miss Austen's texts, particularly her two Bath novels."

Professor Williams walked over to the fireplace and indicated a portrait of a distinguished-looking older man.

"This house was generously left to our program ten years ago by the late Sir Charles Huntington. Lord Huntington, a fellow scholar of nineteenth-century English literature, was the last of the Huntington family line, and he generously arranged for this property to be made available to young scholars of Jane Austen. I would like to offer a toast to my dearly departed colleague. To Lord Huntington."

"To Lord Huntington," repeated the students, glasses raised.

"And to all of you participating in this Austen seminar," Professor Williams raised his glass once again. "To a successful semester at Huntington House."

Janet toasted alongside her classmates. Janet and Amrita spoke about their homes, their studies, and their love for literature. Amrita's father taught English literature at the university in Bombay before coming to England, where Amrita had been born. They returned each year to visit her extended family.

Amrita introduced Janet to Fiona, an Oxford classmate, and to James, a student from Vancouver.

The evening continued with wine and canapés, accompanied by music from the harpsichord and earnest conversation. Slowly, the new classmates began drifting off to their rooms in preparation for their first full day of seminar classes.

Chapter 5

Early the next morning, Janet and Amrita arrived at the formal dining room for breakfast. A few students were already present, and an impressive buffet had been set out on the sideboard. They served themselves and joined their new classmates. Janet took a seat next to James.

"I don't know about you," said James, "but I'm still on Canadian time. I woke up at four a.m., starving. It was all I could do to wait for breakfast."

"I slept like a log last night. Only hope jet lag doesn't catch up with me tonight." Janet buttered her toast, spreading the marmalade thickly. "James, how did you became so interested in Austen?"

"You mean, because I'm male. Didn't it ever occur to you it's a great way to meet women?" He winked.

"Good point. " She sipped her coffee. "I didn't mean to pry. I'm interested in learning everyone's motivations. My father keeps trying to convince me to pursue architecture and not literature."

"You do have to love literature to make a career out of it. The job market for lit majors is pretty bleak. Maybe your father's only trying to protect you. Mine's a mechanical engineer, so I threw him for a loop hating math and wanting to study literature. Jane Austen probably would have done him in. At least my thesis is on Byron. It took a while, but now he's used to it. Kind of." James looked at his watch. "We'd better go. Don't want to be late on our first day."

The chairs in the adjoining lecture hall had information packets on top of them. Janet looked through the curricula and the reading lists, noting their first book for discussion would be *Northanger Abbey*.

Sessions were scheduled on the Gothic novels that influenced *Northanger Abbey*. A scholar would teach a guest lecture on Anne Radcliffe later that week and Janet saw that the *Mysteries of Udolpho* should be completed by that date. Copies were on loan in the center's library. Janet imagined that many of her colleagues would be rereading Ms. Radcliffe's work, but this would be her first time. On so many occasions, she'd wanted to read the book that played so prominently into *Northanger Abbey*, and yet she'd never taken the time to tackle its more than six hundred pages.

If the grey storm clouds shrouding Bath were chased away before the afternoon, she might even have the chance to start her reading out on The Crescent lawn. Perhaps in the same spot where Catherine Morland dipped into that most beloved of Gothic novels two hundred years earlier, filling her head with such troublesome ideas of villains, murder, and subterfuge.

As the students read over the course schedule, Professor Williams entered the room. "Good morning."

Two classmates entered late, the great door creaking as they attempted to close it quietly. The angry look Professor Williams shot them made his views on tardiness clear to everyone.

"I've taught this seminar once a year for the past fifteen years. At first, I taught alongside my dear friend and colleague Lord Huntington. He was always a staunch supporter of this seminar, but when he died, he surprised us all by leaving Huntington House to this program in his will, hoping it could stimulate 'countless future generations of Austen scholars in dedicating their studies to this golden era of English letters.'"

He strode around the room as he spoke. Janet felt both nervous and elated to be seated in the room. One of the thirty students accepted into this program each year. Ever since the acceptance letter arrived, she'd been dreaming about this day, boring her friends to tears by talking of little else.

"I'm certainly not an unbiased observer, but throughout my long academic career, I've found this annual seminar one of the most rewarding opportunities for exchanges among like-minded individuals. I don't know if it is due to the generous opportunity to live within the Georgian splendor of Huntington House, or to be far removed from quotidian concerns, or simply to gather so many eager, young minds under one roof, but each year I am stimulated by the environment, the sense of camaraderie, and the excellent discussions that emerge from these sessions."

Professor Williams paused as the wail of an ambulance filled the room, pulling Janet back to the present. Janet squinted her eyes and tried to imagine what the windows would look like with carriages passing along the narrow road.

"I firmly believe that if Jane Austen herself stumbled upon our little seminar, she would be eager to join us. Alas, no time travel has yet permitted us this honor." There was polite laughter. "This morning, Professor Munroe will introduce us to *Northanger Abbey*. For those who do not have copies with you, I urge you to go to the lending library to request your copy of *The Mysteries of Udolpho*. The author, Ann Radcliffe, was herself a resident of Bath. Wednesday's sessions will be dedicated entirely to the runaway success of the Gothic novel during Jane Austen's lifetime."

Professor Williams displayed a volume to the class. "Specifically, we will be looking at Ms. Radcliffe's most famous work and how these themes are weaved into *Northanger Abbey*. We are fortunate to have one of England's foremost Radcliffe scholars, Professor Daniels, here from the University of Edinburgh. She will lead the seminars on Wednesday and Thursday."

Janet worried about finishing the book on time. Why had she never read it before?

Professor Williams surveyed the class. "I have excellent news for you about our full-day tour of Helmsley Manor. As I mentioned at the reception, Huntington House was the small house in town, but Helmsley Manor was the Huntington's vast estate—forty miles north of Bath. We leave tomorrow morning at eight. A coach will take us to the estate, where we'll tour the grounds and the grand house. Weather permitting, we'll picnic in the gardens. A local historian will show us the manor and explain to us relations between the local population and the local nobility in the nineteenth century. He will also explain the legal basis for entailments in England, and the social responsibilities of the landed classes. This is always a favorite outing for our seminar participants."

Janet glanced over at Amrita, whose excited gaze met her own. Janet had already been feeling grand in Huntington House, and she was anxious to see how this could possibly be considered a mere *pied-à-terre*. Nothing less than a Pemberley could convince her otherwise.

Professor Williams then provided them with details for the next day's outing before introducing them to Professor Munroe, who launched into a detailed lecture, followed by an animated discussion, on *Northanger Abbey*.

Janet enjoyed the discussion and already regretted having given in to her father's demands that she carry out an architectural internship during her seminar. She was eager to explore the school's extensive lending library and to read contemporaries of Jane Austen and social histories from the period.

The discussions from the morning lecture continued on through the lunch hour. Morning rains were supplanted by blue skies, and they toured Bath under the third straight day of blinding sunshine, seeing the Pump Room where Catherine Morland and Isabella Thorpe had looked up the new arrivals, noting with approval the elegant address of the Tilneys. They saw Cheap Street, where ceaseless traffic caused Isabella and Catherine to lose the gentlemen Isabella was following. They gazed on the hills beyond that served as the outing for the country walk with the Tilneys.

Following the afternoon outing, they returned to Huntington House, where Amrita and Janet made their way to the lending library to check out copies of *The Mysteries of Udolpho*. They sat out on The Crescent's lawn, luxuriating in the earthy smell of fresh cut grass while reading the pages that once thrilled generations of young women in Regency England.

Glancing at her watch, Janet startled. She'd forgotten how long the late spring days were. She turned to Amrita.

"What about a tea break? I discovered a great place the other day and I'd love you to see it."

"Brilliant."

The two new friends walked down the gravel path and into the twisting streets of Bath. Janet located the tea shop she'd visited with Malcolm, claiming the last of the outdoor tables.

"What do you think so far?" asked Janet.

"I'm excited." She paused as the tea arrived to their table. "Professor Williams has managed to gather some of the top Austen scholars."

"Your father must be thrilled."

"He is. I don't think he planned for me to follow in his footsteps. He always encouraged me to study whatever I wanted, but I grew up with a steady diet of nineteenth-century English literature. My father taught at Imperial College and I used to go to his lectures sometimes during school holidays. I never truly pictured myself doing anything else."

Janet sipped her tea, and watched the tourists passing by on such a splendid May day. "You're lucky to have parents who let you decide for yourself. My dad's an architect and I have a choice between being an architect—or being an architect. I could only talk him into this semester if I promised to also intern with an architect here in Bath."

Amrita gasped. "How will you manage to keep up with the seminars and the readings and outings if you're expected to intern in a studio?"

Janet shook her head. "It's a good question. My father doesn't have much respect for my literature studies. He thinks it's a little hobby I do on the side."

"Haven't you tried to talk to him about how you feel?"

"He's not all that interested. He keeps hoping my interest in literature will fade. 'Grow up, Janet' is how he usually puts it. He even has a future husband picked out for me, a promising young architect who works in his firm. My whole life sacrificed for the good of my father's firm." She hadn't meant to sound bitter, but when she turned her attention back to the table, she saw the look of pity in Amrita's eyes, and she felt ashamed.

She sipped her tea and forced herself to take a deep breath before speaking. "I'm only feeling sorry for myself. You see how much I'm looking forward to this program and to being fully immersed in Jane Austen at a safe distance from my home." She smiled, hoping her voice sounded lighter, less bitter. "Now tell me something about this Helmsley Manor. How spectacular is it supposed to be?"

The corners of Amrita's lips turned up. "You want to know if it puts Pemberley to shame, don't you?"

"You read my mind." Janet leaned across the table. "Will we see any Fitzwilliam Darcys wandering the grounds?"

"I certainly hope so!" Amrita laughed. "I've never actually seen Helmsley Manor, only through photos. It's praised as a gem of English Palladian architecture. Of course, you'll be able to judge that better than the rest of us."

Amrita and Janet finished the tea at their table in the sunshine. Later they walked back to The Crescent and read their Radcliffe up until dinner. As they got ready for bed, Janet asked, "Do you know anything about this painting?"

"Professor Williams told my father and me about it when I was moving in. It's by the Venetian artist Tiepolo. Painted in 1744, if I remember correctly. Purchased by Sir Edward Huntington during his travels to Venice in the early 1800s."

"Oh, a Tiepolo! I should have known."

"I know, incredible, isn't it? Scholars believe this painting was influenced by the seventeenth-century Bernini statue in Rome's Borghese Gallery. They think Tiepolo would have been familiar with Bernini's work through engravings."

"I love that sculpture." Janet examined the figures closely.

"According to Professor Williams, Tiepolo's painting hung in Helmsley Manor before Sir Huntington moved it here. We're the last students to live with such a valuable painting. Professor Williams says it will soon be gifted to the National Gallery. You know the story of Apollo and Daphne, don't you?"

"The basics, I guess, but I don't remember why Apollo fell in love with Daphne and why she resisted so much."

"I love this myth." Amrita climbed into bed and pulled the comforter up. "It's told in Ovid's *Metamorphoses*. It was all the fault of Cupid. Apollo was angry with him when he found him playing with his weapons. Apollo insulted Cupid, asking what he could possibly understand of warfare. Cupid had a reputation as a troublemaker, and he decided to take revenge. Unfortunately, he ended up sacrificing the beautiful nymph Daphne in the process."

Janet stepped back from the painting, suddenly chilly.

"Daphne was famed for her great beauty, but she'd shunned her many suitors. She longed to remain unattached, like the Goddess of the Hunt, Diana. To get back at Apollo, Cupid selected two arrows. One was a golden arrow. Anyone struck with that would fall in love. The second was a lead-tipped arrow. Anyone struck with that arrow would despise the first person to express his or her admiration."

Janet smiled. She used to love mythology, but she'd forgotten many of the stories. Amrita's words brought details back.

"Cupid struck Apollo with the golden arrow, and Apollo fell hopelessly in love with Daphne. But the mischievous Cupid aimed a lead arrow at Daphne, hardening her heart against Apollo's amorous efforts."

Janet's back was to Amrita. She carefully examined the painting as Amrita recounted the myth. Transported by the story, she tried to ignore a strange sensation in her stomach and a growing dizziness.

"Apollo pursued Daphne and she resisted, but it made no difference to the love-struck Apollo, chasing the beautiful nymph through the forest. As she fled from him, Daphne called out to her father, begging him to deliver her from Apollo's advances. Pitying his daughter, he answered her request. At the exact moment the ardent Apollo captured his beloved in his arms, she was transformed into a laurel tree. From her fingers sprouted branches. The heartbroken Apollo looked on helplessly as her beautiful face transformed into bark."

Janet observed the billowing pink cloth around Daphne's body, the outstretched hands with the first leaves sprouting from her fingertips. She felt the odd dizziness growing stronger as she tried to make sense of the disjointed images.

She couldn't shake the feeling that she'd seen the painting before—not a copy, not a similar scene by a different artist, but this very image. She examined the brushstrokes, acutely aware of the sound of the blood coursing noisily through her own body, the throbbing of her head, the difficulty breathing. Amrita's voice broke her train of thought.

"Apollo was so destroyed by the loss of his beautiful Daphne. He vowed that, from that moment on, the branches of the laurel tree would grace the foreheads of the gods." She paused. "This painting depicts the moment of transformation, of metamorphosis. According to Professor Williams, it was Sir Edward's prized possession, even though he had numerous artworks of greater value. It always hung in Helmsley Manor, in his library, but when Sir Edward was ill and moved to Bath for his health, he refused to take leave of Helmsley Manor without the painting. It was hung here in his bedchamber, where he gazed upon it daily, even from his deathbed. His family didn't have the heart to remove it. It's been here ever since." She laughed. "Little did the Huntingtons know that the riffraff would one day live in their home."

Janet moved to her bed and lay down, relieved the dizziness had subsided. She turned to Amrita in the bed beside hers.

"What a story. I count myself among the fortunate riffraff. Maybe we'll even see its old place of honor in Sir Edward's library tomorrow." She looked at it once more, feeling an overwhelming exhaustion. She switched off the light. "Good night, Amrita."

"Good night." Amrita shifted in her bed. "But remember that the true moral of the story is not to fight off the passionate advances of the handsome Sun god when he's pursuing you."

"Yeah, right. I'll try my best to internalize that one, should the need ever arise," said Janet, her eyes already growing heavy as sleep called to her.

Chapter 6

Following an early breakfast the next day, a bus pulled up to The Crescent. Janet and her classmates filed onboard, excited to be on their way to Helmsley Manor. Janet took a free seat next to Siobhan, a young woman from Trinity College in Dublin.

"What's your room like?" asked Siobhan. "I feel like I've died and gone to heaven. My room back in Dublin is so old and drafty. And now I'm living with grand fireplaces and crystal chandeliers."

"I know! We even have a Tiepolo in our room."

"Lucky you. I'm coming to see it later. You're studying architecture, right? You must be excited to see the manor."

"I am. Everyone keeps telling me how beautiful it is." Janet looked out the bus window at the bright, blue sky. "It's a perfect day to see the gardens."

"They even have a picnic planned. We're stepping into Jane Austen's time. I've left my mobile at home—no modern distractions."

"Yeah, we probably should go for full immersion, although I'd hate to lose indoor plumbing."

"How far along are you in *Udolpho*?" The two women fell into discussion about the adventures of poor Emily St. Aubert as the English countryside passed them by on the drive up to Helmsley Manor.

Professor Williams announced their arrival when the bus turned from the main road under a grand arch, then continued on an unpaved road flanked by giant elm trees.

Janet and Siobhan stopped speaking and pressed their faces to the window. When they turned a corner and glimpsed their first view of the manor and the lake in front of it, Siobhan released an audible sigh. "'Of all this, I might have been mistress.'" She turned to Janet with a sly smile. "We've arrived at Pemberley."

Siobhan was right. The architecture of the manor house, positioned perfectly on a rolling hill, was breathtaking. The manor blended so naturally with the fields and woodlands surrounding it. The grand façade was mirrored in the large lake, as gliding swans added gentle ripples to the reflection. The sun shone off the golden stone, lending an air of grandiosity to the already perfect lines of the stately manor. Janet sighed.

The coach parked in an empty visitor's parking lot, and the students clambered out. Janet stood alongside her classmates, gazing at the façade of the Helmsley Manor. Not for the first time since she'd reached Bath, she wondered if she were in a dream. One of those you don't want to end with the harsh clanging of the alarm clock. The birds chirped above and the sun warmed her shoulders. All that was needed to complete the romantic, bucolic tableau was a dapper gentleman thundering by on his stallion or a farmer passing by with his wheelbarrow.

The spellbound students were eventually jolted back to modern times by the ringing of a cellphone.

Professor Williams answered. "Yes, Mr. Whitshaw, we've arrived ... No, that's fine. We'll wait for you here ... Not a problem at all. The students will be pleased to stretch their legs and enjoy this sunshine ... Of course, of course."

He turned to the students. "Mr. Whitshaw arrives in twenty minutes. Synchronize your watches. Or your cellphones, if you must. It's twenty past nine o'clock. Feel free to wander the grounds, but be back at nine-forty sharp. Do *not* be late."

The students dispersed. Janet walked off in the direction of the lake. Choosing a spot along its edge, she marveled at the fresh air and the smells of spring, particularly the sweet, intoxicating scent of lilies of the valley. She pulled her sketchbook and pencils from her carry bag, eager to take advantage of the brilliant light.

In Rome, Janet had carefully studied Andrea Palladio's famous architectural treatise *Quattro Libri dell'Architectura*, and visited the Veneto region countless times to see and sketch his villas. She loved Palladio's return to classical architecture, and his emphasis on the natural setting as his reference when designing a building.

This influence had been carried out to perfection with Helmsley Manor, with its pleasing proportions, its restrained use of ornamentation, its position on a rising hill, its symmetry, and its elegant porticos that would have allowed its owners to feel at one with the stunning nature around them.

She knew Palladio's sixteenth-century books were only translated into English in 1715. She suspected that Helmsley Manor was an early example of the movement in England.

She continued sketching in silence until a shadow fell across her sketchpad. Looking up, Janet was momentarily blinded by the sunlight, before her eyes adjusted to see James standing before her.

"It's beautiful. Will you make copies for us all?" He sat down beside her.

"Will photocopies do?" She sketched as she spoke. "Have you seen the grounds?"

"A little. It's pretty amazing. I can never get over the idea that people used to live like this."

"I think those of us from the 'New World,'" she said those words with a lame attempt at an English accent, "always find ourselves more stunned. Even if the English don't live like this anymore—at least most of them, anyway—they've grown up surrounded by these grand estates, and the entire idea is less foreign to them."

"That's probably true. You sketch so well. When will you start your architecture internship?"

"Next week. My boss seems really nice, but I was so looking forward to concentrating on literature full time."

"I understand. But you have talent. Who's to say you couldn't be happy being an architect and continuing literature as a hobby—maybe even the odd conference occasionally? You don't have to work in an area to love it, do you?"

"I guess you don't. If only I could find a way to combine the two, I know I would be truly happy."

"Students! Mr. Whitshaw has arrived," called Professor Williams.

Janet packed up her sketchbook and pencils. She and James joined the group.

Mr. Whitshaw looked the part: professorial, glasses, tweed jacket, sturdy boots. "Welcome to Helmsley Manor."

The students formed a semicircle around him.

"Helmsley Manor was built by the Huntington family, a powerful noble family in England from the sixteenth to twentieth century. The sixteenth-century architectural principles of the Italian Andrea Palladio arrived later to England, but the style quickly gained adherents following the publication of Palladio's architectural treatises in English in the early eighteenth century. The Huntington family were early admirers of this architectural movement. Their family manor was built in 1725."

Janet smiled to herself. Just as she had suspected.

"Note the simplicity of form, the elegant lines, the harmony of the building with the nature surrounding it. In particular, the way the porticos extend into the gardens, so that family members and visitors could admire the beauty of the extensive grounds. These were all elements extremely important to Andrea Palladio and his followers in sixteenth-century Italy. The movement would gain momentum in the United Kingdom throughout the eighteenth and early nineteenth centuries. Helmsley Manor, as an early example of Palladian architecture in England, was viewed as a model by both architects and the most illustrious families throughout the country."

Mr. Whitshaw extracted keys from an inside pocket of his coat. "If you will follow me."

He led the group to the front entrance. Janet craned her neck to view the vaulted ceilings and the grand staircase leading to the upper floors. Despite its grand scale, it somehow managed to maintain an atmosphere of simplicity.

Mr. Whitshaw ushered them through the drawing room and the music room, and they peeked into the grand ballroom.

"Look around you, ladies and gentlemen. A ballroom of this size in a private residence was a clear signal of wealth and power. Particularly in rural regions such as this, balls were eagerly anticipated. The local nobility and important families would travel here from far and wide to attend one of the great balls of the Huntington family."

Janet squinted her eyes and tried to picture it: the elegant men and women spinning across the floor, the orchestra on the balcony above, the candlelight flickering in the grand chandelier. She felt dizzy and blinked when she saw swirls of color before her eyes. Her head throbbed. For a moment, she believed she really could hear the strains of the violins tuning up. Janet snapped her eyes open to see her classmates filing out. How odd she felt.

"Now, if you will follow me into the library."

They entered a cavernous library, every square inch covered from floor to ceiling with mahogany bookshelves. Plush chairs were scattered throughout the room, and an ornate desk stood close to a massive fireplace. Several paintings hung along one wall. The stunning Venetian scene appeared to be a Canaletto, and a nearby painting was most likely a Renaissance work. A Lotto? Might the lithographs be Rembrandts?

"Impressive, isn't it?"

Mr. Whitshaw paused as the students admired the artwork and read the spines of the books.

"The Huntington family were well educated. Most of the males of the family studied at Oxford, and they maintained an extensive library. Sir Edward Huntington, who lived from 1786 to 1832, was a collector of many of the impressive first editions in this collection—Austen, Byron, Keats, Shelley, Locke, and Hobbes. Back at Huntington House, there is a fine portrait of Sir Edward hanging along your grand staircase."

Janet recalled the stern gaze of those blue eyes following her as she ran down to catch the bus this morning. His arrogant look never failed to annoy her. And yet, almost despite herself, she was still drawn to his handsome, chiseled face each time she passed by.

"As you see, Sir Edward was also a celebrated art collector. Here along the wall is a charming Canaletto of the Ponte Rialto and the Canale Grande. Here you see an Annunciation scene by the Renaissance master Lorenzo Lotto. Both works were purchased on visits to Venice." He gestured to the opposite wall. "These lithographs are Rembrandt."

The students filed past the works before returning to the center of the room, where Mr. Whitshaw waited. "Sir Edward had an excellent eye for art, but his proudest acquisition was not his most valuable. In Venice, he purchased a mythological scene, depicting Apollo and Daphne, which occupied the position over the fireplace that you see is now bare."

All eyes followed the grand gesture of his arm.

"The Tiepolo now hanging in Huntington House—which is soon destined for the National Gallery—used to hang here in the place of honor in Sir Edward's library. He spent significant amounts of time here, and we know that he considered it his prized possession. He moved it with him when he left for Bath to restore his health. It hung where he could see it clearly from his sickbed. Of course, he never returned to Helmsley Manor. And neither did the Tiepolo."

Janet and Amrita exchanged glances.

Janet sighed. What a lovely place to retreat from the world. She could picture Sir Edward sitting by the roaring fireplace, a book in hand. A first edition of *Pride and Prejudice*, perhaps? His handsome sister—Emma, wasn't it? Her painting was the portrait of a pretty young woman with a dreamy look in her eye Janet noticed on her first day—might be sitting beside him listening to the stories of Elizabeth and Darcy, Jane and Bingley.

How she would have loved to pull up a chair and join them, retreating to their nineteenth-century cocoon of art, literature and family.

Janet cast one last, appraising look at the impressive library as the students filed out to continue their tour upstairs. Once again, Janet squinted her eyes and tried to imagine the room as it was long ago.

As her eyelids lowered, she felt a strange sensation. She was aware of odd images: a fire burning in the fireplace, a billowing pink cloth, a plush chair before the fireplace. Was that a figure in the chair? Her heart beat faster; her hands felt clammy. She heard footsteps approaching. It all seemed strangely familiar. Her heart pounded wildly in her chest. She felt something brush against her lips.

"Janet, are you okay? We've moved on. Hurry up, we're upstairs now."

The words broke the strange sensations.

Janet focused on her friend, shaking off the odd feeling in the pit of her stomach. "Yes." She forced a smile and a calm voice. "I'm fine, Amrita. Just a slight headache. I'm coming."

Upstairs, they visited the bedrooms, before continuing to the kitchen and the grand dining room, the formal gardens, the extensive grounds, and the cottages of the farmers and tenants of the Huntington lands.

After seeing the grand manor house, the cottages, although charming to modern eyes, appeared dark and damp. Whole families would live, sleep, eat and breathe within these walls; the head of the family was out each dawn to toil on the Huntington lands. How did they feel as they gazed upon Huntington Manor, knowing that their endless labor financed the lives of their noble patrons within? Mr. Whitshaw explained about the constant danger of cholera and dysentery in such living conditions, and how cholera had ravaged Helmsley Manor. He spoke about the relatively short life spans for agricultural workers in the nineteenth century, how women often died in childbirth, and how few children lived long enough to celebrate their fifth birthday.

They learned about English law for property inheritances, ensuring that the large manors survived intact by passing on the land to the firstborn son. They learned the legal background of entailments, something so common in Jane Austen's literature, which could entail away the property from the female heirs in the absence of a son.

Following the tour, they all gathered in the formal gardens, taking seats under bright sunshine and a nearly cloudless sky. Janet, James, Siobhan and Amrita all sat close together, enjoying their sandwiches and the regal atmosphere.

"So, what do you think? It's Pemberley, isn't it?" asked Siobhan. "And if the portrait of Sir Edward back at Huntington House is accurate, he looks every bit as dashing as Fitzwilliam Darcy. Bad luck—I missed him by about two hundred years." Siobhan caught James rolling his eyes. "Don't worry, James, if you can join us on our time travel, Miss Emma, Sir Edward's sister, is hot, too."

"Can you believe the artwork and all the first editions in that library?" asked Amrita. "Incredible, isn't it? Come see our Tiepolo tonight."

The rest of the afternoon was spent wandering the grounds. At the end of the day, the exhausted students piled onto the bus for the return trip home.

The odd tingling Janet felt all day in her fingers and legs faded as soon as they pulled away from Helmsley Manor. She chalked it up to delayed exhaustion, the jet lag, and the excitement of beginning the seminar.

I should get to bed early tonight. Otherwise, these headaches and exhaustion will continue.

She craned her neck to catch a last glimpse of the grand manor, bathed in warm, golden afternoon sunlight, tiny in the distance.

Chapter 7

The week continued, full of classes and studying. Janet enjoyed Professor Daniels' discussion of Ann Radcliffe and the Gothic novel.

She was new to the twisted, overwrought plots, the evil, slightly cartoonish villains—why were they always swarthy Italians?—and swooning heroines. She started keeping a running tab on her bookmark, indicating each of Emily St. Aubert's many dramatic fainting spells.

Although the writing overall seemed dated to modern readers, in some segments it was almost modern. They learned about how Austen's *Northanger Abbey* would have been recognized at the time as a spoof of The *Mysteries of Udolpho*. They learned how Radcliffe's writing inspired later authors, including Edgar Allen Poe.

Discussion in the sessions was always lively, and Janet worked hard to keep up with her readings and be prepared for class discussion. A few mornings a week, she jogged with Siobhan, enjoying Bath before the rest of the city awoke. They chatted about the lessons ahead, their lives, and their hopes for the future.

Janet liked her talks with her classmates, the unabashed literature majors who were planning to work in the field. Living amongst them gave her courage. When the course concluded, Janet was determined to confront her father. The following May, she would graduate with her master's in literature and her architecture degree, but she had no intention of continuing her architecture career. Her father would simply have to accept it.

Despite her newfound confidence, her certainty dissipated quickly when she heard her father's booming voice over the phone line.

"Yes, Daddy, it's been wonderful. I'm so happy I came."

"I'm pleased you can cultivate that little hobby of yours. More importantly ..."

Janet heard the clicking of his computer as he spoke to her. She couldn't remember a time when she'd held her father's undivided attention. Multitasking even managed to work its way into family dinners. She'd sit in silence as he barked orders into his cellphone or pored over the latest plans for a project spread out on the table before him. It always left her wondering why she ever bothered to leave her campus to accept his invitations, when they barely exchanged a half a dozen words during an evening together.

"More importantly, how are things going in Perry's studio?"

"Really well. He's fantastic, Daddy." Janet knew she was gushing, but it was such a pleasure to work with Mr. Perry. She treasured his warmth and his genuine interest in his architects. Everything lacking in her own father's studio. "I'm learning so much. It's such a ..." she paused. Would her father be angry? "Such a relaxed, friendly environment. He's supportive. He wants us to learn."

Her father snorted. "Sheldon always was a soft touch. He's too easy on his architects. Always told him as much to his face.

Make sure to put in long hours. He won't be used to it, not with his staff sloughing off all the time."

Her shoulders slumped. She dropped her head into her hands, relieved her father preferred landlines to Skype. "Daddy, I can't put in long hours. You know I'm here for my seminar. None of the other students have outside jobs."

She heard the intake of air that always signaled her father's explosive temper boiling up dangerously close to the surface.

"Damn it! You have the opportunity to make a lasting impression on Mr. Perry, make yourself indispensable. Maybe he'll think of you—and our firm—when he's got big projects. I hoped you could help bolster our client base over there. But instead of taking it seriously ..."

The computer clicking ceased. She was painfully aware of the rising timbre of his voice. The flip side of having her father's undivided attention was that it rarely signaled anything positive.

"... There you are, wasting your time all dreamy-eyed talking about mamsy-pamsy, two-hundred-year-old fashion news and marriage proposals. When the hell will you grow up, Janet, and start to take your life seriously?"

She hated that tone. The only way to stop him was to give in. That's what he expected. What he was accustomed to. What he felt he deserved. But she couldn't keep caving in. How had she ever imagined that an ocean between them could free her from his clutches?

"Malcolm told me to be patient with you, to give you time during this seminar *to reflect* ..."

Sarcasm dripped from his voice. Her head throbbed. Now she had to be grateful to Malcolm for standing up for her? Without his intervention, would she even have been allowed on this seminar?

"But frankly, I never saw the point of any of it. If you're not going to take your internship seriously, what's the point of even being in Bath?"

The damned internship wasn't the point of this semester, you self-centered bastard!

But the words would never cross her lips, unless she one day gathered the courage to be honest with her father. And then what? A break from the only family she had?

She closed her eyes. "I'm sorry you don't understand the point of my being here, Daddy. I'm here because I was accepted into a prestigious literature seminar. That may not be enough for you, but I intend to take it seriously. I'm at Mr. Perry's studio because *you* insisted, but it will not get in the way of my coursework."

"You always were difficult, Janet. Always."

She heard the clicking of his computer resume. His undivided attention had ceased. She was once again a waste of his valuable time.

"I have a meeting in ten minutes. I don't have time for this drivel. Just to let you know, I'll be checking in with Sheldon about your performance. So don't slack off, or I'll know about it."

The hum of the ended call buzzed in her ear. She replaced the receiver and rubbed her throbbing head.

Janet moved to her bed, where she stared at the Tiepolo. In the past weeks, she'd often sat here, silently contemplating details of the painting. It never failed to calm her. As she examined Daphne's alabaster skin and the green leaves sprouting from her fingertips, she felt her heartbeat slow, the throbbing in her head subside. But was it the artwork itself or the metamorphosis? Maybe it was witnessing Daphne's escape from her world that calmed her nerves.

Janet had no idea how long she sat there observing the canvas, but she startled to hear a knock on the open door. "Fiona."

"Hi, am I disturbing you? Were you resting?"

"No, just moping. Disastrous phone call with my dad." She indicated a chair by the window. "Take a seat and take my mind off of it."

"I'm sorry. Do you want to talk about it?"

"Thanks, but you'd be my permanent confidant. It's our normal routine."

Fiona crossed the room and sat down in the sunlight, far from the shadowy wall on which the Tiepolo hung.

Janet stood and walked toward her desk. She cast a last glance at the canvas before offering her classmate another half-smile. "I don't know what it is, but this painting always manages to calm me."

"Make sure to enjoy it before it's off to the National Gallery. Then you'll have to compete with the crowds." Fiona kicked off her shoes and tucked her legs beneath her.

Janet sat at her desk.

Fiona slid to the edge of her chair. "I know how to get your mind off family quarrels. How would you like to meet the perfect guy?"

"Does he exist?"

"In literature, yes. Okay, maybe not perfect, but close. It's my cousin, Reuben. He'll be in town this weekend, and I think the two of you would hit it off. What if we meet up? Something casual, the three of us for drinks. Then, if you want, you two can go to dinner."

Janet shook her head. "Oh, God. I hate blind dates. They're so awkward."

Fiona touched Janet's arm. "But here's the thing. You two have a lot in common. I'm sure you'd like one another. I already told him all about you. Amrita told me you're not going to Oxford with her this weekend because you have to work, but you can join us Sunday evening. C'mon, what do you say?"

Janet shrugged. "I fear I'll regret this, but yes. Against my better judgment, mind you." She smiled at her classmate. "But Fiona, I'm counting on you. If it's a disaster, you need to help me get out of it."

"I promise. But there's no need. You two'll probably be anxious to get rid of me."

Chapter 8

Late Sunday afternoon, Janet stood in the dusty light of a cavernous nineteenth-century library. Her client spoke, yet she made no effort to distinguish his words. She was too wrapped up in a fantasy about possessing the house for herself, and spending countless hours among the shelves filled with first editions she somehow had the means to afford.

The dot-com millionaire stood in the center of the room, texting and talking at the same time. He looked like a scarecrow in expensive, crumpled clothing that swam on his body.

Why didn't you just wear the hoodie and jeans, thought Janet unkindly when they first met in Mr. Perry's office, *rather than trying to play grown-up?*

Ted Benson, senior architect at Mr. Perry's studio, was officially in charge of refurbishing the Bath house. But Mr. Dawson—Tony, as he insisted she call him—felt most at home with his fellow Americans, and he took an immediate liking to Janet. She was quickly added to the project team, and was too often the recipient of Tony's late-night phone calls and cryptic, grammatically challenged text messages.

Janet examined the faded, velvet curtains that covered the five-meter-long windows. Her eyes devoured the floor-to-ceiling mahogany bookshelves that covered every available space in the grand library. How lovely they would look once they were restored to their former grandeur! The water-damaged frescoes on the ceilings would require an expert eye. There was a border that looked intriguing, even if seriously faded. She could make out faint pastoral scenes, and longed for a closer look. Mr. Perry had already provided her with names of local art renovation experts, and she was to make the rounds for estimates.

The grand fireplace could certainly be recovered. She imagined a great desk in front of the flames that would warm this room in the wintertime, plush chairs before the hearth. Peering at the Bohemian crystal overhead, years of neglect were evident, but she had contacts outside of Prague who could hand-craft the missing pieces. She'd worked with them before on earlier projects with her father.

Yes, with hard work and love, this library could certainly be restored to its former splendor. It would be time-consuming, but she was the one to do it. When working on a project like this, when pouring so much love into glorious homes like this, Janet could almost convince herself that architecture was her true calling. Soon enough, however, the spoiled, demanding clients who always seemed to possess these treasures made her rethink that enthusiasm.

As if on cue, a movement from the overgrown boy in the center of the room caught her attention. She looked up to see his thumbs flying over his mini-keyboard, oblivious to the splendor surrounding him. *You don't deserve it, but I'll make you the envy of your friends. This library will look like it did the day it was built by the time I'm done with it.*

She stepped back to the center of the library and met Ted's gaze. He gave an imperceptible shrug. Above his perfectly tailored suit and the crisp, white collar of his shirt, she noticed the rigid set of his jaw. In all the weeks she'd interned at Mr. Perry's studio, she'd never seen Ted flustered, not even once. But his stoicism seemed seriously frayed today. Was it Tony's hyperactive, spoiled-kid behavior that set Ted on edge? She and Ted stood in silence until Tony had completed his messaging and honored them, once again, with his attention.

"So, whaddaya think?" Tony looked at them expectantly.

Ted cleared his throat. "I'm not certain if Janet heard your plans. I believe she was examining the structural damage."

"Yes, I was. Sorry to have missed what you were saying. I was so excited when we walked into this library." She made an effort to consciously slow down her speech. When she felt true enthusiasm for a project, her tongue had a tendency to steam ahead, full-speed. "I have to be honest. There's a lot of damage, but this is one of the most spectacular libraries I've ever seen. I have no doubt we can return it to its former glory ..."

Janet had been gazing around her, and only turned back to Tony when she heard a distinct snort of laughter. Her brow furrowed in confusion and she turned to Ted, who appeared to be issuing her a warning when his grey eyes met hers.

"Its former glory? Why on earth would I wanna do *that*?" Tony's annoying, smart-aleck smile stretched from ear to ear.

Janet paused. "Uh ..." She searched for reassuring words. "I think I understand your concerns, Tony. But I can assure you we'll ensure the structure is sound before undertaking the restoration project. We could get the living quarters in shape first before working on the library, if you're worried about work here slowing things down."

Now it was Tony's turn to look confused. "Earth to Janet. You haven't been listening to me, have you? Why would I have worked so hard to search for a house *not* in the historic register, if I only wanted to recreate some frumpy nineteenth-century gentlemen's club?"

Her throat felt dry. "Pardon? You're not interested in restoring this library?"

"Boy, Janet are you out of it. Didn't you get what I was saying in my text messages? Books are dead, haven't you heard?" Tony shook his head, as if pitying Janet's lack of intelligence.

Janet met Ted's glance, but now she noticed the hardness in his eyes when Tony spoke again.

"This *is* great space—yes, I agree. For an interactive play station. I want to pull all these bookshelves down. It will all need to be rewired, of course." Tony paced around the room. "Everything modern. Think twenty-first-century 'library.'" He made annoying air quotes. "Think multimedia. Think videoconferencing space with three-meter screens. Think giant game consoles lining the entire walls after these hideous bookshelves are torn down." His scarecrow clothes flailed around as he waved his arms. "I'm thinking swings. I'm thinking hammocks. I'm thinking neon. And obviously a bar right in that corner."

He pointed to the spot where Janet had placed her imaginary chairs for evenings engrossed in thick novels. She felt the tears welling up in her eyes, and concentrated all her efforts on not allowing them to spill over.

"The chandelier will have to go, of course. What a dustcatcher." He waved dismissively at the hundreds of shards of hand-cut Bohemian crystals that had hung proudly over generations of learned residents, who read in the very same room Tony now wanted to desecrate. "I have a disco ball that'll look totally dope up there. If you've spent enough sleepless nights coding like I have to achieve what I've achieved ..." he smiled at Janet, "you'd appreciate the irony."

Oh, my God. Strike the twerp down. I beg you, God.

"Hammocks? A disco ball?" was all Janet could manage.

"I know ..." Tony's face was flushed with genuine pleasure. He looked like the nine-year-old child he must have been when the regions of his brain not dedicated to computers and technology stopped developing. "Isn't it, like, cool?"

"I um ... I don't know what to say, Tony." Janet struggled for air. "What do you think, Ted? Is it, like, cool?"

Even Ted's stiff upper lip was challenged. He looked thoroughly uncomfortable as he sought a diplomatic response. "It is certainly ... what I might call ... an *original* vision."

"I know! Like, it is, isn't it?" Tony exclaimed.

Janet worried Tony might want to high-five them both. Feeling more in control, she took a deep breath and tried again. "It's only ... Well, uh, Tony ... your idea *is* visionary—it most *certainly* is ... but I wondered ... um ... why you needed to purchase a nineteenth-century home to carry out such an exemplary, high-tech project?" She cast her glance at Ted and was heartened by his vigorous nodding, encouraging her. "The historic center of Bath is protected, of course." Thank God, Janet wished to add. "But we could find you something to suit your modern tastes at the edge of the city, or maybe build you something more adapted to your—uh—taste. Something spectacular, perhaps outside Bath." Ideally far, far outside Bath. "It could serve as a model of visionary architecture. Maybe attract other tech ... uh ... geniuses to settle around you."

Tony stood at the center of the room, shaking his head and pouting like a petulant child dressed in his father's clothes.

"You two don't get it, do you? I *made it* in London. Me, little Tony Dawson from Wichita. *This*," he said, arms outstretched, indicating the room, "was how the rich showed they'd made it two hundred years ago. Now it's *my* turn. I wanna impress all those London, Oxbridge snobs with my weekend home in Bath. And I wanna build a monument to technology, not restore some boring old library. Now, the question is, can you do it, or not? If not, I'm sure there are plenty of other architects out there who'd be thrilled to work for me ..."

Janet watched Ted's Adam's apple rise and fall, and felt relief when he opened his mouth to speak.

"Mr. Dawson, now that you've explained your plans to us, I'm confident we can design something to your liking. We can come back to you with new plans on Tuesday."

Tony was already busy on his smartphone. Whether he was sending messages or playing video games, Janet could not be certain.

"Great, Ted. Get them to me and we'll speak. Gotta run."

Ted and Janet stood immobile, watching silently from the grand windows as Tony hopped into his Maserati and sped off to London. Janet fought the urge to cry for the second time that day, as she glanced around the soaring walls of the library one last time. They made their way out the door. Ted locked up.

"Couldn't he have stayed in his Kansas cornfields and built some gaudy mansion out there?" Ted's voice was bewildered.

Janet shook her head. "I wish he had."

Chapter 9

In the early evening, Janet entered the pub on High Street. She searched the sea of faces before spotting Fiona toward the back. After making her way through the crowd, she slipped into the booth beside her classmate.

"Janet, you made it!" slurred Fiona, with a wide smile and unfocused eyes.

"How long have you been here?" She observed her friend uncertainly, taking in Fiona's empty pint glass and her friend's flushed cheeks. Fiona was clearly in no state to help her out if this date were a disaster.

"Oh, Reuben arrived early, and we decided to have one or two before meeting up with you. We've been catching up on old times."

One or two? Seems more than that. Let's hope Reuben holds his beer better than you do. What a day—a spoiled brat computer geek, followed by an evening of inane, drunken conversation.

Tomorrow would mean long hours at the studio after a morning of classes, and she thought wistfully about the stack of reading on her bedside dresser that needed to be finished.

As she felt sorry for herself, a lumbering bull of a man, unsteady on his feet, tottered dangerously close to them. A full pint of beer sloshed over his beefy hands. Her silk dress was far too elegant for this pub and its drunken clients. Why hadn't she returned to her room to change into jeans for the pub?

Janet noted with alarm that the bull stopped at their table and slid into the bench in front of her. His shiny cheeks and red nose glowed, even in the pub's dull light. His bloodshot, unfocused eyes honed in on her breasts. Drunk as he was, God knew how many pairs he could see. Judging by the wolfish enthusiasm with which he licked his chapped lips, he was thoroughly enjoying the view.

Since he was otherwise occupied, Janet could observe him freely. His shirt was sweat-stained at the armpits and splattered with what she could only hope was beer. His gut strained against the table. Janet glanced over her shoulder, looking for the athletic rugby player Fiona had promised. She imagined this unappealing drinking buddy of Reuben's was a necessary evil she'd be forced to endure, but she was, after all, adept at small talk.

"Reuben! You were gone in the loo for such a long time, I thought I'd have to call in the rescue squad."

Fiona's slurred voice addressed her cousin, and Janet hopefully examined the men near their table, even though none seemed to be listening to Fiona.

"M'cousin's told me all about you. Pleasure to meet you." The sweating hulk of a man at the table addressed her, and Janet swiveled to turn her attention back to him. Her heart sank. *This* was her date.

"Didn't I tell you what a handsome bloke my cousin is?" Fiona reached across the table to slap the man playfully on the arm, but in the process she hit his glass. Beer and foam sloshed all over the table.

"Bloody 'ell, Fiona! You'll be buying the next round."

Next round? They planned on drinking *more*? Janet wondered if more alcohol than blood now coursed through their bodies. She looked longingly at the fading rays of evening sunlight at the door at the opposite end of the pub.

"So, Jennie ..."

"It's Janet, actually."

"So, Janet actually." Reuben broke out into snorting laughter. Janet looked over to Fiona for assistance, but Fiona was propped in the corner of the booth, her eyes firmly closed, a slight snore escaping from her lips. Compared to Reuben, the filthy-rich computer nerd was starting to look better.

"Fiona here ..." He jabbed a thumb in her direction. "That girl never could hold her beer. Fiona tells me you're some kind of bookworm, too." He stared at her breasts once again. "I was expecting someone more ... well, schoolmarmish, I guess. Fiona was right about you." He winked at her breasts, then seemed to toast them before lifting his glass to his lips and taking a long, steady gulp.

In the city of Captain Wentworth, I manage to find myself on a date with a Neanderthal.

"Yes, Reuben. I'm getting my master's degree in bookworm studies at Harvard."

"Whoaaa. Smart, too." He took another big gulp from his pint and the foam dribbled down his unshaved chin. He wiped it away with his beefy hand. "What're you writing your thesis on?"

"Nineteenth-century social customs."

"Ha!" Reuben's laugh was so explosive that beer in his mouth splattered across the table, catapulting itself onto Janet's dress.

Damn it. A trip to the drycleaner's.

"Whoops. Sorry 'bout that."

He reached across the table to pat the beer stain on her chest. She slapped his sweaty paw away, but it didn't seem to deter him. His drunken gaze remained fixed on her beer-stained cleavage. He winked at her and she fought the urge to vomit.

He licked his lips again. "Those protests won't last long."

She looked longingly at the door beckoning beyond his shoulder. Could she make a break for it?

"So, let me get this straight. You spend hours and hours in libraries studying all that boring, socio- crap from hundreds of years ago. Why?"

Janet breathed in deeply. "Because it's interesting, Reuben. Because your countrymen two hundred years ago cared passionately about literature, art, philosophy and the improvement of the human mind."

"Loada bollocks that was, eh?"

His bloodshot eyes met her own for a moment, before stubbornly returning to their favored resting place.

"So you look for all this socio-culture whatsit in books? Hey, Jennie, didn't anyone tell you books are dead?" Reuben cocked his head to one side and tried to focus his gaze on her.

"So I've been hearing. Well then, let me get this straight. A young, successful man such as yourself does *not* read books?"

"Damned straight I don't. Don't have the time. Too busy following the market, making money for my clients. Who has time to read about ponces in tight pants writing love notes to homely girls?"

Fiona's snoring grew louder from the corner. Janet's cheeks flushed. She knew she shouldn't react, but she couldn't help herself. First Tony, then Reuben. These were the successful men of her generation?

"*That's* what you consider literature, Reuben?"

"Well ..." He sat silently.

Janet imagined his two lonely brain cells circling around one another madly, trying to formulate a coherent response.

"Yeah, pretty much, you might say. But hey," he rummaged through his bag and pulled out an iPad, "if it'll make you happy, look what I have here. You're gonna love this."

He handed his tablet to Janet, and she looked through its virtual library. "Impressive: Dante, Goethe, ah yes, here's the ubiquitous *War and Peace.*"

She looked up. Reuben's grin had returned.

"Tell me, have you actually ever *read* any of these?"

"Well, uh." He drained his beer. "No, not actually. But they're all there, so whenever I *wanna* read 'em, I can."

"Yes, I suppose that's true." Janet looked pointedly at her watch. "As lovely as this evening has been, I have a lot of work to do. You know, that pesky reading of useless books. It's been a real pleasure."

"Hey, Janice." He reached out and held her arm, drawing his face closer, exhaling his sour beer breath. "My firm has me staying in some posh place close by. What do you say we go back together and have some fun?"

He fixed her with bloodshot eyes. His underarm sweat stains had grown larger over the course of their conversation.

Janet offered a tight smile and freed her arm from his meaty grip. She stood. "While it certainly is *incredibly* tempting ... having the chance to see that rugby-chiseled body in one of those plush hotel robes ... I'm afraid I'm going to have to take a pass on that, Reuben." She nodded towards the sleeping Fiona. "I trust you'll look out for your cousin."

"Yeah, yeah." He shook his head, apparently unaccustomed to women refusing his romantic overtures. Reuben tried to get up, his belly catching on the table edge, before he pulled himself up unsteadily to his feet. "But I really think you're making a mistake. You have no idea what you're missing."

As his hulking mass stood before her, blocking her path to the door, her attention was drawn to the gaping hole where two buttons of his beer-stained shirt had gone missing. His sweat-matted belly hair emerged from the hole and she was unable to avoid a horrifying image of his fleshy, sweaty body thrusting against her on crisp, white hotel sheets. She felt a wave of nausea that grew stronger with the smell of his stale sweat in such proximity.

Janet gathered her purse and briefcase from the bench. She calmed the nausea rising in her throat and shook Reuben's hand, eager to prove her civility before making her escape. Freedom beckoned beyond the door.

She thought of the painting in her room. If Reuben's flabby, sweaty form were on top of her, would she pray for deliverance, too? Surely, life as a laurel tree was preferable.

"No doubt, you're right, Reuben. But I'm willing to take that risk, and live with the regret the rest of my life. I've had a lovely time. Thanks."

A sense of relief washed over her as she approached the exit with long strides, fresh air beckoning beyond. Her steps became more determined the closer she came. When she was halfway there, Janet heard Reuben's drunken yell behind her.

"It's your loss! But Jilly, don't forget what I told you. You're wasting your life. Books are dead!"

Later that night, the house was peaceful, with all the students tucked into their beds. The silence was welcome, punctuated only by the occasional squeaks and groans one could expect from an old house. The dimmed hallway lights reassured Janet as she sat alone in her nightgown, hugging her knees and remembering how her mother used to slip her arms around her shoulders when she was younger, to banish away any traces of sadness.

Janet wiped away a tear. From her perch on the empty staircase, she had an unobstructed view of the full-length portraits of Sir Edward and his sister, Emma.

Had Sir Edward and Emma ever met a Tony or a Reuben when they stayed in their home in Bath? Or were their evenings filled with lively, intelligent conversation? Janet studied every chiseled line of Sir Edward's face, his decided gaze, his trim waist not thickened at an early age by sedentary hours at a computer and too many pints of beer. Was it so impossible to find a man like this in her modern world?

She looked once again at the painting beside him, at the peach glow enlivening the canvas that captured Emma. Her golden curls shone on top of her head. The dewy rose bloomed for all eternity in her long, slender fingers. Her lips were ever so slightly upturned. *Perhaps we could have been friends, Emma. If only I'd lived two hundred years ago.* But the lovely face in the painting made no acknowledgement of having heard her thoughts.

Far below, a key turned in the lock, a deadbolt clicked, and footsteps came up the stairs. A few moments later, Amrita stood before her in jeans and sneakers, carrying a small weekend bag over her shoulders. Her mouth opened in surprise when she made out the form of her roommate.

"Janet," she whispered, "you almost gave me a heart attack! What are you still doing up?"

"How was Oxford?" Janet turned her attention from the portraits with a smile.

"Fine, but you didn't answer my question."

"It was an awful day. I couldn't sleep." Janet sighed. "Sometimes I think I was born in the wrong century. Amrita, have you ever wished you could live in the past? Spend time with people like Sir Edward and Emma, rather than dealing with the kind of people we meet today?"

Amrita sank down onto the steps beside her friend and examined the portraits in silence. "All the time, Janet. All the time." She took her friend's hand and stood up. "But now it's time to get you to bed."

Chapter 10

Two weeks later, Janet sat in the architectural studio. A balmy June breeze wafted through the window as she examined the final details of Tony's elaborate, high-tech man cave.

Workers were arriving to Tony's home in five days' time to begin dismantling the library bookshelves. A few days later, the nineteenth-century fresco would be painted over and the hand-cut Bohemian crystal dismantled to make way for the disco ball.

Not technically a crime against humanity, but close enough. She'd cringed as she signed the paperwork authorizing its demolition.

Janet fought the urge to cry every time she stepped into the former library. Once it was shorn of all traces of beauty, it would become just another rich boy's playground. Then it wouldn't pain her so much to enter the room.

Feeling a hand on her shoulder, she turned to see Mr. Perry looking down at her. Kindness shone in his eyes.

"Janet, my dear. You're taking this too hard. Your client has earned his money selling God knows what on the internet. Now he's entitled to spend it as he pleases." He released her shoulder.

"I know I shouldn't let it bother me. But how can you stand it? He wants to destroy a thing of beauty, something that's survived two hundred years and could have been salvaged. And in its place he wants to build an expensive video arcade. This is supposed to be progress?"

Mr. Perry shook his head. The glasses he always wore on a chain around his neck glittered under the chandelier. "Our job is to provide clients with what they want. And since the building wasn't protected as an historic landmark, our client can do as he wishes. Even if I don't agree, I can't be too hard on him." Mr. Perry indicated the room around him. "I'm named for a nineteenth-century ancestor. A doctor. He bought this home, and it's been in our family ever since. He was a man of science, and I've read his journals containing his medical observations. He tended the great gentlemen and ladies of this town. And yet, they considered him as they would any tradesman—unworthy of their regard. There was a big scandal when he purchased this home. Was that progress? I'm certain the wealthy classes asked themselves the same question when they protested a commoner living amongst them."

Janet offered a weak smile to her mentor. "Maybe you're right. But I'm certain that the nineteenth-century Sheldon Perry was worth two million Tonys."

"That may be, my dear. But change is inevitable. We can't live in the past, as much as we may wish to sometimes."

The kindness in his blue eyes shone beneath a shock of messy, white curls. She had grown affectionate toward Mr. Perry's "mad scientist" air, so different from her father's overbearing and decisive style. She found herself wondering again how two such different men had forged a friendship lasting decades.

"I suppose not."

"Good." Mr. Perry clapped his hands together. "Now Janet. It's Friday. Go home. Do the things you young people should be doing on a Friday evening. I'll see you Monday."

"Thank you, Mr. Perry." Janet switched off her computer. "Have a nice weekend."

Janet walked the short distance from The Circus back to The Crescent. The late afternoon sun illuminated both buildings with a golden light, and she recalled her first day in Bath and the Jane Austen walking tour with Malcolm.

She and Malcolm were to Skype later in the evening. There were no classes scheduled for Monday, and most of her classmates had seized the opportunity to spend the weekend in London. They'd booked theatre tickets and had plans for museums and restaurants and pubs, eager to be absorbed into the exciting pace of city life after a month in quiet Bath.

Janet longed to join them. But work on Tony's new home had taken up too much of her time. Now she was behind on the class readings. The London getaway would only cause her to fall further behind. Truth be told, she wasn't entirely sorry to stay in Bath. The easy rhythms of Bath life had grown on her. The neon, the traffic, and the London crowds would all lull her out of her comforting nineteenth-century frame of mind.

When she reached her room, Amrita was placing her last items in a weekend bag. "You're sure, Janet? We could leave you some quiet time to read if you come with us."

"Don't tempt me." Janet flung herself onto her bed and observed her friend. "I'll be much better company once I'm *somewhat* caught up."

Amrita zipped up her bag and hoisted it onto her shoulder. "I still can't believe you're able to complete *anything* at all— keeping up with our seminars, designing houses for heathen internet gazillionaires. I wish you could have a bit of fun, too …"

"Next time, I promise. But I'll want to hear everything about your time in London. Enjoy it for the both of us." Janet hugged her. "I'll miss you." She watched her friend bound down the stairs.

Amrita paused at the portrait of Sir Edward and pointed to it. "You don't fool me at all. You only want to stay here to have Mr. Hot-in-his-britches all to yourself."

Janet shook her head. "Get lost! Otherwise, I'll give Reuben your number and tell him you're in for a bit of fun and heard he was the bloke to call."

Amrita grimaced before running down the stairs to meet the others.

Janet returned to her desk, opened her laptop, and clicked on Skype. She picked up the photo Malcolm sent her, printed on thick, glossy paper. Her first day, standing eagerly beside the Tiepolo. She slipped it into her well-worn copy of *Pride and Prejudice*.

Janet longed for a hot bath and an early bedtime. Her watch said six o'clock. Lunchtime in Boston. Malcolm would either be out with clients or sitting at his desk with a sandwich, working. Leisurely lunch hours weren't tolerated at her father's studio. Honestly, lunch itself was always an issue. On days when she worked there, she often sat outside in the sunshine to eat her bagel and read a book. That twenty-minute break was viewed as an act of rebellion by her father.

She managed to reach Malcolm. His face filled her screen, the familiar walls of her father's studio behind him.

"Hey, Janet. How are you? Have you installed the disco ball yet?"

She groaned. "I was trying to forget. They're coming in to demolish the bookshelves next week. I was going to go to church this weekend to light a candle in its memory. Can't you build the heathen some monstrosity in Boston so he'll stop massacring Bath properties?"

Malcolm chuckled. "He'd be in good company. We're up to our eyeballs in hotshot internet entrepreneurs with more money than taste. Are you still in time to convince him?"

"Let's change topics. How's my dad? Still pissed off at me?"

Malcolm glanced over his shoulder. "Don't exaggerate. He's worried about you," he whispered. "He only wants what's best for you."

"See, here's where you and I disagree. *I* think he only wants what's best for him."

Malcolm looked as if she'd slapped him. He often reminded her of a hurt puppy, and she hated always being the cruel one.

"Okay, forget it. So I'm here practically all alone. Everyone's off in London because we don't have classes on Monday. But I have to catch up on my readings. I've been putting in too many hours in the studio, and I'm falling behind."

"Wow, a whole long weekend as mistress of Huntington House, reading out on The Crescent lawn. Sounds like hell." He smiled. "By the way, how's work on your dissertation going?"

"Ouch! Sore spot. I've done absolutely *nothing* since I've arrived here. Professor Williams recommended all the right archives, but I've had no time at all. Kind of ironic, really. I'm living here in the splendor of the nineteenth century, yet I'm unable to write a word about social customs of the same period. Go figure."

Malcolm shook his head. "Give it time. It'll come to you."

"I hope so. I was counting on getting a lot done this semester."

Malcolm leaned closer to the screen. "I know you. You will. And I hope you'll let me read your drafts."

"I wish I had the same confidence in myself that you seem to have in me."

In the background, her father's booming voice called his senior architects to the meeting room.

When Malcolm turned back to the screen, his eyes were apologetic. "You heard that, right? Gotta go."

"Of course. Say hi to Dad for me."

"Sure. Enjoy your weekend." He leaned closer. "I miss you." He kissed his hand and touched the screen.

Janet touched the image of his fingers. "I miss you, too."

For a moment after the call ended, she sat in silence, gazing out the window onto the lawn and feeling completely alone. She'd never imagined comforting Skype calls with Malcolm. He followed her progress in Bath. He made her laugh. He kept her grounded. It killed her to think that her father might have been right.

It was better not to think about it. She made her way to the bathtub and ran the hot water, eager to relax her limbs after a grueling jog that morning with Siobhan, followed by only the briefest of showers. As she slipped into the steaming water, she felt the tension wash away. The bubbles caressed her sore muscles as she closed her eyes and relaxed.

She forgot about Reuben's leering gaze, Tony's petulant-child demands. She pretended she and Ted weren't responsible for destroying a nineteenth-century home. She banished Malcolm and his tender looks far from her mind. This weekend was all about the nineteenth century. She would be caught up when her classmates returned from London. She sank down deeper into the steaming water and closed her eyes.

When she emerged, fresh and powdered, in clean pyjamas, she felt like a new person. Before climbing into her bed, she sat for a moment on the covers, staring at Apollo and Daphne.

Where are you going, Daphne? Why are you in such a hurry? Was it what you expected it would be? Do you ever regret the old life you left behind?

But Daphne's smooth face provided no answers. Janet stood and stepped closer, hesitating, foolishly expecting some sign. Yet when she stood before the painting, she felt her legs turn of their own accord. They led her back to her dresser and the cosmetics case that sat on top.

She unzipped the case and peered inside. Nail scissors lay within, their gleaming chrome brilliant against the silky, black interior. Her mind raced. The scissors beckoned to her. She stroked the glimmering metal, feeling her heart pounding steadily in her chest. Slowly, she lifted them out and returned to the canvas.

She glanced behind her, sensing a presence. No one. Janet stood with her nose to the brushwork, simply because she could. She'd never get this close to the canvas when it was in the National Gallery. She stared at the image—at the jumble of pink and green and blue.

There had to be some way to prove that the painting was, for a brief time, truly hers. Some little mark only she would know about. Her heart pounded as she gripped the smooth scissors tighter in her fist. She raised the hand clutching the scissors, observing the glint of the lights off the cool metal. Her hand acted on its own as she slashed down quickly, but precisely.

Nausea rose in her throat as she saw the tiny scratch she'd executed in the lower righthand corner. What had made her do it? She'd never done anything like that before, never willingly vandalized property—especially property as valuable as this painting. And yet ...

She examined the tiny mark closely. The scratch was *her* handiwork. An immortal trace of her existence. No one else would ever know of it, but each time she passed the canvas, she would see her mark.

Afraid of what she might be capable of in her excitable state, she placed the scissors back in the cosmetics bag, and shoved it out of reach underneath her bed.

She climbed under her covers, her heart still pounding with guilt for what she'd done. Her eyes grew heavy as they studied Apollo and Daphne.

Chapter 11

Her dreams were troubled that night.

When she woke, not feeling rested at all after a night of feverish tossing and turning, her gaze fell on the Tiepolo. She recalled her actions of the following evening, and it all made sense. For in her dreams she'd been Daphne, running so fast she feared her heart would burst. Apollo was hard on her heels, and she prayed for her metamorphosis. Her passage to her new world.

The strange sensation of the leaves sprouting from her fingertips lingered. She shook her hands to banish the tingling feeling.

You fool. She walked over to the painting and examined the tiny scratch, feeling ashamed of her actions of the previous night.

She dressed quickly and examined herself in the mirror. She wore a simple sundress, but there was something about the Empire-waist and the way it skimmed her body that looked almost as if it could be found in one of the portraits of the era. *While everyone's away, I can play nineteenth-century dress-up.*

She walked down the staircase to the breakfast room, breaking the silence on the landing. "Good morning, Emma,

Sir Edward. A lovely Saturday we're expecting. I may spend it out on the lawn. Would you care to join me?" The portrait likenesses remained immobile. She continued down the staircase.

Bread, marmalade and coffee had been set out by the kitchen staff. She ate in silence, Miss Smith and the other household staff nowhere to be seen. Janet sipped her coffee and thought about the day stretching out before her.

Returning to her room, Janet brushed her teeth and packed a small bag with her copy of *Pride and Prejudice*, her sunglasses, cellphone, a pen and notebook, and her sketchpad and some pencils. She paused at the doorway and returned to stand before the painting. Cautiously, she reached out and touched the scratch, feeling the solidity of the paint beneath her fingers. She stood immobile for some moments, jerking back as a mild jolt of electricity passed through her fingers and up her arm. Confused, Janet shook her hand.

It had to be the solitude playing tricks with her mind. She descended the grand staircase and made her way outside to The Crescent lawn. The smell of fresh-cut grass filled her nostrils. One never noticed that familiar smell in Boston, but here, she loved to breathe in deeply whenever the lawn was mowed. After several days of rain, she delighted in the blue sky and blazing sunshine.

Janet selected a spot on the expanse of green lawn. She looked around her at all the people gathered out on the green, before pulling her book out of her bag. She placed her small bag under her head, careful not to crush her sketchpad, and sank back into the lush green grass.

Looking up, she watched the birds soaring above in the clear blue sky. She wondered how her friends were in London, what their plans were for the day. But she was not envious as she opened her book.

As she opened to her page, she couldn't help but reflect on how glorious it was to be able to reread *Pride and Prejudice* out on The Crescent lawn in preparation for next week's classes. The time flew by, without interruption.

Janet remained on the green for hours, completely absorbed in the story. She arrived to Elizabeth's visit to Rosings Park, and savored the familiar descriptions of the obsequious Mr. Collins and the overbearing Lady Catherine. She read for the hundredth time the visit of Colonel Fitzwilliam and Mr. Darcy, thrilling at the subtle flirtation between Elizabeth and Mr. Darcy, holding her breath as she read Mr. Darcy's haughty declarations of love and Elizabeth's headstrong refusal. She thrilled at the pages of Darcy's letter to Elizabeth, and closed the book with a happy sigh. She had read and reread these pages countless times, but she never tired of them.

She closed her eyes and replayed the scenes from the pages in her mind. Not for the first time, she found herself wishing she could live in Elizabeth's time. The sun warmed her face, and she felt in complete peace out on the green, the sounds and smells of summer all around her. This tranquil feeling was shattered by a sharp sound.

Crack!

Startled, Janet sat up. She turned towards the sound and saw a small group of boys who had set up a cricket pitch on the green. It was the first time she'd seen cricket played here. Perhaps it was time to gather her things to get to the chemist's. After her errand, she could return to the lawn for the afternoon, before moving on to the library for the evening. She loved sinking into the comfortable chairs, surrounded by books and silence. This weekend would deliver more silence than normal.

As she packed her book into her carry bag, the photo of her that Malcolm had sent fell out. She smiled at the image from her first day at Huntington House, beaming under the Tiepolo.

How much she'd changed from that day. The course had provided her with the strength she needed. Each day, the idea of standing up to her father became more plausible. What was the worst he could do to her? Cut her off? Leave everything to Malcolm?

And if she and Malcolm were able to follow her father's wishes by ensuring his son-in-law of choice? Would she be able to pursue her academic career and still participate occasionally with key projects? She would, after all, graduate with her degree in architecture, as her father had insisted. Nothing kept her from practicing occasionally. Might that be an acceptable compromise to her unyielding father?

With these confused thoughts filling her head, she tucked the photo in her book and placed it into her bag before standing. She heard the harsh *crack* of the cricket bat and turned once again toward the piercing sound.

Suddenly, she felt a sickening thud on her skull, and a blinding pain sent her tumbling backwards.

The pain was excruciating, but she was still aware of the motion and sounds around her. Everything happened in slow motion. The people closest to her raced over. From the corner of her eye, she saw that the boy playing cricket dropped the bat and cried out, looking fearful.

The metallic taste in her mouth was unmistakable. She raised her hand to the pain. When she pulled her hand back, she tried in vain to focus on it, but saw everything in double. Even so, the bright red color was unambiguous. She felt a throbbing pain on her head where she'd been hit, but by what? The cricket ball?

Where was the sun? It was crowded out by all the faces only centimeters from her own. What were they doing here? Why were they so close to her, their concerned faces practically pressed to hers? *Please, give me some space*, she pleaded silently, unable to form the words. *I can hardly breathe.*

"Ma'am, are you okay?"

"Miss, does it hurt? I have a handkerchief. Let me try to stop the bleeding." Strong hands pressed against her throbbing head. The voices continued.

"How do you feel?"

"Is there a doctor here?"

"Can someone call an ambulance?"

"No!" she cried out in a voice she didn't recognize. From where had she channeled that powerful voice? She hadn't even believed she had the strength to speak. "No, please," she spoke in a voice barely above a whisper. "I live here at The Crescent. Number Ten. Take me home ... please ..."

It was becoming a struggle to keep her eyes open, hard as she tried. She heard worried voices all around her.

"Should we move her?"

"It's a head injury, not the spine. Moving her shouldn't be a problem. Let's carry her to her home, and they can call the doctor to visit her there."

Who were these people? Would they bring her where she needed to go? Could she trust them? She could hardly do otherwise. What possible control did she have over anything?

Her eyes grew heavier. The searing pain was unbearable. Maybe if she stopped struggling, the pain would subside. She felt her eyes close as the strangers lifted her up in the air. The sound of the birds filled the air, and then all was silent.

Chapter 12

Janet's eyes fluttered open. Frescoed ceiling, grand chandelier, a thick white down comforter, sunlight streaming through the window. When she tried to sit up, sharp pain radiated through her body. She slumped back in bed, an involuntary groan escaping as her head hit the pillow.

"Miss Emma! I think she has finally woken."

Janet turned toward the sound, but the effort was excruciating. Footsteps grew closer as Janet struggled to keep her eyes open, the pounding in her head an incessant jackhammer.

A stout woman with a worried, ruddy face approached the bedside, moving her face closer to Janet's. She wore an odd little cap on her head; tendrils of gray hair curled out from beneath it.

Who on earth was she? Perhaps someone who worked with Miss Smith.

"Oh, ma'am." Relief was evident in the woman's voice and in her kind brown eyes. "You had us so worried. The doctor called several times, but we had given up hope you would wake. How good to see you back with us. Miss Emma has been beside herself."

Miss Emma?

"Ma'am," she continued, "what is your name? We have been so concerned that your family is waiting for news about your whereabouts."

Janet tried to speak, but her mouth was so dry. "My name ... my name is Janet Roberts."

Another woman approached the bed. She wore the same odd, lacy cap. A Bath nurses' cap? But even as Janet noticed her, the lines of the woman's face grew fuzzy. It was a struggle to keep her eyes open.

"What kind of name is that?" said the woman with the grey hair to the other. "Did you hear? Jane Et Roberts?"

"No, no. She must be giving us an initial. Did you mean to say Jane T. Roberts, ma'am?"

Her head throbbed and her vision blurred. She wasn't strong enough to explain to these women. It hardly mattered. She nodded. She closed her eyes, willing the pain to stop, until everything became black again.

Muttering woke her. The room was dark. What time was it? What had happened? She tried to sit up, despite the throbbing in her head. Her movement caused a flurry in the room.

The two women with the lace caps she remembered from earlier scurried to her side. What were they wearing? Did Miss Smith insist on these period maid costumes? It seemed too absurd, but with such pain and dizziness, it hardly mattered.

"Miss Emma!" called one of the women as she raced out of the room. The other woman laid Janet gently back against a pillow she was plumping.

"There now, Miss Jane. You rest here. You've had a blow to your head. Those ruffians were back out on the green, hitting a ball around."

Janet tried to focus on the woman's face. By concentrating fully, the lines grew more distinct, the fuzziness waned. The woman's eyes grew wide as she spoke.

"When you were hurt, they ran away. Simply left you there to bleed to death. What is the problem with youth today? Thank goodness Miss Emma happened upon you. Doctor Perry has been to call, and he has given strict instructions. You are to stay in bed until you've recovered."

Now she remembered. The boys playing cricket on the green. Gingerly, she reached up to her head, to the spot where she'd been struck by the ball. She could feel a bandage wrapped around it. The doctor must have made a house call to Huntington House. She wondered how long she'd been sleeping.

"Thank you, ma'am," she managed in a strong voice. "Could you inform Miss Smith that I've woken? I imagine she's already spoken to Professor Williams."

The woman looked confused. "Miss Smith? Professor Williams? Are those your family members, Miss Jane? Miss Emma has been all around Bath, making inquiries about your family. No one seems to know you, which is quite odd indeed in a city like Bath."

Janet closed her eyes for a moment. Apparently these women didn't work for Miss Smith. Where on earth was she? She remembered having been moved. She clearly remembered having told her rescuers her address before losing consciousness. Had they brought her to the wrong house?

Careful not to lift her pounding head, she slowly tilted her face to either side to survey the room as best she could. It was unmistakably her room. The chandelier. The fireplace. The large windows with their now-familiar views over the green.

But wait. The furniture was different. Where was the second bed? The desks? The second bureau? The computers? Had Amrita moved out in order to leave her alone to recover? She turned slowly to view the fireplace again. Her heart beat faster. Something was wrong.

"The Tiepolo!"

"Pardon, Miss Jane?"

"The Tiepolo!" Panic caused her voice to rise an octave. "Where is it? It used to hang right there!" She raised a trembling finger to point to the empty spot. "Apollo chasing Daphne. You know it. Where did it go? It was there this morning."

The women with the odd caps exchanged concerned glances. It was the grey-haired woman who spoke.

"Ma'am, you've been asleep for two days. You must be confused. You seem to be describing Master Edward's painting back at his library at Helmsley Manor. It has never hung here at Huntington House."

The Tiepolo that now hangs in Huntington House—which is soon destined to the National Gallery—used to hang here in the place of honor in Sir Edward's library. He spent significant amounts of time here, and we know that he considered it his prized possession. He moved it with him when he left for Bath to restore his health. It hung where he could see it clearly from his sickbed. Of course, he never returned to Helmsley Manor, and neither did the Tiepolo.

Mr. Whitshaw's words at Helmsley Manor. What was going on? No, there had to be a reasonable explanation. Maybe the National Gallery had come for the painting earlier than expected. Come while she'd been unconscious.

Janet closed her eyes again and took deep breaths. Surely someone would be able to clear this up. Janet heard the rustle of a dress.

"Miss Emma," said the woman next to the bed. "Thank goodness you have come. Our patient has awoken and she ... she seems confused."

"That hardly seems surprising after a head injury." The young woman stopped at the edge of the bed, her kind eyes fixed on Janet. "Miss Roberts, what a pleasure to see you have woken.

Allow me to introduce myself. I am Emma Huntington. I found you on the lawn after you were hurt, and we had you removed here to our home. We have been so worried. The doctor told us we must be patient for your full recovery." The young woman sat on the edge of Janet's bed as she spoke.

Janet's sight grew unfocused once again, and she was unable to concentrate fully on the woman's words. Why did her sight seem to get better, only to return to shadow and light?

She struggled to see the features of the woman seated at her bedside. When she squinted, her vision seemed clearer. The woman also wore an odd little cap, but she was young and pretty, with tendrils of blonde hair rebelliously escaping down from the unattractive cap. Her blue eyes sparkled and provided a glow to her pale but perfect complexion. She wore an elaborately embroidered, Empire-waisted gown. Was she headed out to a costume party? Her look was kind, her voice sweet and concerned. Yes, this woman would be able to help Janet to find her way home.

"Miss Roberts, I know we have never met previously, but I have spent so much time by your side as you have recovered. May I call you Jane? I would be delighted if you would call me Emma."

Why did she look so familiar? Janet was certain she had seen that face before, but where? If only she could place it. For now, she was more worried about her vision, which seemed to come and go.

"Of course. But Emma, I'm so confused. Is this number ten, The Crescent? Are you any relation to the Huntingtons of Huntington House? I thought the last of the line died some years ago."

There was a strange look in Emma's eyes as she responded. "But what a terrible thing to say! Of course the family line has not come to an end. It is true that my mother died years ago and my father passed away two years ago, but my brother continues the family line. He is Sir Edward Huntington." The tense lines of her features softened again. "But I should not be so cross with you, my dear Jane. It is clear you are a stranger to these parts, and you know not what you say. From where do you hail?"

Janet's head throbbed, from the concussion and from the intense confusion of her current situation. Who was this Emma? Had she accompanied the students on one of their outings? She decided to do her part to keep the conversation flowing, hoping to garner additional information. She also decided to parrot the strange vocabulary. Why did they all speak so oddly?

"I hail from Boston."

Emma gasped. "Boston? The New World? But how extraordinary! That would explain your strange English." She pat Janet on the arm, then gasped and raised her hand to her mouth. "Oh, pardon me. That must sound terribly rude. We are simply not accustomed to hearing Bostonians in these parts. This would also explain why I was unable to learn anything about you while inquiring around Bath."

The New World? Then again, she'd been hit pretty hard by those cricket players. Maybe she was in a coma. Do people dream in a coma? But there was something about that face. The oddest thought occurred to her. *No, too ridiculous.*

Janet took a deep breath before speaking. Her heart raced. "Emma, what's today's date?"

"The date? Today is the fifteenth of June."

"Of what year, Emma?"

"What year?" Her eyes grew wide. "Oh yes, I see. The doctor warned us you may have some confusion at first, and may ask odd questions. Why, it is 1813, of course."

"1813?" Janet's voice was too loud for the tranquil room. "Emma, who put you up to this? Amrita? Professor Williams? Is this part of the program—a full immersion in nineteenth-century manners?" She screamed out towards the general direction of the hallway, "Professor Williams! You can come out now! If my head weren't throbbing with the aftermath of a concussion, I would find this all terribly amusing."

Emma looked concerned. "Dear Jane, you mustn't disturb yourself. The doctor said you would require plenty of rest."

Janet's thoughts were confused. She alternated between crisp vision and shadows. Behind her eyes, the throbbing continued. Perhaps if she slept, she'd wake with Amrita beside her and her classmates returned from London.

"I need to sleep," she croaked, willing herself not to cry.

Despite the throbbing pain, she turned to her side and closed her eyes. She heard Emma blow out the candle at her bedside and leave the room, closing the door silently behind her. *Please, God,* she prayed, *wake me from this nightmare.*

Chapter 13

The sun streamed through the window. Janet opened her eyes and stretched in bed. Her head felt clearer. She remembered the odd dream from the other night, but pushed it from her mind.

Janet heard the door opening and turned toward the sound, attempting to prop herself up. "Amrita?" she said hopefully. The lace-capped woman from the previous day entered with a breakfast tray.

"I'm glad to see you've woken, Miss Jane. It's time to eat. You must regain your strength."

Janet fell back to her pillow in frustration, all the hope of having woken from this endless dream dashed. But did one feel hunger pangs in dreams? Janet didn't know, but she was ravenous, and the smell of soup and fresh bread wafted invitingly from the breakfast tray. She sat up eagerly in bed as, with great ceremony, the becapped woman lay the tray over her lap, then fluffed the pillows behind her.

Her frustration could wait until after breakfast. She attacked her breakfast like a savage.

"Oh my. Well then," said the woman.

Janet noted the fear in the woman's eyes, perhaps wondering if they were sheltering a madwoman. "Perhaps," the woman hesitated, "I should leave you alone to enjoy your meal."

Janet hadn't realized how hungry she was. When had she last eaten? It must have been the morning of the accident. Was that days ago or weeks? Maybe the hunger was causing her confusion. Perhaps if she ate something and spoke again with Emma, everything would make sense again. Surely she'd misunderstood something the other day. *1813, indeed!*

She ate more soup, its rich warmth working its way down to her grumbling stomach. Everything tasted delicious. The kitchen staff was clearly more skilled than the ones that usually cooked here for the students. Or was it the period costumes that made all the difference? After sopping up the last bits of soup with pieces of bread, she pushed the tray aside and raised herself cautiously from the bed.

With tremendous effort and deep, labored breaths, Janet took tiny, unbalanced steps across the room until she reached the grand windows. Feeling dizzy and exhausted from the effort, she pressed her forehead against the cool glass and balanced herself with two hands clutching the window frames. When her head stopped spinning, she focused her gaze onto the green below.

Her knees gave way immediately, but she forced herself to remain standing. She could hardly breathe as she stared, dumbfounded, out the window. Every nerve in her body was still. Her brain attempted to make sense of what her eyes were seeing. The cars, the streetlights, the electrical wires were all gone.

In their place was an entirely new world. A world that made no sense.

Beneath her window strolled corseted women in elegant dresses, men in formal jackets and top hats, servants carrying baskets, and an endless stream of horses and carriages. Not a car in sight. Not even a single power line. Her strength gave out all at once and she slumped helplessly to the floor.

What in God's name was happening to her?

The door opened and she heard footsteps racing toward her.

"Oh, Miss Jane! Please return to bed at once!"

Janet clung to the woman's sturdy shoulder, grateful to be directed back to her bed, where she slumped listlessly into the deep feather pillows.

Could it be true? Had she somehow awoken in 1813? Or was this all a strange, protracted dream?

"I'll fetch Miss Emma."

A few moments later, the woman returned with a concerned-looking Emma. Once again, Emma sat on the edge of Janet's bed, taking her hand.

"Oh, poor Jane. Miller told me about your fall. You mustn't tax yourself so. I have been thinking about you, so confused, so far from your home and your family."

You have no idea, Emma.

"Now that you are improving, I won't leave you alone so much. If you want to get up, let us know. Miller and I can help you. Please promise me that you won't venture around again unassisted. I am fearful it could hinder your recovery. That must be your aim now."

Janet closed her eyes. "Emma, I am so confused. I have blanks in my memory. They seem to be coming back, but maybe you could assist me." Janet opened her eyes, scrutinizing Emma's face. "Now I know why you look so familiar. I didn't want to believe it, but I saw your portrait. In the painting, you're wearing a lovely white dress and holding a rose, with Helmsley Manor behind you." Janet held her breath, half-hoping Emma would deny it. Prove to Janet that it was only confusion that was to be expected following a concussion.

"You are describing the portrait painted by the pupil of Sir Joshua Reynolds. My brother commissioned it. But how could you have seen that? It has always hung in Helmsley Manor. In fact, I noticed among your sketchings a lovely drawing of Helmsley Manor. Have you already been there?"

"How did you see my sketching?" Janet furrowed her brow.

"I apologize. We did not go through your personal items, but your sketchbook fell out of your bag when our servants carried you into our house. We were attempting to discover a clue to your provenance. Your sketches are extraordinary! My brother has procured me a drawing master, but I wish I had only a fraction of your talent. Have you honestly been to all of these places? To France and Italy and Egypt and Japan? I do not know anyone who has travelled as widely."

"I travelled with my father, for his work. He's an architect and after my mother died, he took me with him on all of his assignments."

"But were not the trips difficult on you? Such long sea journeys and endless carriage rides to reach such distant shores."

"Of course, you don't yet have airplanes. Those will really revolutionize things." What on earth was she saying?

"Airplanes?" Emma dragged out the syllables, looking confused. "You have such strange words from the New World. Tell me about Italy. I have always longed to go. My brother has been, but I was too young to accompany him."

"Italy is beautiful. The countryside, the architecture, the art, the food ... and, of course, the men."

Emma blushed and giggled as she met Janet's gaze.

"No seriously, I believe I was probably happiest there. I lived in Rome for a year studying architecture before I returned to Boston to study at the university."

Emma looked puzzled once again. "Study at the university, Jane? Whatever do you mean? Surely even in the New World women are not admitted to the university?"

Careful, Janet. What are you saying? Surely women didn't study in 1813 in America. What were we doing? Embroidering. Sewing. Bearing children. What on earth am I qualified to discuss?

What do I know about America in 1813? Was the War of 1812 with England already over? Didn't it go on for some years? God, I can only get myself in trouble here. Better not to talk about myself and to focus on asking the questions.

"Tell me more about you, Emma. The other day you said you lost both parents. I am sorry. Is it only you and your brother now?"

"Yes, it is. I do not believe I ever would have survived such heartbreak if not for my brother." A smile formed on her lovely face. "He is nine years older than I, almost like a father to me. Edward comes infrequently to Bath. He is extremely involved with work on the manor. It is lovely there, but I often long for a wider society. He understands my longing, and so sends me to Bath. We have an aunt here who also watches over me. Edward may join me in a week or two. And you, Jane? How do you find Bath? How does it compare to your Boston?"

"It's completely different, especially compared to *my* Boston. You have no idea. But I love it here. I feel like I wandered into a Jane Austen novel. Well," she smiled, "especially now."

"Jane Austen? Who is she?"

"The author of *Sense and Sensibility* and, I believe this year, of *Pride and Prejudice.*"

Emma shook her head almost imperceptibly. "It is the first time I have heard that name spoken. I knew only that the novels were written by an anonymous female author. I have read *Sense and Sensibility*, but I have not yet read *Pride and Prejudice.* How do you come to know the author's name?"

"Ah, the New World is rife with rumors. I heard it there. But Emma, you simply *must* read *Pride and Prejudice.* It's my favorite."

"Well then, I shall procure the novel and read it to you as you recuperate. But as for talented women authors, no one can surpass my favorite. Tell me what you think of Mrs. Radcliffe. Have you read *The Mysteries of Udolpho*?"

Janet had never in her life been happier to have read a book. "Oh, yes. I just read it. I did not know much about Gothic novels before."

"Is it not thrilling? I love Mrs. Radcliffe's novels! The *Mysteries of Udolpho* is so exciting, the scenery so vivid, and Montoni is such a wicked villain. It makes one feel transported to France and Italy. Did you not feel that as you were reading it? You who have been there yourself?"

"Mrs. Radcliffe herself had never been to France and Italy, and that is fairly apparent from her prose. The geography is questionable and all the anachronisms bothered me. But perhaps in my present state I can sympathize with Mrs. Radcliffe more. I am glad to have read it. I can see why she is so popular, but I find it inferior to Miss Austen's work."

"That remains to be seen, my dear Jane. I venture to guess that hundreds of years from now, everyone will still be eagerly reading Mrs. Radcliffe's works, while your Jane Austen will have completely slipped from the collective memory."

"I wish we could wager on that." Janet wondered how many people outside of academia even recognized the name of Mrs. Radcliffe in the modern world.

"Tell me more about your travels. Where have you been in France? Have you been to Paris?"

"I adore Paris, but I lived for a year in southern France, in Avignon, when I was fifteen. My father worked on projects and sent me to a French school. He wanted me to learn French well, and to study the architecture of the region."

"This is all so shocking for us." Emma shook her head. "The mere idea that one could live in the land of Napoleon Bonaparte. Have you seen him?"

"Only at his oversized tomb at the *Invalides*."

Emma flinched. "I beg your pardon. His tomb? Excuse me for appearing rude, but why do you speak such nonsense? If only Napoleon *were* dead and buried and no longer a threat to us. Alas, the threat is all too real."

"Of course, I spoke out of turn. We met the architect who was commissioned to design his future tomb. About what one could expect from such a diminutive megalomaniac."

"How shocking you are. It must be the New World influence. His invasion of Russia last year was a disaster, and now we have entered the Sixth Coalition and declared war on France. So many of our young men are on their way to fight, and possibly sacrifice their lives against Napoleon's army. It seems cruel to make light of their noble bravery."

Oh, no. If she really were back in 1813, she'd constantly be inching her way across a loaded minefield. For her, Napoleon had always been a pompous figure from the safe and distant past. How many times had she studied his campaigns, seen majestic portraits hanging on the walls of European museums, and wondered about how he'd effectively terrorized all of Europe? And here, she found herself in the midst of this fear. When was it exactly that he'd be banished to Elba? 1813? 1814? Wasn't his eventual defeat in Waterloo in 1815?

She tried desperately to scour her memory for these facts from her most recent Western Civilization course, the very facts she'd forgotten so quickly after her midterm exam. How could she possibly have imagined that her failure to internalize this knowledge would eventually get her into so much trouble? Who factored in possible time travel when memorizing important historical dates?

Her head ached. For how long would she be here? She longed to wake up in her twenty-first-century room, where she was capable of discussing current events without risking a lynching.

And yet, how extraordinary! She could barely believe her own eyes, but the carriages and residents, the woman before her whose portrait she'd gazed on each day in Huntington House, seemed very real indeed.

She couldn't possibly be dreaming this, could she? Yet, how could she truly be back in 1813? It was too much to process. Better to keep speaking—but not about politics—and to listen carefully and try to understand more.

"I am sorry. Forgive me. We Bostonians are renowned for our gallows humor, and we may sound irreverent. I did not intend to be disrespectful. I do understand the sacrifices England and other countries are being asked to make because of Napoleon's expansionist ambitions."

"And now our countries are at war as well."

Mystery solved. The War of 1812 was apparently longer than one year. Didn't it continue up to the defeat of Napoleon? It must have. Weren't England and France allies once again at that war's conclusion? What she wouldn't give to have her thick, authoritative Western Civilization textbook with her right now. Was there a nineteenth-century equivalent to catch her up to speed?

"Emma, I hope this will not affect us. After all, women hardly decide on the wars."

"Too true." Emma looked out the window and sighed. "We only suffer the consequences. Let us talk of more pleasant matters. Will not your family be alarmed? Shall I contact them?"

My family. Oh, dear. Think, Janet. Won't the war give a good excuse for me to be here? It's not as if telegrams or emails existed. Communication would be sketchy at best in the early nineteenth century, and must be completely cut off between two enemy states.

"No," Janet willed her voice to sound confident and convinced, even if she only felt confused. "I do not wish to alarm my father. He was worried that the fighting might reach Boston." *Please don't let me get myself in trouble here.* "And he felt it would be better for me to remove myself to England and visit friends of his in London. I came on my own to Bath, and then I had the unfortunate accident."

"How irregular! You journeyed to England *unaccompanied*? Your London chaperones *abandoned you* to travel around on your own? My dear Jane, you are no longer living among the Indians. You may not simply flaunt convention as you choose."

Janet kept her face placid. She was so clearly a failure as a nineteenth-century woman.

"I will write my brother and ask that you be taken under our protection while you recover. But Jane, you simply must make an effort to understand the rules of English society. I fear you are accustomed to a level of independence simply not afforded to us here. Although I should never say so aloud— and I will vehemently deny it if you ever broach this subject with my brother—I am afraid that deep down, I do envy you somewhat." She gave Janet's hand a slight squeeze. "Now, I shall leave you to rest. I will return for tea this afternoon, and we can speak more then. If it should please you, I shall purchase *Pride and Prejudice*, and I could read aloud to you."

Something safe, something familiar. "Yes, Emma. I should like that very much."

"Then it is settled. Rest. I shall see you this afternoon."

Janet knew she should rest, but her mind raced. She'd been so ready to laugh this off as a prank, but even she could admit no one would go to all this expense to play a trick that entailed tearing down power wires and reconfiguring a city.

She might even be willing to accept the nineteenth-century makeover was the result of an elaborate, big-budget period production. But how could she possibly explain the appearance of Emma Huntington?

No, there was no mistaking it. Of course she knew that face. She'd gazed at those striking features every day on the school's staircase, wondered about the life such an elegant, beautiful young woman must have lived. How could she rationally explain Emma's appearance now? Janet worried greatly for her sanity as she voiced these thoughts, even if only in her own head, but she feared she'd truly been transported two hundred years back in time to nineteenth-century Bath.

And now what? For how long was she here? How would she return? How would she possibly succeed in not being unmasked as the imposter that she was? Being an admirer of nineteenth-century literature was one thing, but trying to impersonate a nineteenth-century woman was something entirely different. She couldn't possibly get away with it.

Or could she?

It was true that being from the "New World" granted her a certain amount of flexibility. People would expect a lack of familiarity with more genteel manners. Social gaffes would simply be chalked up to her "savage" upbringing.

But how much comprehension would it truly afford her? And what would happen to her if the Huntingtons didn't agree to shelter and protect her? How was a penniless and friendless young woman to survive in nineteenth-century Bath society alone? How could a woman support herself in this society if left to her own defenses? She shuddered.

Yes, she would have to hope that Sir Edward would agree to his sister's proposal to take in Janet. It would be up to Janet to moderate her behavior and not allow Sir Edward or his sister to regret that decision.

At least until she found some way to return to her world.

These thoughts raced through Janet's mind until she fell into a troubled but exhausted sleep.

Chapter 14

"Jane, dear Jane, do wake up." Emma's voice insisted. "I was told you slept all afternoon. Miller is arriving with our tea. I have a nice surprise for you to lift your spirits."

From behind her back, Emma produced a book. Janet turned it over slowly and with great delicacy. Her cheeks flushed with excitement. She could hardly believe it. The weight of it in her hands, the feel of it under her fingertips. The intoxicating smell of fresh leather that permeated the room, the crispness of the virgin pages that sent shivers up her fingertips.

She, Janet Roberts, held in her hands a pristine first edition of *Pride and Prejudice: A novel in three volumes, by the author of "Sense and Sensibility."* What she wouldn't do to take this back with her on her time travel. How much would this be worth to collectors?

"You found it!" She hoped Emma couldn't detect the quiver of emotion in her voice.

"Well, of course I found it. Did you not say it would please you to hear it? This also provides me with an opportunity to read it myself. Shall I begin?"

Janet felt like a child who had lost her mother at the supermarket, only to feel an overwhelming sense of relief to see the familiar face emerge from the anonymous sea of strangers.

Here was something that would ease her fears, something comforting and familiar. How often had she reread those long, familiar pages at difficult moments in her life? How often had those words cheered her up from some long-forgotten disappointment?

"Oh," she sighed. "Yes, please."

"Chapter one. It is a truth universally acknowledged, that a single man in possession of a good fortune, must be in want of a wife.

"However little known the feelings or views of such a man may be on his first entering a neighbourhood, this truth is so well fixed in the minds of the surrounding families, that he is considered the rightful property of one of their daughters.

"'My dear Mr. Bennet,' said his lady to him one day, 'have you heard that Netherfield Park is let at last?'"...

Janet leaned back into her fluffy, goosedown pillows. Her heartbeat slowed to an easy, untroubled rhythm. An overwhelming calm enveloped her as she enjoyed the comfort of oft-read pages, now read in Emma's cultured, nineteenth-century Bath diction, probably remarkably similar to the author's own voice.

The familiar words worked their magic. The throbbing of her head diminished with each turned page. It was soothing to have the written word read to her. When had been the last time someone had read to her aloud? Probably in elementary school. She had fond memories of her mother sitting by her bedside, reading in a voice that had long ago slipped from Janet's memory.

Emma would most likely be well-practiced in this art, not only for invalids such as herself, but as a form of evening entertainment in elegant drawing rooms. What a lovely tradition—sadly lost to the far less intellectual pastimes of the radio and television and the internet. Janet stifled a smile when she thought of Tony presiding over his temple dedicated to so-called progress.

Emma read through the first three chapters before the tea arrived. Miller set out the tray, and Emma poured. "It starts well. How terribly rude Darcy was towards Elizabeth at the ball! She seems quite spirited."

A smile tugged Janet's lips upward. "She is, perhaps, one of the most-spirited heroines in literature, with a universal appeal I suspect will resonate with many generations of readers. Perhaps even more than your Miss St. Aubert, who is consistently fainting at key moments of the story. But of course, we shall have to compare notes two hundred years from now to see who is correct."

"How you tease, Jane! Your color is much better. Doctor Perry will call tomorrow. I hope he declares you well. I should enjoy taking you out for your walks in Bath."

"Nothing would please me more. I apologize for my confusion in these days. All the blanks in my memory scared me. I fear I may have spoken out of turn when I was still confused about my whereabouts." She busied herself straightening the covers. "I apologize if I appeared rude to you or the household staff when you have all taken such good care of me."

Emma placed her hand over Janet's. "The pleasure is all ours. I hope that you feel secure here, as if at home. I know if I had taken ill in Boston, far away from my family and friends, you would have taken care of me."

But would I have done the same?

"Emma, tell me more about yourself. Aside from reading the Gothic novels of Mrs. Radcliffe, what do you enjoy doing?"

"Perhaps I enjoy the Gothic novels far more than I should." She examined her hands. "My brother certainly thinks I do. They take up a good amount of my time. Regarding my other pastimes, I sketch quite ill, even if I enjoy it tremendously." She looked up at Janet, a spark in her bright blue eyes. "Perhaps you could help me to improve?"

"I should like that."

"I enjoy riding and walking the grounds at Helmsley Manor. It is so lovely there. Oh, I do so hope that you shall come and visit us! It is idyllic in the country. Although, when I am in the country for too long, I begin to miss society. I enjoy calling on our friends and acquaintances in Bath and frequenting the assemblies."

Emma walked to the window and looked down to the movement over the green, before turning back to Janet.

"I also enjoy playing the pianoforte, although my playing still requires much improvement. There are a great many concerts here in Bath. Oh, and I love to attend a ball!"

She looked so pretty standing by the window. The sunlight caressed her face, highlighting its girlish enthusiasm.

"I long for my brother to hold a ball at Helmsley Manor. When my father was still alive, we held them often, but I was too young to truly enjoy them. Perhaps I can convince my brother now, and you shall attend."

"I should like that very much. I have never been to an English ball. I am afraid I will not know what to do. They must be so different from what we have in the New World."

Finally! A logical explanation I can use for why I will be such an alien at any eventual balls. This New World excuse should help. I don't think having watched all those BBC productions would really get me through a nineteenth-century ball.

"Emma, say that you will be my guide and help me to prepare."

"It would be my pleasure!" said Emma, with the faint glimmer of tears in her eyes. "I have the feeling we will become like sisters, and I am certain you will like Edward. He is such a kind and fair brother."

Janet forced a smile. She remembered the portrait of Sir Edward hanging beside that of his sister in Huntington House. It was a popular gathering point for her female seminar students, who would generally lament the fact that men like that were no longer available in the modern world. He was tall and handsome, with strong features, but his look was so severe and haughty, with not a hint of warmth. She could not picture him as anything like his sister.

How would he react to her? She would have to rely on his kindness in hosting her for as long as her stay would last. But surely she must be far too foreign for someone so rigid as he appeared to be to accept into his household. She hoped she and Emma developed a strong friendship, and that he saw the importance of keeping his sister happy. There were far too many dangerous variables to consider.

As her mind mused over these complications, she looked up to see that her new friend was expecting a response to her observation. Her enthusiasm sounded forced to her own ears. "Oh, it will be a true pleasure to meet your brother." Silently, she thought, *Edward, don't let me down. I'll be counting on you.*

"Shall I read you another chapter, Jane? Miller will be bringing your dinner plate in about an hour, and then you must rest. Doctor Perry was insistent that you be well rested for his visit tomorrow. We shall see what he says about when you may get up."

Janet put her hand over that of her new friend. "Thank you."

"Now, where were we? Ah, yes, we heard Elizabeth saying what a disagreeable and horrid man Mr. Darcy was. Now we begin chapter four ..."

"'*When Jane and Elizabeth were alone, the former, who had been cautious in her praise of Mr. Bingley before, expressed to her sister how very much she admired him. "He is just what a young man ought to be," said she, "sensible, good humoured, lively; and I never saw such happy manners!—so much ease, with such perfect good breeding!"'"*

Emma read on in a voice practiced in the art of reading aloud. Janet's mind no longer raced with all the concerns that plagued her: where she was, what would become of her if Sir Edward did not take her under his protection, why she had travelled here at all, and how she could return to her modern life. Emma's lovely reading voice quickly banished all quotidian concerns from her mind, and Janet simply allowed herself to be swept into her beloved story. How odd to be hearing it as "contemporary" literature from the lips of her new nineteenth-century friend.

Janet watched in fascination as Emma cut each page with a paper cutter. She was finally seeing how new books were read in the nineteenth century. How would her new friend react if Janet were to explain to her about paperbacks, or better yet, Kindles and iPads? No, not all progress was for the best. This was far superior.

Emma continued to read until the dinner tray arrived, then lay down the book. "I will keep it here for fear that I will be tempted to read on ahead without you. Tomorrow we shall continue where we left off. "

"Goodnight, Emma." After Emma left, Janet accepted the dinner tray Miller proffered. "Thank you, Miller. It all smells so delicious. Please tell Cook how much I enjoy her meals. She will certainly make me well again."

Miller beamed with pleasure. "Of course, Miss Jane. I shall tell her immediately."

Janet was left alone with her dinner. Her head ached much less now; even the dizziness when she sat up had diminished. Janet was eager to see the doctor the following day, even if the thought gave her pause. Could she truly be eager to see a nineteenth-century doctor? She searched her mind for information garnered about social customs of the era, knowledge about the history of medicine. She wished she could recall specifics and feel more confident about what was in store for her. What exactly did they know about medicine back then? What were their qualifications? Perhaps she only felt eager for the visit because she was now feeling stronger. What harm could he do now? Would he bring a container of leeches in his medical bag?

More than anything, she hoped he would officially prescribe walks out in the fresh air. Now that the pain had subsided, she longed to explore nineteenth-century Bath. How could she pass up the chance to see Bath as it was when Jane Austen wrote about it?

Janet lay the empty tray on the table beside her bed and slipped back onto the pillows. Once again, she could barely keep her eyes open, even if her mind continued racing. What had happened to her twenty-first-century life? Was she presumed missing? Dead? Did the days pass back there as they did here, or, were she able to return, would she return to the exact same moment of her disappearance?

She had so many questions, yet there was no one who could possibly answer them. No one with whom she could even discuss them. Confused thoughts tumbled through her mind until late into the night, but Janet was no closer to understanding.

Chapter 15

The sun streamed through the window, lighting up the blue glass vase that stood on the dresser and setting the ceiling ablaze with magical azure reflections. Janet observed the striking pattern before the sound of clinking crockery broke her concentration. Miller struggled through the door with a breakfast tray.

"Miss Jane, breakfast is served. Doctor Perry arrives soon."

Janet rubbed her eyes and pulled herself up to eat breakfast.

Miller returned for the tray, before ushering in a middle-aged man carrying a bag. When he faced Janet, she barely suppressed a gasp.

"Good morning, Miss Roberts. I hear you have given the household staff a scare, trying to get up and about on your own."

Doctor Perry looked exactly the same as *her* Mr. Perry in modern Bath.

The same features, the same stature, the same eyes. She stared at the disheveled, curly grey hair, the eyeglasses dangling on a chain around his neck, the mischievous glint in his eye. How extraordinary that such a striking physical similarity could continue virtually unchanged through so many generations.

Even his voice threw her. If she closed her eyes and listened to Doctor Perry speak, she could picture modern Mr. Perry addressing her from behind his computer.

Doctor Perry stood by the edge of her bed. "I can already observe that the rest and the excellent cooking at Huntington House have made you strong once again."

"Thank you for taking such good care of me when I was first brought here. I hope your visits did not take you too far away from home."

"Not at all, Miss Roberts. I live nearby, at The Circus."

Of course you do. And two hundred years from now, I'll be working there with your descendent. If I ever get back to my real life, would Mr. Perry ever believe me?

"It's a relief I haven't caused too much trouble. Will I be able to go out and take some fresh air?"

"All in good time."

The doctor pulled several instruments from his bag. An odd, hornlike instrument, apparently the precursor to a stethoscope, was pressed to her chest. He listened. He felt her pulse. Thankfully, no leeches emerged from his medical bag. Following the exam, she was declared on the path to recovery. Limited exposure to the outdoors was recommended.

"I will speak to Miss Emma about moderate exercise that you can begin, if you feel up to it. " He packed his bag, but lingered at the edge of the bed. "There are also a few things I wish to discuss with you. We can arrange a follow-up visit, once you are stronger. As a man of science, I am interested in scientific developments in our two countries."

Janet offered a weak smile. What were the scientific developments in American medicine in 1813? If Doctor Perry wanted a magic wand into the future, she could offer him a treasure trove of information that would make his head spin: laser surgery, heart transplants, incubators for premature births, AIDS, breast implants, *in vitro* fertilization, sex-change operations. Where to begin? But she would only get herself in trouble speaking about nineteenth-century medical advances. She bade Doctor Perry goodbye, hoping his suggestion for a medical chat would swiftly be forgotten.

After Doctor Perry left, Miller prepared the bath. Janet had grown reluctantly familiar with the chamber pot in the past days, but this was her first experience with the complications of bathing two centuries ago. Finally, she fully understood the truly miraculous revolution of indoor plumbing.

Nevertheless, as she soaked in the warm water that Miller and the other servants had lugged two stories up from the kitchen stove, she tried to chase away lingering feelings of guilt. Being clean again felt wonderful, despite all the trouble the servants had taken to get her that way.

Janet had her first experience with a corset. "Miss Jane, you are still recovering. I will not fully tighten the stays. You have done enough fainting these days as it is."

Janet gasped as she felt the air forced from her lungs. The whalebone dug painfully into her flesh. Was Miller joking? Was this honestly considered a loosely tied corset in Regency England? She could hardly breathe. She was certain she would die of suffocation. And yet, when she caught a glimpse of herself in the mirror, she couldn't help but admire her perfect figure and notice how the corset coaxed her body into ramrod-straight posture.

Despite these aesthetic benefits, Janet still found herself appreciating the early feminists who did away once and for all with this medieval torture device. No wonder women seemed to be forever clutching at their smelling salts. As she grew accustomed to taking shallower breaths, she even felt a newfound appreciation for poor Miss St. Aubert of *Udolpho* fame.

How could one not constantly succumb to fainting spells when shoe-horned into an apparatus expressly designed to squeeze the breath out of one's lungs? The weaker sex, indeed! Place a man in this instrument of torture and see how long he'd hold out.

"Luckily, you seem to be about the same size as Miss Emma. She has lent you this gown." Miller slipped a yellow gown over her head. Janet observed her reflection in the mirror, and was pleased with the result. With its Empire waist and delicate embroidery work at the neckline, it was exquisite. She sat still, observing as Miller combed her hair and piled it intricately on top of her head.

Janet marveled at her reflection in the mirror. Her light brown hair with its sunny highlights looked elegant swept up; her neck appeared long and delicate. Her green eyes sparkled. She looked older, more sophisticated with her nineteenth-century toilette. She was certainly too suntanned to be fashionable among the creamy-skinned young women of Bath. Her form was perhaps too muscular for nineteenth-century tastes, but sport-sculpted shoulders and legs would be well-covered by the fashions of the day.

It did not require an extreme stretch of the imagination to believe that she might have just stepped out of the Bennet household. If only she could learn the manners and banish anachronisms from her discourse, she might actually get away with it.

Miller was reaching for something. *Please don't ruin everything with a silly lace cap.* But no, she held a handsome bonnet. Janet released a barely audible sigh of relief.

"The doctor insisted. Not too much sun. I see from your color that Americans do not guard their fair complexions as elegant ladies do here in Bath, but now you must follow doctor's orders. Cover yourself well."

Miller placed the bonnet on Janet's head, then tied the ribbon prettily below her chin.

"I could definitely start getting used to this. When I start donning corsets and ribbons, you'll all have to worry."

Hadn't that been what she'd told Malcolm on the green beyond this room? That had been only a few weeks ago, albeit two hundred years in the future. How many things had happened since that afternoon? And here, indeed, she found herself sitting before a mirror, a fine lady donning her corsets and ribbons. It was all so strange.

"Why, Jane! Don't you look lovely! What a miraculous recovery." Emma glided into the room, all smiles and good cheer. "Doctor Perry has given me an excellent report. We are to take a short walk, but I have strict instructions to rest frequently. I have brought my sketching pad and pencils so that we shall have every excuse to sit and rest. Doctor Perry assures me you are strong, and he is confident you should soon be back to your old self."

Janet smiled at her new friend. How kind they were being to her. She followed Emma out of the room, and then out the front door into the glorious, sunny June day.

June 17, 1813.

She could hardly believe it. She, Janet Roberts, writing her master's thesis on nineteenth-century English social customs and manners and how they were reflected in the literature of the period, was now walking around Bath on June 17, 1813. This was a dream come true. How her fellow students and scholars would envy her, if only they knew.

But would they ever know? Would she ever return to her twenty-first-century life to complete that half-finished thesis, the one she needed to finalize by next May? Would she return to finish her Austen seminar? She'd agonized endlessly over her father controlling every aspect of her life—her studies, her career, her choice of a husband—yet here she was, a few days later, and her life was one giant question mark.

Emma slipped her arm through Janet's, and the two women walked along the green of The Crescent, then continued the short distance to The Circus. This was the very same route Janet jogged with Siobhan only a few days earlier, on the morning of the accident that changed her life.

The streets were a riot of sights, sounds, and color. Women in their elegant dresses, servant girls in their coarse, functional smocks and aprons. In Janet's world, it was not always easy to distinguish the classes by fashion. A twenty-first-century internet billionaire—a Tony clone—might work daily in jeans and a hooded sweatshirt, just like the worker cleaning the streets. But here, in this new world, class and privilege were prominently displayed in one's dress and carriage. There were no blurred lines. No room for ambiguity.

Children wandered the streets, carrying heavy parcels and buckets in their delicate, tiny hands. Janet longed to relieve them of their loads. How on earth could such young creatures be working so hard, carrying burdens that must weigh as much as they? Surely they should be in school, or enjoying their brief childhood, or accompanied by an observant adult, someone to ensure that they were vigilant and would not risk being run over and killed by a passing horse and carriage in a careless moment of childish distraction. Goodness, her modern sensibilities found this far too difficult to digest.

As she and Emma promenaded, elegant men stepped aside to allow them to pass. The men smiled and tipped their hats to the passing ladies.

The smell of horse manure was overwhelming. It hung so thickly in the air that Janet felt a wave of nausea wash over her. She saw a few men braving oncoming traffic, shovels in hand, attempting to clear the streets, only able to eliminate a small portion of the mountains of accumulated horse droppings.

Hadn't the automobile been touted as the ideal solution to eliminate pollution? Janet, alongside her middle school classmates, had laughed smugly at the absurdity of that premise. How easy to have been smug in her clean and hygienic modern world. But now that she was actually living in the time period and breathing in the overwhelming odor that must have permeated every major city, she felt more sympathy for those who had welcomed the technology as a possible liberation from the nauseating stench that blanketed cities and towns.

Janet tried in vain to compose her face, but she couldn't help but stare at the sights and sounds all around her.

Emma laughed at her friend. "You must remember to close your mouth and not gape at your surroundings. It looks as if you are out in the world for the first time, my dear Jane. Surely, you have not forgotten in this brief time what the world looks like beyond the confines of the sick bed."

You would be surprised, Emma.

Janet learned quickly from the leering gazes that proper young women did not make direct eye contact with young men. *You can adjust; think about Cairo.* As a young woman walking alone when her father was in meetings, Janet learned to fastidiously avoid eye contact and carry herself with an officious air. She adopted this attitude, though her glance still yearned to take in her surroundings, and much of the time her curiosity got the better of her.

"Now, Jane, the doctor told me not to take you to the Pump Room. We hope to slowly get you back into society, and he does not wish you to be overwhelmed in such a busy environment on your first days out. I am under strict instructions to take you to Sydney Gardens, where we can sit in the shade, and perhaps sketch. Doctor Perry was insistent you not become overtired."

After days of enforced bed rest, Janet felt weak, so she embraced her friend's suggestion wholeheartedly. Emma walked Janet in the direction of Sydney Gardens, where they found a shady bench.

"What progress! You will certainly regain your strength soon."

"I am certain I will, especially with the nursing I receive at Huntington House."

"We are at leisure today. Let me take out my sketchpad and I can try to learn from your more talented hand."

Janet sat beside Emma, helping her friend sketch. "You have a good eye and a steady hand. I think we should do some exercises on perspective. See here? You haven't quite captured the depth of this building. Here, watch me." She took the pencil and drew slowly; Emma followed her example. More than an hour passed. They sat, shaded by the sun on their park bench, laughing and drawing the beauty surrounding them.

As Janet helped Emma to perfect a shading technique, a shadow fell across her sketchbook. Both women looked up simultaneously.

"Good morning. I apologize for having interrupted what appears to be a most productive sketching session, Miss Huntington, but I was extremely pleased to be passing by and to see you here in Bath."

The tall man in elegant clothes raised his top hat to bow. His golden locks fell over a handsome face bronzed by the sun. When he stood straight again, large hazel eyes sparkled as he gazed upon Emma. "What a pleasant surprise to discover you in town!"

"Mr. Bentley," Emma's voice contained the slightest tremor. "The pleasure is all mine. How lovely to see you again. May I introduce you to my new friend, Miss Roberts? Miss Roberts has assumed the daunting task of improving my drawing."

"That, I can hardly believe, is a daunting task." He smiled at Janet and took her hand momentarily in his, raising it six inches beneath his mouth. "Miss Roberts, delighted to make your acquaintance. May I join you?"

Emma beckoned to a seat across from them; he dragged it closer to the bench.

"Miss Emma, I hope you are in good health, I can see that you are. How is your brother?"

"Thank you, I am well and so is Edward. He remains at Helmsley, but hopes to arrive within the fortnight."

"Splendid. I mean to stay in Bath these next weeks."

Emma turned to Janet. "Mr. Bentley has relations close to Helmsley Manor. When he visits, he and my brother enjoy shooting on our grounds."

"Helmsley Manor is stunning," said Mr. Bentley, turning to Janet.

His face was animated, his smile infectious. Janet couldn't help but think what a lovely couple Emma and Mr. Bentley would make.

"And of course, the conversation and company are always so lively. Have you yet been to Helmsley Manor, Miss Roberts?"

"No, Mr. Bentley, I am afraid I have not yet had that pleasure." *Unless, of course, you count that little daytrip I made to see it two hundred years in the future.*

"Ah, but I hear from your speech that you are a stranger to these parts."

Stranger than you could ever imagine, Mr. Bentley. "Yes, I hail from Boston. I am recently arrived in Bath."

Parrot the strange syntax. Banish all contractions from your speech. Don't make too much eye contact with young men. Look demure. Do not fidget or slouch. Ramrod-straight posture at all times. She ran through the lengthy nineteenth-century etiquette checklist in her mind, terrified to miss something important. Would this eventually come naturally?

"All the way from the New World? Well, you are certainly lucky to have found such a charming and delightful guide to Bath in Miss Emma."

He turned his gaze at Emma with affectionate eyes that piqued Janet's curiosity. Was this a beau, or one who wished to be?

"Miss Emma, we shall have to do our best to make Miss Roberts' first impressions of Bath flawless, shall we not? There is to be a concert the day after next. Shall I arrange for us to attend?"

"Sadly, Miss Roberts is recovering from an unfortunate accident. Some ruffians on The Crescent green struck Miss Roberts with a cricket ball, and she was unconscious. Doctor Perry has been overseeing her recovery, and we are out for the first time. Jane, would you feel up to attending the concert? It would have to meet with Doctor Perry's approval, of course. But if he agrees, I would be delighted for you to attend your first Assembly concert."

"I should like that very much."

Mr. Bentley clapped his gloved hands together. "Then it is settled. Unfortunately, I was on my way to an appointment when I was most agreeably detained by you ladies. Miss Emma, may I call on you and Miss Roberts for tea tomorrow?"

"We shall await your visit. Until tomorrow." Emma raised her hand to his and he brought it beneath his lips, before repeating the farewell with Janet and taking his leave.

Watch and learn, Janet. She was a happy fly on the wall, observing firsthand the period customs and manners. Her classmates would drool with envy.

When he left, Janet and Emma resumed their sketching. After drawing in silence, Janet spoke. "Emma, have you known Mr. Bentley long?"

"Oh, yes. His aunt lives not two miles from us. Mr. Bentley may one day take possession of the manor and its extensive grounds."

Emma continued sketching, putting into practice the shading techniques Janet had taught her. She kept her eyes fixed firmly on her work.

"Of course ..." She paused. "Until the manor is properly passed on to him at his aunt's—his aunt's ..." She trailed off. "Let us say that he is ineligible to settle down and find a wife."

Janet noticed Emma flinch ever so slightly.

"My brother has been ... insistent on this point at least."

Emma forced the pencil, scratching a thick, dark line across the elegant sketching she'd worked so hard to achieve.

"I see," said Janet, even if she felt confused. An heir who was certain to inherit at a future date was not an eligible match?

Emma lay her sketchpad down. "I imagine this all sounds very foreign to you, Jane. I know in the New World so many of these traditional ties to family duty and land have been severed."

Janet fought the urge to roll her eyes. "You would be surprised. My own father has already selected his preferred future son-in-law for me. It's the man he most wishes to carry on his architectural work. To my father, whether or not I am in agreement is a minor point."

Emma's face lit up. "Are you engaged? Am I to congratulate you?"

"I am in no rush. Truthfully, I may have been mistaken about my father's heir apparent. He may actually be more worthy than I previously believed, but I need to be sure about my feelings."

"Dear Jane," Emma shook her head, "I fear you are accustomed to far different traditions. Duty and family honor are much stronger ties here. We females have little choice in such matters."

Janet took her friend's hand in her own. "But if you *were* free to choose, would you wish to be with Mr. Bentley?"

Emma's eyes glinted in fear as she looked carefully around her. "Jane, you must be more discreet when you discuss such matters. The shrubbery have ears in Bath." She lowered her voice. "In any case, it is a question I cannot answer. The choice is not fully mine to make."

The sadness in her voice as she spoke those words touched Janet.

Emma closed her sketching pad. "Now, we have stayed far longer than Doctor Perry advised. Shall we return home for your afternoon rest? If you are well, I hope you can come down to dine with me."

"I should like that."

The short outing had tired her more than she wished to admit. Janet took Emma's arm, and the two women slowly made their way back to The Crescent.

Janet dined with Emma in the formal dining room that evening. Following dinner, Emma read aloud to Janet in the library.

Mr. Bentley called in for tea the following day. It was clear from his expressions that Mr. Bentley held Emma in high regard. What an unpleasant situation it was not to be free to act on your feelings as you simply waited for an elderly relation's demise.

The three of them attended the concert at the Assembly Hall. There were arias performed from *Le nozze di Figaro,* and

Janet found herself the official "translator" of the lyrics for Emma and Mr. Bentley, who marveled at her abilities in Italian.

"I am ashamed that my Italian is so poor after so many years of study," said Mr. Bentley. "My lack of progress can certainly not be laid at the feet of my worthy tutor, who was undoubtedly blessed with all the patience in the world."

"I am not certain the merit is truly mine," said Janet. "I lived in Rome for a year and was forced to improve my Italian. Otherwise, I should certainly still be struggling through my grammar book with minimal progress."

"You are far too modest, Jane." Emma turned to Mr. Bentley. "Jane is a French scholar as well. She is reading to me from Rousseau, and helping me to better my woeful French. Edward will be pleased to see the improvement, although he may not approve of the subject matter."

Mr. Bentley laughed. Janet had grown affectionate of his booming laughter. It was so like the genuine joy Emma often expressed. The more time she spent with them, the more Janet felt certain that theirs was the ideal match.

"Miss Emma will be leading the revolution against the landed classes soon, thanks to Miss Roberts' fine Republican principles."

Janet smiled politely before turning to observe the swirl of elegant women and men around them. The room was a riot of colors, fine dresses, plumes and turbans. How she wished she were free to sit quietly in a corner and sketch the lively scene.

She turned when Mr. Bentley said, "I must write to your brother to learn when he might be joining us."

"I received a letter from him only this morning. He is expected to reach us by early next week."

Janet's hand shook and she nearly spilled her tea, recovering in time to place the cup gently down on its saucer.

"My poor Jane. You are looking so well and your constitution is so strong, that I forget that you are still recovering."

"I assure you, I am fine. Do not worry yourself. Slight aches come and go occasionally."

When Emma and Mr. Bentley returned to discuss Edward's arrival and plans for his stay, Janet once again worried about how her presence would be welcomed by the master of Huntington House. It was all too clear to Janet that she had no "Plan B" if Sir Edward did not agree to continue sheltering her under his roof. She was entirely dependent on his charity.

Although Sir Edward's arrival loomed large in Janet's thoughts, the days preceding his arrival were happy. Janet grew stronger each day, and she observed the speech and manners all around her, carefully weaving them into her own conversations.

Mr. Bentley visited often for tea and ferried the ladies around town. They visited the Pump Room and met many individuals of Mr. Bentley's or Emma's acquaintance. Janet and Emma took long walks and worked on Emma's sketching, which improved rapidly.

Janet listened carefully to the conversations, picking up useful information about politics and society of the time. She cultured a greater understanding of what was said, and what was not. She followed the obsessive discussions about Napoleon's military campaigns and the hopes for the Sixth Coalition.

Mr. Bentley accompanied them to concerts. There was even talk of a ball the following week, and Emma promised to teach Janet the dances. Emma and Janet could often be found twirling around the library in the evenings, Emma pretending her friend hadn't hurt her when Janet's two left feet stepped on her instructor's toes, yet again.

Emma insisted on taking Janet shopping and purchased fabric to be made into dresses. They progressed quickly through *Pride and Prejudice*.

The inner workings of Huntington House never failed to amaze Janet—the small army of servants who kept the wheels turning and ensured the grand house's smooth functioning. She often made her way down to the kitchen to speak with Cook and her kitchen assistants. At first, this disturbed the kitchen staff, but gradually they became accustomed to Janet's presence—Janet's American background seemed to smooth over many of the oddities they would never accept from a fellow countrywoman—and they discussed recipes and preparation openly. Slowly, after gaining their confidence, she even pitched in to help prepare recipes. This insight into culinary methods of nineteenth-century Bath was priceless. The recipes and techniques were secretly jotted down into her notebook when everyone was asleep.

The notebook she managed to bring in her bag from modern times—along with her sketchpad and a modern, paperback copy of *Pride and Prejudice*, with the photograph Malcolm had snapped of Janet in her room with Sir Edward's Tiepolo, were hidden in her armoire. If she ever returned to her real life and her thesis, this treasure trove of firsthand information recorded in her scrawled notes would immediately be finding its way into her work.

The days unfolded in this happy way, but Janet lived with the lurking fear that Sir Edward's visit may put an end, once and for all, to the pleasant, easy rhythms of life in Bath.

Chapter 16

"Now Emma, remind me whom we are calling on today? You've introduced me to half of Bath, and my head is simply spinning with names."

Janet walked closely beside her friend down the hill from The Crescent and into town. The air was fresh at the top of the hill, but as they descended, she began to cough, as a thick cloud of coal dust filled her lungs. Each evening, she scrubbed the grime from her pores and wondered how much worse it would be in winter.

"The Whitmores are an old Bath family, and very well-connected. Lady Whitmore was a good friend of my mother, and I always visit her when I am in town. She is too infirm to pay visits herself, but she is a kind woman and enjoys town gossip."

They stopped at the edge of the street, waiting for a carriage to pass by. The traffic light, Janet realized, would be another revolutionary invention.

Some days ago, Janet experienced the danger of Bath streets firsthand, when she saw a young laundress trampled to death by a carriage. The poor girl had been distracted—perhaps thinking of a young man, or dinner later that evening. It all happened so fast. A scream. A screeching of wheels. A basketful of clothes flying through the air. The neighing of a horse. The shouts of a coachman.

Janet raced to the scene, much to Emma's consternation. With knowledge of basic first aid and CPR, Janet hoped to assist until medical attention arrived. But there was nothing to be done. The poor woman's neck had been snapped, and Janet sank beside the young, lifeless body, feeling helpless.

From that moment, Janet became overly cautious at crosswalks. A break in traffic finally occurred, and she and Emma continued.

"You shall be extremely impressed with Lady Whitmore's library. Its fame is hailed throughout Bath. Even Edward is green with envy when he visits."

"Ah, you whet my appetite! I am afraid that in my world, libraries are not as valued as they are in yours." Janet's voice trailed off as she thought of the library she was charged with destroying. Had the demolition work gone on without her? Was construction already underway on Tony's high-tech video arcade?

The women reached a green, and they stepped aside as a shepherd approached with his herd of sheep, tipping his cap as he passed them. Janet imagined sheep crossing though modern-day Bath and the shock it would cause to its residents. But here on the edge of town, the vistas had opened up and public grazing land began. Janet tried to remember the buildings on this stretch of green in her Bath.

Concentrating so hard on trying to recall the modern town layout, she was surprised when Emma announced their arrival.

Janet caught her breath as they stood in front of the imposing house. She examined the façade and grand windows. Her heart beat faster as reality dawned on her. "But it can't be! This is Tony Dawson's house!"

The building in modern Bath was surrounded by late nineteenth-century homes, so the home was no longer isolated by fields with grazing sheep, but there was no doubt in her mind it was the very home she and Ted were renovating for Mr. Perry's internet-millionaire client.

"*This* is Lady Whitmore's home? Are you certain?"

"Of course I am certain! I have been coming here ever since I was a child. Who in Heaven's name is this Tony Dawson person?" Emma leaned in and placed a hand to Janet's forehead. "Jane, you've become terribly pale. Are you well? Perhaps we have done too much walking. Should we return? I can request Lady Whitmore's carriage."

Janet did feel weak, but she would not miss seeing the inside of this building for any reason. She forced her voice to sound confident. "I am fine, Emma. A mere moment of dizziness."

"You must tell me when you are unwell. I should not wish to tax your energies."

"I am most well, I assure you. And very much anticipating our visit to Lady Whitmore."

This is unbelievable! I have the chance to visit my project, two hundred years earlier! How many architects can claim that? A frisson of excitement ran up her spine.

The door opened, and a footman ushered the ladies into the foyer. Janet caught her breath. In home improvement magazines that her clients sometimes brought in to show her, there were often before-and-after photos of miraculous transformations. Janet craned her neck and stared at her surroundings, surprised at how much more stunning the "before" version was of Tony's home.

The fine-grained marble floor of the foyer stretched out endlessly under the shimmering Bohemian crystal chandelier that reflected the light from the foyer window. Janet eyed the floor's glossy surface, willing to bet it was Carrara marble. The transport alone must have cost a fortune. There were horrible, low-quality tiles in the modern version of this home. Could the original marble lie beneath?

Grand mirrors in gilt frames hung in the entrance hall. Massive Chinese vases scattered throughout the room overflowed with fresh flowers. Janet breathed in the heady scent of lilacs. An imposing grandfather clock ticked the minutes. She observed the arching mahogany staircase leading to the second floor. The curving wood of the balustrade shone to highly polished perfection.

"Jane, are you coming?"

Janet heard the urgency in Emma's hissed whisper. Janet was clearly gawking, when she should have been following the footman into the Morning Room. But how extraordinary to observe the original splendor of the home she was renovating two hundred years later! Janet smiled at her friend and hurried behind her.

They were ushered into the Morning Room, an apt name for a room with floor-to-ceiling windows, from which the golden morning light streamed in and set the room aglow. Thick carpets covered the dark wooden floor, and a large fireplace occupied one wall, unused on this warm June day.

Lady Whitmore sat in the center of the room, regal in an ornate precursor to the modern wheelchair. Emma had explained to Janet that the active septuagenarian was no longer mobile, yet her servants took her for a stroll around town each fair day. Janet attempted to be discreet while examining the chair. Its weight must make daily strolls cumbersome for the household staff charged with accompanying Lady Whitmore over Bath's uneven cobblestones.

"Lady Whitmore," said Emma, "it is my great pleasure to introduce you to my new friend, Jane Roberts of Boston."

"Miss Roberts, welcome. I heard all about your unfortunate accident on The Crescent Lawn. I hope you are recovered. Please be seated."

She indicated the divan across from her. Janet eased herself onto the coarse horsehair. These rigid couches had one advantage, at least. They fully supported her ramrod-straight posture, already bolstered by her torturous corset. After such a short time in Old Bath, Janet carried herself like a prima ballerina on stage before thousands. Or so it would seem in her modern world.

"Now, my dears." Lady Whitmore leaned closer to the divan. "You simply *must* tell me all the news of Bath! You young people hear so much more than I do."

Exactly what I need. The well-connected, gossiping busybody. Now this seems like a genuine Jane Austen novel!

Lady Whitmore's voice lowered conspiratorially, and she turned to ensure the servants were not eavesdropping. "I have had it on good authority that Miss Constance Tucker is to arrive in town. Certainly, you remember Miss Tucker." She sniffed. "Her father made a fortune *in trade*."

Janet struggled to suppress a smile as she heard the venom in those words. *Oh, my dear Lady Whitmore. If only you knew about the hideous Kansas internet-millionaire tradesman who will buy your home and wish to strip it bare in two hundred years' time. Miss Tucker will seem like Her Majesty the Queen in comparison ...*

"Now she waltzes around in her brazen way, flaunting her riches and hoping to make a grand match." Lady Whitmore pursed her lips, "Of course, for a commoner, the girl possesses an *almost* genteel complexion ..."

"Ah, Lady Whitmore. You are being unfair to Miss Tucker," chimed in Emma. "Her taste in fashion may be somewhat ...

showy, perhaps, but she seems a sweet young lady, and her face and figure are quite agreeable."

"Yes, my dear. *That* is precisely the problem." Lady Whitmore shook her head. "Gentlemen are helpless to resist a pretty face and attractive body, particularly when it comes attached to such generous purse strings. I fear they may be willing to discard superior breeding and solid English traditions when confronted with a comely smile and an ill-begotten pot of gold."

"Ah, but surely you're exaggerating, Lady Whitmore!" cried Emma, a smile lighting up her lovely face.

"*Exaggerating*, my dear? I?" Lady Whitmore raised her hand to her heart and shook her head again.

Janet had the distinct impression that Lady Whitmore was not used to being contradicted.

"Why, I have it on good authority that Miss Tucker has set her sights on your good family friend, Mr. Bentley."

Lady Whitmore glanced at Emma, a glint of malice sparkling in her eyes. So she suspected an emotional attachment as well. How direct the blow the cunning old battle-axe administered to the innocent young girl.

"Of course," Lady Whitmore continued, "it makes sense from a strictly *practical* point of view. Mr. Bentley is so well-mannered and handsome. But, as we know," her voice dropped, "until his estate is settled with his aunt, and it has been ascertained with certainty that no additional male heirs will crawl out from the woodwork .... Let us only say that not many women could hold out so long. But Miss Tucker obviously has no need of material wealth. She can wait out the fuss and then slither like a snake into the grand manor, to preside over it as if born to the part." She shivered involuntarily. "And so close to your own property, Emma!"

Janet's eyes grew wide at this piece of gossip, and she worried about her friend. She cast a sidelong glance at Emma. But her discretion was perhaps unnecessary.

"My dear, how pale you are!" exclaimed Lady Whitmore. "Are you unwell? Do you wish my smelling salts?"

"I assure you I am well," said Emma, in a faltering voice that did not convey the conviction of her words.

Janet turned to her friend and looked into her eyes. She slid Emma's hand into her own before turning back to the elderly lady. "I am afraid this is entirely my fault, Lady Whitmore. I taxed Miss Emma's strength shamefully when I was ill, and, as a consequence, she is now overtired. I have only myself to blame." She noticed a spark of gratitude in her friend's eyes. "Lady Whitmore, perhaps it would be best to allow Emma to remain quiet for some moments. Would it be too forward of me to ask you to show me the library while Emma rests? I have heard so much about its beauty and its unparalleled collection."

Pride lit up the older woman's face. Emma could have a few minutes to collect herself, and Janet could satisfy her mounting curiosity about the library. Lady Whitmore rang a bell. A servant materialized and pushed the wheelchair out of the room, across the marble hall and to the closed entrance of the library. Two servants went in ahead, fastening the long, velvet drapes back from the windows, allowing the sunlight to spill through the towering windows.

The servant pushed Lady Whitmore's chair into the library and Janet followed. Despite her best intentions to contain her enthusiasm, she caught her breath as she stepped over the threshold. "How extraordinary!"

Her eyes took in the glistening wooden shelves laden with thousands of books, and the shimmering shards of Bohemian crystal on the pristine chandelier that Tony was so quick to consign to the trash heap two centuries later. The carvings on the modern fireplace had been worn away with time, but here in this room, Janet could clearly make out scenes of Bath carved into the golden stone. Thick carpets rested beneath her feet, and plush armchairs sat before the fireplace, positioned as she pictured them on that June afternoon in the library with Ted and Tony. Long velvet curtains skirted along the high windows. Oh, what she wouldn't give to while away afternoons in this library!

"From your outburst, I gather you approve, Miss Roberts," said Lady Whitmore, a sly smile across her face.

"Approve? I think it's possibly the most perfect library I've ever seen!"

Janet craned her head upward to see the ceilings and her heart raced. The terrible condition of the frescoes in the twenty-first century hadn't allowed her to admire them in their full splendor. Tony had refused the idea to engage a team of art restorers who would study the fresco and return it to its former glory. As Janet raised her gaze to the ceiling, she could hardly believe her eyes. How could Tony destroy a work of such unparalleled beauty? Mythological scenes occupied the ceiling—Perseus slaying Medusa, the Greeks descending from the Trojan horse, the weaving contest between Arachne and Hera. Despite the beauty of the mythological scenes, however, it was the quiet contemplation of the landscape paintings around the border that tempted her eyes. How had she missed their glory in Tony's library? They must have been badly damaged, perhaps even hidden under layers of paint applied in poor attempts at restoration.

"This landscape border is so lovely, Lady Whitmore! What expert brushwork, and a lovely composition."

"Well, I should hope so. It was my dear late husband's friend, Thomas Gainsborough, who painted those scenes."

Janet felt her heart beat faster. "Pardon me. Did you say Thomas Gainsborough? The portrait painter?" Janet knew her voice was too loud for the library, her excitement too evident in the high pitch of her voice.

"Poor Thomas," said Lady Whitmore. "Those portraits were his most well-known paintings. The ones he and his rival, Sir Joshua Reynolds, churned out for all the nobility. But these," she indicated the delicate landscape scenes above their heads. "These were his pride and joy. These are the first official landscape paintings he ever did. At the end of his life, he would dedicate all his time to painting landscapes. He said it was the period when he was happiest and most fulfilled as an artist."

"When ... when did he paint these?" Janet managed to stutter. She could feel the excitement rising in her chest. Certainly Gainsborough paintings could not be so easily demolished. Perhaps the library could be salvaged after all.

"Oh, my. Thomas settled in Bath in 1759, I believe. He lived in The Circus, and he and my husband were dear friends. It must have been early on in his Bath period. The early sixties. I can still see him up there on the scaffolding, complaining his back was as stiff as Michelangelo's. I was so anxious to see the completed work. My husband treasured these landscape scenes."

A smile crossed Lady Whitmore's face, making her appear younger. The first Gainsborough landscapes, right here in Tony's planned playroom? If she returned, she was certain the work could be saved.

If she returned ...

"Lady Whitmore, do you think I might visit again one day to sketch these scenes? I am such an admirer of Gainsborough's paintings, and I know so little about his landscapes."

"Of course, my dear. We can arrange a time." She looked at her guest. "Now I think it is best we return to Emma and ring for tea. If she is so weak now, some cake may help lift her spirits."

As they walked back to The Crescent, Janet's mind raced. Priceless paintings in Tony's library! She would return to sketch them, to have a record. She would do so on period paper so that it would look like an official historical record. But how could she get them to Mr. Perry?

And even if she did manage, would it be too late?

Lost in her reveries, Janet paid little attention to Emma, who walked silently at her side. Emma rallied over tea, chatting with Lady Whitmore and sharing Bath news. But as Janet observed her friend, she noticed the light conversation had all been for show. Sadness was etched across Emma's face.

"I hope the gossip didn't upset you. Mr. Bentley is so partial to you, I can't imagine any other woman capturing his attention."

"Can you not, Jane?"

Emma turned her face fully to Janet, and Janet noticed the tears welling up in her eyes.

"Oh, Emma dear." She slipped her arm through her friend's. "I speak the truth when I tell you that I cannot."

"We are only friends. We cannot be anything more than that. Mr. Bentley's situation in life is not settled, and my brother will never accept an ... an understanding that may leave me financially insecure."

"But have you and Mr. Bentley spoken of it? Perhaps you might find some solution."

Emma shook her head. "Jane, sometimes it seems you are from a different planet, not simply our former colony. Mr. Bentley understands this better than anyone. There is nothing to discuss. But I do fear an agreeable young woman with a fortune could offer him something I am unable to provide."

Janet did not know what to say to comfort her friend. She squeezed Emma's arm gently as they continued the walk home in silence.

Chapter 17

Janet sat in the drawing room, examining the sketchings scattered all around her on the divan.

Earlier that day, Janet spent her second morning at Lady Whitmore's, sketching the Gainsborough series of landscapes in the Whitmore-Dawson Library. She'd deliberately used period pencils and paper. Any analysis would be able to date the nineteenth-century materials. Of course, the real question dogging her was how she would transport this information back to Mr. Perry's studio in time to make any difference at all. For all she knew, the masterpiece might have already been destroyed by the techie barbarian.

After sketching the library frescoes, Janet stopped by for a pre-arranged visit with Doctor Perry at his home in The Circus. It was strange to walk through the door and into the medical studio, the same area in which she worked in Mr. Perry's architectural studio in modern Bath. As Doctor Perry asked questions about her stamina, she was distracted by the decorations and layout of the space.

"Miss Roberts ... I have no idea if you are listening to the questions or simply admiring my studio."

"Perhaps a bit of both. It's charming here."

"Thank you." He looked out the window. "My wife and I are pleased with our home, although not everyone felt we belonged. We hope it will be in the family for many years to come."

Janet stifled a laugh. "Somehow I feel confident in venturing that it will be so."

"Now, since you are here and your health has improved, I wish to ask you some questions." Doctor Perry took his glasses off, twirling them like Mr. Perry did when discussing design problems. "In your examinations, there were two oddities I noticed. You seem to have some strange foreign matter filling some teeth. And I also observed that you are missing an organ. Miss Roberts, I do not wish to alarm you, but it seems you are ... missing your tonsils."

How the hell am I going to explain these things to him?

Janet took a deep breath. "Yes, I had cavities in my teeth ..."

"Why did your barber not simply pull the tooth out?"

"Barber?" *Ah, yes, they used to do dental work, didn't they?* "No, in the New World we have dentists, a type of medical doctor who specialize in teeth. They drill out the part with the cavity and salvage the tooth with an artificial substance called a filling. I wish I could tell you what it is made of, but I am afraid I do not know."

"Extraordinary!"

Janet saw the excited glint in his eye she knew so well from her Mr. Perry. "And—uh—with the tonsils ... I had them removed when I was six or seven."

"Whatever for?" His brow was furrowed, the confusion evident on his face.

"Ah, my doctor in America was concerned about frequent illnesses, and he felt it would be best to remove them. It must have had the desired effect. Since their removal, I'm rarely ill."

"An operation? You might have died! How could a mere child have her tonsils removed? Did they force you to drink alcohol until you passed out?"

Oh, goodness. There was no anesthesia back then, was there? Good points, all. How do I get myself out of this?

"You must keep in mind that I was quite young at the time. I believe the doctor was an adherent of the use of traditional Indian medicines. Something called an anesthesia that allowed me to fall asleep for the duration of the operation. I woke up later, and my tonsils were removed. I did not feel much pain and I recovered quickly."

Doctor Perry's brow was furrowed. "Are you certain? I would love to learn what this substance is. Anesthesia, you say? I must ask some of my colleagues from Cambridge. Perhaps they have heard of it. Extraordinary, the things we are learning in modern medicine! Thank you, Miss Roberts, you have given me much to think about."

He walked her to the door. She felt he was in a rush to say goodbye in order to record his new discoveries. Hadn't modern-day Mr. Perry said he still had his ancestor's old medical journals? Mr. Perry described him as a man of science. Might he be a confidant? What if there were other time travelers wandering around Bath? Might he, as a physician, have come into contact with them?

She hesitated. "Pardon me, Doctor Perry, but have you ..." *How to say this?* "Have you ever examined others hailing from elsewhere with organs missing and fillings in their teeth?"

She observed him carefully for signs of understanding.

"Pardon?"

"It's only ..." She struggled. "As a man of science, I wondered if you might have come in contact with similar ... oddities."

She was flirting with danger, and the nineteenth-century mental asylum.

A small smile tilted his lips upward. "No. You are the only oddity I have discovered in Bath."

"Oh, I see." She sighed. "I thought there may have been others. Thank you, Doctor Perry."

She scurried out of the studio and walked the short distance home in a daze.

Back at The Crescent, Janet reviewed her series of drawings spread around her on the divan.

As she studied one of her favorites, Emma burst through the door. "Did you forget that Mr. Bentley is coming to dine, before accompanying us to the Assembly Hall for tonight's concert?"

"Oh, goodness. I *had* forgotten! At what time will he call?"

"In half an hour. And you are not even dressed!" Emma's eyes grew wide.

Janet looked down at her dress, something a thousand-fold more elegant than anything she would wear in her modern life. Yet this was underdressed for the concert. She smiled. "What does it matter, Emma? I know Mr. Bentley will have eyes only for you. The other girls and I will be mere wallflowers in your presence."

A blush spread across Emma's fair cheeks. "How you tease! Off with you. Oh, tonight will be lovely, with two of my favorite people."

Janet gathered up her drawings and made her way to her room to prepare for dinner. Oddly enough, Janet felt the same. Although she stumbled into this nineteenth-century life in the most inexplicable way, she couldn't help feeling so much at home with her new friends Emma and Mr. Bentley.

Although it was odd, each day spent in the past, she found herself missing her modern life a bit less.

Chapter 18

"The concert was so exceptional last night." Emma said as she and Janet crossed over Pultney Bridge on their way to the Sydney Gardens.

The morning's showers had delayed their daily walk, but the sun had unexpectedly emerged and the rapid improvement in the weather beckoned them out of the house. In Bath, one was never sure how long fair weather would last.

"It was truly impressive."

"The only moment ... but perhaps I should not speak of this." A blush spread across Emma's pale cheeks.

Janet suppressed a smile. "Might you be referring to Miss Tucker and her shameless attempts to flirt with Mr. Bentley?"

Emma gasped. "Why Jane! That is not at all what I meant. I am certain Miss Tucker meant only to be friendly. She is new to our ways."

"Yes, she certainly seems to employ her own methods."

And thankfully, Mr. Bentley seems immune to them—at least for now.

Miss Tucker reminded Janet of the shameless women on campus who made sport of chasing the trust-fund boys. Although in her case, she didn't need the money, only the pedigree. She hadn't liked Miss Tucker from the moment she'd set eyes on her. The woman lost not one opportunity to rest her hand on Mr. Bentley's arm or to simper over his every utterance. The whispering behind fans in the Assembly Rooms was that Miss Tucker was a brazen hussy, and Janet found herself hard-pressed to disagree with what seemed an accurate assessment.

After all, when in nineteenth-century Bath.

"How I long to see my brother this evening. I am certain he will grow to love you as much as I have these past two weeks and consider you a welcome addition to our home."

Janet did not share her friend's optimism, but she smiled politely. "And will Mr. Bentley be joining us for dinner this evening?"

"Oh, yes. He was insistent on seeing Edward the moment he arrives."

"I am not wholly convinced that Mr. Bentley's enthusiasm is entirely connected to the possibility of seeing your brother."

Emma blushed. "How you tease. It most certainly is, and you shall not convince me otherwise. I think you have grown to be so romantic now that we have concluded Miss Austen's book. Was it not a beautiful ending? I liked this second novel much more than *Sense and Sensibility*. I do hope this Miss Austen will write other books."

"Oh, I suspect that she might. There are even rumors she may write a book poking fun at the Gothic novels of your beloved Mrs. Radcliffe. If we are lucky, she might set in Bath."

"That would make for a delightful read! Miss Austen is such a wonderful observer of human foibles. Her characters of Mrs. Bennet and Mister Collins are very well done."

"I think the social commentary is what makes the stories so timeless. I believe that these character traits will be equally appreciated by future readers. Hundreds of years from now, readers will still be laughing at Mrs. Bennet's nerves and rolling their eyes at Mr. Collins' proposal."

"It is nice to think there will be some continuity," said Emma.

Janet smiled at Emma's words. She'd always felt an affinity with nineteenth-century literature and the careful manners of that era. Yet how odd to have been thrown into this world. She felt so comfortable beside her new friend, so much closer to her than she felt with many modern friends she'd known for years. Was this a reflection of the continuity among people, even across centuries? Or was it simply a reflection of a simpler life, fewer distractions, and stronger social relationships in nineteenth-century society?

The two friends sketched in the gardens and then walked into town and—in a nod to continuity –drank tea at Janet's favorite tea shop from modern Bath. She'd been thrilled to discover, through her frequent visits with Emma, that it was also a focal point of Bath life in the early 1800s.

Word appeared to travel fast in town. Janet was amazed at the well-informed gossip she heard on the streets. It seemed all of Bath approached Emma to tell her how pleased they were to know that Sir Edward would soon be arriving. How could they possibly know? How could news travel so fast in this pre-telephone, pre-internet society?

Janet and Emma walked around town, stopping by the Pump Room to see some of their acquaintances. Janet always reveled in these visits, thinking of the characters in *Northanger Abbey* who spent afternoons in this room. Later, they made their way up the hill to The Crescent. The butler welcomed them at the entrance. "Sir Edward has arrived. He is in the library."

"Already?" said Emma, her face flushed with happiness.

She hurriedly removed her hatpins and smoothed down her hair. "Come, Jane! Let us go to see him."

Janet hesitated in the foyer. Her heart thumped in her chest as she followed Emma to the library. With each step, she was increasingly aware that Sir Edward had the power to change everything. She took slow, deep breaths and tried to calm her nerves.

Emma and Janet entered the library together, but Janet hung back as Emma raced to his side. "Edward! Welcome. Did you have a pleasant trip?"

Edward placed his book down and stood to see his sister, his back to Janet. "Emma. How well you look! Thank you, I made good time. Rest assured that all is well at Helmsley Manor."

"What excellent news, Edward. May I introduce you to my new friend, Miss Jane Roberts?"

Sir Edward turned to face Janet. How familiar his likeness was. But when he fixed his icy gaze upon her, Janet involuntarily took a step back.

In his portrait hanging on the grand staircase of Huntington House, he was extremely handsome, but regal and remote. Slightly intimidating, perhaps. In real life, Janet could clearly see how truly handsome he was, tall and well-built, with fine features. But the flesh and bones man was even more terrifying than the inanimate portrait. Janet would not wish to fall on the wrong side of his favor. During the moments she was under his scrutiny, she realized that she had been correct to fear his arrival.

"Miss Roberts." He strode toward her. Sir Edward was much taller than Janet. She craned her neck up as he took her hand and raised it below his lips, before releasing it gently. "I trust that you are well after your lengthy recuperation?"

She forced herself to meet his eyes. "Thank you, sir. I am, thanks to the ministrations of your dear sister."

She felt his eyes boring through her and fought the urge to focus on her feet.

"Emma tells me you are quickly regaining your strength. I understand you have also been helping with her sketching. She tells me you are an extremely talented artist."

"Emma may have exaggerated my skill. I do enjoy sketching tremendously, but I have only helped Emma to develop the talent she already has. She possesses a steady hand, and excellent powers of observation."

"I appreciate your efforts. More than likely, I will see great improvement in my sister's art. I look forward to speaking with you more at dinner this evening."

Janet noticed his expression change.

"Perhaps you can also let me know how I might assist in reuniting you with your friends and acquaintances here in England once your recuperation period with us has come to an end. You will be wishing to return to them as soon as possible."

Janet was certain her heart stopped beating as Sir Edward fixed his piercing gaze on her. She had not mistaken the cold finality in those words. He was letting her know that her visit with the family was nearing a natural end. She feared no sound would issue forth if she tried to open her mouth to speak.

"Yes, of course, Sir Edward," she managed to eke out, eyes downcast. She dared not meet those challenging eyes. She'd been spot-on in fearing Sir Edward's arrival, and she wondered what would become of her.

"I beg you to excuse me. I have some pressing matters to which I must attend. I look forward to your society at dinner. Good day." He turned brusquely to his desk without a further glance at Janet and Emma, who both scurried quickly from the room.

Janet left the room, her head spinning. Yes, Sir Edward looked exactly as he did in his portrait at Huntington House, with his thick, dark hair and piercing blue eyes, his regal carriage, fine features and broad shoulders. She'd made one fundamental error in sizing the actual man up from his portrait likeness. She'd interpreted his character as one of noble hauteur. Now she realized his sense of privilege would never warm to someone like Janet. He was simply eager to rid his household of her.

Emma was unusual for a woman of her breeding. Janet would be forever grateful for Emma's kindness to her. But why would someone like Sir Edward trouble himself over someone as unconnected as Janet was? She had hoped her burgeoning friendship with Emma may have tempered his natural animosity toward her, but she could see now that this would not be the case.

"Emma, dear, I feel a slight headache coming on. Would you mind terribly if I rest in my room? I would not wish to be indisposed for dinner."

Emma observed her friend with concern. "Of course not. Please go and rest, Jane. We look forward to your company at the dinner hour."

Chapter 19

Miller entered, a garment draped over her arm. She held it up for Janet to see. "Miss Emma says the new dress she ordered for you has arrived, and she insisted you wear this for dinner tonight. I have strict instructions on how to prepare your hair and what jewelry you are to wear. Shall we begin?"

Dear Emma. Trying to win her brother over with a carefully considered toilette. Apparently, some aspects of life had not changed over the past two hundred years. Janet took a deep breath. And if Sir Edward did not like what he saw? How long would she have until she was out on the streets? At least in her own world, she could hope to earn enough money to survive. And here?

"I surrender myself to your skilled hands, Miller. Please work your miracles."

Janet allowed herself to have the life squeezed out of her with a tight corset. Oxygen seemed a small price to pay for such a lovely figure, not that anyone could see it under the Empire-waisted dresses. Nevertheless, when Miller slipped the midnight blue gown over Janet's head, Janet used the tiny bit of air left in her flattened lungs to breathe a sigh of appreciation.

The gown was so incredibly beautiful, with intricate

embroidery in shimmering threads around the neckline. It complemented her color perfectly. How kind of her friend to have gone to so much trouble and expense for her.

She did not entertain the notion that the efforts would cause Sir Edward to budge one inch in his decision to expedite Janet's departure, but the ministrations lifted her spirits. With skilled hands, Miller piled Janet's hair up high, carefully pinning tendrils, while allowing others to fall down delicately against her neck. Would Janet be able to replicate this elegant look when she returned to her modern life? She studied Miller's work carefully, but doubted she'd ever manage herself.

Next, Miller helped Janet to put on two long, white gloves and placed a delicate necklace with a lovely blue cross around her neck. When she was done, Janet appraised herself once again in the mirror.

She hardly recognized herself. Every day, she seemed to slip further away from the casual college student she'd been, with her canvas sneakers, T-shirts, and hastily combed hair. She was becoming quite a different person, not only in her appearance, but in her mode of address, her manner of speaking, her more reflective nature, and her greater attention to detail.

She would have imagined missing modern conveniences, yet in many ways the simpler rhythms of nineteenth-century Bath seemed richer, more sensible. More human, even. Light years away from the constant distractions of television and the internet and iPhones, she found she missed them not at all. Yet, despite all the changes she had been experiencing, she did not entertain the hope that she was close enough to the nineteenth-century ideal to make a favorable impression on Sir Edward.

"There now, Miss Jane," Miller said as she patted her shoulders. "You look lovely. Miss Emma is waiting for you in her room so that you can go down together."

"Thank you, Miller." She gave the hand on her shoulder a gentle squeeze before walking on to Emma's door, knocking, and letting herself in.

Emma looked up and smiled. "Oh, you look beautiful. I knew the dress would suit you."

"Dear Emma, however can I thank you?"

"There is no need. Let us go and enjoy our dinner." She linked her arm through Janet's and the two women made their way down the grand staircase, the same one that would one day boast the handsome portraits of Emma and her brother and their antecedents.

Tonight would be her first "formal" dinner. Although she still worried about Sir Edward's expanding upon his plans to relieve his household of its unwanted guest, she was equally excited to observe how these dinners worked. How many courses would there be? How would the footmen serve? Who steered conversation? How did the men and women divide into their separate rooms after dinner, and at what appointed hour did they meet again?

These rituals were never entirely spelled out in books from the time, and she yearned to see the customs first-hand. She wished she could have taken her notebook down with her to write surreptitious notes under the table, but she could not risk Sir Edward's catching a glimpse of an anachronistic notebook and ballpoint pen in her possession. Perhaps she'd be branded a witch. Or was that only in colonial America?

These thoughts accompanied Janet into the dining room, where Sir Edward and Mr. Bentley awaited them, greeting their entry with a formal bow. Emma curtsied and Janet clumsily followed suit. She wondered with growing frustration if she would ever get it right.

"Miss Emma, Miss Roberts, how delightful to see you again. How well you are both looking this evening." Mr. Bentley's wide smile helped dispel Janet's lingering fears.

"Yes, you both look exceedingly lovely." Sir Edward's eyes were calculating rather than warm. Niceties dispensed with, he settled them into their chairs.

Janet observed the men in their stiff, elegant jackets, wondering at how formally people dressed to dine in their own homes.

The footmen arrived with the soup. The butler poured the wine as Sir Edward turned to Emma and Janet. "Charles has been telling me how much he has enjoyed your company in these days, and how often you attended the concerts at the Assembly Hall."

"Mr. Bentley has been most attentive, Edward," said Emma. "We have attended some excellent performances. Miss Roberts has been our able translator of the French and Italian lyrics."

"It is rather unusual, is it not, for someone from America to be so fluent in European languages?" Sir Edward turned his sharp gaze on Janet.

Janet swallowed hard. "I suppose it is, but I spent a year with my father living in Avignon while he worked there, and then he sent me to live in Rome for a year when I was eighteen. I learned the languages while there."

"What an itinerant lifestyle." Sir Edward gazed at her, with what looked like disgust in the rigid set of his jaw. "With the exception of Gypsy families, it seems a highly irregular manner in which to raise a young lady—even an American lady. Were you sent to Rome unchaperoned?"

In trouble already. "My father is an architect. He longed for me to study classical architecture, and placed me in the care of an Italian architect friend of his in Rome." Janet slowed her speech and chose her words carefully. "I lived with his family. He had a daughter my age who became a close friend." *No need to hear about the son who was my first serious boyfriend. Clearly inappropriate.*

"Edward." Was Emma's voice faltering slightly, or was it merely Janet's imagination? "You simply *must* see Miss Roberts' drawings. Miss Roberts has travelled widely. Her sketches of the Coliseum and the Pantheon are spectacular."

"I would be pleased to see them."

Janet couldn't help but notice that the look on his face expressed more distaste than pleasure at the prospect. Turning to Emma, Sir Edward displayed the first real sign of warmth, "William has been taking good care of your horse while you have been away. He is riding him regularly so that he will be prepared for your return."

"Oh, it has been so long since I rode! Town life simply does not provide me with opportunities." She turned to her friend. "Jane, I do hope you ride and will be able to join me when you come with us to Helmsley Manor."

Silence hung thickly in the air. From the corner of her eye, she observed Sir Edward's look of obvious displeasure. He turned his attention to her. "You ride, I am certain, Miss Roberts? I am told on good authority that all Americans ride like the Indians."

"That is most probably true, Sir Edward." Janet stifled a smile. "I am afraid we do not have the same refinements of classic English dressage, but one must always be willing to learn from those whose skills are superior. The Indians can certainly teach us a thing or two about excellent riding."

Yes, Sir Edward was clearly glaring at her as the soup plates were swiftly and silently cleared from the table. Why couldn't at least one of the footmen be clumsy and send the silverware noisily clanging to the ground to deflect attention from her?

At least Mr. Bentley remained blissfully ignorant of the barbs being tossed across the table. "I know little about America, but if all the ladies are as full of spirit as Miss Roberts, it must be a fine place indeed."

"I could not agree more, Mr. Bentley." Emma cast a smile on Janet. "Tell me, brother, is there any news from Helmsley Manor?"

"All was well when I left. The tenants are pleased that the summer progresses well, and they anticipate a good harvest in the fall. The women miss your visits. They send their best wishes through Saunders, and look forward to your return. Charles, I paid a call on your aunt before my departure. Her health is well, and she conveys her greetings and hopes to see you with her again soon."

"That was most kind of you. I shall write to her. Nothing would please me more than a visit."

"Shall we all return together?" said Emma, perhaps a little too hopefully. "Would it not be enjoyable to transfer our little party to Helmsley Manor? Jane, I am certain you would love it." She turned to her brother. "Edward, Jane has made a specific study of Palladian architecture, so she would be particularly interested in seeing Helmsley Manor."

There was a painfully long silence before Sir Edward responded. His tone was flat. "While it would be an immense pleasure to obtain Miss Roberts' informed views about Helmsley Manor, I worry a prolonged visit could take her away for too long from her family and friends. Surely you would wish to reunite with them, Miss Roberts?" He fixed her pointedly with the intimidating gaze she was beginning to know all too well.

Janet sat in stunned silence. How was she to respond? Was this a polite invitation for her to decline the offer? Was she obliged to feign other commitments? She didn't know the rules of her new society. Sir Edward was the master of the house, but how much weight could Emma's requests carry in the household? How she wished Sir Edward and Emma could discuss her fate in private.

Janet was saved by the arrival of the second dish. Never would she have imagined to be so pleased to welcome a serving tray piled high with quail. Janet had never understood the sense of eating such tiny birds, but today she thrilled at the possibility of concentrating her full attention on cutting the little bones and attempting to extract the miniscule portions of meat.

"While Jane was recovering, I read to her from *Pride and Prejudice*. How we enjoyed it! It is even better than *Sense and Sensibility*."

"I have read it myself and I agree wholeheartedly with you, Miss Emma." Mr. Bentley cast a quick glance at Sir Edward before he continued. "I know that many men disdain novel reading as inferior to history or poetry, but I believe we are living in a rich era of literature, with many fine novels. Edward, I believe you do not support me in this opinion?"

"I am afraid I do not. I have always urged Emma to read the Greek and Roman classics, poetry, philosophy, and history, although my repeated requests for her to read Gibbons have fallen on deaf ears."

Janet fought the urge to roll her eyes. Poor Emma, declared a simpleton because she could not digest the sleep-inducing *The History of the Decline and Fall of the Roman Empire*. Janet had never managed to get past page fifty of the first volume herself.

"I believe the modern novels, particularly the Gothic novels of Walpole and Radcliffe, fill a young woman's head with fanciful ideas." Sir Edward cast a stern gaze on Emma. "I do not care to read *Pride and Prejudice* and *Sense and Sensibility*, although I would certainly not dictate to my sister what she can and cannot read."

"But how can you condemn something you have not bothered to read, sir?"

Damn! Janet hadn't meant to speak those words aloud. Since she woke up in her room in 1813, she increasingly conducted lengthy internal dialogues, but rarely did those thoughts escape from her mouth as they so unfortunately had now.

"Pardon, Miss Roberts?"

Sir Edward's eyebrows rose higher than Janet believed physically possible. How icy and terrifying his gaze was.

What now? Should she remain silent? Pretend she was deranged and prone to senseless outbursts? Attempt to change the subject? She was, after all, already treading in dangerous waters with Sir Edward. It certainly didn't make sense to antagonize him further, but Janet knew all too well that among her numerous faults was her inability to bite her tongue at key moments.

This appeared to be one such moment. In for a penny, in for a pound.

"I only wished to point out that it is unfair to criticize without having read the works for oneself. I also grew up reading *The Iliad*, *The Odyssey* and other classics, and I adore them. But literature is a long progression of works, is it not?" Janet made an effort to look into the eyes of those gathered at the table. She noticed how Sir Edward maintained his dark scowl, while Emma and Mr. Bentley appeared to be holding their collective breaths. But her tongue made no attempt to stop. "Great authors build upon what has come before them, but they also innovate and set the foundation for future authors. Dante shocked by writing in the vernacular Italian, rather than Latin. Chaucer's *Canterbury Tales* stunned contemporary readers with its ribald depictions. And yet, are not both considered classics of literature today? Can we doubt their influence on modern-day novels?"

She paused as a servant filled her water glass. The sound of the water splashing into the glass thundered like a waterfall in the deadly quiet of the room. Her nervousness propelled her forward, and she was helpless to stop herself.

"I was also not a fan of Gothic literature—perhaps it is still not completely to my liking—but I am convinced that future authors will be influenced by it and look back to these novels as the start of a movement. I am convinced that *Pride and Prejudice* and *Sense and Sensibility* will become classics to be read and reread, even hundreds of years from now. The world will change rapidly, but human nature and human foibles will remain essentially the same, for Miss Austen is a sharp observer of her fellow human beings. The deeper ties of family and society will remain a constant, and therefore these books will continue to speak to us, even if superficial customs and manners change with the passage of time."

A stunned silence hung around the table. After rapidly surveying the damage, Janet returned to the precise, surgical incision of her quail. She fought in vain against the blush rising rapidly on her cheeks. It was eventually Sir Edward who spoke.

"Miss Roberts, you speak with great authority about what the future holds in store for us."

When will you learn, Janet? Why can't you ever keep your mouth shut?

"Our painful experience with our former colony," continued Sir Edward, "is that its residents have never been particularly good at keeping their opinions to themselves. Nor are they renowned for their diplomacy. I was never favorable towards our attempts to wrestle back our former territories, since I believe we have long grown too far apart in both temperament and intellect."

The look of barely masked disgust on his face left Janet in no doubt as to which side he considered to suffer from a depraved temperament and an absence of intellect.

"Nevertheless, I still appreciate your opinions, even if I most adamantly *do not* agree with them. I understand that the subject of literature—like art and architecture—is subjective.

You are entitled to your own opinions, Miss Roberts." He took a slow sip of his wine, and the others sat quietly until he continued. "If you are willing to accept a word of advice, however, I would be cautious in your attempts to predict the future. You will find that I am extremely appreciative of female intellect, but it would be wise to remember that females do not benefit from the broad exposure to politics or worldly events that their brothers, fathers, and husbands possess."

Ouch! Janet's mind raced to the impending moment of being shown the exit. Could a single, penniless woman live on the wages of a drawing instructor in the Bath of 1813? She feared she would soon find out.

Janet fought the tears ready to well up in her eyes. She was often frustrated in conversations with males of her generation, but what on earth had she been thinking to take on Sir Edward?

The plates were cleared and dessert brought to the table. Discussion passed on to Bath society and Janet was, happily, excluded from further conversation. Following dessert, the women separated to the drawing room and the men to the library to drink their brandy, smoke cigars, and discuss political and worldly concerns beyond the realm of female understanding.

Never before had Janet been more eager to experience firsthand these antiquated gender exclusion rituals. If only she were hosted in an Ottoman harem, where she could be entirely banned from the male spheres of the house. At least then, she would not be free to get herself into trouble.

As soon as she and Emma had been seated in the drawing room, Emma took Janet's hand in her own. "Dear Jane, I fear that you are anxious about how events unfolded over dinner."

Janet smiled at the understatement of the year. "Do you mean, do I feel foolish for not having displayed the ability to keep my big, fat mouth shut? Yes, I do. I promise you."

Emma paused. "It is true that your ways are foreign to us, but, as my brother pointed out, you have had an unconventional upbringing. I know you are trying to adapt to our ways. I find it refreshing, but not all will think the same. My brother will come around. Let me speak with him. In the meantime," she offered her lovely smile, "please refrain from antagonizing him *quite* so much. You know how little men enjoy being challenged. I doubt that it is entirely different, even in your America." She offered another smile, a playful one this time. "If I am mistaken, I shall return with you immediately."

Janet felt her tension dissipate. "I will do a better job of holding my tongue. I do not wish to make things uncomfortable for you."

"Leave my brother to me."

The two friends spoke until the men returned, and the rest of the evening unfolded pleasantly. Emma played on the piano and Janet enjoyed the lovely arias from *Le nozze di Figaro*. Janet listened to Emma's skillful performance of *Voi che sapete*, relieved to have the chance to do more listening than speaking.

Janet observed as Mr. Bentley turned Emma's pages. His pleasure at being so close to her was evident on his face. At one point, he leaned in too closely to turn a page and a lock of his blond hair swept across her cheek. The tableau of the handsome couple was so idyllic and appealing that Janet smiled as she noted the blush creeping across her friend's face.

Sir Edward was cordial to her, but she could sense his wariness.

When Sir Edward and Emma fell into a discussion of household matters, Janet was happy to discuss literature with Mr. Bentley. He was insightful and witty. In speaking to him, Janet found herself wishing once again that Sir Edward's concerns for Mr. Bentley's lack of situation could be overcome. Mr. Bentley and Emma would certainly make a happy couple.

Memories of discomfort earlier in the evening faded and she was surprised when it was time for Mr. Bentley to take his leave and for Emma and Janet to retire to their rooms. As Miller helped Janet to undress and prepare for bed, Janet prayed that Emma could convince her brother to accept her presence.

Janet would do her utmost to steer as clear of Sir Edward as much as humanly possible. As she climbed under her covers and lay her head on the thick, goosedown pillow, she hoped Sir Edward could live with this détente.

From her side, Janet was firmly convinced that the less they had to do with one another, the happier both would be.

Chapter 20

Dressed in a pretty, pale blue muslin frock, another "hand-me-down" Janet could hardly believe was not yet another kind gesture from her new friend, Janet made her way down to the breakfast room.

She clutched her sketchpad to her chest. She and Emma had a picnic outing planned, and Emma had promised her beautiful vistas for sketching.

Perched atop the sketchpad was *A Vindication of the Rights of Woman*, selected yesterday from the library. She was anxious to reread Wollstonecraft's controversial treatise. Although nothing within its covers could be considered controversial to a modern reader, she needed to better understand what could be termed as radical political thought of the time.

At least Janet would not have to worry about Sir Edward's critical eyes judging her every move for the next few days. Emma assured Janet that her brother would get an early start on his journey to Oxford for urgent business, departing before dawn. When he returned, Janet would be on her best behavior, better prepared to blend in. Mary Wollstonecraft was a first step in her nineteenth-century reeducation.

Entering the breakfast room, Janet nearly collided with a young parlor maid who assisted in the kitchen. "Pardon, Anna. I am clumsy before my coffee."

"No, Miss Jane. I apologize."

The scared look in the girl's eyes was evident. Janet and Anna had enjoyed long talks during Janet's visits to the kitchen. The young girl with freckles and hazel eyes had confessed to Janet how homesick she was, how she missed her brothers and sisters at their farm not far from Bath, how she felt so scared and alone, in constant fear she would break things in this grand house. Janet told her she could come to her whenever she needed to talk, or even if she only needed to cry it out far from judging eyes. Now she puzzled over Anna's brusque and distant manner.

"Anna, are you alright? Have you received bad news from the farm? Are your brothers and sisters well? Has your mother not fully recovered from her illness?"

Yes, it was clearly panic in her sharp hazel eyes when Anna responded, in a voice slightly too loud and theatrical. A gaze that appeared to issue a warning. "I assure you, Miss Jane, everyone is fine. You should not worry yourself for my welfare. Now, if you will excuse me, I must go see Cook."

Janet shook her head, but decided to let it go. They could discuss it later. "Yes, of course. Please tell Cook I shall come to see her following our picnic. She promised to show me how to make her delicious raspberry tarts. I shall come dressed properly for the kitchen this time and prepared to get my hands dirty."

Fear flashed once again in the girl's eyes. "Yes, ma'am, of course." Faster than an Olympic sprinter, she scurried out of sight.

Janet bit her lip. Why was their conversation so oddly formal? Although all conversations were more formal than in her world, she believed she'd reached a level of intimacy with most of the household staff. She even believed that the kitchen staff embraced her as nearly a friend. Yet Anna's distance raised doubts. Staring at the open door, she puzzled over the situation a moment more before stepping into the breakfast room.

The reason for Anna's apprehension, her fear of appearing too friendly, soon became clear. Two sharp blue eyes glared at her. She fumbled with her sketchpad and her book, but she was too late to catch them before they tumbled noisily to the floor.

Sir Edward sprang quickly to his feet and arrived at the fallen objects before Janet had time to react. He picked up the sketchbook and the book, eyeing the title with raised eyebrows, before returning to his seat and placing the books squarely at his side of the table.

"Miss Roberts." He gestured to the chair across from him. "What a pleasure." His tone conveyed none. "Would you do the honor of joining me?"

Janet slipped quietly into her seat. No wonder Anna had been terrified by the hallway conversation that would most certainly not meet with Sir Edward's approval. Emma had been so convinced her brother would have departed before sunrise. Now Janet's nerves were on edge. Goodness, even in her own mind she was starting to resemble Mrs. Bennet. She saw the coffeepot and poured herself a generous cup before speaking, hoping it would soothe the unease she felt. She willed her voice to remain steady.

"I apologize for my surprise on seeing you, Sir Edward. It is only that your sister assured me you were departing early this morning for Oxford. I did not expect to meet you."

"So I am led to understand by the intimate conversation I overheard with our parlor maid." He tapped his fingers on the table's edge. In the silence of the room, the sound was deafening. "I understand from our butler that you are friendly with all the staff, although I did not realize your familiarity extended to rolling up your sleeves to prepare pastries alongside Cook. I hope that you are not stirring up my household staff to revolt against me?"

She glanced up from stirring the coffee to gauge his expression. His smile revealed perfect rows of teeth—miraculous for this pre-dental-hygiene era—but there was no warmth displayed on the chiseled features of his face. Her gaze slipped down, and she busied herself stirring yet more milk into her coffee cup, wishing labor-intensive quail could be served for breakfast as well. When she gathered the courage to look up, Sir Edward was examining the Wollstonecraft.

"I see your revolutionary ideas extend beyond the role of servants to the rights of women."

"Are they not one and the same?" She lifted her gaze from the coffee cup to meet his. *Careful, Janet. Deep breath.* "That, at least, is Mrs. Wollstonecraft's argument: that a well-bred woman is trained simply to be decorative, that she is not challenged to live up to her full potential. I do not believe her arguments are revolutionary. Strangely, she does not even argue that men and women are equal, but simply that well-bred women should be educated to be better wives, and mothers, and companions. Surely, that is not a revolutionary philosophy?"

Sir Edward observed her carefully. He tilted his head slightly. "Certainly your father must be an adherent, since he raised you as he would a son. Does he truly aspire for you to work alongside him as an architect?"

Janet sipped her coffee. "That is his intention, but perhaps some things are not so different on our separate sides of the Atlantic. Since I am a daughter, I have very little say in my future. I have always been gifted in my studies, but my hopes for my future have never been sought by my father, nor by the other men in my life. Perhaps I have the unique misfortune of being considered both educated and decorative." She placed her cup down on its saucer. "So you see, Sir Edward, even a commitment to and belief in educating females does not necessarily afford them true liberty."

There was a long pause. If she hadn't known Sir Edward's character better, she may have been fooled into thinking that he had been chastened.

They ate in silence, until Sir Edward spoke. "Miss Roberts, may I look at your sketchings?"

How could she refuse him? It was his kindness and understanding she sought.

"Of course."

Attempting to concentrate fully on her toast and coffee, Janet willed herself not to look up at Sir Edward's face as he studied her work. It was not as if she desired his approval. She only hoped his examination would be brief and without commentary. Her heart sank as she realized this was not to be.

"Have you truly been to all of these places? To Rome, and Florence, and Cairo? Athens and Constantinople?"

She raised her eyes slowly. He met her gaze only briefly, absorbed in the sketchbook.

"As I mentioned yesterday, my life was not conventional. When my mother died, my father did not wish to entrust me to nannies. I went with him on his projects, and discovered ancient architecture. I loved it."

"It shows. Your drawings are truly extraordinary. As my sister may have told you, I am not one to dispense of praise lightly."

His eyes met hers for a briefly. She was surprised to feel her heart flutter. Vanity sparked by flattery.

"These sketches of Venice take me back. I spent a delightful few months there after concluding my studies at Oxford, perhaps one of the happiest times of my life."

Janet smiled. Venice never failed to amaze her, no matter how many times she visited. Something they both loved.

Finally, a connection. "I understand, especially for one who collects art. The churches are filled with beautiful masterpieces, and the Scuola Grande di San Rocco! Then, of course, there's the simple pleasure of losing oneself in the city's labyrinthine streets. I could never grow bored in magical Venice."

Janet thought Sir Edward had been listening, but he was studying one of her sketches. His brow furrowed, his lip curled in a grimace. Her heart froze. What had she done now? Had she inadvertently drawn in a car or a bus, or maybe even an anachronistic *vaporetto*? But in her sketching, she generally tried to concentrate on the monuments, blocking out the trappings of modern life.

"And *this*?" He turned the sketchbook toward Janet. "You claim you have been to all of the places you have sketched, but I do not recall having extended any invitation to you in the past to Helmsley Manor."

Janet's stomach dropped. The sketching of Helmsley Manor she'd drawn during her first week in Bath.

The drawing she completed as they waited for Mr. Whitshaw to take them on a tour of the manor house. What on earth could she say to get herself out of this one? Had they been reaching a type of understanding? Had one sketch destroyed the positive gains that might have been made? She hadn't even thought to remove that one drawing. Hadn't Emma already mentioned seeing it and expressed her surprise? She certainly couldn't explain to Sir Edward her visit two hundred years in the future. She'd be locked away in a nineteenth-century insane asylum.

Janet sipped her coffee, willing her hands not to shake as her mind desperately grasped for a plausible explanation. When she spoke, she began slowly, measuring each word. "Ironically, that is the one drawing I did not sketch from the live subject. Strangely, I did not even know the name of the manor. My father visited these parts many years ago, and he told me about the lovely manors he saw."

His scrutiny was unbearable. She gulped before continuing, praying her voice sounded more confident than she felt.

"He was never a guest in any of these houses, but I believe he applied to the housekeepers for the right to sketch these. He has many examples. Since I loved Palladian architecture and studied it in Italy, I pored over his sketches."

Another sip. Pause. Meet his gaze. Channel the calm voice.

"This is a sketch I did of my father's live study. I was surprised when Emma informed me that it is Helmsley Manor. I truly had no idea which manor I had selected as my favorite. Quite the coincidence." She dropped her gaze. Lying was easier if she didn't meet his eyes. "However, as a student of Palladian architecture, I must compliment you on Helmsley Manor's beauty and harmony."

Absolute silence. Janet prayed that Sir Edward could not hear the wild pounding of her heart from across the table.

The slight thawing that may have been underway had definitely been rolled back. His gaze was once again hard. The timbre of his voice expressed no warmth. Standing up, he strode over to Janet and unceremoniously handed her the sketchpad and the book.

"Thank you for allowing me the pleasure of examining your drawings. It is clear that you are prodigiously talented. My sister is fortunate to benefit from your attention to her art. Regrettably, I have stayed too long, and I must be on my way to Oxford. I bid you good day, Miss Roberts."

Following a rapid bow that allowed for no eye contact, he was gone. Janet sat alone in confusion. Was he angry at her? Did he distrust her?

She didn't know what to expect on Sir Edward's return. She willed her heart to slow its wild beating and opened her

Wollstonecraft, trying to make sense of the words spinning on the page.

Emma would soon be down for breakfast, and Janet needed to compose herself. She had to show herself to be a carefree woman who did not fear desperately, with every fiber of her being, her unceremonious and penniless exit into Bath society the moment Sir Edward returned from Oxford.

Janet and Emma sat side by side in the warm sunlight, a light breeze caressing their faces. The sweet smell of lilies of the valley mingled with the musky smell of wet grass. Birds chirped around them as they surveyed the beauty before them. With a final stroke, Janet placed her sketchpad down and lay back on the blanket, observing the cloud patterns overhead.

"Emma, you were right. This spot is so beautiful that I should be sketching page after page, yet all I want to do is be lazy in this glorious sunshine."

"My mother used to bring me here when I was small, yet year after year I am freshly amazed by its beauty and tranquility. I feel there is nothing I cannot conquer when I am seated in this spot and the sunshine warms me as it does today."

"Do you miss your mother?"

"Every day," Emma whispered.

Janet heard the tremor in her friend's voice. She sat up, trying to ignore the discomfort of the whalebone corset digging into her skin. She took Emma's hand in her own. "I feel the same. Sometimes I dream my mother is still alive. I am always so hopeful the first few minutes after I wake up, before I realize ..."

"I suspect that shared sense of loss is one of the reasons I feel so close to you, Jane, and one of the many reasons I already consider you such a dear friend."

They sat for a moment in silence, looking out on the landscape below.

"Emma?" Janet cast a sideways glance at her friend. "Are you absolutely certain I have not made things difficult for you with your brother?"

"Edward is generous and kind, but he is also quick to judge and quite set in his ways. He is not accustomed to women like you. Those who speak their minds. You may," she paused, "wish to further modify your behavior. I long for you to join us at Helmsley Manor. My brother is always so involved in the management of the estate and the lands while we are there, and I am left to my own devices. How I would love to have you as my companion!" Emma placed down her sketchpad and tucked her legs beneath her. "He shall come around. I will speak with him when he returns to Bath. You will be with us at Helmsley Manor in a fortnight's time, I am convinced."

"I should love to see Helmsley Manor."

"How pleased your father will be that you have come to stay with us, after his visit to our estate all those years ago."

Janet tried to relax, but her mind was troubled. Her father. She'd been gone for weeks. What must her father be thinking? Was she missed in her modern world? Were the police looking for her? Was her father following the news from Boston? Or had he arrived in Bath? How she yearned to make sense of this confusion.

"They should arrive soon," said Emma.

Her words interrupted Janet's thoughts. "How pleased I am that Mr. Bentley and your Aunt Maria will be joining us for our picnic."

"It was kind of them to agree."

"I do not believe it was a great sacrifice for Mr. Bentley to agree to spend the afternoon with you." Janet looked over at her friend, whose cheeks turned bright red. "May I ask? Is your Aunt Maria dispatched as a chaperone?"

Emma cleared her throat. "I have become accustomed to your odd questions. Either you are truly oblivious to the rules of society, or you have indeed been raised among the Indians. Mr. Bentley may accompany us in Bath, where we are constantly surrounded by society, but it would be unseemly for him to join two unmarried, unchaperoned young women at this secluded location. Aunt Maria knows this better than anyone, and she offered to join us and to bring Mr. Bentley in her carriage."

"Is it assumed that Mr. Bentley would be a danger to us, or we to him, if left to our own devices?"

Emma laughed. "Jane, you are terrible. Do *not* tease like that before my brother."

"If you were free to choose, would you choose Mr. Bentley as your Mr. Darcy?"

A blush once again crept across her cheeks. "Oh, Jane, do not tease so. You know how fond I am of Mr. Bentley. But I do not know what his feelings are for me. Even if they were favorable, I fear my brother would not smile upon any possible union until Mr. Bentley's future is secured."

"I am convinced of Mr. Bentley's regard for you. How could anyone who observed him in your presence believe otherwise? I wish your brother would realize this. How unfair that Mr. Bentley cannot be judged on his own merits. I would love to raise this point with Sir Edward."

"Do no such thing!" Emma's voice softened. "I ask you, as my dear friend, not to meddle. Customs are different here, and you may make things worse with my brother—both for me and for yourself. Please leave this alone."

"I would not do anything to make you uncomfortable. Although it may not seem so, I am trying hard to fit better into your society and I count on you to guide me. I value your friendship."

"As I do yours. Although it may seem that I am constantly issuing warnings, I admire your independence. Even envy it. I am not certain I would have the courage for life in America, but I find myself fascinated by your observations and points of view. And it often causes me to question my own."

Sitting on this hilltop meadow with her new nineteenth-century friend, Janet felt herself a part of her new surroundings. Her life was less full than her modern life, she had fewer opportunities as a young woman, yet in her short time here, she appreciated the richness of the social and intellectual spheres. Quieter time and fewer distractions that allowed her more time to think and reflect. Had modern progress managed to dilute these spheres in her twenty-first-century life? The sound of carriage wheels approaching interrupted her thoughts.

The coachman brought the horses to a halt and Mr. Bentley alighted before gently helping Aunt Maria down.

"Ladies." He bowed. "How lovely to see you on this splendid day. I am so pleased that you and Mrs. Hale ..." He turned to the elegant, middle-aged lady at his side. "... have allowed me to join you in today's outing. You could not have selected a more perfect day."

A sideways glance confirmed to Janet the presence of the glow that often washed over Emma's complexion whenever Mr. Bentley was nearby. She and Emma curtsied in response to Mr. Bentley's bow. Janet had been practicing her curtsy in front of a mirror, after enlisting help from Emma. She was proud to have learned to do so almost naturally, although nowhere near as gracefully as Emma.

The small group walked around the meadow that afforded expansive views over the lands below. Bath was only a tiny speck in the distance. Janet wondered if this were the spot where the fictional Tilneys had come for their walk with Catherine.

When they returned, Aunt Maria's maid had laid out the food for their picnic under an oak tree. They ate their lunch in the cool shade. Aunt Maria was newly returned from London, and she regaled them with stories of London society.

Janet listened to these conversations, each day gleaning a deeper understanding of the society she'd studied on the written page for years. She yearned for her laptop and her stalled thesis, certain the words would flow effortlessly from her fingertips. She was eager to present her thesis advisor with her revised draft. Yet each passing day in her new home made her wonder about the likelihood of her eventual return.

Following the lunch, wine, and Cook's scrumptious raspberry tarts, Mr. Bentley opened Lord Byron's *Childe Harold's Pilgrimage.* Janet had never read much Byron. Who did in modern America? But here, Byron was all the rage.

To catch up, she'd been raiding the Huntington House library, reviewing the poetry discussed so often in the Assembly Hall and Bath salons. Lord Byron was a contemporary poet in her new world, only gaining a reputation as a celebrated literary figure. The first canto of *Childe Harold's Pilgrimage* had been published the previous year, and seemed to be on everyone's lips.

Janet was captivated by Mr. Bentley's lovely reading voice, so well-suited to poetry. It lulled her into a lazy trance. There were so few men in Janet's modern life who could speak in full, coherent sentences, let alone read poetry in a way that could enthrall a gathering.

> *"And now I'm in the world alone,*
> *upon the wide, wide sea;*
> *But why should I for others groan,*
> *When none will sigh for me?"*

Janet sat up straighter. Lord Byron seemed to speak directly to her through Mr. Bentley's melodious voice. The famed romantic poet was not the only one to feel "in the world alone." How odd to consider Lord Byron as a soul mate, both of them travelers alone in strange lands.

> *"With thee, my bark, I'll swiftly go,*
> *Athwart the foaming brine;*
> *Nor care what land thou bear'st me to,*
> *So not again to mine.*
> *Welcome, welcome, ye dark blue waves!*
> *And when you fail my sight,*
> *Welcome, ye deserts, and ye caves!*
> *My Native Land—Good Night!"*

They sat in silence when Mr. Bentley finished reading. A light breeze caressed Janet's cheek as she considered the poem. *My Native Land—Good Night!*

How extraordinary. Why had those words never moved her before? She'd read *Harold Childe* in a literature class, had probably raced through it to tick it off her reading assignments. The words meant nothing to her back then. Yet now, as Mr. Bentley closed the book and sat down on the picnic blankets with the others, Byron's lovely imagery pierced her soul—she, a twenty-first-century traveler "upon the wide, wide sea."

Yet, like Byron, was she willing to welcome those dark blue waves carrying her to a new world?

After all, a well-off, or at least well-connected, young lord certainly had more options than a penniless, female twenty-first-century explorer. She hoped desperately that Emma could convince her brother to extend his hospitality. How she longed to experience a great country manor and to observe the lifestyle there. She and Childe Harold, adrift in their exotic new worlds.

Emma sighed and disrupted Janet's musings. Her words broke the pleasant silence. "We are living through an exciting age of poetry. Mr. Bentley, you read so well. I believed I truly was in Cintra. How exciting to set off on a journey like Childe Harold's. How unfair that it is only men who can undertake such exotic adventures." She turned toward Janet. "Perhaps I should qualify that to say men, and women from the New World."

"How can I forget that we have our very own Lady Byron here?" Mr. Bentley addressed Janet. "In addition to your stunning drawings, we should be reading your verse about your exotic journeys."

Janet shook her head. "I fear I am relegated to my drawing pencils. I see no need to try to compete with Lord Byron, who expresses himself ever more eloquently than I." *And era-appropriately.*

"Rumor has it that Lord Byron plans to publish additional cantos," said Mr. Bentley. "I am eager to read his second canto, based on his journeys through the Ottoman Empire. He is said to have even been a guest of the despot Ali Pasha. Miss Roberts, I can hardly believe that you yourself have visited the Ottoman Empire!"

Would my new friends believe me if I explained the collapse of Empires?

"Unlike Lord Byron, however, I have not travelled across the Empire on horseback," Janet said. "And no pashas hosted my father and me during our travels. I have only been to Istanbu ... I mean, ... Constantinople. It is one of the prettiest cities I have ever seen. The Blue Mosque must be one of the most dramatic settings of all time."

"Do not tell me, my dear, that you have actually stepped foot into a Mohammedan church! This is most perplexing. Whatever for?" asked Aunt Maria.

"Why yes, they are so beautiful and exotic. An architect can hardly fail to do otherwise. The painted Turkish tiles are a wonder. I have also visited many of the city's minor mosques. They never fail to take my breath away."

"But is it true one must enter barefoot?" Emma's eyes were wide and eager.

"Yes, it is. You leave your shoes outside, but non-Muslims are only allowed to walk in certain parts of the mosques, and, of course, women must veil themselves. There is something magical about the evening prayer hour, as the sun is setting and the muezzins are calling the faithful to prayer. That image of Istanbu ... Constantinople ... has remained forever fixed in my mind."

"How exotic! I wish I could go, too."

"That is out of the question, Emma," said Aunt Maria. "Can you imagine your brother agreeing to your venturing into the land of the Sultans? Better to leave those journeys to Lord Byron. And to Jane, of course, who must have had an able chaperone in her father." The older lady smiled at Janet.

Mr. Bentley picked up the volume again and began to read in his deep, soothing voice. Janet listened, the sun shining down, the countryside stretched before her as far as the eye could see.

The air was clean and fresh. Cars and emissions were many years away. Janet tried to imagine a Tony or a Reuben passing their afternoons in the company of three ladies, reading Byron's poetry in his resonant reading voice. Although, to be fair, there were also more evolved twenty-first-century men, like Malcolm or James. Still, she felt strangely grounded in this distant time. As awkward as she often was, sometimes she felt more at home here than in her true life.

Perhaps the dark blue waves that bore her to this distant land had been her salvation. With each passing day, she was less eager to return to her modern life. *My Native Land—Good Night!*

"When my brother returns from Oxford," said Emma, "I must convince him that Jane is to join us at Helmsley. With you nearby visiting your aunt, wouldn't it be wonderful to all be together again?"

"It most certainly would. Miss Roberts, you simply must come to Helmsley Manor. It is one of the most perfect corners of England."

Mr. Bentley, Emma, and Janet got together later at the 1813 version of Janet's favorite twenty-first-century tearoom. They sat under an awning and watched all of Bath society pass along the streets. Following the afternoon in the countryside, Aunt Maria, Mr. Bentley, Emma, and Janet had returned to Bath. Once within the city limits, Aunt Maria was apparently free to leave the young people unchaperoned on the bustling Bath streets in order to prepare for a soirée.

The three friends sipped tea slowly, eager to prolong the pleasant day.

"I would love to visit Helmsley Manor, of course, but I regret not to have made such a positive first impression on Sir Edward. I am trying hard to fit better into your society, but I fear I am not learning quickly enough. Perhaps I will have improved by the time Sir Edward returns." She smiled as she looked up at two serious faces observing her.

"Poor Jane. I know how hard you have tried to blend in. I will speak to Edward. I would like to have you as my companion. I know my brother will listen to me."

"And I will find an opportunity to speak to Edward as well. Surely Miss Emma and I will succeed in convincing him."

Janet smiled. Talk turned to the Sixth Coalition and its efforts against Napoleon's army. Janet listened carefully, internalizing current events.

As the sun hung low in the evening sky, Mr. Bentley accompanied Emma and Janet on their walk along the gravel path leading up to The Crescent. The gravel path. Janet remembered the famous scene from *Persuasion*, where Anne Elliot and Captain Wentworth walked along this same gravel path to prolong their time alone together after declaring their love. Remarkably, Jane Austen had not even committed the promenade along this path to the page yet.

Mr. Bentley took his leave at the door. That evening, Janet and Emma talked and laughed over dinner, then spent an hour in the library, where Emma continued their reading of *Childe Harold's Pilgrimage*.

The week passed quickly, each day full of diversions: long walks, sketching, their regular outings with Mr. Bentley, concerts at the Assembly Rooms, and calling on Emma's friends and neighbors.

Janet even attended her first ball, where the riot of colors mixed perfectly with the heady mix of music, sights, and sounds. She was content to be a wallflower, admiring the more accomplished dancers while simultaneously observing customs she was long familiar with only on the written page. She surprised herself by fairly successfully managing to dance two quadrilles, thanks to Emma's patient coaching and Mr. Bentley's encouragement as her dance partner.

Cook taught a grateful Janet the secrets to preparing her mouthwatering raspberry tarts, although she made her swear not to share the recipe with anyone else. Janet smiled to think that the promise most probably did not extend to her twenty-first-century friends and acquaintances. Perhaps the recipe and its elaborate preparations would find its way into her thesis.

The week flew by so quickly that Janet was surprised when Mr. Bentley, calling on them one day for afternoon tea, announced, "I look forward to seeing Edward tomorrow. Is he still expected to arrive by afternoon?"

"Yes, according to the letter I received this morning," said Emma. "Are you already engaged for tomorrow evening? I hoped we could all attend the concert at the Assembly Halls that evening, if Edward is not too fatigued from his journey."

Janet did her best to smile pleasantly during the conversation, but her mind kept returning to the next day.

Sir Edward returned. Should she be hopeful or fearful?

Chapter 21

"Edward, I am so pleased to see you." Emma's face glowed as she gazed at her brother over the dinner table. "How was your journey? Are you fatigued, or would you wish to join us at the concert this evening?" Emma paused to take a bite of lamb, her eyes never straying from her brother's face.

Janet greeted Sir Edward warmly when he returned earlier that afternoon, but she'd otherwise avoided him. At dinner, she spoke as little as possible, aware this was her last chance to make a good impression, for the Huntingtons would depart for Helmsley Manor in two days' time.

"The voyage was uneventful, my time in Oxford well-spent. Aside from the business at hand, I also learned about new agricultural methods. I spoke to some of the professors about new irrigation practices that I wish to discuss with Saunders." He turned to face Janet briefly. "He is the foreman at Helmsley Manor."

Janet smiled in a manner she hoped he would interpret as sweet. Sir Edward was far from warm with her, but perhaps he was becoming accustomed to her presence. Of course, his slight change in manner might also be explained by the fact that he viewed her visit with them as finally nearing an end.

"And yes, Emma, I shall be pleased to join you at the concert tonight."

When dessert arrived, Sir Edward spoke with Emma about friends from his time at Oxford. This allowed Janet to listen in rather than be expected to participate in the conversation. Brother and sister enjoyed a close-knit relationship, and Sir Edward clearly doted on Emma.

It was easy to think ill of him when he held the keys to Janet's well-being in his hands, but in observing him, she had to admit he was a caring and nurturing older brother. She believed, as Emma had so often mentioned, that he had fully stepped into the role and responsibilities passed on to him at the death of their father.

"Shall I ring for the carriage?" asked Sir Edward.

"No need, brother. Jane and I have been on long promenades each day; it has done wonders for improving my health. There is no need for a carriage for the short distance to the Assembly Hall."

Later, Sir Edward walked alongside Janet and Emma on the pleasant stroll to The Circus and then to the Assembly Hall. It was still light out during these long summer nights. Janet noted how Sir Edward, like all men who accompanied ladies, always walked on the street-side, thereby sheltering the women from possible splatters from the passing carriages. She smiled inwardly as she noted how he carefully ferried them across street crossings, jockeying once again into the curbside position once he reached the opposite side.

She noticed how gentlemen squeezed aside to allow the two women to pass, and she tried to juxtapose this reality with her rush-hour commutes on the Boston T. Oh, if only she could transport some of these antiquated and lovely manners back to her twenty-first-century life.

Mr. Bentley was waiting outside the building, and his face lit up when they turned the corner. "I am so pleased you could attend, Edward. I hope you are not too weary after your journey."

Janet was learning quickly about distances in her new world. The Oxford-Bath trip might have been a little over an hour by car in her modern world, but in a world in which no one could travel on land faster than a horse's hooves, Sir Edward had undertaken an arduous two-day journey to arrive to Bath.

She had become familiar with nineteenth-century journeys on day trips they had taken from Bath, realizing that trips that took over two hours were short jaunts with modern cars and highways.

No wonder her travels seemed so odd to her new friends. How could she possibly have endured that type of far-flung travel in this nineteenth-century world? How could she explain to her new friends how almost anyone could travel in comfort in her modern world? The simple online purchase of an airline ticket meant no need for dangerous journeys by carriage through the treacherous Alps during the season's first snowfall or voyages in ships tossed across stormy seas with the constant threat of pirates to reach Asia.

The foursome entered the Assembly Hall and took their seats. Janet had hoped to get a seat far from Sir Edward, but Mr. Bentley moved to Emma's far side to greet an acquaintance, leaving Janet on the edge of the row, next to Sir Edward.

From the corner of her eye, she observed how Sir Edward appeared no happier with this arrangement than she, but she was determined to put on a brave face. She needed him to like her, or at least to tolerate her, in order for her to secure an invitation to Helmsley Manor.

Janet swallowed her fear and turned to him. "Sir Edward, it was so kind of you to join us after your long journey. Do you enjoy music?"

"Yes, I do." He stared ahead in silence.

Janet busied herself reading the program.

Finally, Sir Edward spoke. "I see that several arias from *Don Giovanni* are on the program. Have you seen that opera?"

"Yes, I have!" said Janet, perhaps with too much enthusiasm, grateful to not be pointedly ignored.

"Certainly not in America?"

"No." Janet smiled. "We have not yet developed a great opera following, although the patrons of the arts are convinced we may develop a great opera house in New York. Perhaps one day talented performers will dream of their operatic debut at the New York opera." She ignored the dismissive grunt beside her ear and smiled inwardly. "No, I saw a performance at the Stavovské divadlo—the Estates Theatre—where it was premiered."

"In Vienna?" He turned to face her for the first time.

"No, in Prague. Mozart felt that Vienna had snubbed him, so he decided to do the same to his adoptive city by premiering his *Don Giovanni* in Prague. The Estates Theatre is small, but charming. I am told the singers this evening are exceptional. I see that they are going to perform '*Madamina, il catalogo*,' one of my favorite arias. Emma tells me that the bass singing Leporello this evening is prodigiously talented."

He furrowed his brow. "And do you not find the subject matter offensive?"

Janet stifled a giggle, certain he would find it impertinent. "Why should I? It is one of the great operas of all time and I do not believe many women are scandalized to see how Don Giovanni behaves. We have all met gentlemen who aspire to such conquests." She flipped through the libretto to find the words. "Ah, here it is ... '*Non si picca—se sia ricca, Se sia brutta, se sia bella; Purché porti la gonnella, Voi sapete quel che fa*' Ha! I always enjoy this ... It doesn't matter if she is rich, or ugly or beautiful. As long as she wears a skirt, you know what he does.'" She paused and smiled. "Perhaps it's more scandalous to a man's sense of honor, but I doubt many women are shocked by these words. If a woman's heart is broken by such a rogue, she has only herself to blame. The opera itself has always been one of my favorites."

She looked up to see Sir Edward staring at her oddly. Had she ruined things once again? Her nervousness caused the words to spill out. Surely she'd sounded too scandalous for a house guest.

"You speak your mind freely, Miss Roberts," said Sir Edward, following a long pause. "But I must keep reminding myself that it is the result of your unconventional upbringing. Or perhaps the result of your extensive travels. As you yourself told us, you have been in frequent contact with Latins and Ottomans, whose passions are outward and not as guarded as our own."

She bit her lip to stifle a smile threatening to burst free. Blame it on those passionate, corrupting Latins and Ottomans. She glanced around quickly, relieved to observe the musicians making their way to the front of the hall. "The performance is about to begin."

A hush fell over the Assembly Hall crowd as the performers began. At her side, Sir Edward listened attentively. Emma and Mr. Bentley exchanged whispers back and forth. These concerts allowed for little snatches of intimacy for couples such as they. Conversation and physical nearness in a concert hall would not be considered untoward, particularly when the young lady was accompanied by her brother. Janet was pleased for her friend.

"Your pronunciation was excellent when you read me the lyrics. Do you also understand the lyrics as they are sung, Miss Roberts?" Sir Edward asked during a pause in the performance.

"Most of them." Janet turned to see a look of discomfort on his face. Her heart clenched.

"I regret, Miss Roberts, that we may have gotten off on the wrong foot. The opinions you voice so freely—and so frequently, I must admit—may often stun me, but I do admire your wide knowledge. Although I may not demonstrate it, I find it refreshing to see a female so often voicing her opinions on various matters."

Janet sat in stunned silence. Was this a compliment? Or a prelude to an eviction? Perhaps Sir Edward was generously telling her how much he enjoyed her outspoken behavior prior to ejecting her from his house?

Her eyes downcast, she fingered the folds of her dress. Perhaps she could turn this conversation somewhat to her advantage. In two days' time Sir Edward and his sister would be *en route* to Helmsley Manor, and Janet simply had to be in their company.

"Thank you, Sir Edward." She kept her voice soft and delicate, as she had observed Emma do when addressing her brother on matters for which she sought his approval. "I am aware that I may not be doing everything as I should. I feel a little like Lord Byron when he talks about those dark blue waves. I feel they have pulled me far from home, and I am doing my best to understand the local customs and to become a part of Bath society. Believe me, I *am* trying, and Emma has been a most patient teacher. I do not wish to offend with my seeming bluntness. I would not wish to infringe on your generous hospitality. I hope you know how much it means to me to be under your protection, with a dear new friend like Emma, when I am so far from home, and often so uncertain how to best integrate into this society."

Janet willed her eyes to glaze over with a thin veil of tears. As she predicted, Sir Edward's hard features melted slightly, concern evident in the tight lines of his face. Even many modern men felt placated by a damsel in distress, so why should it surprise her that an early-nineteenth-century nobleman would feel the same?

A little vulnerability. Is that all it took to fell the concerns of the mighty Sir Edward? Janet prayed silently that her gambit would have the desired effect—an invitation to the family retreat.

The foursome walked around during the interval. Janet observed that no one had interrupted while she and Sir Edward had been speaking. Yet now that Sir Edward was standing, thereby apparently signaling his availability, many of their fellow concert-goers approached him to have a word.

"How wonderful to have you back, Sir Edward. How was your time at Oxford?"

"Did you have a pleasant journey? Did you hunt in Oxford?"

"Will you be with us a while? No? Back so soon to Helmsley Manor? What a loss for Bath."

Janet hadn't realized Sir Edward's important role in Bath society. Emma was young and charming, and Janet had observed the respect with which she was treated when they were about Bath. For the first time, Janet noticed the deference being paid to the head of the Huntington family as her fellow concert attendees jockeyed to get in a few words with her host. Their faces positively glowed when he turned his attention to them. Did they not think him intimidating? Quick to judge? Apparently not.

Sir Edward introduced her several times as "Our guest from America, Miss Roberts." She observed the respect afforded to her as well, even from some of the same people whose acquaintance she had made in passing with Emma or Mr. Bentley, who seemed to observe her with fresh eyes, introduced as she was directly by Sir Edward.

The performers took their places at the front of the hall once again and the concert-goers bustled to their seats. The music filled the hall. Janet listened with a less burdened heart, pleased in her new surroundings, and slightly more hopeful that her relationship with the Huntington family might be on more solid ground.

Following the concert, Emma, Sir Edward, Mr. Bentley, and Janet filed out into the fresh night air, heavy with the intoxicating scent of honeysuckle. The stars were crystal clear, tiny diamonds dotting the inky night sky. They spoke about the performance on the Assembly Hall steps as concert-goers exited around them. A gentleman approached Sir Edward, asking for a word in private.

"Charles, would you accompany the ladies safely home?"

"I'd be delighted."

The three friends set out on the walk back to The Crescent, the bright moon and stars guiding their passage. Mr. Bentley and Emma fell deep into conversation as Janet glanced upon the windows of The Crescent. Most of the time, she found herself fully engaged in her current life, but her mind was often grasping to understand how she came to be here in the first place. How could time exist on two separate planes?

Here she was, glancing at these familiar windows, but were Amrita, Siobhan, James, and Professor Williams within those same walls in some parallel world? Was time simply one continuum, existing simultaneously? Was her modern life already the ancient past for some future residents of The Crescent, residing in yet another parallel plane? She wondered how many people could pass between centuries as she'd done. Were there other time travelers walking around nineteenth-century Bath? Had she inadvertently met such travelers in her twenty-first-century life?

She could not make sense of it. Worse, she feared that no one would be able to clear up her confusion. Would she ever get back? Was this what happened to people who vanished without a trace?

She heard her name and turned from the lights to see Mr. Bentley and Emma staring at her.

"Jane, you seemed far away from us," said Emma.

"I'm sorry. I am afraid I was. Far away. I was staring at this perfect night sky and the lights in all the windows and wishing I had some paints to capture this view."

"Perhaps not tonight, Jane. There is a slight chill in the air, and we must keep you strong. We need to ensure that Edward agrees to your joining us at Helmsley Manor. Mr. Bentley will be at his aunt's home next week. So, you see—our agreeable little party can continue in the fresh country air."

Janet smiled, not wanting to show her friend that her own optimism for such an outcome was significantly less. They exchanged good nights before Emma and Janet entered the house. Janet forced her voice to sound light as Emma chatted about the concert and the performances as they made their way upstairs, but she was relieved to retreat to her own room.

Miller helped her undress. As she did each evening, Janet released an enormous sigh of relief as the whalebone of the corset that dug into her skin each day was removed.

An exhausted Janet lay down in her bed, but her mind was too disturbed to sleep. Somewhere in the same house, indeed in this same room, but in a different century, her roommate Amrita was also retiring to bed.

Chapter 22

The next morning, Janet entered the breakfast room and found Emma and Sir Edward deep in conversation.

"Good morning, Jane. We have excellent news. May I tell her, Edward?"

He nodded.

"You are to be my special guest at Helmsley Manor!"

A sense of relief washed over Janet. "Thank you, Sir Edward, for your hospitality and kindness."

"Not at all, Miss Roberts. My sister has done nothing since my arrival in Bath but convince me that you must accompany us. It seems she cannot live without you."

"I am truly grateful."

"I have things to attend to before our departure. If you will both excuse me." With a bow, he took his leave.

Emma was silent as his footsteps receded. "Oh, Jane! How happy I am. Now we shall truly be like sisters. You must hurry and have your breakfast. We have so many neighbors to call upon this morning. This afternoon we must supervise the packing of the trunks, for we leave before dawn. Come, Jane. Make haste."

The coffee fortified Janet for the hectic morning, seemingly taking leave of every resident of Bath. She couldn't help but smile when she realized that all this fuss had to be taken prior to a short journey. She listened to endless exhortations to travel safely, to bolster oneself for the arduous journey—as though they were travelling six thousand miles through crocodile-infested swamps, rather than a mere forty miles north of the city.

The day passed by in a blur, with visit after visit, followed by packing for the trip, and preparing for the closing of the house. Dinner was a light and rushed affair, in anticipation of the early departure time the following day.

The next day, Miller woke Janet well before dawn. Dressing quickly in the dark, she went down for coffee and a light breakfast. Despite her numerous day trips, she was not fully accustomed to the carriages and the bumpy journey they afforded. Better to play it safe by having as little in one's stomach as possible.

The footmen finished loading the carriage, and then handed Emma and Janet inside. Sir Edward rode on horseback beside them.

They left Bath under cover of night, heading northward to the Huntingtons' vast estate. Just over two months ago, Janet made this same journey in a rented, air-conditioned coach, travelling on a characterless, yet smooth and easy highway. How she missed that hermetically sealed bus as she jostled along the dirt road in the rising heat. Sweat trickled down her forehead. Dust from the road seeped in every time they tried to open the window slightly, in order to gulp the cooler air in an attempt to ease the nausea.

This type of travel could easily cure Janet of the Wanderlust she'd suffered throughout her life. How on earth could she endure weeks of this to reach her beloved Italy? Certainly she would become a nineteenth-century homebody in her new world. It was the only sensible thing to do.

At first, Emma maintained a light, nonstop chatter, but soon the two ladies were too exhausted to keep up the pretense. Despite the nausea and the general discomfort of coach travel, Janet was transfixed by the landscape passing by the carriage's windows. She'd missed this on her twenty-first-century coach ride.

The towns, the tangle of people walking alongside the horses and buggies jostling for road space, and the peasants tending the fields all held her attention and filled her head with descriptive language for her thesis.

About halfway along the route, they stopped at a post exchange to change horses. Emma and Janet descended from their travelling torture chamber. Solid ground once again! A young servant boy materialized with a basin of water and two cloths. Emma tipped him and the two ladies scrubbed their faces and necks with the fresh, clean water in an attempt to scrape off the grime. As she held the cloth in her hand, Janet startled at how grey it had become. Perhaps she could better understand the farewell visits and the very real concern from their neighbors that the two ladies make a safe and pleasurable trip.

As they changed horses, Sir Edward, Emma, and Janet proceeded to the dining room. The space was dark, and slightly rough around the edges. Unshaven men in tattered clothes eyed the ladies' fine gowns as they passed. Instinctively, Janet clutched her purse tighter. Sir Edward, grumbling that the private room above was unavailable, steered them clear of the shadier elements in the room and secured a secluded table in the back.

Relieved to be out of the bouncing carriage and on solid ground once again, Janet looked around her with interest.

Many of the men sitting at the tables drinking ale were rough-looking. If Sir Edward were not in the party, Emma and Janet may have been in for some unwanted attention. *So this is the nineteenth-century version of a truck stop?* If she could spend time here, she could surely listen in on conversations to add to her understanding of the period. She could probably fill her entire thesis with the social commentary she'd pick up at this post house during a boisterous drinking session.

"Jane? Did you not hear me?"

Janet turned her attention back to the table. "I am sorry. I was curious to see an English post station."

"If only there were a way to avoid it. Let us hope a bar brawl does not break out."

"But Emma, if I am to better learn about your world, shouldn't I observe all aspects of your society? Where better to learn?"

The waiter arrived with their steaming stew. Janet, wary of the jostling ride that awaited her, ate little, but she was surprised at how tasty it was. They passed an hour like that, eating and drinking ale and talking.

Surprisingly, Sir Edward turned out to be almost friendly. His demeanor was still haughty, but perhaps their longer acquaintance softened his negative judgment of her. At moments, she thought he was even somewhat warm, but perhaps it was the effect of the ale and the relaxed atmosphere of the post station pub.

Soon enough, it was time to continue their journey. Janet may have grown accustomed to the jostling rhythms, or perhaps the food in her stomach improved her mood, but she did not feel as queasy as she had that morning.

Out the carriage window, she observed the people working in the fields. So many of them were young children who, back in her world, would be having a story read to them in nursery school, or running around happily in a playground. Here, she watched these tiny bodies work alongside adults, dangerously close to sharp blades, pickaxes, and sledgehammers. Baby-proofing consultants apparently hadn't set up shop in 1813.

As evening fell, Emma reached across the carriage to touch Janet's hand. "Jane, we are almost arrived." A hint of excitement rose in her voice.

Sir Edward rode on ahead. The trees were thick and birds flew overhead. Janet remembered her coach trip from Bath with her classmates, the drive along the highway, which would one day cut through this swath of lovely forest. Gas pumps and convenience stations felling century-old oaks. Exhaust fumes replacing the crisp forest air.

They turned off the main road onto a smaller path. Janet remembered the large, arched gate marking the start of the Huntington's manor. How could she ever have imagined she would be returning here, in a nineteenth-century horse-drawn coach, alongside the woman whose face she had glimpsed each day on the walls of her twenty-first-century student housing?

Emma pressed her face to the window. "Here we are!"

"Yes, it's exactly as I remember it," Janet whispered, before sensing Emma's confusion. "I mean, the way I imagined it when I copied my father's sketching and he described his visit."

The furrows in Emma's brow smoothed and an eager smile lit up her face. "I do love my time in Bath, but I am always pleased to return home. I long for you to love it here as much as I do."

"I am certain I shall."

Janet caught a glimpse of the lake in the distance. The last rays of sunlight hung in the air, casting a golden reflection over the mirror-still waters. As the carriage grew closer, Janet spotted the grand manor home. So familiar, yet so different.

The carriage pulled up to the front door and a footman materialized to help Janet and Emma step down. A line of servants outside the home stood ready to greet its residents and guests, just like in the films. How large a household staff was required for a manor of this size? Janet hoped to glean a better understanding of the day-to-day household and field management that Mr. Whitshaw had discussed with them at this same spot not long ago.

"Jane, Turner will assist you to bathe and settle into your room. Dinner will be served later tonight, at nine. I will accompany you to dinner."

Janet surrendered herself to competent hands. She'd travelled across the world, but never had she been more exhausted than the forty miles of swaying and bouncing across nineteenth-century English roads.

She'd never look at literature in the same way again. She'd no longer laugh at the prolonged wishes for a safe journey, now that she knew what those journeys entailed. Byron was her new hero. She wondered how he had ever managed to survive such journeys. Then again, perhaps he hadn't. Wouldn't he soon die of fever in Greece?

Janet followed Turner up the dramatic staircase she remembered from her class visit. How beautiful to see the house lit up with candles. She'd last seen it in the glow of a lovely spring day and with blinding electric lights, but she appreciated the romanticism of the candlelit manor.

Turner led her through the seemingly endless hallways to a bedroom. A fire blazed in the fireplace, and the large window looked out onto the lake from which she'd sketched this house on a day that seemed a lifetime ago.

A large bed beckoned her with its down comforter and thick pillows. An enormous and intricately carved armoire stood along one wall, its doors propped open, ready to welcome her newly acquired finery. A table and chair were positioned next to the window and the lovely view it proffered. Or would in daylight. If only she had her laptop. Her thesis would fly off her fingertips in no time in such a setting. Then again, she smiled at the thought that perhaps her thesis adviser would be impressed by a thesis on nineteenth-century manners in English literature penned with quill and ink.

She allowed herself to be bathed, dressed and have her hair styled, although memories of showers and hair dryers still made her sigh with pleasure in quiet moments alone. Ready well in advance of dinner, Janet sat at the window, staring into the dusky evening.

She rose and dug deep down into her trunk, retrieving the tiny bag that accompanied her on her time travel. She returned to the table with her paperback edition of *Pride and Prejudice*, this reprinting from 2005. How on earth could she explain it? She should've discarded the book long ago. Yet how could she destroy the only tenuous connection to her real life? Perhaps it held some key to her return.

She slipped a photograph from the book– another item whose possible discovery by one of the maids struck terror in her heart—the one of her standing in front of the Tiepolo. The photo Malcolm took at her request that first day at Huntington House.

Of course, the Tiepolo was now hanging in Helmsley Manor. Might this be the connection between her two worlds? Perhaps the painting could lead her back. If Mr. Whitshaw had been right, it used to hang in the library. She would finally see it again.

She gazed at the girl in the photo. Her modern twin. How different she looked, with her unstyled hair, her mascara, her tanned face, her lack of corsets and bonnets.

Another world, another century. Another Janet.

With a sigh, she tucked her former self into the paperback.

Returning to her trunk, she retrieved the diary Emma had given her. Emma commented upon the fact that Janet never wrote in a diary, and she'd taken it upon herself to present one to her friend. Now Janet set aside time each day to write her impressions on the page. This time was considered sacred, and she was never disturbed. She knew her privacy would be safeguarded, so while she still veiled certain references, she freely wrote down her impressions and comments about her surroundings. This diary would serve as a treasure trove of information should she manage a return to her modern life.

Janet treasured the moments of solitude dedicated to quiet reflection and the written word. When had such lovely traditions been lost? Surely her mother must have still kept a diary, alongside those of her generation. Janet's generation simply turned to blogs or Facebook to record every mundane thought emerging from their heads. No reflection required.

Yet how much was missed by writing words meant only for yourself, of reflecting carefully on events and quietly making sense of your world? Even the ancient practice of dipping her quill into the inkwell and gliding the instrument across the page caused her to slow down and reflect, to commit only serious thoughts to paper. It was entirely different from tapping away at a keyboard, knowing that everything could be erased at the click of a delete button. This felt more special, more poetic. More lasting.

Janet finished her description of the day's travel when there was a knock on the door. Emma entered, looking lovely in a crimson dress.

"I am pleased to see you putting your new diary to good use. Shall we go to dinner?"

They descended the grand staircase and continued on past the doorway Janet recalled as the library, and on to the formal dining room, lit by what appeared to be hundreds of candles. Sir Edward bowed as they entered the room and Janet automatically curtsied, stifling a smile as she wondered if this reflex would lose itself immediately if she returned to her modern world. Or would she encounter scores of stunned bank clerks and supermarket cashiers before she broke the habit?

"Miss Roberts, I hope you are well after your long journey."

"I assure you I am, Sir Edward. And what a charming prospect of the lake from my room! Now I only see it in the dusk, but I look forward to admiring it in all its glory tomorrow morning. "

"I am pleased."

The servants arrived with the evening's feast. Janet cast her eye upon the absurd amounts of food piled high on the platters. All this to feed three people? She hoped, not for the first time, that the leftovers in this pre-refrigeration era would feed the servants and their families later that night.

"I know that Emma is eager to show you around the grounds tomorrow. If the weather is fair, I am certain she is even more eager to ride her horse. If you would care to join her, I will ensure that William arranges everything."

"William is the stable boy," explained Emma.

"Thank you. Seeing the grounds of Helmsley Manor on horseback will make for a wonderful first impression."

Emma and Sir Edward fell into conversation about household matters, and Janet silently observed the room. The table could comfortably seat twenty. The candles flickered brightly, setting off the gold and crystal in the room. She looked up at the frescoed ceiling with its mythological scenes—Diana at the hunt. How like a Domenichino it looked.

"Miss Roberts?"

"I was admiring this fresco. But surely it is not Domenichino?"

Sir Edward observed her closely. "I wish it were, but I know the painting to which you refer. I can understand why Cardinal Scipione coveted it so much. No, this is a pale copy."

"Pale? I should say not. It is spectacular." Janet craned her neck to observe it.

"Perhaps you would like to view my small collection in the library after dinner?"

"I should like that. Emma has told me about the Tiepolo. I am extremely anxious to see it."

A definite smile, albeit a small one, spread across Sir Edward's face. Although he was handsome, the stern look he often wore gave him a proud, intimidating look. Instead, when he smiled, his face softened and there was a glint in his blue eyes. If one didn't know him well, one might almost define the look as playful. Emma often spoke warmly about her brother and Janet was frequently skeptical, but seeing this look, so much friendlier, so much more open than the gruff exterior to which she had become accustomed, she could see glimpses of that warmth.

Following dinner, Emma said, "You know we are only being invited into the library tonight because Edward is out of sorts. With no gentlemen around to share brandy, cigars and political conversation, we must do."

Her brother grinned good-naturedly as he ushered them in.

Janet caught her breath. Of course, she remembered this impressive room from her former visit here, but it was so utterly different. No longer a museum environment, but a room lived in, a room loved. A blaze in the fireplace cast a warm glow over the room. Dozens of candles flickered. Goodness, so many candles in a library! It was unthinkable nowadays. If this was common practice back then, it was truly a miracle so many first editions managed to survive to modern times.

Janet recognized the ornate desk, the inviting, plush chairs scattered around the library, beckoning readers to sit and enjoy the treasures on hand. And what a treasure trove it was! Mahogany bookshelves lined the walls, overflowing with hundreds—no, thousands—of books.

The walls were hung with untold millions of pounds worth of art. If only she could master a time-travel art heist, her future would be secure. *Imagine a private collection such as this in one's personal library today!* Here were the paintings Janet remembered from her earlier visit—the Ponte Rialto by Canaletto, the Rembrandt lithographs, the Lotto Annunciation. Yet there were more she hadn't yet seen. And, of course, the place of honor over the fireplace—oh, in her mind, so worryingly close to the lapping flames—was the spectacular Tiepolo.

She hadn't realized how long she'd been staring at the familiar painting, but she sensed Sir Edward beside her, observing her. His voice was gentle when he spoke.

"I see you have gravitated toward my personal favorite."

She turned to him, her cheeks feeling flushed. "It's so beautiful. So soothing. I can see why you treasure it. The colors, the composition, the slight ambiguity of her expression. She seems almost on the verge of turning around, perhaps she is experiencing a nagging doubt about her decision to transform herself in order to escape Apollo. But we shall never know."

She felt his eyes upon her, but her gaze remained firmly on the Tiepolo.

"No, I imagine we shall not."

She thought she detected a tenderness in his voice, but it was probably only the effect of the dim lights, the exhaustion, and the strong claret she'd had at dinner. "And you can see the influence of Bernini's statue on Tiepolo's work. I understand he was familiar with the lithographs of Bernini's masterpiece."

"You have seen it then?" His voice sounded eager. "Seen it yourself? I mean, Bernini's sculpture."

Janet turned to face him. "Oh, yes. I adore that sculpture."

"And the Villa Borghese must have been where you saw the Domenichino. I was there when I was in Rome, following my time in Venice."

"Did you purchase this painting in Venice?"

"I did." A softness appeared on his face as he spoke. "I believe I told you about my sojourn in Venice when I completed Oxford. I also purchased this Lotto." He indicated the Annunciation Janet had seen with Mr. Whitshaw. "You are familiar with Lorenzo Lotto?"

"Oh, yes! I have been to Bergamo, and I saw a wonderful exhibi—many of his works there. This is lovely."

"Edward," said Emma, "the tea has arrived. Yes, please place that over here. Perhaps we can sit and enjoy it, while we continue admiring your art."

"Emma is always teasing me about my new acquisitions." He gestured to the chair.

Janet sank into plush velvet. She'd covetously admired these chairs on her previous visit to Helmsley Manor. Back then, she'd imagined Sir Edward and Emma seated together in the library before a roaring fire. Little had she imagined she'd complete their gathering.

Emma passed her a teacup and Janet sat in silence, looking up once again at the familiar Tiepolo. This must be the key between her two lives. But how could it lead her back?

"As you see ..." Sir Edward began.

Janet startled at his words, tugged back to her present life.

"We have a large collection of books. Feel free to borrow them. In a gesture to my sister, we even have a small collection of Gothic novels, including Radcliffe and Walpole. Oh, and

Miss Roberts, you will be pleased to note that we also have a first edition of *The Vindication of the Rights of Women*."

She turned to face him, catching a definite smile on his lips. If he was teasing her, he could not be plotting to cast her out. Perhaps he had grown to tolerate her eccentricities. Perhaps— dare she hope it?—they might even turn a corner and become friends during her visit.

"Thank you, Sir Edward. I shall bear that in mind. And thank you for the generous offer to borrow your books. I cannot wait to explore your collection."

Sir Edward turned to Emma. "I understand that you, Miss Roberts, and Charles have been reading Byron's new poem. Would you care to read aloud to us before we retire for the evening?"

"I would love to, Edward. Where is it?"

"There, on the edge of my desk."

"Ah, yes." Emma found the page. "We left off here last time, with Childe Harold's arrival in Ottoman territories."

Sir Edward nodded and Emma's clear, resonant voice spoke of Childe Harold's adventures among the brave, 'savage men.'

> *"Land of Albania! let me bend mine eyes*
> *On thee, thou rugged nurse of savage men!*
> *The cross descends, thy minarets arise,*
> *And the pale crescent sparkles in the glen,*
> *Through many a cypress grove within each city's ken."*

Janet was swept off to the wild, rugged mountains of early-nineteenth-century Albania. She had been exhausted by her forty-mile journey that day; how had Lord Byron ever survived treacherous paths through Balkan mountains? His poetry, which had always seemed so archaic in her modern world and had never moved her, now spoke to her once again. She felt herself transported alongside him on his Balkan journey.

Emma's melodic voice enunciated Byron's words so beautifully as Janet looked up at the Ticpolo. The familiar Tiepolo. She felt eyes upon her and turned to see Sir Edward examining her. He did not allow his gaze to drop as she met his eyes. Instead, with a slight blush, Janet was the first to cast her gaze down.

That piercing blue stare made her nervous. It had to be what she feared most. He was starting to suspect she was an imposter. How could he not?

Each day, she felt more tightly bound in her new life, but surely it couldn't last. Someone would discover that she didn't truly belong. Sir Edward was not one to be easily fooled. He most certainly suspected something at the very moment he appeared to be warming to her. Or at least tolerating her.

Despite her hesitation, she had even begun to think of him with, if not yet admiration, at least no longer with dread. Behind the harsh lines of his square jaw seemed to lurk a glimmer of playfulness. She had seen it manifest itself several times. He was confident and forceful, and that could cause him to appear intimidating, but she observed that he was also intelligent and measured and fair with his staff. They respected him, and aimed to please him. But weren't all servants trained to behave this way with their masters?

Sir Edward was extremely handsome and well-spoken. If she'd met someone similar on her campus or as a client at her father's firm, she would have been friendly, even flirtatious, interested in getting to know him better. Yet this nineteenth-century version of a cultivated man daunted her, and left her desiring an escape from his intense gaze.

She looked up at the Tiepolo again, feeling the nervous thudding of her heart begin to subside as her eyes rested upon the familiar, billowing pink gowns of Daphne. The firm step of

Apollo in fruitless pursuit. The room had grown silent.

"I am too exhausted to read," said Emma. "The words are spinning on the page. Edward, might we continue tomorrow?"

Sir Edward gazed at Emma. Confusion etched his confident face. He recovered quickly. "Of course, everyone needs rest after the exhausting journey. We shall continue tomorrow. Emma, Miss Roberts, I bid you good night."

He stood as Emma and Janet rose to make their way to the door. Janet followed behind Emma and allowed herself to be led to her room, where Turner undressed her and helped her into her nightgown.

Janet tumbled unceremoniously into her big bed, where she quickly fell into a troubled sleep. Even in her dreams, however, that piercing blue stare followed her. Yet she felt oddly protected and content as she ceased struggling against it, allowing the dark blue waves to carry her where she was meant to be.

Chapter 23

Janet woke with a start, her eyes flicking around the dark.

The dream had seemed so real. She'd been at a ball, dancing with a handsome man. They were twirling around the dance floor. The velvet of her dress brushed against her leg at each turn. She listened to the strain of the violins as they played the triumphant last notes. It felt effortless. Then her dance partner leaned down to kiss her.

She looked up into his shadowy face, lost in his deep blue eyes the moment before his lips met hers. But something was wrong. She pulled back, and the bright, flickering candlelight from the chandelier illuminated his face as it slowly came into focus. Sir Edward.

She jolted up in her bed. Breathed slowly. Forced calming thoughts into her mind. A dream. Only a dream.

The silence of the predawn house was absolute. Romantic dreams about Sir Edward? She turned over and tried to get back to sleep. Tossing, turning, and endlessly repositioning herself in bed did nothing to help.

Get a grip, Janet. It was only a silly dream, probably the effect of all these romantic poets. A little less Byron, a little more Locke,

Hobbes and Wollstonecraft. Gibbons will singlehandedly put an end to any romantic silliness.

She slid her legs over the side of the bed, pushed bare feet into her slippers and walked over to the window, pulling back the curtains. It was still dark, with only a glimmer of light along the horizon signaling the start to the new day. The fading night sky was clear. An ideal day for riding - something she had learned young, alongside her mother who loved to ride.

Nothing cleared her head better than a gallop through the countryside. She wished she could go off on her own, before everyone was up. Instead, she sat at her table and dipped her quill into the inkwell. Scratching the quill against parchment, she recorded her observations from last night as the sun emerged and cast its golden light upon the waters of the pond.

Penning her thoughts cleared her head, and she felt better when Turner entered the room.

"Miss Jane! You are up so early. Why did you not ring for me?"

"There was no need. I was enjoying the silence before the start of the day. I feel refreshed now."

"I have brought you one of Miss Emma's riding habits for your morning excursion." She stroked the fabric. "This should fit you beautifully."

Janet felt a wave of nausea. "*This* is how I am supposed to ride? A dress and jacket? Won't the dress get caught up in the horse's legs?"

"Miss Jane, the extra folds get tucked under your legs when you are riding sidesaddle. Surely you must do the same in the New World? There is even a petticoat that will cover what the habit cannot." Her cheeks flushed. She looked down. "Your ankles, my dear. It would be most inappropriate to have them on view for all to see."

How had Janet failed to consider the riding habit and sidesaddle when agreeing to ride with Emma? How many BBC films had she seen? And what exactly had she expected to wear to ride two hundred years ago? Surely not a jockey's silks. How on earth could she ride in this get-up and not kill herself? No, she couldn't risk it. She'd allow Turner to dress her, and then bow out at the moment of saddling. It was hardly worth risking a broken neck—quite literally—in exchange for a bit of exercise.

Turner was pulling tight the stays of the torturous corset Janet had hoped would be unnecessary for riding. She should have known better. The habit was swept over her head. A little jacket was added afterwards. Its tight arms limited mobility. Aside from its more somber colors, the habit appeared to Janet almost the same as the dresses she wore on a daily basis. How in God's name could women ride in this get-up? How she longed for her no-nonsense, twenty-first-century riding britches and boots.

Janet sat sulkily at the breakfast table, long before the rest of the family was ready. She drank her coffee slowly, devising ways to extricate herself from her morning ride without causing offense. A headache? Upset stomach? An attack of Mrs. Bennet-like nerves?

"You are up already! You must be eager for our ride," said Emma as she breezed into the breakfast room. Elegant in her riding habit and certainly capable of sitting expertly in it in her sidesaddle, Emma took her seat across from Janet.

Janet wondered how to explain the sudden change of mind to her friend. She poured coffee into Emma's empty cup. As soon as they had finished breakfast, they walked the short distance to the stable.

A small boy with curly dark hair, perhaps the son of the stable hand, was standing at the door as they approached.

"Good morning, William," Emma addressed him. "I have missed seeing you. Have you been taking good care of Bucephalus?"

"Ever such good care. I've galloped him every day," said the boy in a lilting voice. There was something about the voice Janet could not quite place.

"William, I would like you to meet my friend, Miss Jane."

The little boy bowed.

"Miss Jane will be staying with us for some time and we will need to find a horse for her to ride. Which do you think would be best for an experienced rider? We rely on your judgement."

William smiled and excused himself.

"That is William, your stable hand? How old is he?"

"Ten. He is small for his age. His father does carpentry work at Helmsley. He also used to serve as our stable hand, but William is talented, and has taken over most of his father's duties. Now his father is free to also cultivate his fields. It is a tremendous help to the family, since William has seven younger brothers and sisters."

"Bucephalus? You named your horse after the one tamed by Alexander the Great?"

Emma smiled and blushed. "You can probably surmise that the horse—and its name—were a gift from my brother. Teasing me for reading my Gothic novels and neglecting the classics."

William returned with two horses. "Whoa, Bucephalus, good boy. Here is Miss Emma." Emma held the rein and stroked her horse's neck. "And for Miss Jane, this is Ebony." He tied the rein to a post. The horse was beautiful, but skittish. As he became more agitated, William stood beside him, stroking him gently. "*Tranquillo. Sta tutto bene*," he whispered in his ear.

That was the slight lilt she heard in William's English.

"*Sei italiano, William. Ti chiami Guglielmo?*" asked Janet.

He looked at Janet in surprise. "*Sì, siamo venuti dalla Toscana quando ero piccolo, però mi sono cresciuto qui.*" He glanced at Emma, perhaps a bit nervously, before continuing in English. "No one calls me Guglielmo except for my *mamma* and *babbo*."

"I love Tuscany. I visited when I lived in Rome. It's a wonderful place to go riding."

He observed her with surprise. "So I understand. I was so little when we left that I do not remember it, but my parents often talk about its beauty. I hope to return one day." William looked at Emma and gasped. "Not to say I am not very pleased to be here."

Emma smiled. "Oh, William. Anyone would prefer to be in sunny, exotic Tuscany! You do not have to be ashamed to say that before me."

William saddled Bucephalus, positioning a stepladder and helping Emma to mount. She composed herself daintily as Janet looked on more nervously than before.

"Okay, *Signorina Gianna*," said William.

Janet smiled at her new Italian name.

"It is your turn." He picked up the saddle to prepare Ebony.

"Wait!" She fought the rising panic when she spoke. "I am sorry. Emma, William. I can't ride like this. I do not know how. If I try, I shall certainly break my neck."

Emma furrowed her brow. "But Jane, you assured me you know how to ride. Whatever do you mean?"

Janet nodded. "I *do* know how to ride, but, well ..." She saw the confusion in Emma's expression. "Remember when your brother asked if I learned to ride like the Indians? Let us just say that I did. I ride astride the horse. I have never ridden in a riding habit before, nor have I ever ridden sidesaddle. And I am certain I shall be thrown by the horse if I attempt it. We are alone at this hour. Could I not simply ride as I do back home, with a man's saddle?"

Emma's eyes grew large, and William looked as if he were stifling a laugh.

"But Jane, how could we? It is improper. What if someone were to see us? Whatever would Edward say if he found out? You may have different rules in America, but here it is simply not done."

"And if we swore William to secrecy? *Guglielmo, sai tenere un segreto, vero?*"

William smiled, but Emma did not look at all amused.

"I am sorry, Emma. I do not want to stir up trouble. I will simply wait for you here. Do not rush on my account. I will admire all your beautiful horses."

"No." Her voice was firm. "It is your first day, and you must come with me. But no one must know. William, you must promise to keep this secret."

He nodded his agreement.

"And Jane, if anyone approaches, you must dismount and walk the horse."

"Of course, Emma."

"Alright, then. William, please saddle up Miss Jane's horse," she sighed and rolled her eyes,"... as she requests."

Janet mounted her horse as delicately as she could, careful to show the minimum amount of her petticoat as she kicked her leg over and balled the abundant folds of fabric beneath her. William adjusted the stirrups, biting his lips the entire time to suppress laughter. When he finalized the adjustment, he gave Ebony a firm pat and said, "*Allora, Signorina Gianna. Tutto a posto. Sarà il nostro segreto.*"

Janet gave him a smile, appreciating the mischievous glint in his dark eyes. With a quick kick to Ebony, she tore off happily through the field, the wind disheveling her hair and rushing against her face, her heart pounding until she was sure her corset would burst. Ebony was a good horse, strong and quick.

Then she remembered Emma, "Whoa, boy!" She reined in Ebony, and waited for Emma's arrival.

Emma trotted up beside her friend. "What you told my brother is true. You did learn to ride with the Indians. I have never before seen a woman ride in this manner. The New World must be a shocking place, but your secret is safe with me."

The two friends trotted while Emma pointed out the grounds to Jane. It was beautiful, far more beautiful than Janet imagined. In the modern version, much of the land had been sold off and developed. Modern, soulless developments buttressing the bucolic idyll. In the nineteenth-century version, rolling green hills stretched as far as the eye could see. To think that one family owned all of this!

Emma was a good rider. Janet was impressed by how fast she could ride sidesaddle, while still looking so perfectly composed and elegant—something Janet knew she could never replicate. They galloped through fields and up a hilltop to enjoy a clear view of the lands and the home far below.

"It's beautiful here." Janet surveyed the view below. "I can see why you love it so much."

"Yes, I do. But my time here is limited. My brother will have to marry, and a newlywed wife is generally not pleased to have a sister-in-law in her new home. I will have to make my new life in another man's home." She smiled, but no joy reached her eyes. "Probably causing discomfort to another sister."

"But Mr. Bentley has no sister."

"Jane, please. Mr. Bentley has never declared himself, and it seems unlikely it will ever come to pass. Mr. Bentley and my brother are so close, yet Edward has never encouraged me to consider him. I do not wish to be bartered off to the highest bidder. Yet what are members of our sex to do when we have no ability to support ourselves? You do not realize how lucky you are to have a father who trains you in a profession and wishes you to work alongside him, even if he prefers a husband of his choosing. "

Janet took a deep breath. "I do realize I am luckier than most, but I would prefer to make my own decisions about my future husband."

"What is he like—your *promesso sposo*?"

"Malcolm?" She looked away from Emma, watching the trees swaying in the gentle breeze. She'd barely thought of him in these weeks. "He is different from your acquaintances. He was born into a poor family and became a well-regarded architect. He is intelligent and has achieved everything on his own." She turned to her friend. "He also loves literature, and is an admirer of Jane Austen."

"Why are you not interested in him?"

"I do not know. He is perfectly nice, truly a gentleman, but there is no real spark. Maybe there never will be." She sighed. "I probably expect too much."

"Everyone teases me for my Gothic novels, but who is the romantic now? You are accustomed to far more freedom than females in England. Only the lucky few can marry for love. We have our family obligations. We must do what is expected of us." Emma looked out over the idyllic landscape. "I have said too much. It grows late. Shall we race back to the stables?"

Emma gave Bucephalus a gentle kick and galloped full-speed down the hill, dress billowing behind her, leaving Janet astonished by her friend's skill in the impossible sidesaddle. Janet galloped in pursuit, all the riding habit's fabric balled up unattractively between her legs. Unattractive, perhaps, but still better that than a broken neck. The fresh air hit her face. The sun warmed her shoulders. The exercise was exhilarating.

That morning was one of many early morning rides. All week long, the weather was fair. They only ran into some of the tenants a few times on those early jaunts—generally steering clear of the fields and favoring the hills and woodlands. When they spotted a farmer, Janet would slowly slide down from the saddle and walk her horse along.

In the late afternoons, Sir Edward joined them for walks around the grounds or into the tiny town. He discussed a wide range of topics—literature, music, travel, politics, agriculture, botany—Janet was impressed by his breadth of knowledge. With fewer distractions, how much more people actually spoke with one another constantly surprised her. The art of conversation had clearly been lost across the centuries.

They always returned to rest before dressing for dinner, and this was when she recorded observations in her diary. If she returned to her modern life, would she continue to set aside this quiet time for daily reflection?

She filled pages with her observations—conversations overheard between Sir Edward and his tenants or local farmers about weather patterns, crops, or market conditions. There were talks with neighbors about the successes and defeats of the Eighth Coalition, or news from big and faraway London. Then there were conversations Janet had with the servants about their daily tasks, or new recipes, or gossip from town.

Each day added to her treasure trove of knowledge, a more complete understanding of the intricacies of nineteenth-century life.

One perfect morning following their daily ride, Emma asked Janet to join her for a walk. "There's a lovely place I wish to show you."

They walked in silence, listening to the birds chirping and the sounds of twigs snapping under their footsteps. Emma knew her way through the trees, and soon they emerged in a clearing in the woods, filled with colorful wildflowers. Janet caught her breath. In the distance was a large, sparkling pond.

"Oh, Emma. It's beautiful!" The sunlight reflected off the pond's surface. "Shall we sit and enjoy it?"

They stretched out along the water's edge, enjoying the warm sunshine and the soothing gurgling of the small brook that fed the pond.

"I have received a letter this morning," said Emma. "It is from Mr. Bentley. He tells me he hopes to join us in a few weeks' time."

"How nice it will be to have Mr. Bentley here with us, even if it may put an end to our morning riding."

"He will certainly be expected to pass the breakfast hour with his aunt. We should be safe." Emma smiled.

"Shall you be happy to see him?"

"Yes. I always enjoy his visits. However, I must convince my brother to hold a ball. It's time we dusted out the old ballroom."

"If that is the case, we shall come here often under the cover of the forest so that you can teach me more dances. I do not wish to make a fool of myself."

"Your quadrille in Bath was lovely."

"I am not certain poor Mr. Bentley agrees with you. How I tortured the poor man's feet! He bore it heroically, and I was disposed to like him forever for his chivalry."

"I forgot to tell you, my brother mentioned it to me in passing. Tonight one of our neighbors, Sir John, will visit us for dinner. He has been away in London. Having recently returned, he wishes to pay a call."

"I imagine he is intimately acquainted with your family."

"Yes, his family has resided here for generations. He is polite, although his company is not as enjoyable as, say, Mr. Bentley's."

"I imagine few could match Mr. Bentley's charms."

Emma's cheeks colored. "That is not what I meant. Sir John is very agreeable, but do not expect him to be witty or clever. Hunting is the favored conversation when he comes to dine."

"Then I shall be prepared." Janet gazed out on the water. "Emma, it is hot today, and I see we are remarkably secluded here in this secret clearing. What would you say about a little dip in the water?"

"Bathing, Jane?" Emma's eyes grew wide in disbelief. "Have you gone mad?"

"You do not swim here?"

"We most certainly *do not*." Emma's agitation was evident in her trembling voice. "Some go for therapeutic reasons along the seacoast, I have been told, but it is not common. Besides, we have no swimming gowns."

"Swimming gowns? Do they have as much fabric as these ridiculous riding habits?"

"I do not like the sound of this New World of yours at all. Are you attempting to tell me that ladies swim in form-fitting garments—alongside gentlemen—in your Boston?"

Janet took a deep breath as an image from the previous summer with friends on a Nantucket beach holiday flickered through her mind. Perhaps Emma was not ready to hear about the advent of the bikini, the thong, and the fashion for suntanned limbs.

"Perhaps rules are more relaxed. I simply thought with no one here, it would do no harm to cool off."

Emma's look softened. "So you truly know how to float on the water and move across without touching?"

"Of course I do. I've been doing it since I was a child. I even competed." *Yikes—why did you have to go and say that?*

"Competed! Against men?"

"No," said Janet, happy not to have to tell yet another lie. "The competitions were divided by gender. Females compete against other females."

"This is all very shocking." Emma wrung her hands. "I am certain I shall regret saying this, but if you still wish to go …

bathing ... then you may. I will serve as your lookout to ensure no one is coming. If someone does approach, you must hide in those bushes there at the edge of the pond until he passes. But Jane, I hope you do truly know how to float. If you start to go under, and I must seek help, how will I ever explain to someone what you were doing?"

"I'll be fine. I promise." Janet shed off her riding habit and asked Emma, who was nervously looking around her, to loosen the stays on her corset. She wore a type of cotton chemise and a pair of ankle-length bloomers, meant to cover her ankles if her riding habit should billow up. Janet had never before been so covered up when swimming. Nevertheless, that did not stop Emma from emitting a low, shocked whistle. Poor Emma, what would happen if she could time travel to spring break in Florida or to see modern-day British tourists in Ibiza?

Janet walked to the edge of the pond and dove into the water. Emerging some distance later, she waved to Emma, noting relief wash over her friend's worried face. Emma nervously swiveled her head from left to right, watching for anyone who might be passing by the secluded spot.

Janet should probably not have put her friend in this uncomfortable position, yet what harm could be done by an innocent swim? The cool water caressed her body.

Wouldn't the beach resorts catch on soon anyway? When Emma grew older, she'd remember her friend on the cutting edge of fashion back in 1813.

Janet picked up her pace, swimming back and forth across the small pond—crawl, breaststroke, butterfly—the flash of arms, her quick breaths, the thrilling sensation of propelling herself forward in the refreshing water. She could have stayed there for hours, but she did not wish to needlessly prolong her friend's anxiety. Janet floated for a moment on top of the water, examining the fluffy clouds in the blue sky above. She stretched her arms far over her head, floating effortlessly as she listened to the distorted sounds under the water.

She returned to shore, looking carefully to each side before climbing out of the water and making her way to Emma. The two sat silently in the sun, the warmth drying Janet's garments.

After some minutes of silence, Emma spoke. "I was certain my heart would burst in fear that someone would discover us. But I must admit you were splendid. I have never seen anyone swim like that. You looked so ... happy and free."

"That's how I feel in the water. Join me next time. I'll teach you."

Emma shook her head. "Just dry off in the sun. I will help you with your corset and riding habit as soon as you are dry. We should be getting back."

After lunch, Janet joined Emma on her rounds of the cottages. They paid calls on the tenants, delivering baskets with milk and cheese, cured meats, and preserves. The women accepted the baskets gratefully, eager to supplement their meager pantry.

While chatting with the women, Janet took in the damp cottages, with their poor insulation and crammed living quarters. *When would the cholera outbreaks hit England? Wasn't it later in the century? Certainly something could be done to improve their living conditions.*

The women were simple, but proud. They were clearly fond of Emma. The young children would shyly approach Janet and Emma, smiling and wanting to stroke their hands or the sleeves of their gowns. Hadn't Mr. Whitshaw spoken about the interdependencies between the noble families and their tenants, how intertwined their lives were?

Later in the day, as Emma discussed household matters with the housekeeper, Janet took advantage of the gentle breeze for a walk around the grounds. The golden afternoon light glowed warmly off the facade of Helmsley Manor. She remembered her first glimpse of the house during her seminar daytrip. How could she ever have imagined she would one day be calling this home, even if only temporarily?

She turned her back to the manor house and set out on her walk, swinging her volume of Shakespeare's *Julius Caesar*. The Huntington library was a goldmine of books, and she found herself filling her days with literature she had never taken the time to read and others she hadn't read since high school assignments.

A slower pace to the days and fewer commitments were the norm. She didn't own a watch in her nineteenth-century life. She'd learned to observe the level of the sun and she woke earlier, feeling far more rested than she did back home. Walking and riding provided her necessary exercise each day. There was no need for forced jogs or visits to the gym. Her time in the past might even succeed in rendering her a fish out of water when she returned to modern Bath.

She walked by the fields now, where farmers were still hard at work, long after their early mornings out tending their fields. They stood and tipped their caps as she passed. She longed to stop and chat with them about their crops and yields, but she knew enough not to bother them at their work. They would feel obliged to stop and speak with her, based solely on her station, and this would mean a later return home to the families who awaited them for their early dinner and bedtime, before the start of another grueling day.

How difficult life was for these tenant farmers. Janet and her modern-day friends never even thought about the work that went into growing the food they bought in the supermarkets. But passing these fields on this summer day, with the men, women, and children breaking their backs to tend the crops under the blazing sun made her pause. No mechanization, no automated irrigation systems or tractors. These things had changed in modern England and America, of course, but these same traditions were still alive and well in most of the developing world.

She thought of little William, Guglielmo. He'd taken over most of the work in the stables. What kind of future would he have at Helmsley Manor? Would he be able to provide for his large family if his father grew infirm? The other day she'd read to him from an Italian book she'd found in the library, and he told her how much he'd love to read. How happy it would make his mother to have him read words to her in her native language.

She felt foolish not having realized it earlier. Guglielmo was illiterate. How could he have ever learned to read? She promised to teach him, said she'd stop by in the afternoons as he finished his work. He'd been shocked, yet there was a noticeable glint in his sharp eyes. She'd broach the subject slowly, if that's what it took, but she *would* teach Guglielmo to read.

Janet reached a meadow she passed each day on horseback with Emma. She slumped down ungraciously into a heap on the ground. Her posture had never been better than during these past weeks, wearing her undergarment armor. Now, far from the eyes of society, Janet sprawled on the grass. She opened her book to its well-worn pages, transported to Ancient Rome, back in the Roman Forum she'd passed each day during her year in the Eternal City.

Engrossed in the story, she gasped when a shadow fell over the page. Looking up, she saw a face shrouded in darkness. As her eyes adjusted to the bright light, a pair of bright blue eyes came into focus.

"I have given you a shock while reading. I hope it's not a Gothic novel."

Janet hastily straightened her garments and struggled to sit up. Flustered, she prayed there were no stray blades of grass entwined in her hair. "I apologize, Sir Edward. I am afraid you find me when I did not think to meet anyone."

"So I surmise," said Sir Edward, with a barely disguised smile.

"That certainly does not mean the interruption is unpleasant. Would you care to join me if you have a moment?" Janet gestured to a spot on the grass beside her, then gasped. Was she being too forward? Perhaps he'd now feel obliged to join her when he most certainly had other matters to which he should attend. But he sat down at the spot she indicated and examined the book's spine.

"Ah, *Julius Caesar*. A fine work."

"I agree. Although, shamefully, it has been years since I have read it. I had quite forgotten this work. In school, we performed this on stage, but I only remember the beginning of Antony's speech. '*Friends, Romans, countrymen, lend me your ears. I come to bury Caesar, not to praise him*'..." She trailed off, trying in vain to remember the next lines.

"'*The evil that men do lives after them, the good is oft interred in their bones; So let it be with Caesar. The noble Brutus hath told you that Caesar was ambitious: If it were so, it was a grievous fault, And greviously hath Caesar answer'd it*'..." Sir Edward's voice was deep and sonorous; it seemed to ring off the hills. His diction was perfect.

"You know it all, don't you? I am impressed."

"Don't be. When I was younger, my tutor derived enormous pleasure from forcing me to memorize long passages of Shakespeare. Apparently, the memorization exercises had the desired effect. The passages are now permanently imprinted on my brain. When I finally saw the Roman Forum with my own eyes, all I could do was replay the words of Brutus and Antony in my mind."

Janet laughed. "We were in desperate need of you at our school play. You should have joined us."

Sir Edward smiled. "I am certain I will live to regret my missed opportunity of a career on the American stage."

They sat in comfortable silence.

"Miss Roberts, I hope you are enjoying your time at Helmsley Manor. My sister is pleased to have you with us."

"Thank you. Emma has become such a dear friend. I treasure our time together."

"You are turning my sister into quite the artist. Her sketches are much improved."

Sir Edward leaned back on his left hand, raising his right leg up and resting his right arm on the knee, hat in hand. The relaxed pose of a country gentleman on his estate. If Sir Joshua Reynolds were still alive, he'd be hard at work capturing the ideal portrait. How Janet wished she could strike a relaxed pose like his in her tight corset, but she was sure that lay beyond the bounds of propriety. Or even physical possibility.

"You flatter me, Sir Edward. I had little to do. Emma is very talented. We have simply carved out time each day to concentrate on our drawing."

"Are you happy here? Do you not miss your home?"

She looked directly at him. His face was kind and open. The late-afternoon sun shone down on his strong features, lighting up his thick hair. He looked so handsome sitting before her, genuine concern carved into his fine features. How could she ever respond to his question? *Did* she miss her home?

"You are a man of the world, Sir Edward." Her voice sounded soft, even to her own ears. "You know better than I that when one travels, one always misses home. But that does not necessarily mean I do not feel equally at home here, even while I pine away for some of the familiar aspects of my world."

A slow smile spread over his face. "Well said. Spoken like a true diplomat. I do not know many people as adaptable as you. I hope that my sister can learn from you. She is so rooted to Helmsley Manor, but, she is a young lady after all." He looked beyond her at some point in the distance, carefully weighing his words. "She may one day move far away. I fear that may be difficult for her."

Janet wished she could truly speak with Sir Edward, explain to him Emma's admiration for Mr. Bentley. Try to understand if he saw a future for that deserving young couple. Instead, she sat still, fingering the pages of Shakespeare. She was still an outsider looking in, albeit one who was beginning to understand the language and the customs of society. One who was finally beginning to glean the rules.

She and Sir Edward would appear to outsiders as two old friends, content to be in one another's company on a late summer day.

"I can easily understand Emma's love for Helmsley. The manor and grounds are so beautiful. We have been enjoying our morning rides tremendously."

"So I have been told repeatedly by my sister. Last year her health was poor. She had severe pneumonia, and we worried she might not recover." He looked over at Janet, registering the fear in her eyes. His face softened. "Please do not be alarmed. I was desperate last year, but there is no cause for concern now. She has regained her health after a difficult year. I think it is one of the reasons she was initially so eager to assist with your recovery. Her daily walks and rides with you have done wonders for her health. I wanted to thank you. I see my sister becoming stronger each day."

"No thanks are required. It is a pleasure to spend time with Emma. I feel almost as if I have gained a sister through my misfortune on The Crescent Lawn."

What Janet said was true. Emma had become so dear to her in such a short period of time.

Sir Edward considered her carefully for a moment before speaking. "Miss Roberts, I wonder if I might ask a favor of you. My estate manager, Saunders, and I intend to carry out maintenance work on the tenants' cottages. As a student of architecture, you may be able to provide us with valuable insight. Would you care to join us?"

Janet caught her breath. "Oh, yes."

"Then that is settled." He stood. "I leave you to enjoy Antony stirring up trouble among the plebeians. I must attend to some affairs. We shall see you at the dinner hour."

"Until dinner."

His elegant, confident strides carried him back to the house. Perhaps he was warming to her. At least he appreciated her friendship with his sister. As his defensiveness melted, she found herself wondering if they were becoming friends.

She smiled inwardly at the idea of striking up a genuine friendship with the handsome but haughty man in the portrait her Bath friends had enjoyed commenting on. She remembered the offhand comments of her classmates about how there were no longer any men like that in the modern world. They'd never believe it.

Stranger things had happened. She was living proof of that.

Janet returned to Shakespeare's Roman Forum, Sir Edward's resonant voice sounding in her mind as she reread Antony's speech.

Janet descended the grand staircase, elegant in yet another of Emma's purported hand-me-downs—a lovely, green silk gown. Turner had taken extra care in dressing her hair, and Janet felt transformed before the mirror.

She remembered how she and her classmates had traipsed along the same staircase a few months ago, in shorts, T-shirts and sneakers.

Voices drifted from the drawing room. She entered to find Emma and Sir Edward deep in conversation with a short, portly man. All three turned when they heard her footsteps at the threshold.

It was Sir Edward who spoke first. "Miss Roberts. I would like to introduce you to our neighbor and good friend, Sir John. Sir John's estate adjoins Helmsley Manor, and he is a frequent visitor. Sir John, may I present Miss Roberts, a dear friend of my sister."

Janet curtsied and Sir John bowed. "It is an honor to meet you, Miss Roberts. Emma has been enthusiastic in recounting your visit." With a handkerchief, he mopped his perspiring brow.

"I have been truly fortunate to enjoy the Huntingtons' hospitality," said Janet. "I believe Emma and I have ridden close to your property, Sir John. You have lovely woodland."

"You and Emma must pay a visit the next time you are riding nearby. Tell me, Miss Roberts, do you enjoy hunting?" He placed his hands on his ample belly.

"Woefully, I know little about it, Sir John."

"A shame, a shame." Sir John faced Sir Edward. "Absurd that young women cannot join in on hunts, I always say. Healthy exercise, strong traditions. You should have your sister and Miss Roberts join us tomorrow."

Janet noticed a slight, pained look pass across Emma's face.

"Now, John. You know as well as I that my sister and Miss Roberts are probably most pleased to be rid of us. I doubt the ladies wish to join men on our hunting outings."

"You may be right there, Edward." Sir John swiped a hand along his receding hairline. "I was recently in London with our mutual friend, Sir Robert, at his estate in Greenwich. Excellent pheasant that day."

Sir John droned on about his numerous hunting expeditions near London. Hunting banter continued as they moved into the dining room, recounting the plans for his outing with Sir Edward the following day. Janet was happy for Emma's warning about the evening's conversation. Emma attempted to put on a brave face and follow conversation. Sir Edward tried several times, without success, to steer the conversation away from the massive slaughter of game. Janet imagined no poetry reading was envisioned for that evening.

"Do you agree, Miss Roberts?"

"Pardon, Sir John?" Janet's mind had wandered some time ago.

"Do you agree that there is no better start to the autumn than killing the first stag of the season? It is a rite of passage, is it not?"

"Oh, certainly, Sir John," She met Emma's eyes. A look of complicity passed between them.

"Edward, when is the lovely Miss Chadwick arriving to grace Helmsley Manor with her presence?"

Janet wondered if this was someone she should know. She glanced at Emma, catching the surprised, unguarded look she cast at her brother.

Sir Edward was slow to respond. A new course arrived and he waited until everyone was served and the servants left. "I have received a letter from Miss Chadwick. She hopes to pay us a visit in two weeks' time." He turned to Emma. "I had not yet had the opportunity to speak to you. Emma, dear, would it please you to entertain Victoria during her visit?"

Janet noticed the tight smile Emma sometimes used when a topic displeased her. Did her brother not notice?

"Nothing would please me more, brother. It is always such an immense pleasure to welcome Miss Chadwick to our home."

Conversation turned to hunting once again, and Janet bided her time until the men would depart for brandy in the library.

Arms linked, Janet and Emma made their way to the music room. Janet sat at the pianoforte and shuffled through the sheet music, selecting Beethoven. She'd become accustomed to listening to Emma's accomplished playing in the evenings.

"Emma," she said, eyes still downcast, seemingly studying the music. "At dinner you did not seem enthusiastic about the news of Miss Chadwick's visit. May I venture to ask why it does not please you?"

In silence, Emma moved to the piano bench and took her seat, fingering the keys without pressing down to usher a sound. Janet remained still. She suspected Emma wished to say something unpleasant, and was most likely struggling with how to voice her thoughts.

When she did speak, her tone was measured. "Perhaps I was unfair. I trust that only you noted the hesitation in my countenance. Miss Chadwick and I ... perhaps have not started our acquaintance on the best footing. I know she is immensely fond of my brother."

Much to her dismay, Janet felt her heartbeat accelerate.

"I should try to make her feel more welcome. She is—how shall I say it?—less comfortable with our country manners, forever comparing life at Helmsley unfavorably with the more sophisticated pleasures of London. Perhaps she has simply not been made to feel at home. I will make a greater effort."

Emma had not looked once in Janet's direction. She continued silently fingering the piano keys.

"And is she very beautiful and elegant?" Janet held her breath.

Emma smiled. "Ah, yes, but you shall see for yourself. Miss Chadwick never travels without enough trunks to clothe the entire British regiment, were the soldiers to wear feathers and silks. I am afraid our relaxed days are coming to a close." She looked up at Janet, a serious look in her eyes. "And I need not tell you that our ... unconventional riding ... must come to an end during Miss Chadwick's visit."

"But of course, Emma. Shall I turn the pages for you?"

Emma's music filled the room, but Janet's thoughts were taken over by concerns regarding Miss Chadwick's imminent appearance. She tried to tell herself it was simple nervousness toward a new arrival, but she couldn't deny the pangs of jealousy she'd felt when Sir Edward mentioned her name, or when Emma talked about Miss Chadwick's beauty and her fondness for her brother. Certainly, Janet couldn't be developing feelings for Sir Edward. It made no sense. She concentrated on the music that soothed her.

The gentlemen entered. Emma continued her playing while talk returned to the next day's hunt.

Janet spent a pleasant evening, feeling once again as if she'd stepped onto the set of a BBC costume drama, but the characters were flesh and blood, at home in their elegant dresses and finely cut suits. The manners were so completely different from those of their twenty-first-century descendants.

Sir John took over the task of turning pages for Emma, and Janet retired to the divan. She stifled a smile as she heard Sir John rattling off his kills in Greenwich. She recognized the rigid set to Emma's shoulders as she listened to his recounting and tried to concentrate on the music at the same time. How tiresome to play for someone who did not appreciate the efforts.

Sir Edward took the seat beside her. "Sir John may require more regular female companionship to appreciate music."

"I don't think much will change with female companionship. His wife will simply learn to block out the nonstop diatribes about his successful slaughter of hedgehogs and sparrows." Janet felt the lump in her throat forming. How on earth had she managed to do it again? Saying aloud what should have remained buried in the deepest recesses of her mind. What was wrong with her?

At least they were far away from Emma and Sir John. With Sir John's excited banter and Emma's brave attempts to continue with the music, they could not have heard.

But Sir Edward heard her loud and clear. She felt his eyes boring into her, and she wished she could sink under the chair and crawl to the door unseen.

"Miss Roberts, I will remind you that Sir John is my friend," Sir Edward whispered. "I will not have him insulted under my roof."

Even whispering, his voice managed to sound menacing to her ears. The one person anyone in her right mind would not wish to cross. Janet gathered her courage and fought the crimson blush she could feel rising across her cheeks. She turned slowly toward Sir Edward and looked squarely into his eyes. "You are right, Sir Edward. I apologize. It was unforgivably rude to say such things."

He nodded, looking like a priest forgiving a wayward parishioner. "I accept your apology. After all, Emma may find it in her heart to notice Sir John's attentions one day."

He spoke quietly, but Janet was unable to control herself. She took a deep, angry breath. Emma turned from her sheet music to look back, and Janet tried to smile reassuringly. She willed herself to be calm, before leaning in closer to Sir Edward. "But surely you don't mean ...?" For once, Janet was at a loss for words.

Sir Edward shook his head dismissively. When he spoke again, his voice was so low that she had to strain to hear every syllable. "Women have such romantic notions about marriage. Excessive novel reading contributes to this, I am most certain. Sir John is a fine man, with a title and a large estate. He could maintain my sister very comfortably. Besides, such a match would mean that our estates would be practically joined."

His look was so icy and unbending. Where was the cultured Sir Edward who read poetry and recited *Julius Caesar*? The one who showed her his art collection in the library, spoke with her of his love for Venice? How could he be so cold-hearted and mercenary when it came to his sister's happiness? Was it a mere business proposition? His sister doomed to speak about hunting for an eternity in order to forge stronger economic ties between the two estates?

Janet knew she should shut her big mouth, but her friend's future was on the line. She paused for a moment, noting that Sir John was fully engrossed in telling Emma about a friend posted in India and the tiger hunts he enjoyed there. There was no danger he could be distracted by snatches of quiet, nonhunting conversation.

"But Emma is so vibrant, so full of enthusiasm and joy." Janet fought to control her voice. "Certainly you would not wish her into a union with someone so entirely unsuited for her? They share no common interests. Surely even you can see that such a marriage would crush the life and beauty out of your sister? Would she not be happier with someone of a more similar character, even if he is not as prosperous as Sir John?"

Two hard blue eyes observed her. Only a few hours ago, they'd sat together in the shady field and spoken about literature, and Rome, and Emma's happiness, as if they were the closest of friends. But no traces of that kind person resided in the rigid body of the man before her. Had she been standing, the furor of that glare would have thrown her off-balance. The firm divan rescued her, but she longed to move back from this cruel man, one who was so cavalier about dashing his sister's hopes for happiness.

"Miss Roberts." His quiet, clipped tone expressed his distaste. "I am loathe to remind you that you are a guest in our home. You are entitled to your own opinions, but that does not mean that my motives should be called into question by you. I am the head of this household and, as such, I alone decide on the welfare of my family. If that does not meet with your approval, I would prefer you to keep silent on the matter. And I ask you not to attempt to influence my sister in matters which do not concern you."

The tips of her ears burned in anger. Still, she managed to hold her gaze on the ice-cold eyes of the starch-shirted, pompous ass who sat before her in all his vain glory.

One day soon, you and all your type will be irrelevant. That day cannot come quickly enough, as far as I'm concerned.

She fought the bile rising in her throat. Mr. Bentley, with his fine manners and kindness and lack of a fixed estate, was worth thousands of Sir Edwards and Sir Johns. She startled at a cough at the other side of the room and noticed that the music had ceased.

"My, my." Sir John turned his fleshy, ruddy face in Janet's direction. "So serious over there at the other side of the room. Discussing the fate of nations?"

"Not at all, Sir John." Janet willed her voice to sound confident. "Although I agree with you, a more pleasant topic of conversation is in order. Sir Edward was just recounting to me how eagerly he longed for a detail-laden discussion on the merits of fox hunting in each English region. Even better, on the relative merits of the quality of hunting on each estate. Alas, I am the wrong partner for such weighty conversation."

She plastered a sweet smile on her face as she turned to the piano. "Emma, perhaps I may turn the pages for you while the men discuss their blood sports?"

Janet rose from her seat to approach Emma's piano bench. Sir John passed her by with impressive speed for a man of his girth, and an excited glint in his beady eyes, ready to hold forth at length with Sir Edward on his only topic of conversation.

Janet kept her anger at bay, turning pages for Emma and allowing the music to enter into her body and calm her frayed nerves. Poor, sweet Emma, poised to be thrown under the bus by her imperious brother. And how could Emma defy him? Janet's own father would feel at home in such a world as this.

In the background, Sir John rattled on endlessly about hunting rifles, foxes, and merry hunting parties at the homes of other dim-witted, privileged gentlemen with far too much leisure time on their hands. Despite the anger welling up inside her, Janet took a perverse joy in knowing that Sir Edward was helpless to get a word in edgewise for the rest of the long, dull evening. It certainly served him right.

She hoped with every fiber of her being that Miss Chadwick was an arrogant, spoiled shrew, who would enrich the coffers of Sir Edward's family treasury in exchange for a life of dull conversation about superior bloodlines, feathers and lace, and the immense pride to be gained in snubbing one's neighbors if they did not possess the proper pedigree.

The festive BBC costume drama atmosphere had a dark side as well, and Janet would do well to never forget it.

Chapter 24

Birds chirped from the branches, shading Janet and Emma as they made their way to the stables. Janet had not slept well. Her heart was heavy for her friend.

"I saw that you and my brother were deep in discussion last night." Emma hitched her riding habit up daintily to step over a fallen branch.

"Yes," said Janet absently, "we were. He was singing the praises of Sir John. Apparently any girl would be lucky to snare him ... no hunting pun intended."

"Oh, Jane." Emma sighed. "You worry yourself unnecessarily. I suppose you are angered because Edward mentioned what a fortunate match a union between our two families would be."

Janet gasped. "You know? I was so worried about mentioning anything, for fear of upsetting you."

"My dear friend." Emma's smile appeared forced. "Who is the true romantic now? You speak about marrying for love, as Lizzie and Jane Bennet do. Most women of my acquaintance feel more affinity with Charlotte Lucas, who does not expect much from marriage, and hopes only for a man who is not cruel."

"Mister Collins over Mister Darcy?"

"No, Jane. We all long for true love, but family duty does not always allow us to act as we may wish. My own mother and father did not marry for love."

"I see."

Had her own parents married for love? If they had, it dissipated as quickly as it developed. Who was she to offer lessons? Still, she so longed to see her friend happy with Mr. Bentley. Perhaps it was better that he was not yet with his aunt near Helmsley Manor. His proximity might simply cause Emma pain.

Emma recently received a letter from Lady Whitmore, mentioning that Mr. Bentley had been seen speaking to Miss Tucker in the Pump Room and again at a concert at the Assembly Hall. Janet assured her friend it was nothing, but had Emma read these observations aloud to Janet on purpose to prove that her heart could survive such a blow?

Janet tilted her face up to the weak morning sunlight. The stables came into view, and there was no need for further conversation on the topic. After all, Janet had nothing to say to cheer her friend.

William did not greet them with his customary smile. He went about his work with his usual efficiency, but Janet felt something was worrying him. She took him aside when Emma went to check on Edward's horse.

"It's my baby brother, *Signorina* Gianna. He's sick and Mamma's worried. He's broken out in a rash and he won't eat or sleep. It came on so sudden."

"William, why don't you ride on with Emma? I'll go see your mother and your brother."

"I don't want you to get sick, too, Miss."

"I'll be alright, William. I'm vaccinated … uh … I have been exposed to many illnesses in the New World." She saw Emma returning. "Would you mind if I begged out of our ride this morning and William takes my place to accompany you? I slept so poorly last night. I am in no condition to ride."

"Of course not. Do rest."

Janet waved them off before making her way to William's family cottage. Inconsolable wails pierced the peaceful surroundings, growing louder as she approached.

She knocked on the door, let herself in, and introduced herself in Italian to William's startled mother. The cottage was clean, but Janet shivered in the dank interior, feeling the drafts from the poor-quality shutters, even on a warm day. What must it be like in winter? These cottages were in desperate need of a proper sanitation system and better insulation against the harsh elements.

Janet smiled kindly at the petite, dark woman who was clutching a wailing child in her arms. Her black curls had been pinned up hurriedly, and the lines around her eyes made her appear far older than she must be—years of sickness, hardship, relentless work, multiple pregnancies and difficult childbirths had taken their toll on her, Janet suspected. But when she smiled, her face lit up. Janet glimpsed hints of the fetching young woman Guglielmo's mother must once have been.

"*Sì*, Guglielmo told me about you," she said in Italian. "You lived in our homeland and speak our language. But, Miss, you should not be here. What if you were to fall ill?"

"I shall be fine," Janet spoke with the authority in her voice that she knew would settle this mother's worries. "May I examine your baby? Paolo, isn't it?"

The frightened mother nodded, almost imperceptibly, and Janet reached her arms out to take the child in her embrace. She felt his feverish forehead. She examined the baby's bloodshot eyes and runny nose. She opened his tiny mouth to see the telltale white spots inside, and then she turned her attention to the rash that covered his face, neck and was starting to form on his shoulders and upper chest, working its way down.

Janet's grandfather, a pediatrician, had constantly quizzed her on illnesses from his medical textbooks when she was a child in the hope she might one day study medicine—something she always knew would never happen. But for once, she was thankful for his obsessive quizzing.

"*Signora Rossi*, I believe your baby has the measles. The disease is spread through the air, through coughing and sneezing. It is highly contagious. Paolo should be separated from your family. I could take him to the manor and care for him. I have already had the disease, so I am immune."

Fear flashed in the woman's eyes. Her hand caressed the edge of the baby's blanket.

"*Signora*," Janet spoke with kindness. "He requires fluids and proper foods to keep him strong. I'll speak with Miss Emma about having the doctor come to call. We need to ensure your other children do not catch the disease." Janet saw the woman's expression change with the last sentence. In this cottage, the disease would spread rapidly. She could only pray it hadn't already.

Slowly, almost imperceptibly, *Signora* Rossi nodded her head.

Janet made an effort to sound efficient. "I will return with Paolo after he has recovered. In the meantime, you must get to work airing out the cottage, washing the sheets and all the clothes and air drying them. Give the cottage a good scrubbing. It is important that the other children not return home until all this has been done."

She nodded, but her eyes conveyed an unfathomable sadness.

Mothers and children, thought Janet, remembering her own mother's protective embrace and soothing words when Janet was ill. Janet touched the anxious mother's hand as she rose from her seat. "I will take good care of Paolo. I promise you."

"May God bless you, *Signorina Gianna*," she said, making the sign of the cross and stroking Paolo's face. A single tear slipped down her cheek.

Janet rocked the whimpering Paolo in her arms. She exited the cottage and strode across the lawn to the manor house. Nineteenth-century diseases and mortality rates were something she preferred to consider merely through the lens of history rather than firsthand.

Please, God, look over little Paolo, and let me deliver him safely back to his mother.

She shifted the young boy onto her left hip and, like Paolo's mother, made the sign of the cross before hurrying back to the manor house.

"But Miss Jane, this is highly irregular." Turner twisted her apron. "What will the Master say?"

Janet had never seen Turner so discomposed. Little Paolo slept on her bed. Only two years old, he'd cried for his mamma, but Janet sang Italian songs she remembered and it seemed to calm him, until he fell asleep.

"I will speak to Sir Edward, and explain it was my idea alone. But for now, I need your help." Her voice was firm. "I do not wish to expose you or any of the other servants to the disease, so you may leave everything here before the door during these days. I will take care of cleaning my own room."

"You, Miss Jane?"

Janet smiled faintly. "Do not worry about me. I shall manage. In America we are expected to handle many household duties on our own." There was an understatement.

Turner looked as if she'd swallowed something distasteful.

"The important thing is that I receive cool compresses to help bring Paul's fever down. I will need plenty of water to keep him hydrated. We must ensure he has Vitamin A—carrots, spinach, eggs. Could you let the kitchen staff know?"

Turner nodded, although she did not look convinced. She'd eventually grow used to the idea, Janet was certain. When Turner left, Janet considered how to best break the news to Sir Edward. She wondered if she should request a visit from the family doctor. Was he competent? Or would he simply suggest cures such as bloodletting? As long as there were no complications, Paolo should emerge no worse for wear. Her room was certainly preferable to that damp cottage. She could keep his forehead and chest cool when his fever spiked. She would ensure he was hydrated. Yes, she could do this alone.

Throughout the day, Janet nursed Paolo. Turner returned numerous times with basins of cold water and provided Janet with linen nightdresses for the child, elaborately embroidered around the neck. Had these once belonged to Sir Edward or Emma? They were made of fine fabric, clothes of far better quality than the oft-mended hand-me-downs Paolo was wearing.

Janet sat at Paolo's bedside, wringing out the cloth and dabbing cool water against his chest. She swabbed his forehead. It seemed to do the trick. His forehead was slightly cooler. She removed his threadbare clothing and replaced them with the borrowed finery. He looked so angelic against her thick, goose down pillow. He didn't have the baby fat one expected on two-year-olds. She didn't imagine there was enough food to go around in Guglielmo's large family.

Janet wrung out the cloth, startling to hear a sharp rap at the door. "Just a moment, Turner." Using the wet cloth, she wiped at mashed carrots on her chest, only making it worse. She'd long undone her hairpins, and her hair fell over her shoulders in a messy cascade. No time to worry about it now.

Opening the door, she caught her breath when she saw who stood on the other side. "Sir Edward." How she must look with her wild hair and disheveled clothes. The hard glint in his blue eyes reminded her of his haughty portrait. "You must forgive me. I was not expecting you."

"I should say not. I suspect a visit by the estate owner is the last thing on your mind. I have the impression you act however you choose, without considering the consequences. Or the effect of your actions on others."

She sensed his distaste as he examined her carrot stains, wild hair, perspiring brow, and flushed cheeks. *Oh God, can he tell I loosened my stays?* She'd been convinced no one could tell under the riding habit. She may as well waltz around in a negligée, advertising her brazenness.

"Where is the child?" he demanded in a voice one didn't question.

"Here, inside." She cast her eyes down. "He is sleeping on my bed. His fever is down, although I do not believe we are safe yet." She heard her voice, so meek. The good servant responding to her master.

"And what is wrong with him?"

"He has the measles." She dared not meet his angry eyes. She gazed on the sleeping child. "The rash has spread all over his body. The cottage is so damp and poorly aired, and I worried that the other children could come down with the disease. I thought I could care for him better here."

"You thought? *You* thought?" he thundered.

She looked up, catching the flash of anger in his eyes.

"Miss Roberts, I have tolerated you because you are my sister's friend, but you forget yourself. This is *not* your home. This is not *your* decision to make."

She blushed at his reprimand.

"What if your recklessness endangers my household servants? Do you realize these people have families who depend on them, depend on their wages? Did you consider their welfare? What about my sister? I informed you about her delicate health. Will you thoughtlessly endanger her as well?"

"Sir Edward, I would *never* do anything to harm Emma or the household staff." She raised her gaze to meet his. "I intend to stay here alone with Paolo—with Paul. I have already asked Turner to leave things I need outside. I will manage my own cleaning and handle all my own personal needs." She ignored his pointed examination of her haphazard toilette. "I will not be a carrier of the disease since I cannot contract it." Her voice was firm, unbending. She had conquered her fear over the glowering autocrat before her.

His eyes became narrow slits. "How are you so convinced you cannot contract the disease?"

She paused. Sir Edward was an intelligent man. What if she confided in him? At least partially. It would be a relief to prune back the tangled web of lies she'd planted.

She took a deep breath. "I have told everyone I have already had the disease. Because the truth seemed more complicated. But I think I can trust you to understand."

Was it an impression, or did she see a slight softening in the rigid set of his jaw? Did his eyes burn slightly less? Or was it her own wishful thinking? She shifted her weight from one leg to the other as she considered how to proceed.

"There is an experimental technique, not yet widespread in American medical circles. My father has some acquaintances in Boston who practice this technique. It is called vaccination."

Confusion spread across his face.

She continued, carefully weighing each word. "Some ... some ... doctors believe that the body can become immune to deadly diseases by being exposed to them at an early age." *So far, so good.* "So these doctors collect ... uh... cultures of the disease and they prepare small doses, which they, um ... inject into the bodies of healthy, young children. These children grow up with an altered immune system." She took a deep breath. "The antibodies of these diseases are present in their bodies from a young age. Therefore, when their bodies are exposed to these viruses at a later date, they are unaffected by them."

She saw how strangely he observed her. Anger marred his face. He must understand—that she was not one of them, that she came from a different time. This wasn't what she'd wanted. She'd simply longed to voice some honesty.

"You wish me to believe, Miss Roberts, that your father *knowingly* injected you with a deadly virus as a ... a ..." His voice rose in anger. "A type of medical experiment? It's an abomination!"

She breathed a sigh of relief. "It is ... *different* from what you are used to, but I know you are a man of the world—a man of science, and open to new ideas. That is why I have explained this to you. It is—" she looked up at him, "—still experimental, but I believe one day these vaccinations will be widespread. Just imagine, future generations will be protected from some of our deadliest diseases." Her eyes challenged his. She could see it from the anger still smoldering in his gaze. She decided to press her luck. "Sir Edward, we can discuss this at a future date, but I would like to discuss with you the state of the cottages."

He looked wary. "I do not understand."

She composed her face, allowed her voice to assume a softer timbre. "I believe some changes might help improve the health of your tenants: better ventilation, increased insulation, a more effective drainage ditch. Some minor adjustments could do wonders for improving their current state." She looked down. "I used to work alongside my father on similar projects, and I would be happy to lead this type of work here at Helmsley Manor."

She heard his sharp intake of air. When she looked up, that hard glint had returned to his eyes. She couldn't have quit while she was ahead.

"Miss Roberts, it is obvious that we come from entirely different worlds. While you clearly find your upbringing and experiences superior, I find them simply distasteful. I would thank you to never raise this issue with me again."

She heard the hard edge in his voice and sensed the danger. Her cheeks burned as he continued.

"I handle my own estate affairs, and I find it disturbing that you wish to constantly meddle in what does not concern you in the slightest." He stepped back, offering a curt bow without meeting her eyes. "I bid you good day, Miss Roberts. I will take you at your word that you will not involve my sister in your nursing efforts. I do not wish her health compromised by your reckless decisions."

When she blinked her eyes, he was gone. Janet shook her head and returned to her patient.

Learn to bite your tongue.

Why was she constantly making things difficult for herself? It seemed she was a disaster in any time period.

Chapter 25

The dappled light spilled through the window as Janet and Guglielmo sat in the antechamber, reviewing his letters.

"Let's review. A-B-C-D."

Guglielmo had never had the measles, so Janet did not allow him beyond the wall to see Paolo, but he did stop by to fetch word for his mother each day. During those visits, Janet reviewed his progress in reading and writing. As she suspected, he was bright and progressed quickly in his lessons.

She pointed to a sentence he'd written. "You have a fine hand, William. Your cursive is extraordinary. Copy these sentences—fifty times each. Feel the flow of the quill as you write these and sound them aloud as you repeat them." She handed him a small booklet. "Here is your text. Remember to read each evening before you go to bed."

He nodded. "I read aloud to the littl'uns, *Signorina* Gianna, before they fall asleep. It helps to cheer them with Paolo away. We all miss him. My mother is so grateful. She thanks you for all your kindness."

Janet blushed. "There is no need. Paolo improves." She closed the copybook and handed it to Guglielmo. "The doctor pays a visit tomorrow. I hope Paolo shall return home soon.

If you will excuse me, it is time to feed him." She tousled Guglielmo's hair, trying to picture this mature and earnest ten-year-old in her own world.

In the bedroom, Paolo slept. She wiped her hands on her apron. These past days had been solitary ones, alone with the child. The servants delivered plates of food and quietly collected them from the antechamber. The feverish child seemed to improve.

After the unfortunate exchange with Sir Edward, Janet had not heard from him again. Even Emma had been mostly absent, speaking several times to Janet through the closed doorway and sliding books for her into the antechamber. She told Janet she was busy preparing the house for Miss Chadwick's arrival.

Janet hadn't minded the solitude. For one, she stopped wearing the corset, since no one but Paolo could bear witness to her brazenness. She wrote observations in her journal, of life around her, customs, medical thinking. Ideas for her stalled thesis filled her mind. And, when he was awake, she enjoyed taking care of Paolo, cuddling his warm body against hers, comforting him when he called for his mother, soothing his fears. She'd set up a cot in her room, but Paolo would wake during the night and call for his mother. Afterwards, he'd often crawl into bed beside her.

The only thing Janet missed was Emma's company. Emma wasn't simply her rescuer in this new world. In her absence, Janet realized how much she counted on their daily chats and the depth of their friendship.

It was different from her modern friendships, where various activities and media competed for time and attention. Her pace of life was slower in this world, and Janet felt she had more time to dedicate to her burgeoning friendship with Emma. As she sat at the window in the dawn light, she longed to be once again with her new friend, to discuss books, to listen to Emma's lithe fingers expertly perform Mozart or Bach on the pianoforte.

A knock on the door interrupted her thoughts, and Turner ushered in the doctor. An old man stood before her. She noted his wiry, white hair, ruddy complexion and large hands. He smiled as he bowed to her. "A pleasure, Miss Roberts."

"I appreciate your visit." Janet self-consciously threw a large shawl around herself, hoping to cover her lack of a corset. "Here is our patient, Paul. He slept well last night. I believe the fever has gone down. He eats more and he is more alert. I have been keeping him well-hydrated." Paolo began to stir as she undid the top of his nightdress to show the doctor the child's chest. "I did not wish to get my hopes up, but I assumed that Paul has been through the worst."

The doctor sat beside the child, feeling his forehead, measuring his pulse, examining the fading spots on his chest and body. He opened the child's eyes and examined them, lay an instrument to Paul's chest to listen to his breathing. Finally, he turned to Janet. "You have been a fine nurse. It appears the worst is indeed over. Sir Edward informed me the child's mother is nearby in the cottages. I would recommend another three days of rest here at the manor, before he returns home. I will speak to cook about his broths."

They both looked down at the child, who had fallen back to sleep and snored gently.

"You did well to bring him here and isolate him from the rest of the family. In those cramped living quarters, these diseases spread quickly. We may have had an outbreak on our hands, just as harvest season approaches. The situation could have been dire indeed, if not for your quick thinking."

The doctor took his leave. Relieved, Janet sat at the windowsill. Would Sir Edward soften at this news? Their argument still weighed on her.

The tiny lake glittered beyond the giant elm tree. There was the spot where she'd sketched this manor home so long ago. Closed up in this room, she thought more often about returning to her old life. After all, she couldn't stay here forever, relying on Sir Edward's hospitality.

But how could she return? No matter how long she turned the question over in her mind, she never came closer to an answer.

That night Janet woke with a start. Traces of the familiar dream were fresh in her mind, the same she dreamed her first night in Bath. She remembered the velvet gown swishing against her stockinged legs. She recalled holding a candle as she wound through Helmsley Manor hallways, for it was clear that is where her dream took place. The distant sound of music, her hand reaching out to the door. The sense of relief when she entered. The disjointed images. The cloud of pink, the alabaster faces, the green leaves. Yes, now it was clear. It *had* been the Tiepolo in her dreams. The Tiepolo she'd never even laid eyes upon when she first dreamed about it.

She'd gazed on the painting each day in her life in modern Bath, and here it was under this same roof, in Sir Edward's library. Two centuries earlier. Could it truly be the connection between the two worlds?

The curtains had been left open and a full moon illuminated her room. Paolo snored gently beside her. He wouldn't notice if she absented herself briefly. She slipped her bare feet into slippers and wrapped a shawl around her shoulders. It buffered the light cotton of her nightdress from the house's deep chill.

Seizing a candleholder from the hall table, she held the wick to a lantern. She held her light aloft and made her way down the grand staircase. The old house groaned. She feared waking the servants, or Emma and her brother, who would inquire about her nighttime ramblings.

She approached the library, opened the door, and caught her breath as the door moaned. Stepping in, she closed it gently behind her. The candle, held high, cast a tiny circle of light. She approached the mantelpiece and rested the candle below the painting. It did not shed much light on the images, but the drapes had been left open, and the full moon partially illuminated the room.

Janet gazed at the image. How had she overlooked this before? It was so obvious now. Her dream clearly consisted of snatched images from the painting. The billowing pink and yellow cloth of Daphne's dress, the pink of Apollo's robes, Daphne's alabaster skin and rosy cheeks, the surprise in Apollo's face, the sprouts of green emerging from her fingertips, the deep blue sky.

"Yes," she said aloud, "this is it."

This is what she'd dreamed, what must have been months ago on her first night in Bath. How could her subconscious have known of this painting before she stepped into Huntington House and viewed it for the first time? It had to be some sort of sign. If only she could discover the significance. She examined the painting more closely, willing it to yield clues.

Janet heard a rustling behind her. Her heart beat frenetically as she turned to see a figure rising from an armchair. For a moment, she couldn't make out the features, only a shadowy form.

"If I may inquire, Miss Roberts. What did you mean by 'This is it' as you were gazing on the Tiepolo?"

Janet's hand flew to her chest. "Oh, Sir Edward! You startled me."

He stepped closer, and she could make out a slight curve to his lips. Was Sir Edward being friendly with her again, when she only recently feared he would cast her out? He was an impossible man to read. His tall form looked trim in an exquisitely tailored dressing gown. She wondered when men had stopped wearing them; they looked so elegant. He fixed her with his piercing stare, and Janet realized he awaited a response.

She turned back to the painting, trying to ignore his presence beside her. He stood so close he was almost brushing against the thin cotton of her nightdress, involuntarily sending shivers up her spine. Self-consciously, she pulled her shawl tighter around her shoulders. She felt almost naked, even if she'd never owned a nightdress as chaste as the one she now wore.

"I dreamt of this painting." Her eyes remained carefully focused on the canvas. "It's not the first time, and I never understood what the disjointed images meant." Her voice gained steady strength as she explained, happy to unburden her thoughts to someone else, even if not ready to reveal the whole truth. "I dreamt of billowing pink cloth, alabaster skin, the flushed cheeks of Daphne, the green buds ... all seen individually. The imagery was so powerful. It woke me. It's the first time I made the connection with the Tiepolo."

There was complete silence before Sir Edward spoke, his voice gentle yet resonant as it filled the silent room. "You said there was another time you dreamt of the painting. Was that while you were at Helmsley Manor?"

Janet turned toward Sir Edward. His expression was impassive as he regarded the canvas. His high cheekbones and sculpted face were a dramatic chiaroscuro in the play of candlelight. Could she risk it? Might he understand?

"Honestly ..." Her voice was hoarse and uncertain, barely more than a whisper. "I have had this dream before. A long time ago." She took a deep breath, afraid to go on, yet, at the same time, needing to tell someone who might understand. "When I first arrived in Bath. Before my accident ... before I met Emma ... before I ever laid eyes on this painting. Something about this painting calls to me. I do not pretend to understand it."

Sir Edward was silent, and Janet felt self-conscious.

The clock ticked on the mantelpiece, the steady sound of the second hand reverberating throughout the room. Janet's breathing sounded too loud to her own ears. Sir Edward stood too near. He'd hear it. She felt his hot breath brush against her face. Her heart beat faster now. Janet was terrified, yet she turned to face him, her face tilted up to his. She held his gaze.

"Miss Roberts ... Miss Jane. It is not odd."

He gazed at her intently and she caught her breath.

"I have felt the same. This painting called to me, in Venice. It came to me in my dreams each night after I viewed it for the first time, and I could not rest until I possessed it."

He faced the canvas once again, running his hands through his hair. Janet startled. It seemed such a modern gesture. She'd never noticed such casual behavior in well-bred society since her arrival in this world. Twisting her hair, or scratching her nose, or flopping down unceremoniously into a chair were all actions she'd banished from her daily nineteenth-century life. Something about this familiar gesture made her smile. Sir Edward turned and noticed it.

"You are laughing at me. My friends and family do not understand my fixation with this painting. Yet it is my most prized possession. I come here often at night to gaze upon it. I do not even know what it is precisely that leads me here."

He stepped closer, his body so close to her own. The proximity caused flutters in her chest that she tried to ignore.

"Will you humor me, Miss Jane?"

It wasn't even her real name, but she thrilled to hear Sir Edward speak it rather than the formal mode of address. "Jane" traipsed off his tongue. There was a softness about his voice when he said it. Not trusting her own voice, she nodded.

He picked up her candle from the mantel, turning to her once again. One corner of his mouth twitched up and transformed his face into that of a mischievous boy. "Even objects of perfect beauty have their flaws. And sometimes, those imperfections can render them even more beautiful in the eyes of the beholder."

He raised the candle closer to the bottom of the canvas, to the shadowy lower-right corner. The grassy foreground. The candle came closer and closer to that familiar point. She gasped.

"Yes, you noticed it. You're a woman of exquisite taste to notice such a tiny flaw in this dark room. You see, it is a scratch."

Her head spun. How could it be? How was it possible that the scratch *she* inflicted on the painting also managed to be on the same canvas two hundred years earlier?

"And the scratch ..." Her voice was a hoarse whisper. "It was there when you purchased the painting in Venice?"

He studied the mark as he spoke. "Yes. I'm embarrassed to say it, but this scratch attracted me to the painting even more than the perfection of the composition. There was something about it ... I couldn't explain the hold it had on me. It called to me somehow. I come here often and touch this point when I'm here alone ..."

The dizziness was overwhelming. Janet slumped into the chair behind her.

Sir Edward must have heard the ungraceful thud, for he turned. His mouth opened in surprise. He placed the candle on the mantelpiece and knelt before her. "Are you unwell, Jane? Listen to me raving on like a madman. I hope I did not frighten you."

Janet felt calmer. Her voice was still breathy, but the lightheadedness had subsided. "No, it is not you. Sometimes I experience dizziness."

She registered the concern in his eyes. It looked almost like tenderness, but it was so unlikely to come from Sir Edward. More likely, it was the play of the candlelight.

"Stay right here." His voice was authoritative. "Let me get you some brandy to calm your nerves."

He raced away. Nerves. She was no better than Emily St. Aubert, a heroine she'd once laughed at. Yet who was in a swoon now?

Returning with a glass of brandy, he handed it to her. His fingers brushed hers as she grasped the glass. She felt a spark of electricity, similar to what she felt back in her room in modern Bath when she touched the scratch on the painting. *You're imagining things.*

She took a sip of the brandy and felt its warmth seep through her body, slowing the beat of her heart. She took another and then sank back in her chair, closing her eyes for a moment. She felt a hand on her forearm. The sleeve of her nightdress had slipped away and she felt the distinct touch of strong fingers against her bare skin, a comforting warmth. Janet forced herself to meet Sir Edward's gaze, afraid her eyes might reveal more than she wished. He sat in the chair beside hers, concerned.

"I apologize for scaring you, Sir Edward. Thank you for the brandy. The dizziness has passed. I feel much better now."

"I am pleased."

He withdrew his hand from her forearm, and she immediately felt its absence. She took another slow sip of her brandy and breathed deeply. She needed the courage to speak.

"Perhaps it is not only the scratch that draws you back to this painting." Her voice was low, husky. "Perhaps it is something else entirely."

"And what might that be, Jane?"

How sweet the name sounded on his lips. She felt his gaze on her.

"Metamorphosis," said Janet, without a trace of doubt in her voice.

"Pardon?" His eyes questioned hers.

She needed to say this. He might understand. "Perhaps it is the subject matter. The metamorphosis. The ability to change form ... to move between one world and another."

He seemed to be searching her eyes. She noticed again how handsome he was in the candlelight.

"Like the Byron," she continued. "The dark blue waves that carry you to distant worlds so far removed from your own. Does that not attract you?"

He leaned toward her. His eyes were so close to hers. She thought she saw recognition in them. Did he understand her?

"Look at Daphne's face," she said. "She is at peace, is she not?"

He smiled. She was certain this time. Sir Edward used it rarely, but he had a beautiful smile. His whole face lit up.

"I am not convinced," he said. "Observe her carefully. I have always thought she regrets her decision. Does she not seem wistful? Apollo has almost caught up to her, yet it is too late to return to the world she chose to leave behind. She is changing before his eyes. And still, her face seems—to me, at least—to be filled with regret at the choice she has made. I believe she regrets leaving her world. Perhaps she suspects she could find happiness with Apollo, but it is too late. It is she who called out to her father and set the wheels in motion. She chose to leave Apollo behind."

Janet was silent, examining Daphne's expression carefully. Was that regret in her expression? Did she fear her metamorphosis, her transition into her new world? Or might she be happier in her new reality?

"Miss Jane ... did you not hear me?"

Janet turned to see Sir Edward's gaze firmly on her. Had she been daydreaming? Had she missed something he said? "Pardon, Sir Edward. I was wrapped up in my own reveries."

"Ah, I understand. I am often in that state. Do you think such a metamorphosis is possible, outside of mythology and literature? Do you believe we can experience something similar in real life?"

Janet met his gaze and stared deeply into those blue eyes. How she longed to speak to him openly. Perhaps someone of Sir Edward's stature and intellect could understand something she could barely comprehend herself, even if she were living it daily. Instead, she simply nodded.

"I do, Sir Edward. The world is large, and there are many different realities. I believe it is a mistake to stay too wedded to our own narrow experiences." She stood and moved closer to the painting. "Perhaps, like Daphne, we have to be more willing to embrace those changes, our personal metamorphoses."

When she turned, he was no longer seated in the chair. He stood directly behind her. Her chest practically touched his. He was so close that she could feel his warm breath caressing her cheek. Inexplicably, Janet felt the desire to tilt her face towards his, to feel the warmth of his lips against hers. She longed for him to stroke her hair and tell her everything would be alright.

Her heart pounded wildly in her chest, her breathing grew more labored. He looked so strong standing before her, his chiseled features accentuated by the play of light and shadows from the flickering candlelight. His face moved closer to hers, and she struggled to stay still. Her eyelids closed in anticipation. She tilted her face towards his.

She stood that way for several moments. When she opened her eyes again, Sir Edward was no longer before her. He was pacing the room at the far end of the library. Her cheeks burned. What a fool she'd been! Had he recoiled at what seemed forward behavior on her side?

He turned and strode across the room, although not, she couldn't help but notice, as close as before. His fingers were laced together; he gazed at some invisible point beyond her shoulder. *He doesn't even want to look at me.*

When he spoke, his voice was quiet, but firm. "I must take my leave, I fear. It has long been time for me to retire, with such a busy day ahead of me."

Janet felt uncomfortable trying to hold a gaze that had no intention of meeting her own. She turned her attention back to studying Tiepolo's intricate brushwork. She willed her voice to sound cool, distant. "Of course, Sir Edward. I bid you a good night. I, too, shall retire in a few moments."

She did not hear the rustle of his departure. From the corner of her eye, she saw he was still standing rigidly in his place.

Sir Edward cleared his throat. "Before I take my leave, I hope you will permit me to offer my apologies for the comments I made the other day about your nursing of young Paul."

She turned and saw him regarding her.

"I was wrong to think you would endanger my sister or the staff. The doctor informed me that Paul recovers well, and that in a day or two he should be ready to join his family once again." He was silent for a moment as he examined the mantelpiece clock. "He also tells me you averted a larger tragedy—that the disease could have spread among my tenants. And that he was extremely impressed by your professional manner of nursing the child and your medical knowledge."

"That was kind of him."

"Miss Roberts ... Miss Jane."

Janet looked up as he said these words, offering her an olive branch.

"I once spoke about your assisting my foreman, Saunders, and me when we renovate some of the tenants' homes. You have already expressed some of your views on this matter when we spoke the other day."

Janet blushed when she recalled what must have sounded like recriminations, as if Sir Edward were to blame for little Paul's measles.

"Perhaps you would join us the day after tomorrow and contribute your architectural expertise to our planning stages? It would only be an hour or so. Now that Paul is recovered and no longer contagious, Turner could keep an eye on the child."

He awaited a response. He'd forgiven her, or was attempting to. He was even requesting her collaboration. Her moment of folly was not as disastrous as she'd imagined.

"Of course, Sir Edward. I shall be available."

"Thank you, Miss Jane," he said, before leaving the room.

She stayed a few moments longer to observe the painting. "My dear Daphne," she whispered. "You and I are hopelessly uprooted. Let's hope all works out for us. Will you know how to lead me back to my own world if I ask you?"

Slowly, she placed the tip of her index finger and middle finger over the scratch. She closed her eyes, bracing herself for the jolt of electricity she'd feel penetrate her body, like the one she felt prior to her time travel. She stood still like that for some time before daring to open her eyes. Nothing.

She examined the nymph's face for a sign, but none appeared. Did the magic only work in one direction? Would the painting be able to lead her home, or was she here forever?

Picking up her candle, she walked out of the library, closing the heavy door behind her. Confused thoughts tumbled through her mind as she made her way to her bedroom, extinguished the candle, and climbed into bed. Paul snored gently beside her.

It must have been the talk of metamorphoses, the candlelight and the conversation that turned my head tonight. I'm not developing feelings for Sir Edward. What a ridiculous idea. I'll be on guard for such silly, romantic ideas in the future.

What he must think of me! It's enough that he no longer wishes to remove me from Helmsley Manor. It was simply my gratitude that caused my head to spin. It absolutely won't happen again.

Chapter 26

The sun was still warm, but the air filling Janet's nostrils was crisp. Visits with the tenants confirmed harvest preparations were approaching, and all hands were required—men, women and children.

The staff were frantic, while Emma was ecstatic about plans for a Harvest Ball. "Jane, it is the first time the ballroom will be used since father fell ill. I can scarcely believe Edward suggested it. The staff is hard at work organizing." She smiled as she took her friend's hands in her own. "You shall see Helmsley Manor at its best!"

That morning, little Paolo returned to his family. Janet herself carried the child to his overjoyed mother. Signora Rossi examined his rosy face, his rounder features from all the fine food he'd eaten in the manor house, and she formed the sign of the cross over her narrow torso and shoulders, before throwing her arms around Janet and repeating, "*Grazie, Signorina Gianna. Che Dio ti benedica.*"

Janet turned to see the sunlight shining down on Signora Rossi and little Paolo, as mother kissed her son. Paolo was back where he belonged.

Janet and Emma spent the morning at the tenants' homes, distributing baskets and chatting with the wives. Paolo's miraculous recovery was on everyone's lips. They regarded Janet with favor. Although she deflected their praise, it did nothing to diminish their open admiration.

Observing the cottages with a critical eye, she noticed their dampness, lack of ventilation, and overcrowded conditions. She would be meeting with Sir Edward and Saunders later that morning, and wanted to come armed with ideas for possible new cottages.

Now, after having accompanied Emma back to the manor house, Janet returned to the cottages the third time that day for her meeting with Sir Edward.

As she approached, two men stood together over what appeared to be a map. Sir Edward looked elegant in a handsome grey coat, a top hat perched upon his head. Beside him was a shorter, more compact man, dressed in fine, if less elegant, clothes, his brown hair worn long and tied with a ribbon. Deep in conversation, they didn't notice Janet until she stopped in front of them.

"Miss Jane," said Sir Edward, "thank you for joining us. May I present Saunders? Saunders has been with us for many years, and he will be overseeing the project on the cottages."

"A pleasure to meet you, Miss Roberts."

He bowed and she curtsied. She stifled a smile when she realized it was becoming almost second nature to her.

"Sir Edward told me your father is an architect. That you worked with him. I admit to skepticism about working with a woman, but Sir Edward has great faith in your capabilities."

Sir Edward thought highly of her abilities? She wished she could catch a glimpse of him, see his expression, but it would seem too awkward. "Thank you, sir. I hope I may be of assistance."

"Just call me Saunders. I've been on this property ever since I was a wee lad, my father a foreman before me. I know this terrain like the back of my hand." He smiled and set his face off in a spider web of lines and wrinkles. "Perhaps you will wish to see some of the tenant cottages. I have asked some of the families in the vicinity if we could take a look."

"Thank you, Saunders, but that will not be necessary. I have been a frequent visitor with Miss Emma. I'm familiar with the cottages." She pulled papers from under her arm, unfolding them. Sir Edward stepped beside Saunders to examine the sketches and she tried to quell her nerves as she explained. How often had she made presentations before her father's clients? Why did she feel so nervous now? "I hope it will not seem forward, but I have taken the liberty of sketching ideas for new cottages, concentrating on better ventilation, detached cooking areas ... perhaps shared between two or three cottages. Better rain gutters, drainage systems, and improved outhouse facilities. I have been in touch with Doctor Perry on these matters, particularly concerning sanitation."

Sir Edward looked up. His look was no longer amused. "You have been in touch with Doctor Perry? About *my* estate?"

"Well, yes, Sir Edward. Not your estate, per se, but we entered into an epistolary relationship when Paul was ill, and I asked for his general views about sanitation and curtailing the outbreak of disease, and improving the overall health, especially that of the children." She pointed to one of the renderings. She was so used to designing on her computer programs that it had been a challenge to go back to the literal drafting board. "You will see my attempts to incorporate some of his ideas into these designs, introducing better insulation in the cottages. I know from the tenants that the winters can be cold and damp."

The moments ticked by and Janet felt her heart beat faster in anticipation. Finally, she heard a low whistle and turned to see Saunders observing her.

"This is quite impressive for a lady. I will examine this before I come back with comments. This may be more expensive than we foresaw, but I'll see if we might be able to make this work. If Sir Edward agrees, of course."

Sir Edward was bent low over the designs. He raised his head and his eyes met hers. The sun shone in them, the sunlight making them appear an even deeper shade of blue. The golden light caressed his square jaw and high cheekbones. She caught her breath and cursed herself for behaving like a teenager with a crush. It was Sir Edward who stood before her. The man who could decide her fate.

"Miss Jane. These are indeed impressive. I will allow Saunders to review these, before discussing expenses and whether such a large-scale project can be undertaken."

Her heart fluttered to hear those words of praise. Sir Edward liked her work. He approved.

He offered his arm and suggested they survey the cottages.

She'd never sought approval from any man with the same intensity she longed for it from Sir Edward. Now it looked as if she were on the cusp of receiving it, and her heart soared at the thought. Although she convinced herself it was only fear of her future at Helmsley Manor that heightened her joy, not any feelings that may be developing in her heart.

Chapter 27

The days passed quickly.

On Sundays, Janet joined the family at church service. The whole parish awaited the arrival of Sir Edward and Miss Emma, and she joined them as they took their places up front. After the services, Janet joined Emma in the small Sunday school for the children of the tenant farmers, who learned their letters in order to read passages from the Bible.

One sunny Sunday, the two women walked back to Helmsley Manor together. "Emma, why do the children only have schooling Sunday mornings?"

Emma creased her brow. "It is their day of rest. During the week the children are hard at work with their families. They would not have time to attend the village school with the sons of town merchants." She tilted her head and a small grimace marred her lovely face. "You have seen how hard the tenant families work. The older children help to care for the younger ones. They help with the cooking and cleaning. School is simply not a priority."

But what if a school were nearby?

The two women entered the entrance hall. "Emma, would you excuse me? I should like to go rest in my room for a few moments."

"Of course, Jane. But you will join us for lunch, I hope."

"Yes, certainly." Janet raced up the stairs, taking them an unladylike two at a time.

Once in her room, Janet spread the paper along her desk. She'd borrowed a slab of wood from the Helmsley Manor carpenter and set it at an angle, with some books below it to form a makeshift drafting table. With her quill, she worked quickly. After years of working with computer programs, somehow, her creativity felt liberated with a simple paper and feather quill. She sketched and sketched, oblivious to the ink stains blossoming on her hands, until Miller announced that luncheon was served.

The golden sun slipped low in the sky. After a late-afternoon ride, Janet found an excuse to stay in the stables while Emma returned to the house to discuss menus with cook.

Janet brushed down the horses herself as William read his composition aloud. Janet had snuck away occasionally to teach her lone student, and William was proving to be as bright as she'd suspected.

He looked up from his reading at Janet brushing Bucephalus. "Miss Gianna, that is not work for a lady. I should not have allowed it."

"Nonsense, William. I do far more at home. We do not stand on such ceremony back in Boston. Besides, I wanted to hear your progress, and I am impressed. You capture the sensory details perfectly, but we still need to work on your punctuation. I shall take this home to correct it, and then I will want you to copy it neatly, concentrating on the correct grammar and punctuation."

He nodded solemnly and Janet smiled at his earnestness.

"Miss Gianna." He picked up the pitchfork, laying fresh hay in the stables as he spoke. "Mamma is grateful for what you've done for Paul and for me. She wondered if ..." He smiled sheepishly. "Well, we don't have much. But we have made some *parmigiano* and she makes fresh pasta and grows tomatoes. She remembers you saying you liked to cook pasta, and she wanted to know if you might wish her to prepare these things for you."

Janet stroked his cheek. "That would be lovely. It has been ages since I had Italian pasta. I should enjoy that. Perhaps I can prepare a special dinner for Emma and Sir Edward. An Italian feast. It may please them." She continued brushing the horse. "William, what would you think about a school for the tenant children here at the manor?"

"How would the children have time for school?"

"I know the timing would be difficult. Perhaps an hour or two a day might be feasible. I should like to discuss it with Sir Edward, but I wanted to have your opinion first."

"I do not know. It has never been attempted before. It would have to be brief, since we all have so many tasks to carry out each day. Perhaps some of the tenant children from the neighboring manor houses could join us ... although I do not know if it would be appreciated by all."

Apollo and Daphne stared down at Janet as her heart raced faster than if she were running in the Boston marathon. Sir Edward examined the designs she'd spread across his desk. His face, far from the mantelpiece candles, was shrouded in darkness. It was difficult to read his expression, so she looked up to observe the light dancing across the forms of Apollo and Daphne.

Janet had returned to this room several times when she believed she was alone, but she felt no tingling as she touched the painting's scratch. She didn't even know if the painting had the power to bring her back to her world, but there was no other explanation.

"Miss Roberts."

His voice caused Janet to look down quickly from the painting.

"Ah, I see you are far away. Dreaming of your metamorphosis, I assume?"

"Not quite." Even if that had been exactly what she'd been doing.

"Please, be seated." He indicated the plush chair before his desk. "This is excellent work. And I do not doubt your enthusiasm for the project. But we are already hard at work on the improvements to the cottages, and I am not sure I should undertake the additional time and expense of constructing a schoolhouse." He began to roll up the blueprints.

Janet hastily placed her hand down to stop him, inadvertently brushing his wrist with her fingers. She startled at the touch of his skin against hers. But this was no time to be distracted. "Sir Edward, I believe it is. Please hear me out." Sitting made her nervous. Janet stood and began pacing before his desk. "You will note the simple design I have chosen for the schoolroom, a mere one-room schoolhouse. All I require is the funding for the lumber and some equipment." She approached the desk, pointing to a corner where the figures were clearly indicated. "This is the budget I devised with your carpenter's help. I will oversee the project. The tenants, and even the women and children, can help me with the construction. I have kept the design simple for that purpose. The tenants will construct desks and chairs for their pupils."

He observed her, but his expression revealed nothing. "I see you have thought everything through. And shall we hire a schoolteacher? Are the children expected to be excused from their farm work? Can't you see how that would impoverish these families, who rely on their labor?"

"I would be pleased to serve as their teacher, with Emma's assistance. We have spoken to the women at the neighboring manors. And the reverend's daughter. They welcome the chance to undertake such charity work for the benefit of the children." She walked back and forth, afraid to meet Sir Edward's eyes. "The school schedule would not interfere with the children's work in the fields. I have thought seriously about this. During harvest season, classes would be held during the lunch hour, with longer lessons held in the winter, but it would never take away from their time for work or chores."

He shook his head. "I do not wish to anger the other landowners. What will they say to a tenant school? They may worry about having to create their own."

"I have discussed this with Saunders ..."

"You *what*?" he barked.

She blanched at the set of his jaw. That look always meant opposition. "You have been introducing new methods in tilling, fertilization, crop rotation and irrigation systems. We would be covering these methods in lessons on science and math. Of course, we would aim for basic literacy, but I would work with Saunders to ensure that the curriculum is extremely practical and supports the modernization efforts you are undertaking. We would expect the children to review their lessons with their families. So, you see, it would be a true win-win situation."

"Win-win?" He furrowed his brow.

"Ah, yes. A little American colloquialism meaning that the arrangement would be favorable to all concerned parties. Saunders hopes that the children could reinforce the new agricultural methods with their parents, and, of course, we would be forming a new generation of skilled tenants to carry on with work at Helmsley Manor. Educated farmers who could adapt to new methods and increase yields."

He sat back in his chair, the palms of his hands pressed together. His eyes did not meet Janet's, but remained fixed on the blueprints spread across his desk.

Janet stood still, wanting desperately to sit in the chair across from Sir Edward but hesitant to bring attention to herself and to interrupt his thoughts. The billowing pink robes of the painting caught her eye: Daphne's rosy cheeks, the slight sadness in her gaze. She felt a strange tingling through her body. Could it be? The feeling was gone as quickly as it came, but it was certainly the same sensation she'd felt in Bath before her accident on The Crescent Lawn. She looked up at Daphne once more.

"Miss Roberts?"

Turning toward the voice, she feared her face revealed all the fear and confusion swirling within her. "Pardon, Sir Edward?"

"You really are in another world. I said I agreed with your plan, but you must promise me it won't detract from the tenants' schedules as we approach harvest season. We must go ahead right away."

Janet forgot the odd sensations. "Thank you, Sir Edward! You won't regret it."

"I hope not. Now, I have some work to complete this evening. May we continue this conversation tomorrow?"

"Of course, I bid you good night."

Janet made her way up the staircase, the joy of the approved school tempered only by the return of the strange sensation.

Was her time here coming to a close?

Chapter 28

In three days' time, a rudimentary Helmsley Manor school was completed. Sir Edward insisted the work had to be undertaken immediately, so as not to not interfere with harvesting.

Janet and Saunders were present throughout construction, overseeing the work. The tenants were skilled at their tasks, and the simple schoolhouse took form quickly.

On the fourth day, the school's official inauguration, Janet left Helmsley Manor arm in arm with Emma.

"It is so exciting, Jane. We have done it. Helmsley Manor's very own school."

"I know." Janet tilted her head up to feel the warm sun on her face. "It came together quickly. Everyone worked well, even the children. William tells me they are excited to begin classes."

A crowd milled about the school. The tenants were dressed in their Sunday best, even if they'd been out in the fields all morning and would have to change once again into their work clothes following the dedication ceremony. Emma waved to Reverend White. The children were wide-eyed, gazing at the school as if it were an impressive monument, when Janet knew it looked more like a glorified shed. Yes, she had ensured that the building was sturdy, but she also made it as simple as possible to keep expenses low.

Gazing on it, she appreciated the simplicity. The men had built the stone walls to be strong, and the grey stone matched that of the surrounding cottages, like the thatched roof she found so charming. She'd had no idea how to construct a thatched roof, something she'd always admired in the villages around England. Saunders and the villagers taught her. The interior utilized the lumber purchased from town—and would help keep the school warmer in winter, since Janet doubted that tiny wood stove in the corner would be particularly effective. The families were each constructing their own pupils' desks, and those would soon fill the classroom. She breathed in the smell of freshly cut wood before stepping out into the crowd gathered before the tiny school.

A small band of local men played trumpets, clarinets and drums, adding to the festive atmosphere. Sir Edward stood on the top step of the schoolhouse entryway and the crowd broke out in cheers.

"Ladies and gentlemen, I am honored to welcome you to Helmsley Manor's new school. Mr. Saunders will work with all of you to ensure that school hours do not interfere with harvest and household chores, but we are pleased to see the enthusiasm. Your support will be key to its success."

Wild applause interrupted him. Helmsley Manor was ahead of its time, offering basic education to its tenants' children. Janet was proud to have been a small part of it. When she lifted her gaze to Sir Edward, his eyes rested on her.

He quieted the crowd with his hands. "Please join me in extending heartfelt thanks to Miss Jane Roberts, our guest and a talented architect, who worked so hard to plan this schoolhouse."

Janet felt her heart swell. She'd worked on numerous projects, many of them "prestigious," but the simple schoolhouse she'd built in three short days alongside these men, women, and children was far and away her most rewarding work.

"Miss Roberts, would you care to join me?"

The crowd parted to allow Janet access. When she reached the bottom step, Sir Edward stretched out his hand. The warmth of his skin and the pressure of his fingers as they enveloped her hand caused her heart to flutter. She prayed her cheeks would not flush and give her away in front of this crowd as she stood beside him.

"Miss Roberts, as a small token of our appreciation, you will note that the space for the foundation stone at the bottom has remained empty."

Janet looked down. When she'd asked about that, the workers had been evasive, saying it required a special stone in keeping with village traditions. With so many other pressing items, she hadn't pursued it.

Now she saw Joseph, a farmer and skilled stonecutter, whose help had been precious these past days, approach the school. He and another man carried the large foundation stone with its carefully carved letters. She marveled at when he would have found the time to produce such a striking work after hours of labor in the fields and building the school. She wiped away a tear as Sir Edward read aloud:

"The Helmsley Manor School is dedicated to the manor children and its talented architect, Miss Jane Roberts, on this day of 28 August 1813."

The crowd clapped. The stone was set in its place of honor. Janet fought to stem the tears she felt welling up. From the corner of her eye, she saw Sir Edward smiling upon her. Turning her face to meet his gaze, she mouthed, "Thank you."

He looked out over the crowd. "Enjoy the music and the refreshments." He ferried Janet down the steps, where the crowd enveloped them. The small band played music. The children raced eagerly to a table laden with cakes and breads. Janet talked to the villagers, tenants, and children.

As the crowd began to disperse, Guglielmo's mother approached her. "*Signorina Gianna*," she addressed her in Italian, for her English required more effort. "Guglielmo is so excited about his lessons with you. I cannot thank you enough for saving Paolo's life. God blessed us by bringing you into our lives."

"*Signora* Rossi, you embarrass me. It was no trouble. Your children are delightful."

"*Ti prego*, let me thank you. William will deliver a basket filled with fresh ingredients and Chianti wine."

"*Grazie*." Janet kissed the woman on both cheeks and held her tight for a moment, feeling very much at home.

Chapter 29

The wind whipped through Janet's hair as she urged her horse to gallop faster. She knew Turner would scold her for creating extra work. About this, Janet was sorry. Yet, every time she tried to dress her own hair, Turner *tsked* and insisted on doing it again herself. The correct way.

The breeze on her face and the perfect gallop across an endless expanse of grass was too tempting to resist. She reined in her horse, waiting for Emma to catch up with her.

"My, Jane." Emma brought Bucephalus to an abrupt halt. "You have an unfair advantage not riding sidesaddle. You can travel as fast as the wind. We'll have to make a proper English lady of you yet, so I am not at such a disadvantage when we ride together."

"Even you, my dear Emma, are not patient enough to teach me to ride sidesaddle. It would be a thorough disaster, I assure you."

"If we are to be on time, we must turn back so that we can change."

"Is it not exciting? The first day of lessons at school."

"Yes. And is what Cook tells me true? Are you to prepare dinner tonight—a feast from the Italian peninsula?"

"It is. *Signora* Rossi has provided me with wonderful delicacies, and I am determined to finally do something useful in the household. I have already arranged for everything with Cook and the kitchen staff."

Emma shook her head. "How can you claim not to be useful? Just look at what you've done for little Paul, and the cottages, and the school. Still, I look forward to this evening. Edward will be most pleased. He waxes on about his time in Italy. I am always so envious."

"Race you back?"

"What is that odd little American expression you taught me about the egg?"

"We'll make a Yank of you yet. Last one back's a rotten egg. Ready? Set? Go!" Janet gave her horse a sharp kick and raced toward the stable. Glancing behind her, she saw Emma far behind. Generally, Janet rode away from the road, but no one was around, and this was the quickest route back to the stables. She galloped onto the dirt road, the hooves thundering as she gathered speed. Her concentration meant she didn't hear the carriage coming up behind her until it was too late. *Damn it!*

She pulled on her reins when the coachman called out for her to move aside. As the horse slowed, her pulse quickened. In all this time, no one had seen her riding. Why had she been so careless today? She prayed it was someone travelling through the region, not a local family who knew Sir Edward. What on earth had she done?

She brought her horse to a complete halt, fighting off the blush creeping across her cheeks and hoping the carriage would pass on without remark. Although her eyes were downcast, she glimpsed a woman's hand reach through the carriage window. Large, precious stones on long fingers caught the bright sunlight. A woman of means. Even worse.

The hand hit the side of the carriage and a voice called out. "Coachman, stop at once!"

It took some time to stop the four horses as they resisted and neighed, but the carriage eventually came to a halt on the road about fifty meters from Janet. What now? Could she risk galloping off in the opposite direction? As her mind reeled through the possibilities, a face emerged from the carriage window. And what a lovely face it was. Golden hair was piled atop the woman's head, its coils catching the brilliant sunlight and setting it aglow in a halo. Two sharp, blue eyes observed Janet with confusion.

"You there, urchin girl. Come here."

Janet glanced over her shoulder, but she was all alone on the meadow. Was she supposed to be the urchin the woman addressed? She eased her horse up to the side of the carriage. She must have done a poor job of masking her confusion as she said, "Yes, ma'am?"

The woman observed her with distaste. "What in heaven's name are you doing riding in this shocking manner? Where is your sidesaddle, girl?"

The harsh voice was at odds with the lovely face, and Janet felt her rage boiling deep within. Did she know this woman? She did not recognize her from the town, so why should she remain here to be reprimanded?

"Are you lost, ma'am?" Janet mustered her sweetest voice. "Could I point your coachman in the right direction?"

"I always know *exactly* where I'm going ... and, more importantly, the *proper* way in which to travel," she snapped. "Which is far more than I can say for the likes of you."

Janet's blood boiled. Yes, this woman was lovely, but her beauty could not make up for her cruel manner of address. Janet was formulating a few choice words in her mind, ready to retort to the well-heeled Regency Barbie doll with an acid tongue. As she opened her mouth to let loose her tirade, hooves thundered up behind her.

"Miss Chadwick!" exclaimed Emma breathlessly as she approached the carriage on Bucephalus. "What an unexpected pleasure to see you."

Miss Chadwick? The famous Miss Victoria Chadwick?

"Unexpected?" The cruel voice dissipated. Miss Chadwick's polished syllables were sweet as honey as she addressed Emma. "Did you not receive my latest letter, anticipating my arrival to today?"

Emma's eyes grew wide. "No, I am afraid we did not. We were not expecting you for another few days."

"Ah." Miss Chadwick shrugged. "Is that all? What is a few days at a grand house like Helmsley Manor? Surely the household staff has prepared my wing in advance?"

Janet couldn't help but notice the tight set of Emma's jaw.

"Now tell me, dear Emma." Miss Chadwick nodded her springy golden curls in Janet's direction. "What is this abomination? Have you sent your stable boy home and hired a local farmer's daughter?"

Janet clutched her reins tighter, afraid if she weren't clinging onto the well-worn leather with all her strength, her hand might spring free of its own volition to smack the witch.

"Miss Chadwick, may I introduce you to our guest, my dear friend, Miss Jane Roberts."

Deep blue eyes flashed with an icy anger. "*This ... this person* is a friend of yours, and a *guest* in your home?"

Janet's fingernails dug deeper into the leather. *Calm, calm. White beaches, rolling waves. Relax. No strangling on Helmsley Manor property, remember?*

"Is this the way you ride where you come from, Miss Roberts?" Miss Chadwick asked, her eyes narrowing.

"Jane comes from Boston, and this is how she learned to ride."

Miss Chadwick's eyes were narrow slits as she looked Janet up and down, obviously not pleased with what she saw. She turned once more to Emma. "And your brother is aware of this savage behavior taking place on his estate?"

Damn it, just lie Emma!

Emma's cheeks turned red and she looked down. "Not exactly, no. We have been careful, riding in the fields so as not be spotted."

"Ah-ha!" said Miss Chadwick.

Janet watched the woman's eyes open up to their full, lovely shape. A triumphant spark of victory glinted in them.

In that moment, Janet realized everything would change at Helmsley Manor.

Miss Chadwick smiled at Emma. "My dear, Emma. It shall be our little secret. But if you allow yourself to be led astray again by such ..." she cast a disapproving glance at Janet "... foreign eccentricities, I may be forced to raise the issue with your brother." She turned to face Janet and the rigid smile melted from her face. "Miss Roberts, I imagine you can be trusted to curb your savage impulses, at least during my stay at Helmsley?"

Janet's heart raced faster; she felt her blood pressure rising. How could such a treacherous creature be trapped in such a decorative outer shell? The next few days would be trying indeed.

"Lesson learned, Miss Chadwick," said Janet in clipped tones. "Now, if you will excuse us, Emma and I will be late for the opening of the new tenants' school."

"A tenants' school?" Miss Chadwick's face twisted into a grimace.

"Miss Chadwick, Jane is right. Shall we ride back with you and I will announce you? When you have unpacked and rested, I shall be back. We can have tea together and chat."

Janet noticed the pleading tone in Emma's voice. Poor, sweet Emma would be stifled by a controlling shrew like Miss Chadwick.

Miss Chadwick smiled, and her face was once more a portrait of beauty. The sun had broken though a cloud and its rays shone down on their new visitor, setting her hair aglow in a golden light.

Had she no occasion to open her mouth, one might even mistake her for an angel.

"Yes, Emma, my dear. That is a fine idea," said the sweet voice in the carriage. "I am exhausted from my journey. When you return from your charitable work, we can sit together," she cast a quick glance at Janet, "*alone,* and have a long-overdue chat." She hit the side of the carriage with an imperious hand. "Driver! Onward."

Emma kept her horse still for a moment before loosening the reins. She looked Janet squarely in the eye. "Did I not tell you it would be challenging once Miss Chadwick arrived at Helmsley?"

The heat from the kitchen was sweltering. Janet swatted away a stray lock of hair that refused to stay pinned up under the kerchief. She set three papers before her, meeting the stunned gazes of the kitchen staff.

I have written the recipes down here," she said. "As for timing, we will have to work backwards. The *tiramisu* will be prepared first to set in the icebox."

"Tear-a-what?" said Cook, her eyes wide in her round, flushed face.

Janet smiled. "*Tiramisu.* It means 'Pull me up' in Italian, and it is a delicious dessert. We will make two so that you can try one at the servants' dinner. We do not have the mascarpone cheese it requires, but I will show you how to substitute with cream cheese, heavy cream and butter. It is not the same, but it shall have to do." Janet saw all eyes upon her. Everyone looked so nervous, but she needed to walk through the entire afternoon before they voiced their concerns. "The *abbachio alla romana*—the lamb served Roman style—is the second course, but it will be prepared before the first dish. We have the garlic, olive oil, rosemary, white wine and vinegar right here. I will walk us through that in a moment. Cooking time is one hour."

The kitchen staff exchanged nervous glances. Janet plunged on.

"The pasta dish is first—*pasta all'amatriciana*. Mrs. Rossi has provided me with the chili peppers. And we will substitute bacon. I have already stewed the tomatoes. They're delicious, though not exactly what we could have in Italy. And I have borrowed an instrument from Mrs. Rossi to grate the *parmigiano*. The sauce and cheese will be ready in advance, but the pasta only takes a few minutes to cook in boiling water, so it must wait until the dinner hour." She smiled at the nervous-looking faces. "Shall we review the recipes before we start with the dessert?"

Cook cleared her throat. "Miss Jane, I can see you have thought things out. And you know how much we've grown to like you here in the kitchen. But I still don't feel it's proper to prepare a dinner that hasn't been attempted before, especially as we now have ... uh ... a rather particular guest."

"You are referring to Miss Chadwick, of course." Janet sighed. "Yes, that was an unfortunate stroke of luck, but the food will spoil if we don't cook it. So she will be exposed to one exotic meal during her stay. I shall take the blame if Miss Chadwick is not satisfied."

The kitchen staff exchanged looks before Cook spoke. "Even if we took out the wine, the rosemary, the garlic and olive oil and served English lamb, Miss Chadwick would find a way to express her dissatisfaction." The kitchen staff suppressed smiles. "Let's go ahead with the Italian feast tonight, but tomorrow it is good, old-fashioned kidney pie."

"Thank you, Cook. Thank you all for helping me. Please review the recipes, and I will get started on mixing the mascarpone substitute."

Janet began mixing and directed Mary, a young kitchen maid, to mix the egg yolks and sugar. The kitchen was a heady mix of heat, sounds, yelled directions and sizzling pans. Janet and Cook walked around to the teams handling each course.

When the *tiramisu* was finished, everyone admired it. Both the upstairs dessert and the one to be shared after hours by the kitchen staff were placed in the icebox to set.

They began slicing the garlic and mixing it in a bowl with the rosemary, salt, vinegar, anchovies, and olive oil for the basting sauce of the *abbacchio*. Cook raised her eyebrows at the anchovies but hadn't argued as Janet had expected her to do. She and Mary were slicing garlic by the bulb. Mary looked troubled.

"Miss Jane, aren't you worried the smell will remain on your hands? Maybe you should leave that to me."

"Ah, I'd forgotten. But it's too late to fret now. My hands always smelled like garlic when I lived in Rome. They say all that garlic helps keep you healthy."

"The horrid smell scares the colds away?"

Janet smiled. "Something like that."

"Miss Jane, I have a cousin who started at the new school today. How did it go?"

Janet looked up from her chopping. "Oh yes, little Matthew. He told me. He's a sweet boy. It is all so exciting! All the children were eager to learn. And they are so adorable. I look forward to returning tomorrow."

As they prepared the mixture, others browned the lamb in garlic and butter. "Miss Jane," said Cook, "we are close to done over here."

Janet gave Cook the mixture to be added to the skillet.

Cook grunted. "We have everything under control. Should you not be in your room dressing for dinner?"

Janet looked down at her apron splattered with tomato sauce and oil, and rubbed a forearm across her sweat-stained forehead. She must look a mess. She'd live up to Miss Chadwick's expectations of dining with an urchin. "Perhaps you are right. But I want to explain the *bruschetta* to Mary. These should come out before the pasta. The tomatoes are chopped, the oil and garlic are ready."

Cook untied Janet's apron and shoved her out the door. "I still think it is an odd dish to serve as an *hors d'oeuvre*, but we shall manage. Now—be gone with you. Go wipe the kitchen grime and grease off you, and leave us to battle the garlic and olive oil."

Janet placed a rough hand across Cook's cheek. "Thank you, Cook, for all your help today." She looked up at the kitchen staff, so hard at work. "Thank you, all of you."

As she ran up the stairs, she heard Cook sigh. "Lovely girl, that Miss Jane. If only the Master could get it in his head to be sweet on her, rather than that high-strung Miss Chadwick, we would rejoice."

With a grimace and a shake of her head, Janet continued to run up the stairs and down the hallway to her room.

"Turner, you've worked your miracles once again!" Janet exclaimed as she sat before the mirror. Gone was the hot and sweaty kitchen helper. Sheer powder evened out her complexion, and she marveled at the elegant, porcelain-skinned lady who stared back at her.

Turner had reprimanded Janet for flinching when the hot iron was removed from the flames to create little ringlets over her forehead and above her ears. Janet wondered how many women walked around nineteenth-century England with heat-scalded skin as the result of grooming errors.

The hair in the back was pulled into an attractive chignon, held in place by a delicate headband with tiny, red silk flowers, perfect for the stunning crimson gown Emma insisted she wear. The color and the rich silk sheen suited her complexion perfectly.

"And," Emma had laughed, "if you spill your spaghetti sauce on it, no one will notice."

There was a knock on the door as Turner pinned up the final locks. Through the mirror, Janet saw Emma peek her face around the door. "You look lovely, Emma."

She did. The sky-blue dress matched her eyes perfectly, a delicate shawl draped gently around her shoulders. Her piled-up hair was a golden version of Janet's own.

A smile spread across Emma's luminous face. "And so do you. You shall look even more splendid wearing this."

From behind her back she produced a sparkling necklace with a large ruby. Janet stared at it in the mirror, gaping.

"Is that real? It's as large as a robin's egg. I could never wear anything so valuable."

Emma laughed. "But you must. To please me."

She slipped it around Janet's throat, the large stone cool against her skin. Emma brought her face closer and met Janet's eyes in the mirror.

"You were born for such jewels. It is only a loan. We mustn't have Miss Chadwick calling you an urchin now."

Janet sighed. "Emma, dear. Miss Chadwick will think me an urchin no matter what I do. I fear wearing precious jewels will only make things worse. I would prefer to just fly under the radar with her."

"Fly under the …?" Confusion flashed in Emma's eyes.

"Nothing, a silly expression all the rage in America."

"About the necklace. Please make your friend happy this evening." Emma walked to Janet's bed, sitting on the edge. Her eyes were downcast. "Help lift my spirits. I spent the afternoon having tea with Miss Chadwick, who lectured me about how the manor is not up to her exacting standards. One would think she were already the mistress." Emma played with a fold in her dress. "And now Sir John is expected to dinner." She took a deep breath. "Of course, I am pleased to see our neighbor. But it would seem Miss Chadwick is already anxious to be rid of me."

Janet crossed the room. She sat beside Emma and put an arm around her shoulders, just as she had always longed to do with a real sister during the lonely years of her childhood. If only she could absorb Emma's pain and leave her friend lighter.

She reached down and lifted Emma's chin up with her right hand. "Emma, we have a strange expression back home: *It ain't over 'til the fat lady sings*. I won't even attempt to explain the Wagnerian origins of that one, but it means you cannot give up. Do not let *her* dictate to *you* what your life will be. There are Miss Chadwicks everywhere, but we mustn't let them get to us."

Emma's big, blue eyes looked into hers, reminding Janet of the glowing portrait she'd gazed at daily in modern Bath. She couldn't let her new friend down.

"Now come," Janet pulled Emma up, "let us go down and conquer the invaders."

Emma giggled.

"And we have an Italian feast to consume. We will bust these awful corsets with delicious pasta."

Emma tucked her arm under Janet's, and they made their way downstairs. As she stepped into the drawing room, Janet could hardly believe the perfect hostess had been so distraught only moments earlier.

Emma's smile was wide and sincere-appearing as she glided into the room. "Edward! Ah, Sir John, what a pleasure to enjoy your company this evening. Word has travelled far about our Italian feast, has it not? Jane, please come here to welcome Sir John. Jane has been hard at work in the kitchen overseeing the recipes, so it shall be truly authentic."

"Thank you for the invitation." Despite his rotund frame, he executed a perfect bow. "I should not miss it for the world."

"Ah," said Sir Edward. "I had forgotten about our Italian feast. I wonder if it might not be overwhelming on Miss Chadwick's first night, however? But of course, Victoria is easygoing. Sir John, you are in for more of a surprise than you imagined. Miss Roberts has managed to shake up our household extraordinarily."

He glanced at Janet, a mischievous glint in his eye. Despite herself, her heart skipped a beat. *Stop right now. Bad idea, Janet. This is the future Mr. Victoria Chadwick, and the shrew'd kill you in a heartbeat to keep you from getting in her way.*

"Sir John, have you been hunting since we last met?" asked Janet sweetly. This evening would go perfectly, she vowed.

"How kind of you to ask, Miss Roberts. Why, yes …"

They were interrupted by voices at the entry hall. "Oh, Emma dear," said Sir Edward. "We have a last-minute guest. The servants have already added another place. Excuse me for a moment."

Emma sighed. "It is so tiresome to have a brother who is constantly changing plans without informing me." Her tone was light and jocular.

Sir John smiled. "I suppose things will be quite different when you are the mistress of your own household, Miss Emma. Your husband will be anxious to defer to your judgment on all household matters." He tilted his head and looked at her adoringly.

Yowza! Janet glanced quickly at Emma and saw her immediate reaction before she masked her astonishment. They were saved by the arrival of Edward, a guest by his side.

Oh, dear God. Can it get any worse?

There, beside Sir Edward, stood a beaming Mr. Bentley, also casting an adoring gaze on Emma. This was the surprise visitor Sir Edward couldn't have mentioned earlier? Did he want to kill his sister?

From the corner of her eye, Janet glanced at Emma. Her friend's hand trembled, a flush worked its way across her face. Would she faint? Quick as a fox, Janet strode over to her friend, supporting her by the elbow in what would appear to observers as a mere friendly gesture. "How charming, Emma. Our Bath party is intact once again now with Mr. Bentley amongst us. Don't you agree?"

Her friend's body trembled. Janet was certain Emma would collapse if she should step away.

But breeding trumped emotions, and Emma smiled and found her voice, despite her agitation. "But of course. Mr. Bentley, what a pleasure to welcome you to Helmsley Manor. I hope you have been well. And what of your aunt, and all our acquaintances in Bath?"

The wide smile appeared permanently fixed on Mr. Bentley's face. "Thank you, Miss Emma. My aunt is well, and all our acquaintances in Bath send their warmest regards. What a pleasure to be with you again. And with Miss Roberts, of course." He bowed. "I was so pleased when Edward extended to me the invitation." He saw Sir John by the mantelpiece and walked toward him. "Sir John, how pleasant to see you again."

Janet took advantage of the moment to whisper in Emma's ear. "Why don't we sit for a moment?" She led her friend to the divan. Poor Emma. Sir John dropping hints, the prospect of Miss Chadwick casting barbs, and the whole time Mr. Bentley sitting across from her like an eager puppy. The pleasant dinner Janet planned was poised to become an absolute nightmare.

Sir Edward observed the clock. "We should make our way to the dining room, but Miss Chadwick appears to be fashionably late this evening, as is her wont."

As soon as he spoke the words, Miss Chadwick appeared at the doorway. "Good evening, everyone. I do apologize for my delay. My maids have been in a flurry unpacking my trunks, and I was worried I would have nothing to wear."

Janet fought the urge to roll her eyes. Miss Chadwick appeared to bask in the room's attention. She stood regally in an intricate gown of fine white muslin and lace. Janet knew enough from her time in this world that pure white dresses such as hers signaled wealth and leisure. She flinched for the fate of the poor maids, if even a drop of tomato sauce should land on the dress. She suspected Miss Chadwick might flog them personally if any stains weren't removed to her complete satisfaction.

The low, square neckline of Miss Chadwick's gown displayed a revealing amount of white flesh, and the swelling of breasts under the fabric. Yet an artfully draped coordinating shawl, with embroidery and tassels along its edge, somehow made the décolleté appear less brazen. Her golden curls were arranged fetchingly to frame her angelic face.

Miss Chadwick's height was dramatized by an intricate turban and a tall plume that shimmered in the candlelight. How could the woman walk through doors with that appendage on her head? Janet looked down, and her eyes grazed her borrowed jewel. Now she understood why Emma had insisted. She must have known Janet would require something stunning to not appear shabby besides Miss Chadwick's exaggerated splendor.

Sir Edward found his voice. He must have been admiring Miss Chadwick's grandeur like the rest of them. "Victoria, it pleases me that you are not too tired to join us this evening."

Her eyes glowed as she turned them onto Sir Edward, her face all sweetness and light. Janet battled the nausea working its way up her throat.

"Oh, Edward." There was a softness to the way she pronounced his name. "I wouldn't miss it for the world. The chance to meet your respected friends and spend time with your dear sister."

Janet's heart stopped when Miss Chadwick's eyes fell upon her. The sweetness dissipated, replaced by a steely hardness in the deep blue irises. Surely their natural state.

"And your assorted guests."

Oh, tonight would be fun.

"Victoria." Sir Edward moved closer, placing a gentle hand on her shoulder.

Such an intimate gesture. *But surely this wasn't permitted?* Janet's mind reeled wildly. She was allowing the friendship she'd felt developing with Sir Edward to cloud her judgment. *This woman will be his wife. Watch your step and stop this ridiculous jealousy.*

"Victoria, may I present my neighbor, Sir John?"

Sir John bowed and Miss Chadwick executed a perfect curtsy. Janet had to give her credit for pulling it off with a plume the size of a giraffe's neck resting on her head. Few women could manage such a feat.

Miss Chadwick's face positively glowed. "Oh, Sir John. I have long wished to meet you. Earl Wyndham has spoken so highly of you, and your unparalleled prowess on the hunt."

Sir John smiled, extracting a handkerchief from an interior pocket to pat his ruddy cheeks and perspiring forehead. "So kind of you, Miss Chadwick. Such a pleasure to finally meet you in person. Your beauty is spoken of far and wide. And now I have the privilege to see such praise is justly deserved."

He was simpering like a love-struck schoolboy.

"*We* shall talk more over dinner, Sir John." Miss Chadwick tapped his puffed-up chest lightly with her fan. Her voice seemed to indicate the promise of intimacy, and hapless Sir John lapped it up like an obedient puppy. Miss Chadwick was clearly a master, even Janet had to give her that. "You must explain *everything* to me about the hunting season on the horizon. I have ever so much to learn."

Oh, please. Was she for real?

"And this," said Sir Edward, "is our dear friend Charles Bentley."

"Ah, Mr. Bentley. A pleasure."

Janet couldn't help but notice that her curtsy was not as low and ingratiating as the one she offered Sir John. Butter no longer melted in her mouth as she addressed him.

"I am acquainted with your aunt, of course. I assume you are relying on her kindness to host you here. Any friend of Edward's is, of course, a friend of mine."

Ice Queen alert. Gold digger in our midst. Sir John was wealthy and titled. Mr. Bentley was not. That Mr. Bentley, with his wit and kindness, was worth thousands of Sir Johns was irrelevant in Miss Chadwick's limited mind. These were the characters Jane Austen dissected so expertly. *Listen and learn tonight.*

The butler appeared. "Dinner is served."

There was an awkward moment when both Emma and Miss Chadwick approached the chair at the foot of the table. Hurt sprang to Emma's eyes, but Miss Chadwick placed one gloved hand up to her mouth and giggled in an Oscar-worthy performance. "Oh, Emma dear. How clumsy I am, and utterly confused after my long journey. Of course, my dear. This is *your* place." She gestured to the chair before walking to her own seat.

You are a piece of work. Making it clear to everyone it will not be Emma's place for long when you rule the castle, Janet noted.

Sir John rushed to pull Miss Chadwick's chair out. She sat beside him and at the right-hand side of Sir Edward, presiding over the head of the table. Janet noted the sly smile on Miss Chadwick's lips as she settled prettily opposite Janet and began to remove her long gloves, with the practiced hand of a vaudeville striptease performer. She had the full attention of Sir Edward and Sir John. Only Mr. Bentley, seated beside Janet, kept his eyes stubbornly fixed on his empty plate.

Dear Mr. Bentley, rescue Emma from this.

The footmen arrived with platters of *bruschetta*, and Janet's mood cheered with the colorful trays of toasted bread laden with chopped, bright red tomatoes, drizzled with olive oil and flecked with dark green basil. When she looked across from her, her gaze crossed with that of Miss Chadwick. Disdain oozed from her pores.

"Why, Edward. What is this? Surely this year's harvest is not forecast to be so disastrous that you are forced to serve us this peasant's feast?"

Sir John smiled and gazed on her adoringly. Janet may have misread it, but she thought she'd detected a flash of anger in Sir Edward's eyes. But if it had been there, it disappeared as quickly.

"Not at all, Victoria," he said in his deepest, most authoritative voice. "Miss Roberts nursed the child of Italian tenants of ours back to health when he had the measles. And for that, and Miss Roberts' work in opening the new school to educate the tenant children, the family has rewarded her with a basket of Italian ingredients. Miss Roberts has been hard at work with the kitchen staff, overseeing an Italian dinner." He nodded to Janet, a slight grin tugging his lips upward before he turned back to Miss Chadwick. "We did not know of your anticipated arrival when we planned this dinner. But I assured Miss Roberts of your openness to foreign cultures and cuisine, and your renowned flexibility."

Oooh, pushing it, Eddie. You'd forgotten all about the dinner yourself. Let's see how she extricates herself from this.

"Yes, well, of course. I am as easy to please as they come." She smiled at Sir Edward.

Janet fought the urge to laugh out loud. Miss Chadwick's gaze soon fell on her, and any trace of warmth was long gone.

"You are a woman of many talents, Miss Roberts. Nursing sick immigrant children, setting up schools for the peasants, cooking dinner. You must feel at home among your kind. Where exactly in Boston did you say you were from?"

"I didn't, Miss Chadwick." Janet offered a smile as insincere as Miss Chadwick's own. "But perhaps we can discuss it later. I can assure you the kitchen staff has been hard at work today, and I do not wish to delay our enjoyment of the *bruschette*."

"By all means." Sir Edward nodded to the footmen to serve. "And I understand we even have Chianti wine to accompany our meals tonight—straight from the Tuscan hills."

"*Buon appetito*," said Janet.

Across the table, there was an exaggerated sigh. "Please tell me we won't be speaking Italian tonight. I simply cannot tolerate that language. One seems to be singing rather than speaking." Miss Chadwick shook her pretty curls. "If one cannot speak English—and let us admit that anyone worthy of our regard, certainly does—then let it be a civilized language like French, even if their leader at the moment is anything but civilized."

Janet bit her tongue. Geopolitics seemed not to be the lovely Miss Chadwick's strong suit.

"Passionately said, Victoria," said Sir Edward. "But you will find our guest, Miss Roberts, has also lived in France and speaks the language exceptionally well." He turned to Mr. Bentley. "So, Charles? Does this remind you of our visit to Tuscany?"

"It does indeed. Applause to Miss Roberts and the kitchen staff. I cannot tell you how pleased I am to eat an Italian dinner once again."

"You were in Tuscany with Sir Edward?" asked Janet.

"Yes. We both completed Oxford the same year, although my Grand Tour was not as long. I joined Edward at the tail end of his stay in Venice. Do you remember, Edward? You had just bought your beautiful Tiepolo. I was the first to see your purchase, and teased you mercilessly about the scratch."

Janet spun to face Sir Edward. His blue eyes met her own. It was the same recognition she'd detected that evening alone in the library. *Do not think of it.*

"Yes, Charles, I recall everything perfectly. And I can report that, years later, I am happy not to have followed your advice— to have left the tiny flaw intact."

Sir Edward spoke to Mr. Bentley, but gazed at Janet. Her body temperature rose at his words and his eye contact. Could everyone else in the room sense it? Could Miss Chadwick? She turned away quickly.

"And, Mr. Bentley," she said. "Where did you go after Venice?"

His face broke out in a wide smile. "To Florence, and Arezzo, Assisi, Tivoli, Rome, and Naples. It was remarkable."

Emma laughed. "I remember Edward's letters during that voyage and how envious I was. I was still very young at the time, and I longed so desperately to be with you."

"If there were one single thing that could have perfected our journey to that stunning land," said Mr. Bentley, his eyes aglow in the candlelight, "it would have been your presence."

Emma's cheeks turned pink and she lowered her head over her *bruschetta*, concentrating all her effort in cutting the pieces.

Even Mr. Bentley's cheeks appeared flushed. Sitting beside him, Janet could hear his breaths quicken, and her heart soared for her friend. Emma and Mr. Bentley simply had to be brought together. Surely even stubborn Sir Edward could see that.

"I never cared for Italy," said Sir John, shaking his head. His loud, monotone voice filled the room. "No decent hunting on the Italian peninsula. A shame. Now Prussia, Bohemia. Those are worthy cultural destinations. Lots of game for a skilled hunter there. Why, Lord Atham says it's some of the best hunting he has ever enjoyed."

"What an ideal place for a young woman to be taken on her wedding trip!" exclaimed Miss Chadwick, apropos of nothing. She beamed widely, her perfect, white teeth prominently on display. "Wouldn't you agree, Emma?"

The first dish arrived in the nick of time, interrupting conversation. "*Pasta all'amatriciana,*" announced Frederick, the handsome young footman, placing their plates before them. He'd asked her at least a dozen times for the correct pronunciation, and she winked at him to signal he'd done well. When she turned her attention back to the table, Miss Chadwick was appraising her, before glancing at the departing figure of the strapping young man filling out his crisp breeches.

"My, my, Miss Roberts." There was a glint in her eyes. "You do seem on extremely *intimate* terms with the household youth … I mean, staff."

Janet fought the urge to leap across the table, lunging for the ridiculous skyscraper-inspired plume. The corset made calming, deep breaths more difficult, but Janet was becoming something of an expert. Ignoring Miss Chadwick was a Herculean task, but one she was determined to master. She smiled and looked around the table. "This is a Roman specialty. You sprinkle the parmesan cheese over the top."

"We are to pile cheese on top of this odd tomato paste-like mixture?" Miss Chadwick wrinkled her nose in disgust.

Janet was tempted to inform her making faces would bring on premature wrinkles, but she chose to keep silent. "I assure you, Miss Chadwick. It is most tasty."

The parmesan went around the table and they began their course. Sir Edward, Mr. Bentley and Emma were full of praise for the pasta and the wine. Sir John and Miss Chadwick remained sullenly silent, picking at their food like spoiled children.

"It's so *spicy*," whined Miss Chadwick, fanning one hand before her mouth. "I simply cannot abide spicy food. When I think of the *horrors* our countrymen are exposed to when they venture to India. Not only are they elbow to elbow with those backward people, with their lack of culture and breeding, but oh! Even the food they endure must be a source of suffering for our brave men who venture there! Curries and spices, and all manner of unthinkable foods. Thank goodness that England can have a modifying influence on those primitive, culinary traditions."

Sir John nodded along heartily. "But, of course, we must not forget all the wonderful hunting to be found on the Indian subcontinent. Wasted on the locals, obviously."

"How truly lucky the Indians are," said Janet. "Not only do they have the opportunity to welcome the English colonizers into their country, and to be enlightened and civilized by them, but they also have the added benefit of abandoning their varied, spicy cuisine in favor of bland lamb stew and mincemeat pie." Janet caught Sir Edward's eye issuing her a silent warning.

"How surprising, Miss Roberts, that you and I appear to see eye to eye on something. But it is not only a question of eating strange foods when one goes abroad." She glanced down at her untouched pasta and made a decidedly unattractive face.

"It's the whole issue of language and culture and … unsavory cultural practices." She looked to Janet's left. "Mr. Bentley, when you were in Italy, were you not disturbed by the excessive passions of its people?"

"Not at all, Miss Chadwick. It brought me pleasure to be in a society with a mentality and culture so different from our own. They are a warm and open people, perhaps influenced by their sunny, Mediterranean climate. Perhaps I suffered most my first weeks back in England. When I returned home, at first everything seemed so grey and joyless to me. I pined for the milder Mediterranean climate."

Emma's face glowed as she gazed on Mr. Bentley.

"Yes, yes," said Miss Chadwick, in clipped tones. "*Perhaps* I can agree with you that they are blessed with more days of sunshine than are we."

Very generous of you, Vicky, to agree that the weather is better in Italy than in England. Really going out on a limb with that one.

"Yet everyone knows that an abundance of sunshine produces a lazy and slothful people."

Where's the off button on this woman?

"I am not convinced," said Sir Edward, "that if you walk into the churches of Milan, Florence or the Sistine Chapel in Rome, that you are struck by how lazy and slothful were Raphael, Leonardo da Vinci, Bernini or Michelangelo."

"Yes. A valid point, Edward." Miss Chadwick sounded as if she were addressing a group of children. "Their art and architecture are sublime, of course. Proving that genius can emerge from even the most unworthy and decadent societies."

Is it my imagination, or is she fixing me with her psychotic gaze?

"But the tragedy is that one must enter directly into a *Papist lair* to view those masterpieces. I should categorically refuse to ever step foot in those dens of deprivation."

"Oh, Victoria," sighed Edward. "You are exaggerating, surely."

"Am I, Edward? Did you feel *at ease* being surrounded by all those hateful Papists?" Her voice rose to a decided level of hysteria. "One may pity them their ignorance and superstitions, but one does not wish to come into close contact with them." She turned to Janet. "Did *you*, Miss Roberts, feel at ease living among those ... those *pathetic creatures*?"

Janet took a slow and deliberate sip of her wine, enjoying its taste as it made its way down her throat. Thank goodness for the Chianti during a conversation such as this.

She took a deep breath and fixed the Plumed Ignorant One with her most confident stare, smiling as she might when speaking to a slow child. "Miss Chadwick, I assure you I never once felt uncomfortable among those ... *pathetic creatures*, as you choose to call them. Perhaps, however, my tolerance for and ability to relate with the savage race may have been aided by the fact that I, too, am a Papist." Four sets of stunned eyes stared at her. The silence in the dining room was absolute. "Of course, back where I come from, we prefer to simply call ourselves Roman Catholics."

Miss Chadwick looked as if she'd been slapped. Sir John's mouth dropped. It was Emma who spoke first.

"But Jane, you have been coming to church with us each Sunday. I simply assumed you were Anglican. Why did you never say anything?"

"I am your guest, and happy to partake in all household activities, including church services. I have been to all manner of Protestant masses, Orthodox churches, Jewish synagogues, Muslim mosques, and even Buddhist temples. I have no reservations about understanding how other people live and believe."

"Edward," Miss Chadwick finally found her voice, "are you not disturbed by this news? Are you willing to expose your sister to Catholic dogma and prejudice? What can your guest be teaching those poor, ignorant tenant children?"

Sir Edward's gaze met Janet's own and they observed one another in silence. This was not at all how she'd envisioned the dinner.

"Miss Roberts." His voice was gentle. "When you entered a Buddhist temple and heard their chants and prayers, did you instantly become Buddhist?"

"No, Sir Edward."

"And are you, by any chance, the direct envoy of the Pope, sent here to convert the masses at Helmsley Manor?"

"If I were the Pope's emissary, I would have the benefit of visiting the Sistine Chapel without the crowds, with Michelangelo's ceilings and Last Judgment all to myself. Alas, that has never happened." She caught his eye and saw a glint of amusement there.

"For that privilege," said Sir Edward, "I might even be tempted to become a Papist myself."

Miss Chadwick gasped.

"I believe I can declare with the utmost confidence that we are all safe from the dangers of conversion." Sir Edward looked away from her when he heard movement at the entryway. "Ah, what excellent timing, Chambers. I see our second course is ready. Perhaps we can put an end to this theological discussion and enjoy our *abbacchio*. I have not tasted this specialty since I was in Rome. Excellent choice, Miss Roberts."

The *abbacchio* and roasted potatoes received compliments, even from Sir John. Mr. Bentley and Sir Edward recounted their stay in Rome. A third bottle of Chianti was opened before the *tiramisu* was brought out. Even without the mascarpone, it was delicious. Janet felt the stays of her corset straining. Everyone praised the Italian dinner. All except for Miss Chadwick, who continued to glower at Janet from across the table.

When it was time for the men to drink brandy and smoke cigars and the women to retire to the drawing room, Janet's misgivings returned to her. She stood and took a deep breath, gathering her courage before stepping across the threshold.

Into the lioness' den.

Miss Chadwick's coolness was far more evident in the drawing room.

"Emma, come sit by me." She patted the place beside her on the divan. "I must not neglect you during this visit. You evidently need my support and guidance, my dear." She shot an icy gaze at Janet. "Now, tell me all about that handsome young man at dinner. I see how he looks at you. He can hardly keep his eyes off you."

A nervous glint shone in Emma's eyes, her hands tremored slightly. "Pardon, Miss Chadwick? There must be some misunderstanding."

"Ah, my dear, innocent girl." Miss Chadwick patted Emma's hand. Her ridiculous feather bobbed up and down with the physical effort. "Do not tell me you did not notice how that dashing Sir John admires you?"

"Sir ... Sir John?"

It was excruciating to watch the tremor in Emma's jaw and the moistness in her eyes.

"Oh, my dear. Your modesty does you credit. But you are ... though certainly not a great *beauty* ..."

Janet thought back to kickboxing classes and wondered if she were still capable of delivering a powerful roundhouse kick to Miss Chadwick's ribs while constrained by her whalebone corset.

"... you are what *some* men might term pretty, and, of course, so charming and well-bred. You and Sir John would be the toast of the county. At least until you had competition. That is, if wedding bells were to ring twice in your county."

The wench! Christ, even my brain is starting to sound nineteenth century.

"Miss Chadwick, I am afraid you are mistaken. I am only eighteen and not yet ready to marry, and Sir John is nothing but a friend of my brother's and a kind neighbor. There is nothing else, I assure you."

"You mark my words, Emma. You and Sir John are made for one another. Such a combination of wit and breeding, intelligence and culture. I know I am right. I *always* am."

What did Sir Edward see in her? Yes, she was beautiful, Janet would give her that, but even her beauty faded before her unpleasant personality, mean spirit, and appalling ignorance.

"Now, you there ... oh, Miss Roberts, apologies. Not a name of consequence that one would recall easily." She smoothed out the folds of her muslin. "Where in Boston did you say you were from?"

Damn. The question she'd been dreading. Boston in 1813?

Janet smiled sweetly. "Do you know Boston, Miss Chadwick?"

"No, I have never been." She made an unattractive face. "Nor do I have any desire to visit such a backwater village."

Thank goodness. "Ah, then it is of little interest to you. We live on Beacon Hill. My father is an architect and he renovated—pardon, built a home there, where he also practices."

"Ah, a tradesman." Miss Chadwick sniffled.

Spoken by a woman who spends her days berating servants, trying on clothes and having her hair dressed.

"Yes, Miss Chadwick. A rather talented tradesman. And I have been training with him in the hopes of becoming a tradeswoman in the same profession."

Miss Chadwick's mouth formed a large "O." "You intend to exchange *your labor* for *money*? I believe there is a word for that, although I blush to even think it, let alone allow it to pass my lips. Is there *no shame* in our former colony?" Miss Chadwick shook her head while observing Emma.

Oh, put a sock in it, Vicky.

"I am not sure I agree," said Emma, her voice meek but steady. "Jane is a talented artist, and she has improved my drawing tremendously."

"*She?*" Miss Chadwick nodded her head in Janet's direction. "But you studied with the esteemed Monsieur Lemaire. He has the finest reputation among ladies of a certain standing. It is extremely difficult to secure him as a drawing master because, of course, he is the best." Miss Chadwick fixed her icy gaze on Janet. "I, myself, studied with him. *Bien sûr.*"

Janet turned away to study a piece of sheet music, allowing herself to roll her eyes at Miss Chadwick's ridiculous remark. Janet had seen the exercises the esteemed Monsieur Lemaire, fleecer of upper-class families, carried out with Emma. The man was a fraud. A two-bit talent, if that. But if one aristocratic family sung the man's praises, all the others followed suit like mindless lemmings—and paid handsomely for the privilege.

"I do not agree with you, Miss Chadwick."

Janet snapped her neck around to catch sight of Emma. Her friend's cheeks were pink and there was a strange glow in her eye, but she was standing up to the dragon lady.

"I did not know any better before." Emma looked briefly to Janet and took a deep breath before continuing. "But I am not convinced that Monsieur Lemaire deserves his vaunted reputation. After improving my techniques under Jane's tutelage, I'm prepared to say Monsieur Lemaire's talent and teaching methods are simply ... *ordinary.*" Emma's hand trembled.

Miss Chadwick looked as if she'd been slapped. Her mouth opened in an unattractive gasp, the lofty feather bobbed wildly on her head. "I am *shocked* to hear such statements from you, Emma. I can see the dangerous influences the lower classes have upon you." She cast a withering gaze at Janet. "I must talk to your brother at once."

Where the hell were the men when you needed them? How much brandy could they possibly consume? Were they smoking all the cigars produced in Cuba?

The strength that allowed Emma to voice her honest opinions was fully spent. She sat silently with her head down, a former shell of her courageous self. Poor Emma stood no chance when eclipsed by Miss Chadwick's domineering personality. Now Janet understood what Sir Edward had hinted at, about the need for Emma to leave Helmsley Manor to make her own life. He understood the dangers, too, even if it was he who freely chose to invite them in.

Emma stood slowly and her face transformed into the pleasant, smiling mask Janet often observed her friend wear in company. How many times had Janet worn a similar mask entertaining her father's clients, or while playing the dutiful daughter at his side at dinners and award ceremonies? She and Emma were more similar than she would have imagined before her time travel.

Emma took a deep breath and fixed Miss Chadwick with her gaze. "Miss Chadwick, you are a valued guest at our home, but I think there will be times when we are not of the same opinion. I am afraid that our views on Monsieur Lemaire's talent is one such example. Surely we are two intelligent people allowed to have different views. I would request that you do not concern my brother in issues that do not require his intervention."

You go, girl! Janet bit the inside of her mouth to fight off a smile. Emma's burst of strength stunned her. Judging from the sour-puss look on Miss Chadwick's face, Janet wasn't the only one.

"I believe some music is in order." Emma glided to the pianoforte and began to play Mozart, the music that always calmed her.

Thankfully, the men seemed to have had their fill of brandy and cigars; they entered the drawing room.

"May we join you?" said Sir Edward from the entryway.

Emma looked up for a moment from the piano, but continued to play.

Sir Edward strode across the room and took the free spot on the divan next to Miss Chadwick. "Is this not pleasant? Ladies are so much more civilized than gentlemen. Here we were arguing like fools about politics, while you are simply content to be in one another's company, creating beautiful music for us."

Miss Chadwick's face took on a pinched look, but she remained silent.

Mr. Bentley hung at the edge of the room, sitting in a chair beside the entryway. Janet crossed the room to sit beside him.

"Mr. Bentley, Emma informed me of your impending arrival, but we did not expect it to be so soon."

Mr. Bentley looked up, but his smile appeared forced. "No, I found myself unable to wait. I anticipated my visit." He looked toward the pianoforte where Emma continued to play.

Sir John sat beside her on the bench, where he turned pages poorly. He must not have read music, since Emma had to nod theatrically to warn him of every page turn.

"Perhaps I should not have bothered," he muttered as he observed the pair. "From what I gathered from Edward and Sir John, plans are well underway to secure Emma's happiness." He grimaced. "Sir John is the luckiest man to walk the earth."

Janet heard the bitterness in his voice as he pronounced the last words. She shook her head. "Mr. Bentley, please do not speak so, as if it's a *fait accompli*. Emma has had no say in these decisions. I know she has no feelings toward Sir John."

"Poor Miss Roberts, such an outsider to our ways." Mr. Bentley shook his head. "Do you not realize? It does not matter what Emma wants. It has been decided between her brother and his titled neighbor. Now it only requires sufficient time to convince the bride."

She'd never heard him speak in such hopeless terms. Mr. Bentley was always so optimistic, witty and charming in conversation. His spark was disappearing as quickly as Emma's.

"Please cheer up." Janet heard the desperation in her own voice. "It won't do to have two friends with long faces." Her mind raced. What could she do? "Mr. Bentley, tomorrow at a quarter to eight Emma and I shall be at the stables." She was careful to keep her voice low. "At eight on the dot, we shall be at the beautiful little pond at the edge of the meadow. Do you know the one?"

Confusion marred his handsome face. "Yes, I believe I do."

"Be there, please. Emma and I will wait for you."

Mr. Bentley looked stunned, but he nodded.

Nineteenth-century romantic intrigue. How many times had she read of it? But did it ever work out far away from the world of novels? Might the famed Scottish elopement location of Gretna Green be an option if Sir Edward refused to budge? Janet had no idea what she was doing or whether or not she risked making things worse for her friend. But how could she be party to tearing apart a couple so clearly made for one another?

Tomorrow it would be. Emma and Mr. Bentley would meet in secret to come up with a plan. Praying for fair weather, Janet stood to make her way to the group.

Chapter 30

"Jane." Emma walked quickly beside Janet, the length of her riding habit gathered on her left arm. "I do not understand why we are riding this morning. You know very well you cannot risk being seen a second time if you refuse to ride sidesaddle. Miss Chadwick already dislikes you. Do we need to make things worse?"

Janet's nervousness boiled over and the words spilled out. "Do not be angry at me. I did not want to tell you in the house for fear of being overheard, but we are meeting Mr. Bentley."

Emma's eyes grew wide. "What? How could you arrange this?"

"I spoke to Mr. Bentley last night, and he was so distraught at the idea of your marrying Sir John. He seemed so ..." She searched for the correct word. "Lost. Hopeless. It broke my heart. I told him I would arrange a meeting. At eight. At the pond."

"Oh, Jane. How could you do such a thing? What if someone should see us? Just think how it will look."

"It will look like two people who are fond of one another, enjoying one another's company." Janet's voice was indignant.

"It is no one's business but your own, in any case. How dare others think it is right to marry you off to a landed neighbor who is so bereft of culture or interests or humor? How should you stand it, Emma?"

Tears formed in Emma's eyes. She hid her face in her hands. "I shan't! How can I bear to be Sir John's wife? But how can I defend myself from Miss Chadwick's reproaches if I refuse him? She will marry my brother and slowly turn him against me for my choice. And then where shall I turn? What would become of me?" Her sobs came quickly.

Janet hugged her friend. "Do not cry. Mr. Bentley does not want to see a tear-stained face. He wants to see the Emma he is so fond of, the one he fears to lose. Talk to him."

"I am frightened."

Janet placed a hand on Emma's cheek. "Will you not be more frightened if you do nothing? You are strong. I loved how you gave it to that horrible Miss Chadwick last night. You really shut up the old cow. I only wish you could have told her where to stick her ridiculous plume."

"Oh, Jane. What a wicked influence you are." She clasped Janet's hand and squeezed it. "And how happy I am to have you." She took a deep breath. "Now come along, make haste. Before I lose my courage."

Janet and Emma reined their horses to a halt at the pond's edge and waited. Neither said a word. The silence was punctuated by the occasional neighing of a horse or the chirping of a bird. Would he come?

"I'm so nervous." Emma's eyes scanned the distance. "Propriety dictates that I should not meet with Mr. Bentley in this manner, and yet I feel so desperate seeing my brother, and now even Miss Chadwick, insisting on my marriage with

Sir John, that it almost justifies my action. I do not know if anything can change, but I cannot always be so passive. You have helped me to be strong."

"I am not very strong myself. If ... I mean, when ... I go back to my life in America, I, too, must make many changes."

"Whatever those changes are, Jane, you shall succeed. I have full confidence in you. Now, are you certain Mr. Bentley wished to meet with me? The idea is so forward. What if he feels obliged because you insisted?" Panic shone in her eyes.

"I assure you, Mr. Bentley was desperate last night, ready to return to Bath. Before yesterday, he had no idea your brother wished you married to Sir John. I realized the two of you needed to speak in private." Janet heard the sound of distant hooves.

From over the edge of the meadow, a tall figure on a black horse galloped in their direction. The rider was a fine horseman, elegant in his saddle. He wore a top hat, but the glint of his golden hair in the morning sunlight was unmistakable. Mr. Bentley.

He reined in his horse beside the women and gave the horse's neck two gentle pats. "Good morning, ladies." He tipped his hat.

They nodded their heads in greeting.

"I apologize. Leaving my aunt's company at this hour was more difficult than I envisioned. Shall we ride on together?" He beamed at them.

Mr. Bentley must have been confused indeed to not have noticed Janet sat astride her horse. "Mr. Bentley, my horse is slightly nervous this morning. Perhaps I should stay a moment to calm him before I join you. Please, you and Emma ride on ahead."

"But Jane," Emma's eyes were filled with fear, "surely he'll be alright once we are riding. Please join us."

"I shall. Ride ahead to the meadows. I will join you there."

"Shall we, Miss Emma?" said Mr. Bentley, an eagerness to his voice.

Emma cast one last look at Janet, displaying a glint of uncertainty, before she and Mr. Bentley trotted off in the direction of the meadow. Janet watched their golden heads disappear over the distant hill before dismounting and tying her horse to a nearby tree. She walked the few steps to the pond. The water glistened in the sunlight.

What would happen now? What did she truly hope? That Mr. Bentley would ask Emma to marry him? That they would both forsake their families and live on ... what, exactly? What kind of living could Mr. Bentley make if he were cut off from his society? Would Sir Edward truly disown Emma just to teach her a lesson? On his own, definitely not. But if Miss Chadwick were to become his wife, it would certainly be the way things would unfold.

What had she set in motion? Janet Roberts, a twenty-first-century traveler sent back in time to ruin everyone's lives. The minutes ticked by. She tapped her foot, then began pacing back and forth. Nervous energy gnawed inside her. She'd never been able to function with so much stress, unless ... She glimpsed the shimmering surface of the pond. *Oh, what the hell.*

It was still early enough to ensure solitude. Peeking quickly around her and seeing no one, she began to peel off her riding habit. A few laps would calm her down. She'd dry off and dress in plenty of time. It was a risk, but the tension would kill her otherwise.

Sliding the riding habit off, she managed to unfasten her stays alone. All these weeks living in the nineteenth century had taught her a thing or two. After loosening her hairpins, she strode to the beckoning water, and dove in. As the water hit her face and enveloped her body, the tension dissolved instantly.

Each lap across the pond improved her mood. Swimming always did this. Back and forth, strong and confident: crawl, backstroke, breaststroke, butterfly. With each labored breath, her concerns melted away. The sun rose in the morning sky. Days warm enough for swimming were almost over, and with Miss Chadwick's suspicious eyes seemingly everywhere, she certainly wouldn't risk getting caught another time.

For herself, she couldn't care less. Miss Chadwick could hardly dislike her any more than she already did. But it was unfair to place Emma in difficult circumstances. As she flipped and executed a rapid crawl stroke across the pond, she wondered where the shame lay in swimming if a woman were covered in undergarments from neck to ankles, as she was now, with no men around to observe her.

Nevertheless, it was probably time to exit. She would have to dry in the sun and put on her riding habit before Emma and Mr. Bentley returned. Better to go out with a bang. She took a deep breath and raised her arms over her head to do the butterfly back to shore: arms overhead, two kicks, arms overhead, two kicks. Her muscles groaned with the effort. Her lungs burned. She reached the edge breathing hard, and emerged from the pond. Water ran in rivulets off her hair as she wiped her face. Stepping gingerly over the rocks, she reached the grass and extracted the blanket from her saddle pack. Drying her face, she gasped at the image before her.

"I simply *cannot* believe what I am seeing! A brazen harlot nude as the day she was born, her flesh on display for all passing male eyes." Miss Chadwick spoke from the saddle of her horse, her long skirts tucked modestly under her legs on the sidesaddle.

Confused, Janet looked down to ensure her undergarments had not torn or frayed during the exercise. But no, she was fully covered from her neck down. Only her ankles and wrists were on brazen, harlot-worthy display.

Nevertheless, she wrapped herself tightly in the blanket, pleased it was long enough to cover her entire torso. In her shock, she had not noticed the horseman beside Miss Chadwick. There before her, in his riding jacket and his fine jodhpurs that stretched tight against defined quadriceps and calves, was Sir Edward, looking incredibly handsome and worryingly severe.

"Edward, how can you entrust your impressionable sister to such a ... such a *savage*?" Miss Chadwick's cries echoed through the trees.

Janet's breathing sounded too loud in the silence.

"Miss Roberts," said Sir Edward.

Janet recognized the I'm-displeased-with-you-young-lady tone. She'd certainly heard it often enough these past weeks.

"Judging from your technique, am I to assume this is something you do quite often?" His gaze was sharp, the line of his mouth rigid.

"I have only been a few times since arriving at Helmsley Manor." It took all her strength to meet his gaze.

"And my sister? Has she joined you in your bathing exercises?"

"*Never*, Sir Edward. I promise you." Janet wrapped her blanket tighter.

"And you *believe* her, Edward? What has Miss Roberts ever said that is the truth? She is probably a spy for the Americans, here to pass on information to her country's ragtag generals."

"Victoria, please." His tone was terse. "Even if that were true, what strategic information from Helmsley Manor would help the troops across the Atlantic?" He turned back to Janet. "We shall discuss this later. Where is my sister now?"

Damn! Emma. Thank goodness being wet from the pond would mask the perspiration she felt breaking out across her forehead. How on earth could she get herself out of this? And what if Emma and Mr. Bentley came riding back together? Why was she always getting everyone into trouble? And now she'd managed to ruin her friend's hopes for happiness.

"Emma ... uh ... rode on ahead. Here in the meadow." Her voice sounded shaky to her own ears. "My horse was nervous this morning and I decided to stop for a few moments here. I told Emma to go on without me."

"Edward, it is clear that this ... this ... woman ... is incapable of doing anything in the correct manner." Miss Chadwick's face was red. Her voice grew more shrill with each word. "You know I *never* wish to interfere, but here I feel I am justified. I think it is high time this ... *person* and Emma were separated, and she is sent back to where she belongs. Do you not see how she can damage your sister? Your sister's reputation? And now Emma is out riding all on her own?"

"Please, Victoria. This is not helping to solve the matter at hand." He looked tired.

Get used to it, Eddie. Consider this a preview of your marriage to the shrew.

"Now, Miss Roberts. How long ago did you and Emma part? In which direction did she ride?"

Thundering hooves approached them. *One* set of horse's hooves. Janet released an audible sigh of relief as she looked up and saw Emma—alone—riding towards them.

Emma reined in her horse and Janet noticed how flushed her cheeks were. Emma looked from Miss Chadwick to her brother, her eyes as big as saucers.

"Oh, Emma," Janet forced her voice to sound cheery. "I lost sight of you at the end, riding in circles around the meadow.

How dull it must have been for you riding over such a small area all alone. I was watching you from the pond and timing my laps by yours. But you must have gone over the edge of the hill when Miss Chadwick and Sir Edward arrived."

Emma stared in silence for a hopelessly long moment, and Janet feared she was too stunned to follow Janet's lead. *Lie, Emma. For once in your life, tell a lie!*

"Ah ... yes. Bucephalus spotted a rabbit, and gave it a good chase. Miss Chadwick, Edward, what a pleasant surprise seeing you out here."

"Emma, we shall speak at home." His voice was firm. "Miss Roberts should not be standing out here all wet. Please help her to dress."

Janet heard the distaste with which he pronounced the last words.

"Victoria, shall we continue our turn around the grounds?"

Not waiting for an answer, he administered a sharp kick to his horse and trotted ahead. Miss Chadwick cast a withering look at Janet from over her shoulder.

This isn't over in her book.

Emma helped Janet to dress in silence, and the two women returned to the stables. Both were too stunned to speak.

Only later that afternoon did Janet manage to extract the full story from Emma. The two women walked along the path from the schoolhouse, where they'd taught a noontime lesson. The children were hard at work in this pre-harvest season, and soon classes would break during the harvest.

Once they were far from the tenant households, Janet turned to Emma. "You have not yet told me what happened between you and Mr. Bentley this morning."

Emma's eyes darted around her. She reached for Janet's hand and pulled her to a clearing at the edge of the path. Her eyes glowed with excitement. "Oh, Jane! Mr. Bentley—Charles—declared his love for me. Told me he's always loved me."

Janet wrapped her arms around her friend. The risk they'd taken this morning had not been in vain. She pulled back and examined Emma's face, the pink flush on her cheeks. "I am so happy for you. I knew it was true the first time I saw Mr. Bentley gaze on you in Sydney Gardens, and then that first walk we took together in Bath. I was convinced of his regard for you. And have you told him you feel the same?"

"I have. My heart has been bursting with happiness, but I have no one with whom to share my joy, except you, my dear Jane. Charles is so grateful to you. And so am I."

"I did nothing—simply arranged for two people to meet. Annoying Miss Chadwick in the bargain was simply the icing on the cake."

Emma stifled a giggle.

"But what will you do now?"

Emma bit her lip. "This is the vexing question. Charles wants to speak with Edward, get him to understand. But we both agree it would be better to wait until Miss Chadwick has left. We do not wish her to influence his response."

"That seems like a wise decision."

"In the meantime, we must keep quiet about this. Jane, please ignore Miss Chadwick's references to Sir John, as will I. It will be our secret."

"Oh, Emma." Janet took Emma's hand in her own. "You have made me so happy with your news. I shall bear the wrath of the dragon lady so much easier now that I know two of my favorite people are in love and, I am certain, one day soon will be together."

"Come. We must make haste. I have tea with Miss Chadwick and I expect a vicious scolding. I, too, shall bear her barbs more easily now that I know Charles' true feelings for me. Nothing she says will ever hurt me again." She pulled Janet back to the path and in the direction of Helmsley Manor.

Chapter 31

The moon shone through the library window, casting its mysterious light on the Tiepolo. Janet pulled her shawl tighter around her shoulders to ward off the dampness of the house. Summer was nearing an end, and the evenings had already turned cool.

She gazed up at the painting and felt the strange tingling in her arms and fingers. She'd felt it earlier, while speaking to Sir Edward. She'd stood in this room this very afternoon as Sir Edward upbraided her for her swimming escapades. As he spoke, an odd sensation swirled in her stomach, one she remembered feeling in twenty-first-century Bath before she'd scratched the painting. But Sir Edward had broken the spell, calling Janet back to their discussion, and the strangeness dissipated as quickly as it appeared.

Still, the uncertainty lingered for the rest of the day. When the house fell silent that night, she tossed and turned in her bed. Sleep refused to claim her. Midnight came and went, and eventually she abandoned the useless struggle and crept down the stairs.

In the dusty moonlight, she observed Apollo and Daphne, willing the feeling to return. She examined the faces of the star-crossed lovers, searched their eyes, followed the swaying form of their billowing robes, but the tingling sensation did not return.

In frustration, she sank down into the plush armchair facing the painting and closed her eyes. Breathing deeply through her nose, she felt her chest rise and fall with the effort. *Daphne, what am I doing wrong? Guide me.*

She breathed in deeply again, feeling her heartbeat slow. The clock on the mantelpiece ticked loudly, announcing each second. Janet startled to the sound of footsteps behind her, but when she turned the room was out of focus, as if peering through a fog. Had someone left a window open, allowing the mist to seep in? The footsteps came closer, and she held her breath. She squinted to see better. Approaching her was a white-haired man, in a familiar tweed jacket with corduroy patches on the elbows. She blinked twice to ensure it wasn't a dream, but he was still there. So close she could almost touch him.

With trembling fingers, she reached out to touch his sleeve, but her hand went through his arm as if it were air. She gasped. She must be dreaming. Sleepwalking, maybe? She reached up to her forehead. A fever? But her forehead was cool and clammy. She pulled her legs up to the chair and wrapped her arms around them. Her heart beat so wildly she feared it would burst from her chest. Is this how people had heart attacks? The kind where you heard, "She seemed so young and healthy, no health problems at all. We never suspected."

Her breath came quickly now. The man was mere inches from her, yet it seemed he could not see her, hear her, could not even sense her presence. There was something familiar about the man, but she couldn't quite place it. Her panic made it impossible to study him clearly. If she screamed, would the others come? Would they see this figure, too?

The man was reaching inside his jacket and slowly extracting something from an interior pocket. A knife? A dueling pistol? She saw the flash of metal and hid her face with her hands.

Familiar beeping sounds.

"Hello, Inspector Lander," said the man. "This is Miles Whitshaw at Helmsley Manor."

Mr. Whitshaw? Twenty-first-century Mr. Whitshaw? Speaking on a cellphone?

She gathered the courage to drop her hands and saw the familiar outline of his face. As her gaze dropped, she saw that he was wearing jeans and decidedly plastic wellies on his feet. What on earth was going on? A slow descent into madness?

"Yes, I think the caretaker was right. Must have been teenagers, but they don't seem to have broken in."

Teenage intruders?

"Well, yes, as you know, the caretaker is on crutches after his operation. To be on the safe side, it's better if I stay the night. I have the office set up off the drawing room."

Office off the drawing room? There's no such thing.

"Yes, the alarm system is on, connected directly to you. If anyone tries again, we'll catch them. Still think we're dealing with teenage pranks. But I'll rest much better when all this artwork is shipped off to the National Gallery. Thank goodness the Tiepolo isn't here anymore."

But it is, Mr. Whitshaw! Can't you see it right there in front of you?

"You, too, Inspector Lander. I'll stop by tomorrow to file the report. Thank you. Goodnight." Flipping his phone shut, he placed it back in his pocket and walked out the door. His footsteps receded across the foyer.

She stood, trying to ignore the trembling in her legs. *Remember when you were in this house and you thought you heard music from a ball? Remember your dizziness and the odd flashes? It was just before you time travelled. Could you be in limbo? Somehow straddling centuries?*

The idea grew stronger and it calmed her. The flashes and dizziness happened before. Was this flash of modern Helmsley Manor signaling her return? She stood before the painting, her hand suspended in mid-air. She could have been Bernini's marble Daphne, her hand was so still and steady.

Taking a deep breath, she pressed one finger to the painting's scratch. When the shock flowed through her body, she closed her eyes and bit the inside of her mouth to keep from yelling out loud. The pain ebbed quickly. Gingerly, she opened one eye.

Nothing had changed. She was still in the nineteenth-century library. She touched the scratch again. Nothing.

She made her way to the drawing room. No small office lay beyond it. *This is crazy. You're confused. Just go to bed.*

Heart pounding uncontrollably, she made her way up the stairs. She felt exhausted. Maybe it would all seem an odd dream in the morning.

After tiptoeing through her door, she blew out the candle and placed the candleholder on top of her bedside table. Pulling down the comforter, she felt grateful for the beckoning warmth of her bed. When she looked up, she saw a shadowy figure sitting in the chair. She opened her mouth to scream, but no sound issued forth. Her heart hammering double-pace, she edged back to the door. As she touched the handle, the moon broke through the clouds. The moonlight shone on the pale features of Miss Chadwick, sitting still as a queen, dressed in a ridiculously formal velvet and brocade dressing gown.

Her hand dropped to her side; she stepped forward. "Miss Chadwick, what are you doing here? Is something wrong? Is Emma alright?"

Miss Chadwick shook her head, looking exasperated. "This is not about Emma. Although your midnight wanderings around the house do much to endanger your friend."

"And you are here in my bedchambers because ...?" Why Miss Chadwick was in her bedroom in the middle of the night was beyond her comprehension. Having to face her during the days was torture enough, surely.

"Consider it a friendly warning, Miss Roberts. I heard you go downstairs, most likely for some amorous encounter with your handsome but ill-bred footman. I found it too loathsome to follow you and see such vice committed in this virtuous home, but I am issuing you a warning."

Her voice was measured and full of venom. Janet looked upon that face in the pale moonlight and saw traces of what it would one day become, following years of the mouth turning downwards, the mean wrinkles at the eyes, the heart hardened by berating servants and henpecking a husband and children who would never live up to her precise and demanding expectations. The dangers of a mean-hearted woman of leisure with nothing to do but fill her days casting misery on the lives of others.

No, she did not envy Sir Edward his choice.

"Leave. Leave now before you cast shame on this home." Her voice sounded vaguely menacing. "Before you endanger Emma's chances for a favorable marriage with Sir John."

"Why are you so intent on seeing Emma married off, when she is not ready?"

"*You* would never understand. A woman must secure a favorable marriage when the opportunity is presented to her. The occasion may not return, and men are not as patient as women. No doubt that is something that even you understand in your world. It seems that unwed females from your class background have a good deal of carnal knowledge of men.

Shall we word it kindly and call it experience?" Her lips curled into a cruel smile.

Janet opened her mouth to protest, but changed her mind. Strangely enough, Miss Chadwick had finally hit the mark. In Janet's world, women did indeed have a more intimate knowledge of men. Without even meaning to, Miss Chadwick had made one accurate observation, and Janet was too tired to argue.

"Miss Chadwick, you have insulted me long enough. I could not sleep, and went down to the library to read, hoping it would make me drowsy. I now long for bed, and I would ask you to quit my room and never return in the absence of an invitation." *And don't hold your breath expecting one of those, Wicked Witch of the West.* "I bid you goodnight."

She climbed into bed, turned her back to Miss Chadwick, and closed her eyes, listening to the swish of heavy velvet passing her. There was an angry click of the door as Miss Chadwick, unused to being dismissed, took her leave of the chamber.

I cannot stay here much longer. She may be a snake, but she's not stupid. She'll be the first in this household to figure things out.

Chapter 32

Emma and Janet sat on the blanket, enjoying the weak rays of sunshine. The days were growing shorter. There was a crispness to the air in the early mornings and evenings that hadn't been present only a week ago. The unusually warm start to September would soon come to an abrupt halt.

Neither woman was accomplishing much reading. Their books had been cast aside long ago in favor of conversation.

"I know this sounds terribly mean-spirited of me," said Emma. "But since Miss Chadwick has departed for London, I feel an enormous burden has been lifted from me."

"It's not mean-spirited at all. I do not possess your angelic nature, so I can honestly say, without one ounce of guilt, that she is one of the most infuriating women I've ever met. And I have known many of them."

"She is still a guest, and I will not speak ill of her, nor listen to others do so. Not even you, dear Jane. But I do wish she would relax more when she comes to visit. She always wants to run everything, and my efforts are never good enough for her."

"There is nothing you can do to please that woman. Do not exhaust yourself trying. Even her drama about having to get to town was unnecessary. Can you imagine with how many new gowns and plumed hats she will return?"

Emma laughed. "Her dressmaker is designing her gown for the Harvest Ball. I am certain none will outshine her, but she is clearly taking no chances."

"Has your brother shared with you news of his engagement?" Janet concentrated on smoothing the pleats on her dress.

"No." Emma sighed. "It is odd. He has made hints before, but during this visit, he doesn't seem to wish to talk about it. At least with me. I cannot decide if this is one of the reasons for Miss Chadwick's sudden departure—perhaps she believes her absence will make him realize he must act to secure her affections."

"I see." Janet looked out over the meadow.

"If he is to ask her, the Harvest Ball would be the place to make the announcement. This is the first ball we have held in years. All the prominent families in the county will be there."

"Ah, so soon." Janet felt her heart drop. But it couldn't be for anything she felt for Sir Edward. It was surely due to the fact that Miss Chadwick—already insufferable enough—would become the original, nineteenth-century Bridezilla once wedding preparations were underway.

Still, Janet wondered if she'd be at Helmsley Manor for the ball.

After her strange sighting of Mr. Whitshaw, Janet returned several evenings to the library. The tingling sensations did not appear all the time, but each time they did, the feeling was stronger. She often recalled the slow buildup of the tingling sensations in modern Bath, before her time travel. She hadn't understood at the time, but now she was attuned to the signs. Emma's voice startled her from her thoughts.

"Although my brother does not talk to me much about Miss Chadwick, he does often speak to me of you, Jane."

"Of me?" Janet's voice was a surprised whisper.

"He has so much respect for your work on the cottages. For Edward, asking a woman to assist on an architectural project was very much out of character. Yet he was intrigued by your upbringing. He is taken with your sketches, too. Said he's never seen such a fine hand, that you possess the clear eye of an architect."

Janet felt the blush spread across her cheeks. "He's simply saying those things because he knows we are friends, Emma, and he wishes to please you."

Emma fixed her with a stern gaze. "Jane, you know my brother. He does not believe in false flattery. If he does not believe it, he will simply not say it. Edward may be abrupt, but he is always truthful. A compliment from him is a compliment deserved."

Emma's words were true. Sir Edward often seemed harsh, but when he said kind words, she always knew they were truly meant. And those words never failed to make her feel proud. Even special.

"Edward has been most enthusiastic, speaking at length about your improvements, even if all the technical explanations make my head spin. He believes the changes will be a vast improvement for the tenant farmers."

Janet smiled inwardly. "He did not tell me any of this. I have mostly worked with Saunders on our project."

"No, I do not imagine he would have shared his thoughts with you." Emma fixed Janet with her gaze. "Edward is very much like our father. He keeps his true feelings locked inside. Even when our father admired something we did, we would often hear it from others, never directly from him. Like Edward, Father was so guarded in expressing his emotions and feelings."

Janet thought back to some of the most intimate conversations they'd had. Speaking in the meadows over Shakespeare, alone in his library the evening Sir Edward had shown her the scratch on the Tiepolo. Those moments were when she'd felt closest to him, when he'd let his guard down. And in subsequent conversations, he'd seemed to retreat from those moments of intimacy as quickly as he'd arrived to them. She'd assumed he'd been retreating from her, but perhaps his candor had embarrassed him.

"I see." Janet felt Emma's gaze upon her. She longed to change the subject. "Emma, as much as I hate to suggest leaving this spot, we do have dinner tonight at Sir John's. Should we not return to get dressed?"

Emma made a face. "Ah, I had almost forgotten. Yes, you are right. I am not looking forward to this, but duty calls."

The dove-grey muslin dress Janet wore was simple, but her face lit up as she twirled before the mirror and examined her reflection. She loved the elegant lines of its Empire waist, the full-length pelisse made of the same material, with its elaborate embroidery around the edges. The dainty jacket was belted high at the waist.

As day faded to evening in her new world, sleeves shortened and necklines plunged. Emma warned Janet that Sir John's house was often drafty. Janet was tired of being chilly at evening gatherings where short sleeves were de rigueur, so she'd been pleased to obtain a lined pelisse to keep her warm. But she still startled at the low bustlines of women's dresses. Never one for plunging necklines in her modern culture, nineteenth-century evening gowns seemed so immodest. How had this never occurred to her in her studies?

Sometimes she missed comfortable yoga pants and hoodies, but she was becoming accustomed to nineteenth-century fashion. Putting on such beautiful clothes transformed her, made her feel elegant and sophisticated. The corset was still as annoying as ever, but even that had become a habit. She no longer groaned in protest as Turner laced her up each day.

Looking over her shoulder, she winked to her reflection in the mirror and walked down the grand staircase. She entered the library, the meeting point before the carriage arrived. Janet knew that Emma was discussing ball preparations with Cook. Sir Edward would likely be speaking with Saunders. That left Janet precious moments alone with the Tiepolo to see if the sensations materialized in daytime as well, or only in the solitude of the night.

She sat in the armchair positioned before the painting. She examined every inch of the canvas—the blue sky and clouds, the trees blowing in the wind, the twisted figure in the foreground, Apollo and Daphne at the center, their billowing robes, the green sprouts budding from her fingertips. She squinted her eyes, and took shallower breaths, but nothing appeared to change. No tingling, no odd sensations, no dizziness. Had there been only a narrow opportunity? Was it gone forever? The harder she stared at Daphne's face, the more frustrated she grew.

"So studious." Footsteps approached. "How is Daphne today?"

Sir Edward materialized beside her. He sat in the armchair beside her own, looking elegant in his dinner jacket.

She was acutely aware of his presence. He awaited her response, but her mouth was dry.

Janet cleared her throat. "Daphne doesn't want to speak to me today."

"Daphne regularly speaks to you, Miss Roberts?"

"Not really, no. But there are days when we feel more ... connected. I don't know how to describe it. Apparently this is not one of those occasions."

"You are probably tired. Little wonder, what with your duties at the school, and all the assistance I know you are providing to Emma for the Harvest Ball."

"Yes, perhaps that is true. I had no idea the amount of work that went into organizing such events." *The ball where you will propose to Miss Chadwick.*

"Nor do I, to be truthful. My mother used to handle all the details, and now, of course, Emma is so competent in organizing everything that I must not lift a finger. And one day, of course, it will be handled ... well ..." He trailed off, gazing at Janet.

He's trying to break it to me gently—about his announcement at the ball. As soon as it's official, Miss Chadwick won't accept my presence here. Will I be back in my own time by then?

Janet sighed audibly and looked back to Daphne and Apollo, studying the faces of the would-be lovers who missed their chance.

"How melancholy you both are. Sitting in silence like an old couple, admiring their prized possession." Emma approached her brother and placed a hand on his shoulder. "I see you much more relaxed these days, Edward. All must be progressing well with the harvest."

"Yes, it will be a good year. But I don't believe my improved mood is solely due to estate work." He looked up at the painting.

Emma turned to Janet and winked. Janet knew they were thinking the same thing. The departure of the shrew to London brightened everyone's mood.

Sir Edward stood and Janet was ashamed to notice how nicely he filled out his britches. She felt a telltale blush rising across her cheeks, and quickly looked down to examine an imaginary thread on her sleeve.

"The carriage will be arriving. We should make our way to the entrance."

He stood and ushered Emma out. Janet hung back for a moment and approached the painting. Gingerly, she placed her index finger on the scratch, anticipating the tingling sensation she'd feel throughout her body.

But all she felt was a cool, hard layer of paint.

"And *this*," Sir John gestured proudly to yet another trophy head hanging on a wall laden with the weight of dead creatures, "has a fine story behind it. I shall never forget the day I felled this beauty." He stroked its furry neck lovingly.

Janet fought the urge to grimace. Every space on the wall was covered with antlers, glassy eyes, claws, and hides of various colors, textures and patterns. The spoils from the killing fields were proudly displayed on each of Sir John's numerous walls. How many hours must the servants spend dusting these monstrosities? Could Sir Edward truly envision his sister living happily in this macabre mansion?

"And this is the library."

The windows were small, allowing little light to enter. The furniture was heavy and dark. Looking around her, Janet was surprised by the dearth of books, but it was more than made up for by the abundance of dead animals. She shivered at the thought of navigating this space at night. Moose heads jockeyed with deer and antelope heads mounted on the walls. A brown bear stood by the fireplace, his claws ready to attack. An elephant's leg served as a makeshift table. A wolf crouched along the edge of the single, sparsely populated bookshelf. A cursory glance confirmed it contained weighty tomes on hunting and wild animals.

"*This* is my pride and joy."

Could he truly have some enviable first edition he was ready to show off? A Gutenberg Bible amidst the carnage? Janet found herself drawn to the conversation for the first time since arriving at Sir John's estate.

But no, he was indicating the floor beside his desk. "The hide of a Bengali tiger, given to me by my dear friend Lord Willer when he assumed his post in India. Extraordinary, is it not?" His eyes glowed with excitement.

Emma and Janet exchanged glances. The pinched expression on Emma's face concerned Janet. How her beauty, joy and kindness would fade away in this gruesome mausoleum.

Sir John's fleshy face grew red with excitement. His jacket stretched across his wide berth, the buttons straining with effort. "I keep telling Edward he should do what I've done and remove all those bookshelves to make way for hunting trophies. Too much time spent reading books is time wasted, I say. I'm a man of action." His beady eyes slid over Emma's slim form.

Janet fought the urge to vomit. What could Sir Edward be thinking? Sir John was a paunchier nineteenth-century version of her client, Tony. Instead of tearing down a library for video games, Sir John defaced this space with an Ode to Taxidermy.

Janet wondered if, back in her world, the Thomas Gainsborough paintings were destroyed now, replaced by digital wiring and a disco ball. And back in her room at Helmsley she had the sketches, that historically accurate, yet useless evidence that might have saved them.

Janet's shoulders slumped and she stepped backward and winced in pain.

"Oh!" Sir John's surprisingly effeminate cry filled the library. "Miss Roberts, do have a care! You brushed against my wild boar. An exquisite example, if I may be immodest."

Janet looked down into two beady, glassy eyes peering out at her from a solid, furry body. She rubbed her calf, which had been pricked by the boar's ugly, curved tusks. When she looked up, she caught Sir Edward's eyes upon her. There was no mistaking the look of apology she read in those deep blue eyes, although she wished the apology could instead be addressed to his sister.

"Shall we go in to dinner?" asked Sir John, taking Emma by the arm and walking ahead.

Janet shook her head and sighed. Sir Edward noticed.

"I fear you are not pleased with me, Miss Roberts."

Janet was ready to deny it, but then she looked around the room, with its oppressive weight of hunted heads and blood trophies, its lack of books and beauty. "No, Sir Edward. I most certainly am not pleased with you. Look around you. Can you truly envisage Emma at home here among the birds and deer and elephant legs and," she kicked the ugly boar in its abdomen, "ridiculous, tusked wild boar? Send her here and soon enough she'll start resembling these gruesome cadavers."

Now she'd surely face Sir Edward's wrath, but how could she stay silent and witness her friend's happiness dispensed with so easily? Tears blurred her vision as she made her way to the exit. In her haste, her shoe snagged the tiger skin's mouth, and she tumbled forward with a groan.

"Miss Roberts, are you alright?" Sir Edward knelt beside her.

"I'm fine. Terribly clumsy of me." She sat and attempted to push herself up, but the pain was excruciating.

"Do not attempt to move," said Sir Edward.

"Or what? The tiger might eat me?"

His face, so close to her own, broke out in a smile. His eyes lit up. He placed his hand on hers, and she felt a tingling throughout her body.

"Any number of creatures could eat you or peck your eyes out in here." He shook his head. "I have never enjoyed this library, even back when it used to bear some resemblance to one." His eyes met hers once again. "Now, where exactly does it hurt?"

"I think it is my ankle."

His hands reached down to the edge of her dress, and he grasped her hem upward. "Ah, I apologize Miss Roberts." His cheeks were flushed. "Might I examine your ankle?"

The nineteenth-century equivalent of ripping off her clothes and having his wicked way with her. Janet suppressed a smile. Should she blush and look as if she were struggling with such a forward request from a gentleman? Her acting skills weren't up to it, and the pain was too intense.

"Please, Sir Edward. I would be grateful."

Gingerly, he lifted the hem of her skirt, exposing her stockinged legs. In keeping with the fashions of the time, bosoms were on ample display, but the ankles were oddly intimate. He slipped off her shoe.

Cinderella gone wrong.

He lifted her leg slightly and touched the ankle, ever so tenderly. His touch caused a flush to spread across her face. She'd been here far too long if a man touching her ankle could have this effect on her. Or was it Sir Edward touching her ankle that had such an effect? Sir Edward, who was arrogant and infuriating. And soon to be engaged to someone else. Someone from the same century.

He caressed her ankle again, rubbing up and down in small circles all the way around the leg. She closed her eyes and attempted to distract her thoughts. How many hunting trophies did Sir John's house contain? Hundreds? Thousands? Perhaps she could count them.

Despite her best efforts, it wasn't working. Sir Edward's fingers were causing heat to rise through her body, in a far too familiar way. Exactly how thorough did this exam need to be?

"Sir Edward." Her voice came out hoarse. His deep blue eyes met her gaze and she feared she'd melt. She breathed deeply. "Surely you have had ample time to discover if anything is broken. After your massage, the pain has subsided."

"So I was useful to you, Miss Roberts." His lips turned upward. "I am pleased to report that the tiger has done no lasting damage. Your legs are far too lovely for even an inanimate tiger to attempt to hurt them."

He winked, and Janet was certain her heart had stopped. Sir Edward, flirting? He picked up her shoe and slipped it gently onto her foot as her heart beat wildly again. *Cinderella restored.*

"Even though it does not appear broken or strained, it would be best to keep your weight off of it." He leaned toward her, sliding one arm beneath her and placing one at her back. He stood as if she weighed nothing at all, cradling her into his solid chest. "I apologize for my audacity, but as you are a dear friend of Emma's, I thought I might take the liberty."

His face was so close to her own and his gaze so intent, that Janet felt breathless. She smelled his musky soap and felt the warmth of his chest against her body. Miss Chadwick may be a disagreeable person, but she was a lucky one.

"To the dining room, Miss Roberts?"

"I can walk, if you support my arm. I must be heavy for you."

"Not at all. You are light as a feather."

He strode to the dining room. Sir John's voice drifted out to the hallway.

"And this stag, Miss Emma, is my pride and joy. I shot him when I was just a lad—eight years old. I was, you can imagine, ecstatic. There's nothing more important for a boy than his first kill. One day, when I'm a father, it will fill my heart with pride to stand beside my own son when he fells his first stag."

Sir Edward rolled his eyes at Sir John's words. He grimaced when he caught her gaze on him. "You are still light as a feather. I only experienced a momentary cramp."

"Cramp, my foot!" She fixed him with her most scolding look.

"Is this one of your charming New World expressions?" He cocked one eyebrow.

They stopped in the hallway. Janet knew Sir Edward's arms must be giving out, but she couldn't miss this chance. "*You* were expressing your boredom with yet more hunting banter," she whispered. "Perhaps you feel that Emma is much more fascinated by such talk? And will be similarly enthralled for the next thirty or forty years?" She kept her eyes fixed on his.

"Do not push your luck, Miss Roberts. As light as you continue to be, I must set you down at once."

Sir Edward teasing rather than snapping at her? This was surely a new phase in their relationship.

As he entered the room, Emma turned away from a moose head. "Oh, Jane! Have you hurt yourself?"

"Miss Roberts is fine. Only a slight tumble. It is her ankle, but I assure you, Emma, nothing is broken. I thought it better she not put any weight on it. Miss Roberts, you may want to keep off your leg tomorrow as well. We shall call for the doctor. You do not want to risk being injured for the ball." He placed her down on a chair.

Why should he care if I attend the ball? It will be Miss Chadwick's moment of glory, and she would surely prefer me indisposed in my room.

Perhaps Sir Edward was truly not aware how much his fiancée disliked her.

"I am very sorry about your injury. Please make yourself comfortable here at the table. Tonight we enjoy a hunter's feast." Sir John rubbed his hands together in anticipation, a glint clearly visible in his beady eyes. "All our courses have been carefully prepared with game I have personally hunted on my property. This will be a culinary adventure for you, Miss Roberts. All the best game our county can offer."

Janet smiled as politely as she could. She caught Sir Edward's eye, but he remained impassive.

Sir John rested his hands on his ample belly. A film of perspiration glistened on his ruddy cheeks. "For Miss Emma, of course, it is not as exotic. But I hope she will appreciate that the bounty of my manor is very similar to what she is accustomed to at Helmsley." He fixed Emma with an expectant gaze.

Emma offered a tight smile, then dropped her gaze, busying herself adjusting the perfectly ordered silverware.

Later that evening, Sir Edward carried an exhausted Janet up the grand staircase to her bedchambers. "Pardon the intrusion," he said to a stunned Turner. "Miss Roberts twisted her ankle and she must keep her weight off it."

Turner's look turned to one of compassion. "Of course, Sir Edward. I shall fetch hot water compresses right away, if you would kindly place her on the bed."

Sir Edward met Janet's gaze. "With pleasure."

The glint of mischief in his eyes was unmistakable. Her heart skipped a beat.

"Here we are, Miss Roberts." He placed her gently down, reaching behind her to fluff the pillows, before sinking to the edge of the bed.

Surely it was improper to sit on the edge of the bed where she lay, with no chaperone present, but he made no move to leave. The flickering of the candlelight heightened the twinkling in his eyes. She felt the telltale tingling throughout her body, uncertain if it was some signal of time travel or something Sir Edward's nearness provoked.

"I will call for the doctor to examine your ankle tomorrow. I need you to be in perfect health for the ball. I shall expect a dance with you." He lay his hand against her cheek. "Good night, Jane." He stood and left the room.

Janet remained immobile, a tingling feeling of warmth lingered against her cheek. She couldn't remember how to breathe.

"Miss Jane," said Turner, bustling in. "Let me help you to undress. Cook is preparing the hot water bottle. Why, you're white as a sheet! We must take care of you and ensure you are recovered in time for the ball."

"Thank you, Turner," said Janet absentmindedly. She glanced at the door, still uncertain about what exactly had happened. Her voice came out in a whisper. "I wouldn't miss it for the world."

Chapter 33

Miss Chadwick sat at the breakfast table in a bright, crimson-colored dress with a matching military-style jacket she'd told Emma was all the rage in London. Janet couldn't tear her eyes away from the gaudy, shiny buttons and gold-trim braiding. She was certain this fashion trend would be doomed to be remembered as the bell bottoms of 1813.

"I understand you were indisposed, Miss Roberts." Miss Chadwick sipped her tea and cast a dismissive glance across the table. "What was it this time? Riding like a messenger boy? Swimming against the river current with the urchin children?" Her giggle sounded more like a snort.

"Not at all, Victoria." Sir Edward's voice was crisp. He placed down the letter he'd been reading and fixed Janet with his sparkling blue eyes. "This time Miss Roberts was hunting tigers."

From the corner of her eye, Janet saw the daggers Miss Chadwick shot her across the table.

"Ladies, if you will excuse me. Harvest time is busy for us all, and I must join Saunders in the fields today. I bid you good day."

"Edward, my dear," said Victoria. "Are we not to ride today? I have asked my maid to prepare my riding habit. I bought it expressly in London, and I am anxious to wear it for you."

Her face was sweet, but Janet sensed a hardness in her voice.

"I'm sorry, Victoria. I've no doubt your riding habit puts the Parisian ladies to shame, but the tenant farmers await me. I shall be eager for your company at dinner." With a quick bow, he was gone.

Miss Chadwick pouted unattractively. She sat immobile, staring at the empty door with a worrisome flash in her eyes. Clearly, she was not a woman accustomed to being refused.

"I do not know why I bothered returning from London at all. Edward is so wrapped up with those dull tenants. Certainly in London, people do not forsake moments of pleasure to pass entire days with their servants." She shook her head dismissively.

Emma caught Janet's glance, and a look of understanding passed between them. "Miss Chadwick, I apologize for my brother's haste. But surely you know this is the busiest time of year on the estate. The tenants count on Edward. He always participates in the harvesting. My father and grandfather did the same. It is a tradition for the men in our family."

Miss Chadwick shook her head, looking very much like a petulant child. "Edward has spoiled them. Those peasants ... *farmers*, as you choose to call them, work for *him*. They are lucky to have found their way into his good graces. That wretched Italian family, for example. Who else would take in Papists such as they?" She raised a hand to her mouth and gasped in impressive B-movie fashion. "Oh, that was truly unforgiveable of me, Miss Roberts. I beg you, do forget I ever said anything." She looked at Janet with eyes that appeared anything but apologetic.

"Rest assured, Miss Chadwick, forgetting your words will be something I shall do with great pleasure."

Emma looked down, and Janet swore she was stifling a giggle.

Miss Chadwick had been back at Helmsley Manor less than twenty-four hours, but in that short time, she'd made her presence known. And how. She'd complained to Cook about the previous night's dinner, she had the kitchen staff in disarray with her incessant demands, and she'd berated the footmen for having slightly scratched one of her dozens of trunks.

Since Miss Chadwick's return, Emma had a constantly furrowed brow, though she'd bitten her lip and remained silent when Miss Chadwick said she hoped that the "commoner" Mr. Bentley would not be attending the ball. "I know he is an old friend of Edward's," she'd told a stricken Emma yesterday, "but it is such a shame to lower the tenor of the event with such ... *such people* in attendance." She'd looked directly into Janet's eyes as she spoke the words, and it took all of Janet's discipline not to sock the woman herself.

"I suppose," Miss Chadwick sipped her tea and observed Janet, "that thanks to Emma and Edward's continued generosity, you have once again procured something to wear to the ball—at minimal expense to yourself."

Janet fixed her gaze on the cold blue eyes observing her. She took a deep breath. "Yes, Miss Chadwick. I am once again indebted to Emma, and I make no secret of it. She has ordered me a lovely gown for the ball."

"Let us hope you are able to get some use out of it." She sipped her tea. "I understand the footmen will be hard at work all evening and unable to dance."

Janet counted to ten, then plastered a fake smile on her face. "Some do not need to constantly draw attention to themselves." She let her gaze linger upon the nineteenth-century bling sparkling on Miss Chadwick's chest. "I am satisfied to be an observer, Miss Chadwick."

"That is convenient for you, Miss Roberts. Where I am from, we tend to call women like that wallflowers, but I like that you have tried to put it in a positive light. While in London, I did meet several acquaintances who lived in Boston." She glanced up and met Janet's gaze. "Oddly enough, none had ever heard of you or your family. Is that not unusual?"

Janet lowered her hands into her lap to hide the tremor. "That is odd, Miss Chadwick, although I admit I am infrequently in society. It tends to bore me. But my father has many prominent clients, and I would assume he is widely known."

Miss Chadwick's eyes narrowed. "And yet, he is not. Is that not singular?"

The clock struck nine, and Janet nearly jumped for joy. "Emma, our lessons. We should not be late."

"Of course." Emma looked at the clock. "But I shall have to return to my room to collect the new quills I ordered."

"Run along, Emma. Take your time. I shall play hostess and keep Miss Roberts company." Miss Chadwick smiled brightly.

Janet swallowed hard and tapped her fingers against her leg. She'd avoided Miss Chadwick ever since her return from London yesterday, but she hadn't missed the cold looks cast her way at last night's dinner. And now she seemed intent to close in on the kill.

Both women sat in silence as Emma's footsteps receded. It was Miss Chadwick who spoke first. "Miss Roberts, I have been kind to you because I knew you to be a special friend of Emma, even if I have questioned your influence over her."

Miss Chadwick's icy gaze held Janet in place. Her severe look would have been more terrifying had the golden, military-style buttons and braiding not caught the bright morning light, looking ridiculously garish.

"She will not require your presence much longer. Edward will announce our engagement at the ball, and neither of us wishes for a long engagement." She squinted her eyes. "One who gives away her virtue so freely would not understand, but when a man is so in love with a chaste woman, he cannot be expected to wait long to claim his prize."

Janet bit her lip and laced her fingers together. *I hope the wedding night is all fireworks, because your poor husband will be stuck with you the rest of his life. In comparison, the grave might hold some promise.*

"I believe you have monopolized Emma's attentions during your time with us, and it would be best for Emma and me to have time alone together—to learn to be sisters." She twirled the ring on her finger. "I hate to be unpleasant, but Sir Edward would never tell you to leave, even if it is what he most ardently desires."

You hate to be unpleasant, my foot.

"And Sir Edward asked you to convey all of this to me? It seems so odd when he specifically requested I reserve dances at the ball for him. Indeed, it was only the other day."

Janet regretted her words immediately. Miss Chadwick's eyes flashed with the aggression that must shine from those of a lioness about to attack her prey.

"No doubt, Miss Roberts, you *know* men far better than I. Edward is about to be married, surely some harmless flirtations with ladies of ..." she sighed "... questionable character, might occur. Do not flatter yourself it is anything more than that. Edward and I speak with one voice. It is time you moved on." She leaned in closer and lowered her voice to a whisper. "And besides, I have been checking on you. You are quick to dismiss the fact that no one in Boston seems to know you, but I have a wide circle of acquaintances, some of whom have resided in your Beacon Hill." Her voice sounded harsh. "I *will* find out about you, Miss Roberts. I offer you friendly advice and suggest you slink away before the ugly truth comes out."

Janet's heart beat frantically. Her throat felt dry. She struggled to keep her voice calm, to not drop her eyes from Miss Chadwick's intimidating gaze. If Miss Chadwick truly had acquaintances in Boston, surely it was only a matter of time until she was unveiled as an imposter.

After all, she was.

The thought of Emma and Sir Edward interrogating her was too much to bear. How could she possibly make them understand?

She fought the lump forming in her throat. "Miss Chadwick, doubtless you will do what you feel you must, but I will not be chased out until my hosts request I leave." She struggled to imbue those words with all the confidence she did not truly feel.

"Suit yourself, Miss Roberts." She smiled sweetly. "I was providing you with the opportunity for a graceful exit. A scandal will suit me just as well." She raised her teacup and took a slow sip.

"Ah, Emma!" exclaimed Janet, feeling like a drowning victim spotting a life raft.

"Miss Chadwick, I will join you later for tea. Jane, we should be off."

"With pleasure." Janet jumped to her feet. "If you will excuse me, Miss Chadwick." She forced herself to drag her feet in order to stop herself from sprinting to the door.

As she and Emma stepped out into the fresh air, Janet breathed a deep sigh of relief. The cool breeze soothed her shattered nerves. Mrs. Bennet had nothing on her.

Later that evening, Janet stood in the darkened library, her candle the only source of light as she examined the Tiepolo. Slowly, she reached her index and middle finger toward the painting's scratch and pressed firmly against it.

"Please, Daphne," she whispered. "It's time to go home. What shall I do if I'm thrown out on the streets? I'm sorry to leave—*very* sorry to leave—but it seems my time here is coming to an end. Help me, Daphne. I beg you."

She closed her eyes and breathed in deeply. After a moment, she felt an unmistakable tingling throughout her body, the same sensation she'd felt in those days preceding her time travel. She pressed the canvas harder and felt a jolt run up her arm. She stood silently, opened her eyes. The library was the same. When she pressed again, this time even harder, no tingling sensation returned.

Janet shook her head in frustration. It wasn't time. Daphne's pleas had been heard at her hour of need. Would Daphne, too, be prepared to save Janet when she called for her assistance?

Chapter 34

Janet prepared the same bag she'd had on her arrival to this world. Inside, she placed her copy of *Pride and Prejudice*, her cellphone with its impossibly dead battery, her inkless ballpoint pen, sunglasses, the journal given to her by Emma and, most importantly, the sketches of the Gainsborough frescoes in Tony's house. There was no mistaking the tingling sensation, and she needed to be ready if it grew stronger.

Since her conversation with Miss Chadwick two days earlier, Janet kept as much to herself as possible. It was easier to do in Helmsley Manor with preparations underway for the ball. The household staff were in a tizzy, preparing the ballroom, the food, and the decorations. Emma was exhausted from the preparations and the constant harping by Miss Chadwick that things were not being handled properly. Oddly, Miss Chadwick never offered concrete assistance. Constant complaints appeared to be her sole contribution to the preparations. Not surprisingly, Sir Edward was eager to stay away, assisting with the harvest and leaving the responsibility for the ball entirely to the women.

Janet tucked the prepared bag into her armoire and looked again at the ball gown laid out on her bed. The midnight-blue velvet absorbed the afternoon light flooding through the windows. The bodice was intricately embroidered with a silvery thread. Tiny crystals caught the light and shimmered brightly.

A blue sapphire necklace rested on her dressing table, the jewel the size of something a Russian oligarch's wife might wear in her modern world. Janet begged Emma not to lend such a precious gem to her, but Emma insisted. "I am so happy, Jane, and it is your friendship that gave me the courage to follow my dreams. Mr. Bentley has already claimed the first three dances. We must wait until Edward and Miss Chadwick announce their engagement, but then we shall tell him of our feelings for one another, of our desire to marry. If Edward will accept it, he could speak to Charles' aunt. Charles and I are so close to claiming our happiness, and you have been my staunchest ally."

She placed the necklace back down on the dressing table. Feeling a strange dizziness, she touched her forehead. She stumbled to the bed, using her last energy to push aside the gown before falling backwards onto the mattress. The tingling returned to her arms. Her head throbbed. She heard voices all around her in the silence of her room, the voices of young people, the ringing of a cellphone. She closed her eyes and balled her hands into two fists, pressing them on her eyelids in a useless attempt to ease the pain. The sounds were unmistakable, but where were they coming from? Taking deep breaths, she tried to calm herself. Slowly, the sounds faded, and the strange tingling ebbed.

She heard the door open. "Miss Jane, whatever are you doing there? Do not tell me you are unwell."

Janet opened her eyes to see Turner's round face looking down at her, concern in her dark brown eyes. Janet ignored her pounding heart and managed a weak smile. "I feel better now. Thank you."

"Thank goodness. Perhaps a spell of nerves. You simply cannot be unwell for the ball. The ballroom is sparkling. The room is overflowing with flowers, and the orchestra is setting up on the mezzanine. I am to prepare you so you can receive with Sir Edward and Emma."

Janet lifted herself up and shook her head. "I do not think that would be wise. Surely, Miss Chadwick would not be well-pleased."

Turner grunted. "Miss Chadwick is often not pleased. But Sir Edward and Emma agreed that, as their longtime guest, they should extend the honor to you." Turner bustled around the room, gathering items for Janet's toilette. "I suppose Miss Chadwick will soon enough be making all the decisions in the household. The servants are far more happy to enjoy one last evening in which you will assume that responsibility. You have made many friends here, Miss Jane. We all wish ... well ..." She blushed. "It is certainly not my place to say. I only want you to know we all agree it has been a pleasure having you with us."

Janet took Turner's hand in her own and gave a gentle squeeze. "Thank you, Turner. You have all been so kind to me. I fear my time with you may be coming to a close, but I have been extremely happy here."

"Now, now. We have a ball to prepare for."

Nearly an hour later, Janet admired the ringlets that tumbled down from her carefully styled hair. Turner pinned a delicate headdress into her upswept hair. Its blue ribbons and crystals mirrored the intricate designs of her gown.

Tucker slapped Janet's hand playfully when she tried to tug up the bodice of her dress. "Stop being so modest, Miss Jane. There is nothing wrong with displaying your endowments. Miss Emma must have thought the same when picking out your dress." She winked.

She twirled before the mirror as Turner stood behind her.

Turner clasped the sapphire around Janet's neck. "You look like a princess. Now go to Miss Emma and Sir Edward. They are eager to greet the guests with you."

Why, when Sir Edward will want to dispose of me so quickly after his announcement? Miss Chadwick would certainly have preferred me up here packing my bags tonight.

But she banished her melancholy. "If I look beautiful tonight, it is thanks to all your hard work, Turner. You have transformed me better than any fairy godmother. Thank you." She leaned toward the older lady and kissed her cheek.

Turner stumbled back, a blush on her face. "You embarrass me, Miss Jane." A smile spread across her face as Janet waved from the door.

Janet caught her breath as she entered the ballroom, truly feeling like Cinderella. The candles of the chandelier burned brightly. The recently waxed floors glistened. Fresh flowers were placed around the room, and tables boasted punch bowls and glasses. An orchestra was set up on the mezzanine, in clear view for the dancers who would gather on the ballroom floor. Her stomach fluttered. A ball at Helmsley Manor. The balls at Bath's Assembly Hall had been crowded, public affairs. But the chance to attend a private ball in such a grand manor was a dream come true.

The musicians placed their instruments down and left the mezzanine. The servants were no longer bustling around the room. Janet had the ballroom entirely to herself. She raised her head up to the chandelier and smiled at its beauty. Arms outstretched, she spun around and around until dizziness nearly caused her to collapse.

Strong arms gripped her waist and twirled her around once more. She gasped and looked before her. Two deep blue eyes met her gaze.

"I see you have started the ball before the guests have even arrived," said Sir Edward.

Janet struggled to stay in place, not wishing to appear rude by stepping backwards. Sir Edward looked down on her with those piercing blue eyes, a smile lighting up a face that was too often stern. He was dashing in his formal coat with tails. His broad shoulders and upright posture emphasized his fine build. His hands remained firmly in place on her waist, and she thrilled at his touch.

"Soon, this room will be filled with guests. Miss Roberts, would you do the honor of christening this ballroom floor with me before the festivities begin?"

"Oh, Sir Edward." Janet's voice sounded breathy to her own ears. "I am such a poor dancer. I would not wish to start the evening off unpleasantly for you."

"I assure you, you could never do that." He winked. "And, I know your secret."

Janet's eyes grew wide. She swallowed with difficulty.

"I have seen you and my sister practicing dancing in this ballroom many times. I know you have perfected the quadrille."

Relief flowed through her. "You were spying on us?"

"Spying? In my own house? I think not." He stepped back and executed a deep bow. "But my ... observations, shall we call them? ... have served me well. I knew I would wish to dance a quadrille with you before any other gentleman has even had the chance to ask."

Janet curtsied. "I'd be honored, sir. Although we are missing six dance partners."

"Good, then I need not envy the other three men when they lead you."

Janet peeked up at Sir Edward's eyes, but his gaze was as impenetrable as always. He nodded up to the lone violinist who had returned to the mezzanine, and Janet heard the musician tune his instrument.

As Sir Edward led Janet to the center of the dance floor, she heard the instructions in her mind. It was true that Emma had taught her well, but dancing with Sir Edward was as easy as breathing. He led so exquisitely. They passed by one another to their invisible partners, spinning and twirling with an elegance Janet would never have thought possible only a few months earlier.

But after they executed their turns and spins with their imaginary partners and she and Sir Edward came together, his hand resting on the small of her back as he twirled her, her breath caught in her throat. Butterflies raged in her stomach.

You're no better than one of those silly girls in nineteenth-century novels, melting over even the slightest glance from a handsome gentleman. Don't get your hopes up. After tonight, he'll be officially spoken for. I hate to listen to anything Miss Chadwick says, but this appears to be his attempt at bidding farewell to bachelorhood.

The violinist played his final notes. Sir Edward bowed, a lock of hair breaking free and falling over his forehead, making him appear boyish. Janet curtsied and reached out her hand, which he took in his own.

She startled to hear applause from the doorway. Turning quickly, she was relieved to see Emma, and not someone else, standing at the entrance.

"My dear brother. I do not know that I have ever seen you dancing so willingly with any other partner."

She approached them and gazed upon Janet. Sir Edward dropped Janet's hand, and she felt strangely abandoned.

Emma smiled. "Edward always dances as if he's carrying out a necessary chore. He must be partial to your dancing, Jane. However, I do believe our first guests are arriving. Shall we make our way to the entrance?"

An hour later, Janet's feet hurt from standing still in the receiving line as guest after guest passed through the door. Emma and Sir Edward received them all with a smile and a kind word, introducing Janet as their special American guest. Janet was stunned by the beautiful gowns, intricate hairstyles, and precious jewels worn by the women. For years, she'd read about balls, but the experience standing at the receiving line and seeing the guests pass before her was well worth the temporary numbness in her toes.

As the arriving guests dwindled, Emma announced they could make their way to the ballroom. Janet asked where Miss Chadwick was.

"Ah." Emma shook her head. "Miss Chadwick is biding her time. She will want to make a grand entrance when the dancing begins. That ensures more eyes focused exclusively on her."

They entered the ballroom, overflowing with elegant ladies and gentlemen. The side doors had been opened, and the guests tumbled out to the portico to drink punch and seek the relief of the cool evening air. The room looked lovely bathed in golden candlelight. The musicians were seated on the mezzanine, ready to play their first notes when commanded. Janet smiled as she surveyed the room. Her first grand ball. How her classmates in modern Bath would die of envy ... if they would ever know.

All at once, whispers passed around the crowds near the entryway, and people began to turn toward the grand staircase. Confused, Janet followed the movement around her, wondering what the attraction might be.

An old woman beside her lifted her face upward, a look of rapt adoration on her face. "Oh, lovely, simply lovely!" Janet followed her gaze to the top of the grand staircase.

There on the landing, Miss Chadwick stood, immobile as a statue.

One arm was elegantly draped on the mahogany balustrade, her head turned away from those gathered below, gazing at the paintings on the wall to her right. A silk fan was propped dramatically against her upturned chin. The exaggerated pose reminded Janet of the silent movies, and she fought the urge to groan. Still, looking around her, Janet had to admit that Miss Chadwick's penchant for drama seemed to have the desired effect. Everyone stood still, admiring her glowing image. Just as she'd planned.

Quiet gasps could be heard all around as Miss Chadwick stood stubbornly still in her puce gown—a strange purplish-pink shade that, much to Janet's bafflement, appeared to be coveted by elegant, young ladies of the era. Despite the unfortunate color, even Janet could agree the dress was lovely. An Empire-waisted gown, with an extremely lowcut bust and puffed, short sleeves that reminded Janet vaguely of the Disney version of Snow White. The bodice was encrusted with shimmering jewels that caught the light of the chandelier above Miss Chadwick's head. Had Miss Chadwick carefully arranged the blocking for this grand entrance with her French maid or some of the household staff, as an actress would prepare with the lighting experts before performing on stage?

The stones and crystals burst into light, an aura of heavenly illumination. Now Janet understood why Miss Chadwick had no desire to be on the receiving line, where she would never garner the captive audience's attention as she could with this Hollywood-worthy entrance.

"Victoria and her dramatic entrances," a familiar voice muttered behind her. "I never could stand them."

Janet turned to see Sir Edward immediately behind her. She felt his breath against her cheek. Their eyes met, and a look of understanding passed between them.

Sir Edward leaned down, his mouth close to Janet's ear. "I will have to dance the first three dances with Victoria. It is to be expected." He paused. "But I happen to know the fourth dance will be a quadrille. I wonder if you would do me the honor of being my dance partner?"

Janet's stomach somersaulted, but she found her voice, responding to Sir Edward while keeping her eyes fixed on the immobile Miss Chadwick. "I should like that very much."

"I am honored, Miss Roberts. Do not allow any other man to whisk you away. I shall be back to claim your hand on the fourth dance." He stood up straight. "It is now time to put a stop to this theatrical nonsense."

He strode over to the base of the mahogany staircase, the crowd parting to allow him to pass. Whispers passed among the observers.

"Victoria," Sir Edward said in his deep, booming voice. "What a pleasure to see you so deep in contemplation over the paintings you pass by each day without notice."

There were scattered twitters of laughter amongst the women gathered around Janet. The spell appeared to have been broken.

"Perhaps you might wish to join us in the ballroom? The dancing is about to begin."

It was a mere split-second, but a sneer marred Miss Chadwick's perfect countenance before she raised her fan delicately to her throat and composed her face into a more flattering look of studied surprise. "Oh, Edward. I did not see you there. I was transported to another world as I gazed on your art."

She looked down on the crowd and flashed a wide smile. Janet managed to stifle the groan that longed to escape her lips. Miss Chadwick aspired to the role of Queen; nothing less would do. Shoulders thrust back, posture perfect, Miss

Chadwick floated down the long mahogany staircase, her jewel-encrusted gown capturing the light during her descent. All eyes remained on her. Likely, they knew they would endure many such dramatic moments once Miss Chadwick became Sir Edward's wife. Watching the spectacle and displaying the proper awe would simply be the price of admission to the evening's festivities. And countless evenings afterwards.

On the landing, Miss Chadwick slid her arm under Sir Edward's. Janet felt a pang in her stomach when even *her* brain, so conditioned to dislike Miss Chadwick, processed what a handsome couple they made. Sir Edward and Miss Chadwick would be the toast of the county, the glamorous, glittering couple everyone sought to secure at their dinners, and balls, and hunting parties.

The hot tears pricked her eyes. She moved along the side of the room until she reached the open doors at the edge of the ballroom. Taking a glass of punch to the portico, she felt a sense of calm as the cool night air enveloped her body.

He is spoken for. He'll dance with you tonight to be polite to a guest and a dear friend of his sister's, but that's all there is to it.

Tonight is their night. The night they will announce their engagement. Your time here must come to a close.

Chapter 35

Standing in the moonlight, with the house illuminated behind her, Janet gulped the fresh night air, allowing it to enter deep into her lungs. She sipped the strong punch, shaking her head. It was even stronger than the spiked variety her classmates created at high school dances. Still, she was not one to complain about the strong spirits. The alcohol calmed her frayed nerves and quelled the tears forming in her eyes.

Footsteps approached her, and she made out a shadowy form.

"Why might it be that a beautiful woman stands alone, drowning her sorrows in punch, when all the gaiety she could wish for plays out just behind her?"

The man stepped from the shadows into the glow of light. His brilliant red uniform and its shiny gold buttons momentarily blinded Janet. If this were still the uniform across the ocean in the War of 1812 and against Napoleon's troops on the continent, it certainly made for easy target practice.

He removed his hat with a flourish and bowed deeply. "George Wickham, always at the service of young, distraught women." He stood straight, a smile playing at his lips. A lock of black hair dropped across his chocolate-brown eyes.

"Lieutenant George Wickham?" Janet's voice was incredulous as she drew out each syllable.

The sounds of the first notes of the orchestra drifted from the ballroom. Janet felt her heart racing. What was happening?

He broke out in a wide smile. "I see you have read *Pride and Prejudice*, too. Lieutenant George *Williams* at your service. I should not tease in such a manner with well-read young ladies. But the urge was irresistible." He smiled, displaying dimples.

Her heart rate slowed. The tremor in her hand ceased. She curtsied. "Jane Roberts."

"Ah! The Miss Roberts who hails from Boston! You are well-known in these parts. The name of Sir Edward and Miss Emma's long-term houseguest from America is on everyone's lips."

"It must be a rather dull neighborhood if I am the big news."

Lieutenant Williams laughed, a deep, booming baritone. "I should preface my comment by saying that no discussion centered on you could ever be dull. But I shall not argue with you that we are somewhat starved for good gossip in these parts. Your new school is another source of tittle-tattle. You've come to provoke class warfare, Miss Roberts?" His eyes twinkled.

"Most certainly not, Lieutenant Williams. I was only intent on helping a few talented children of the tenant farmers. They are eager and bright students, despite their parents' economic circumstances."

"I am certain they are." The lieutenant winked. "But I am not so convinced that Sir Edward would have been so eager to meet the unusual request had the suggestion come from a less attractive petitioner."

Janet shook her head. These nineteenth-century single men had a thing or two to teach their twenty-first-century descendants. They both turned to the ballroom, standing in silence and observing the dancing couples within.

"Miss Roberts, may I be so bold as to request the next dance?"

Janet smiled inwardly. She was so certain Sir Edward's charitable request, and perhaps a similar act of kindness by Mr. Bentley, would have been her only chances to dance that evening. After so much training with Emma, she was pleased for the opportunity to put her new skills to use.

"I should like that very much, Lieutenant." She took the arm he proffered and they made their way to the ballroom.

They stood on the room's edge and watched the dancers. A puce dress swirled at the center of the dance floor, its gems catching the light. The dancer carried herself as if she were performing onstage with the Bolshoi.

Tonight Miss Chadwick was on her way to becoming Sir Edward's wife. How many balls would she preside over in this very ballroom? Would she learn to love his Tiepolo and to speak with her husband about metamorphoses, and literature, and travel? Would she be at his deathbed in Huntington House, comforting him as he gazed on his Tiepolo and recalling the life they'd built together?

As much as Janet disliked Miss Chadwick, she did want her to make Sir Edward happy, and to learn to love Emma. For how could one not treasure a friendship with dear Emma, as she had been fortunate enough to do these past months? Perhaps Miss Chadwick would grow into her new role and be worthy of it.

The music stopped and the dance floor buzzed with activity, with some couples sweeping away from the floor and towards the refreshments, and others eagerly taking their places. Lieutenant Williams held up his arm and clasped Janet's hand in his own, leading her to the middle.

But not too close to Sir Edward and Miss Chadwick.

As they formed in groups, Janet observed Emma and Mr. Bentley taking their places across from her. Ah, so Mr. Bentley had managed to wrest Emma away from Sir John. Emma's creamy complexion was aglow in the candlelight, and Mr. Bentley gazed into her eyes as if no one else in the world existed.

Lieutenant Williams smiled upon her. "A moment of fulfillment before the dance begins? A fitting way to pass through life, I should say."

"Yes, I suppose it is. I was simply observing the happiness of my dear friends."

The music struck up in that precise moment, and Janet concentrated carefully on the complicated twirls and spins. Janet still wasn't much of a dancer, but the men led so well it hardly mattered. Janet passed expertly from partner to partner. She felt beautiful and elegant in her gown, with her hair piled up, a priceless gem grazing her clavicles, and her posture ramrod-straight. Her head spun as she made her way through the dance steps, hearing the swell of the violins.

Emma passed by her when she was handed off to Lieutenant Williams, and she winked at Janet and smiled. The women and men changed partners and executed their turns and promenades so expertly. Janet was so concentrated on carrying it off that she was stunned when the last notes played and she returned before her partner, who bowed deeply as she curtsied.

When the lieutenant straightened before her, he looked not upon her, but at a point beyond her shoulder. His eyes glowed with pleasure. "Sir Edward. What an honor."

"Yes, Lieutenant. I see you are returned to visit your uncle."

Janet felt her chest constrict. She turned to see him.

"I had requested the next dance with Miss Roberts. Might I disturb you?"

"Of course, Sir Edward. Miss Roberts is a divine dance partner." Lieutenant Williams bowed and took his leave.

Sir Edward and Janet stood still, facing one another in silence as couples came and went on the dance floor, in preparation for the next dance.

"Who introduced you to the lieutenant? I did *not* introduce you earlier." Sir Edward's voice was low, but harsh. There was a rigid set to his jaw.

"Why, no one. I stepped out for some fresh air and he began chatting with me."

"Miss Roberts, that is not the proper way to be introduced in society. He took liberties in asking you to dance." He kept his voice low. "Lieutenant Williams has a reputation for ..." He coughed. "... taking advantage of innocent young ladies. Knowing that you are my guest, no one would have introduced you to the lieutenant, nor allowed you to dance with him. If you had simply followed the rules, this unpleasantness never would have occurred."

Janet's cheeks flushed. First Miss Chadwick, then Sir Edward. She was tired of being on the receiving end of endless reprimands in this home. "But I am a grown woman, Sir Edward. One with a functioning brain, I might add." Her voice was quiet, but firm. "I have had dealings with flirtatious young men in the past, and I know how to conduct myself. I do not require your brand of protection from so-called unpleasantness."

The couples were all in formation, and the first notes sounded.

Sir Edward bowed and Janet curtsied. They stepped together and Sir Edward lifted her right hand above her head and swirled Janet. The butterflies did not return when his gloved hand touched hers.

"Miss Roberts, while you are under my roof, I will *not* be talked about." His voice had a harsh edge to it. "Your dance has set tongues wagging, make no doubt."

Janet was passed off to another partner and she took the opportunity to observe the crowds. Women were clustered in groups, and many were indeed looking her way and speaking to one another in animated gestures. But was it because she was dancing with Sir Edward? Or because she'd thrown the house into shame by dancing with the local Lothario?

As she joined the promenade line, she saw an unmistakable puce-colored gown at the center of a large group of ladies, gesturing with her fan in Janet's direction and giggling at comments made around her. Miss Chadwick had only been biding her time to rid Helmsley Manor of Janet, and now Janet had done much of the groundwork herself.

When she and Sir Edward were reunited, he took her hands and glided effortlessly through the steps. Janet felt hot tears gathering behind her eyes, but she was determined not to allow them to flow over. "Sir Edward, I am sorry if I have caused embarrassment to you or Emma. That was not my intention. I meant only to be polite to your guests. I do not wish to spoil this special evening for you and Miss Chadwick. I will stay a short while longer, and then I will retire to my room. I feel I have trespassed on your hospitality long enough, and I should start to make alternate arrangements." When she garnered the courage to look into his eyes, she saw only hardness there.

There was no chance to gauge his reaction, since she was passed off to the next partner. In the film versions, it always seemed so easy to carry out conversations in a quadrille. But she was learning quickly that there was a world of difference between dramatic reenactments on stage sets and in real life.

The elation she'd felt earlier in the evening faded quickly. When the dance ended, she allowed herself to be led off the dance floor.

Sir Edward sighed. "That did not go as I had hoped."

"Nor I." Her anger was eager to boil up to the surface were she not keeping it firmly in check.

"Perhaps we could go somewhere quiet to talk for a moment?"

His voice was soft and pleading, but Janet felt no kindness towards him. If all eyes were upon her now, what would happen if she left to speak with Sir Edward? And Sir Edward was so angry that a private chat with him would only end badly. She needed time alone to think.

"No, I have kept you long enough from your fiancée." Janet drew out the word, making it something ugly. "I feel a headache coming on, and I would prefer to be alone to get some fresh air." With a brief curtsy, she turned and walked to the exit.

People mingled outside the doors, but Janet stuck to the edge of the shrubbery and moved slightly further away, to a bench where she often sat when she sought solace, safely shrouded from the household. She sank her head into her hands. Taking deep breaths through her nose, she attempted to stave off the tears threatening to burst forth.

Things were going so well. How much I looked forward to this ball. And now what shall I do?

Her thoughts were interrupted by the snap of a twig. Janet sat up straight. She heard drunken laughter, safely relegated to the other side of the hedges.

"About time they held a ball at Helmsley Manor. It's been ages. Takes the pressure off me if they start entertaining again." A drunken snort followed this observation.

"John, you always were worried about your own finances more than the entertainment of your neighbors," said another man, followed by drunken peals of laughter.

Janet held her breath and leaned in closer to the hedgerow. The first voice sounded very much like Sir John. She'd seen him earlier with a group of men near the punch bowl, leering at Miss Chadwick and discussing hunting. How had he managed to drink so much in such a short span of time?

"Lotta good that's done me," said Sir John, his words sounding even more slurred. "Bad harvests. Poor management.

Too many expensive hunting trips. It all adds up, and now I risk losing the estate without an infusion of cash ... and soon."

"Too bad the lovely Miss Chadwick'll be spoken for by evening's end. I understand she's flush."

"Yes," said Sir John. "That she is. And she *is* a thoroughbred. Edward does not deserve her. He is not even a decent shot. A *real* man could show that racehorse a thing or two, break her in the way she deserves ..."

Janet placed her hand over her mouth, afraid to usher forth a sound.

"But I may have found another solution ... another golden-haired angel to come to my rescue, though ever less comely and pleasing than the hunting trophy I desired."

Emma less pleasing than Miss Chadwick? Emma as some kind of second-rate consolation prize?

"Settling down at last, John? I thought those pretty does arranged for during our hunting parties were enough to keep you satisfied. Hehe ... I remember those shapely twins at Lord Willer's. They seemed to keep you occupied all night long ..." The men dissolved into more drunken laughter.

Female deer as slang for prostitutes? A hunting bore even in his sexual banter.

"Why must that change with a wife? She will not accompany me on my hunting expeditions, so I expect the supply to remain as abundant and varied as it is now. Even better, funded by her silver. Aside from the financial benefits, it is also time I sired an heir. I have at least half a dozen bastard offspring scattered about, but what good do they do me? I need a legitimate heir, and Emma will do fine to bear me my sons."

Drunken laughter broke out from behind the shrubbery, footsteps receding.

Janet released her breath. Her whole body trembled. Emma would be married off to the monster, only to discover the truth before the honeymoon had even come to an end. And then what? Divorce would be unthinkable. Emma would be condemned to a life of misery and servitude. Financing her husband's debauchery, no less. And all because her brother believed the bankrupt Sir John to be a good catch.

A single tear slipped down Janet's cheek, followed by another. She wiped them away, but her body still trembled with anger. She was powerless to change anything.

"Miss Roberts, is that you? Do not tell me you are crying?"

She looked up to see the moonlight shining on golden hair, and she attempted to smile. It must have been a poor attempt indeed, for Mr. Bentley's face grew even more anxious.

He lowered himself beside her. "Miss Roberts, you have done so much to secure my happiness. Please let me assist you. Why have I come upon you so melancholic?"

She laughed and wiped at her eyes. "Melancholic. There is a word one no longer hears much in my world." They sat in silence and Janet took deep breaths, attempting to calm her nerves. Those nerves again. She and Mrs. Bennet grew more alike by the day. "It is Emma, Mr. Bentley. I am worried for her."

Fear flashed in Mr. Bentley's eyes. "But why? I only left her now. She is well!"

Janet nodded. "She is now. But I have overheard drunken Sir John's plans for her. You must not allow that scoundrel to marry Emma. You must do everything in your power to prevent it. He is no gentleman. He is only after the family's money." She turned to face him, feeling the tears well up again. "You must rescue her."

Mr. Bentley's face fell. He dropped his chin to his chest. "I suspected as much. There have been rumors of his debts, of course." He looked up, meeting her gaze. "You know how much I care for Emma, how I would strive my whole life to ensure her happiness. She is all I have ever desired. I will do anything to make Edward understand."

"You must, Mr. Bentley." She reached out to grasp his hand in her own. "Promise me. I am counting on you."

She startled to hear footsteps beside them. Rookie's error about how nineteenth-century balls worked. When she'd retreated behind the bushes seeking solitude, she hadn't anticipated it would be transformed into Grand Central.

"Well, well, well. What have we here? Lovers' promises in the shadows of the shrubbery? That seems fitting for your type, Miss Roberts ... and Mr. Bentley. Not the footman tonight, I see."

Janet looked up to see the puce color, so unattractive in the ballroom, appear even less appealing in the cool glow of the moonlight. How she wished to tell Miss Chadwick how unflattering the color was with her skin tone, but what was the point? The woman lived in her own delusional world of make-believe, where she was the undisputed center of the universe and the others mere bit players—existing onstage solely to adore her. Janet longed to retire to her room, but now she knew she had longer to endure painful conversations on this out-of-the-way bench.

Janet turned again to Mr. Bentley. "I have the feeling that Miss Chadwick's talk is meant for my ears only. There is no reason to keep you from the ball, too. Please go and enjoy yourself, Mr. Bentley. And remember what I told you."

Mr. Bentley allowed his worried gaze to flit between the two women, but Janet managed a reassuring smile. He bowed and reluctantly took his leave.

"Very intriguing, Miss Roberts." Miss Chadwick eased herself into the bench beside her.

Janet took pleasure in the knowledge that, with the stays Miss Chadwick must be wearing in order to be shoehorned into her dress, the pain must be excruciating.

"And a smile, too? You must be reliving special, intimate memories. First the handsome footman, then the local Don Juan. And now the neighborhood gadfly."

"Miss Chadwick, back where I am from, we have a lovely expression to use in instances like this. 'Put a sock in it.' I hope you can garner the meaning without a lengthy explanation from my side. For someone who claims to be so virtuous, you seem to constantly have your mind in the gutter. Mr. Bentley and I were not meeting in a lovers' tryst. We are two friends discussing matters that do not concern you, and you had no right to eavesdrop."

"My, my! Someone has a bee in her bonnet this evening. *Everything* that happens in this household, where I will soon be mistress, concerns me. And you are determined to be a thorn in my side as long as you insist on staying here."

"No, please, Miss Chadwick. Do not feel the need to mince words with niceties. Speak candidly, I beg you." Anger boiled within.

"Are you insane, Miss Roberts? That would explain so many things."

"No, Miss Chadwick. I am not. I am simply exhausted, and I came here to seek solace. Let's cut to the chase, shall we? Have you come to simply insult me, or do you have something specific you wish to discuss?"

"The topic I wish to discuss is your immediate departure. Tonight, Sir Edward will announce our engagement. Not surprisingly, I wish the focus to be on us and the anticipation of our spectacular wedding, not on why some visitor continues to linger on in our home. I know that everyone is talking about you." She made an unattractive face. "And, frankly, they should all be talking about *me* ..."

Janet stared carefully into Miss Chadwick's eyes. Her type would not change over the centuries. The model for self-centered people remained essentially the same, even if the era of internet and worldwide social media promotion may have made things even worse in recent years. That is why Jane Austen's social commentary still read so well, even in her modern world.

"Miss Chadwick, there is not much going on here. People will certainly be fascinated for a period of time when your engagement is announced. Then there will be the wedding to plan and the first rounds of visits to make. But what then?" Janet knew she might only make things worse, but her frustrations had been pent up for so long. What harm could it do now if she tried to pry open that closed brain of the silly woman sitting beside her in her silks and jewels? "What will keep you happy once you are no longer the belle of the ball? Will Sir Edward be enough for you then? Will you take any pleasure in his sister's company? Try to appreciate Emma for the gentle, kind soul that she is? Will you ever learn to look *beyond* yourself and take an interest in others?"

Janet saw a slight change in the haughty face beside her. It was a momentary shift in expression, an odd glint to the eyes, a softness perhaps, but she was certain she'd witnessed it.

Miss Chadwick squinted and the telltale, hard glint returned to her eyes. There was no longer any chink in her armor. "Do not worry for me, Miss Roberts. I shall be fine. I always am. Let us cut to this chase you were talking about." She reached inside the bodice of her dress and extracted a letter. "I received this missive only this morning from my dear friend, Lord Alton. He has spent much time in Boston and has many friends and acquaintances there."

She extracted the letter from its envelope and opened it. Janet caught sight of the gorgeous penmanship. These lords and ladies may have left her skeptical on most matters, but their handwriting never failed to impress.

"Ah, yes, this is the part that refers to you." She looked up and her eyes sparkled with mirth. "'I am well-acquainted with Beacon Hill, having lived there for fifteen years. With the outbreak of War, I was forced to return to London and my home now remains empty, and, judging by the avaricious nature of our former colonists, has by now most likely been looted and destroyed. But I am most certain that there is no resident tradesman by the name of Richard Roberts who builds houses, and no daughter with the name of Jane Roberts. That class of people simply do not reside in such an elegant part of town. I can assure you that I would never have chosen to build my home side-by-side with tradesmen. I can only assume that your Miss Roberts is some type of imposter. Perhaps a clever daughter of a haberdasher or a milk delivery man, trying to rise above her station in life. I am willing to corroborate my story with Sir Edward, and to provide him the names of many of my former neighbors, who can all vouch for the accuracy of my statements.'"

She sat quietly, folding up her letter. A spark of triumph glistened in her eyes. Janet's heart beat frantically.

"I will not waste time asking how you can explain this letter. Your type lives by deception."

Janet's voice was low and measured. "You would not understand."

"No." She shook her head. "I would not. I will not ruin the mood of this festive evening and its anticipated announcement with such sordid news. I will, however, issue a warning, which you will follow. You will go up to your room and pack the few belongings that are yours." Her voice was calm and authoritative. Miss Chadwick hit her stride when issuing orders. "You will leave all the gowns, and jewels, and generous gifts that Emma and Edward have bestowed upon you under false pretenses. You will make your way to the stables, where

I have generously arranged for my coach to await your arrival. The coachman is under orders to take you wherever you wish to go. This is far more than you are owed, but I am willing to be generous, since I wish to have you out of my sight at once."

She stood and paced back and forth before the bench. The moonlight bathed her in a cool light. Her voice was firm and precise. Janet couldn't tear her eyes away.

"You will tell no one. You will not speak to Emma or Edward. A quill and paper await you in your room. You will draft a letter of thanks to your hosts, with the envelope unsealed. I will personally review the contents of that note this evening. If anything is amiss, I shall shred the letter and you will have escaped like a thief in the night. By tomorrow morning, Emma and Edward will be apprised of the contents of Lord Alton's correspondence to me, so your farewell note is your only opportunity to beg for their forgiveness for your obvious deception."

"You have everything figured out, don't you? I am not sure you have ever impressed me more than you have this evening," said Janet, her words belying the fear that gnawed at her insides. But her admiration was real. In her modern world, Miss Chadwick, with the benefit of a broader education, could be the CEO of a multinational corporation or a politician. Most certainly a politician.

"From a swindler like you, I shall take that as a compliment, Miss Roberts. If that is even your real name." She ushered a deep-throated laugh. "I have long been bored with your little saint routine—nursing the sick, befriending the kitchen staff, rebuilding the cottages, teaching the filthy, ignorant tenant children to believe they are above their station in life. It amuses me to think that all your hard work was in vain. People will remember you for the charlatan you are, not the saintly image you have tried to construct for yourself."

Janet felt the telltale tingling in her hands and legs. She needed to make her way to her room and then down to the library. With any luck, she would not require Miss Chadwick's carriage at all this evening.

Janet stood. "I bid you farewell, Miss Chadwick. But you are mistaken in analyzing everything from your own narrow and self-absorbed worldview. I undertook none of those activities in the hopes that people would think well of me. I acted out of a sense of respect and love for others, and the genuine belief that my humble talents could make a difference to those less fortunate than I. It saddens me that you will never experience that sense of fulfillment in your life, that spirit of generosity and true friendship that makes this life—in whichever century we find ourselves—worth living." She took a deep breath and her voice took on a gentler tone. "Until I arrived here, I am not certain I fully understood it myself."

Miss Chadwick shook her head, her curls bouncing with the effort. Her countenance was dismissive. "Do not waste your pity on me, Miss Roberts. I have no use for such a sentiment from the likes of you."

Janet took a deep breath. "I beg to differ. I think you do. Goodnight, Miss Chadwick, and farewell." She executed the sloppiest curtsy she could manage and turned on her heel, racing towards the manor house as quickly as her gown would allow.

The tingling grew stronger with each step.

Chapter 36

Janet banged her leg against the bedpost and winced in pain. With almost each of the manor home's candles burning in the ballroom, only one small candle remained for her room. She removed her carry bag from the armoire and made her way to the desk, where Miss Chadwick had laid out a paper and quill.

She sat silently before the paper. What could she say? How could she express her gratitude, explain how much she'd valued her time with Emma and Sir Edward? How could she let them know how much she'd miss them, how much she'd longed to stay?

She picked up the quill and dipped it into the inkwell. She chewed her lip, worried about penning lines that would meet with Miss Chadwick's approval. Finally placing quill to paper, she wrote.

Dearest Emma and Sir Edward,

Thank you for welcoming me into your world. Not a day shall pass in which I will not think of the precious time spent with you. Thank you for your kindness and friendship.

With love,

Jane

Her arms began to tingle. Placing the quill down, she picked up the bag she had already prepared. It was time. She couldn't risk the moment passing.

With a last look around the room, she raised the candleholder high and made her way through the hallways. The halls were dark, but the weak circle of light guided her. The velvet of her gown brushed against her legs as she wound through the familiar corridors and crept quietly down a back servants' staircase, where she was less likely to be spotted. A distant piano was playing in the ballroom. *Voi che sapete.* A lull in the dancing.

The tingling grew stronger and she longed to reach the library. With each step, the sensation increased. Finally, her hand reached out for the door. Her fingers closed around the doorknob and she pushed it open in one decisive move. More cautiously, she pulled it closed behind her, afraid to make noise that could attract attention.

Once inside, her eyes slowly adjusted to the dark. The curtains were partially drawn. Better to leave them that way. She approached the painting with her weak candlelight. As she drew nearer, she made out the familiar images. The flowing pink and yellow cloth. The alabaster skin. The sprouts of green breaking through Daphne's fingertips. Her heartbeat calmed, her breathing slowed. She placed her index finger on the scratch. No tingling began, but a sense of peace enveloped her.

She heard stirring behind her, spun around. On the chair sat a shadowy figure. A man. He stood, his tall form undefined in the poorly lit room. He strode towards her, but something impaired her vision. She saw his face as if through a fog.

Yet still, she'd never mistake this man for another. As he approached, her heart fluttered, as it often did in his presence. As it did in the dream before she'd even met him. It was his painting with the scratch she'd inflicted that led her here. It was his face that caused her comfort in her dreams.

Now she would never see him again, except as an inanimate painting on the wall of Huntington House. A single tear slipped down her cheek.

"Jane, do not cry."

Sir Edward stood before her. He reached out and held her arms. She felt the telltale jolt of electricity. She bit her bottom lip.

"Victoria tells me you are leaving us. That it is a very complicated matter and an explanation will have to wait until tomorrow. I could not find you in the ballroom, but I knew you would not leave before visiting our favorite painting. I have been waiting for you."

Our favorite painting. And now we will both gaze on it, two hundred years apart.

He breathed in deeply and his strong hands steadied her. His eyes were so intense. They never strayed from her own.

"Jane, I must give you something."

He removed his hands from her arms and she felt the absence of his touch. He picked up a volume at his desk and returned to her side.

"I have a present for you."

She held the leather volume in her hands. Lifting it closer, she delighted in the scent of new leather, and read the cover page in the dim light. She furrowed her brow and looked up at him quizzically. "*Pride and Prejudice*? But I thought you disliked such frivolous novels."

"I did. But I read it and, although I dislike to admit it, you were right and I was wrong. It is well-written and witty. I devoured it in sittings here in the library during the evenings, half-hoping you might discover me when you came down to gaze at the Tiepolo."

Janet felt a warmth within her at these words. Sir Edward had been waiting for her, hoping to be caught at his novel reading?

He stepped to the mantelpiece and placed a hand on it. "I do not know why, but I felt some sense of connection to the proud and haughty Mr. Darcy character. Strange, is it not?"

He looked at her with serious eyes, but soon his face broke out in a grin. Self-deprecating humor from Sir Edward? This was shaping up to be the strangest of evenings.

"And I was impressed by another character in the book." His voice grew quiet. "Elizabeth Bennet, who comes from outside Mr. Darcy's privileged but narrow world and is sparkling and outspoken, and helps to bring out the best in him. I can see why he falls in love with her."

Janet's heart raced.

"You have not read my dedication, Jane." His eyes were soft as he observed her.

Gingerly, afraid her fingers might tremble, Janet opened the book to see a dedication penned in thick, black ink in an elegant hand.

'To Jane, the most beautiful and fascinating woman I have ever had the privilege to meet. May these words accompany you on your journeys, if I am unable to be at your side. With undying affection and admiration. Yours, Edward.

> "With thee, my bark, I'll swiftly go,
> Athwart the foaming brine;
> Nor care what land thou bear'st me to,
> So not again to mine.
> Welcome, welcome, ye dark blue waves!
> And when you fail my sight,
> Welcome, ye deserts, and ye caves!
> My Native Land—Good Night!'"

Beyond the library, hundreds of guests danced, and drank, and flirted, and chatted, but here in the quiet of the darkened room, Janet fell into a silent trance. Only the ticking of the clock and the wild beating of her heart punctuated the silence. Breathing was an effort as she kept her eyes fixed on the page, unable to comprehend the words before her.

"You are silent, Jane. Have I taken too many liberties? When I learned you were to leave us, I truly understood all I risked to lose."

She looked up with moist eyes to see him watching her closely.

"It is beautiful, Sir Edward ... Edward."

He smiled at her and stepped closer as she said his name. A softness transformed his expression.

She took a deep breath. "I love this quote of Byron. I feel it describes me perfectly." She looked down at her feet. "But why now? Why on the eve of your engagement do you feel the need to tell me this?" She looked up at him once again, knowing her face must reflect all the doubts swirling around in her mind. Did Daphne feel as conflicted during Apollo's chase? Did Cupid's arrow succeed in hardening her heart entirely, or did a sliver of doubt remain?

He placed one hand on her shoulder and shook his head. "I did not plan this, I swear. You infuriated me much of the time, but my admiration for you grew slowly. Your presence filled a longing I have felt for years, a longing I first felt when I gazed on this very painting we both treasure so much." He turned to the canvas. "When I saw you dancing with Lieutenant Williams tonight, I was overcome first by jealousy, then by the fear that I would never have the chance to tell you how I felt about you. And to learn if you might feel the same. Victoria's announcement terrified me. That is when I decided to wait here for you, to tell you about my feelings." His face came closer to hers. "Even if you are still determined to leave me."

Leaving Edward was the last thing she wished to do. Janet's head spun. The tingling spread all over her body, whether from Edward's revelations or the painting calling her back home, or a combination of the two, she was unsure.

"Your words are beautiful. Even if I was afraid to admit it to myself, I longed to hear them, too."

He stroked her cheek, his warm fingers tracing her cheekbone. She felt a jolt pass through her body and took a step back. She held up one hand to halt him from approaching.

"Edward, you must allow me to explain."

He shook his head. "Explain what? All I long to do is hold you in my arms."

He closed the distance between them and enveloped her, crushing her against him. She could hear his heart exploding in his chest, feel the warmth of his body against hers. All she longed for was to remain in this position, safe, and warm, and protected from the outside world. Secure in the knowledge that Sir Edward loved her, and that she loved him. But the time for lies had come to an end. With a sigh, she extricated herself from his protective embrace and pushed back.

"You must hear me out." She breathed in deeply to steady herself. "Miss Chadwick will say that I am an imposter, here under false pretenses."

Edward shook his head. "Jane, do not distress yourself. Victoria will be disappointed at first, but I will not take heed of what she says."

"But she is right."

A dark cloud passed over Edward's face, the look Janet knew all too well when he was provoked. After all, she'd elicited this expression in him by her own actions on far too many occasions.

"Explain yourself, please." His voice was low, but firm.

Janet took a deep breath, willing her pounding heart to slow. "It is not as she understands it, but I cannot blame her. I come from Boston ... but not the Boston of 1813." She searched his face, hoping for a glimmer of understanding, but there was only confusion. She slipped Sir Edward's book in the bag she carried, the bag for her departure. She clasped her hands together and paced before the fireplace. "I would never have believed it myself, if it hadn't happened to me. I come from the future, Edward. From *two hundred years* in the future. I traveled back here, to your world. To *you*, I realize that only now. I travelled through your painting. It spoke to me, too, and I believe I must have unwittingly allowed it to lead me here."

Sir Edward shook his head. He stumbled back, his face a mixture of anger and confusion. Janet winced inwardly, but there was no turning back now. She needed to say everything. Consequences be damned.

"I know you must be angry and confused. So overwhelmingly confused. I know I was myself during my first days here, when I thought I was going mad. How I longed to tell you and Emma. Do you remember when I told you about the vaccinations, Edward?" Her eyes pleaded with him to understand.

He looked up at her, but his eyes were cold.

"I came *so* close to telling you the truth. I needed to voice it to someone who could understand. In my world, we do have vaccinations against some of the most deadly diseases. I have travelled so widely because it is easier to do so in my world. We no longer travel by carriage. We have machines to carry us faster than horses by ground, and even to fly us through the air."

He flinched and she stepped forward. She took his hands in her own, feeling their warmth and solidity.

"I know how strange all this sounds. I did not want to spring this on you all at once, but I need to be completely honest with you. I need you to understand the world I come from, and why I sometimes seem so out of place here. And why Miss Chadwick was not wrong to assume I am not who I claimed to be."

He met her gaze. "But surely this is madness. How is this possible? How can it be true?" He shook his head and a furrow deepened in his brow, but he did not let go of her hands.

"I truly do not know. But in my world, I lived in a room in Huntington House, a room that housed that painting." She turned to her right, catching Daphne's eye. Daphne's flushed face observed her, urging her on. "In my modern world, I felt drawn to the painting and one evening, when I was alone ..." She took a deep breath and closed her eyes. "I scratched it with a pair of scissors." With her right hand, she gingerly touched the scratch. A dull tingling ran through her arm and she retracted it quickly. "The next day, I touched the scratch again, and later I was hit in the head by a ball on the Green. I woke up in your world."

He clenched her hands tighter and she almost cried out in pain. His labored breaths grew louder.

"Edward, I know I sound like a raving madwoman now. I know you need time to process this, but the tingling I felt before my arrival in your world is back. I fear it may be time to return. I need you to understand. Perhaps I should have told you earlier ..."

There was so much pain etched on his face. She could see traces of the older man he would become, the man she longed to be beside their whole lives.

She reached into her bag and extracted her sunglasses. "Look Edward, these are sunglasses. They are not made of glass, but plastic. A chemical substance invented in the mid-1900s." She reached in again. "And this is a ballpoint pen. We also use it to write. Also made of plastic, with ink inside. I used up all the ink and was forced to use the quill and inkwell."

She handed them to him and he stared at each item, slowly turning them over in his hands. He was silent, and the silence scared her. He placed the items on the mantelpiece and kept his gaze fixed on the ground.

"Edward, this is a modern paperback version of the book. Yours is a first edition, but Jane Austen's books are widely read in my world. Look here." She pointed to the copyright page. "This edition is from 2010." Her voice had a desperate edge to it, but he had to understand. "And here. This is a photograph. Taken with a machine that can capture your image. It will be invented later in this century. Here I am in front of the Tiepolo. This is me in my modern world, dressed without a corset or a gown. We no longer wear them. Living in the center where I study nineteenth-century literature, women studying beside men, working in professions beside men." She couldn't stop herself from speaking, desperate to fill the void that came from his stubborn silence.

She took back the book and the photo, slipping them away in her bag. He needed time to think things through calmly. He wouldn't be repeating his declarations of love for her. She'd ruined everything, but somehow she still felt freer in having shared her burden with someone else.

The silence hung over the room like a wet, dark blanket. It extinguished all the lovers' hope that had blossomed there earlier. The candle burned lower and its weak light began to flicker. Soon it would extinguish entirely.

Edward cleared his throat and she looked up, certain desperation was evident in her eyes.

"This is all ..." His confident voice wavered. "... very strange. If it were not you standing across from me, I would not believe a word. I will need time to reflect, to try to make sense of things." His voice grew more secure as he met her eyes. "But it does not change the way I feel about you, Jane."

Janet longed to tell him her real name, but she'd dropped enough bombs on him for one day. This could wait. Now all she desired was to feel his arms around her, to feel that happiness she'd never truly felt with other men. They'd never had the power to melt her insides with a single touch, like Edward. She'd never feared losing any other man as desperately as she feared losing Sir Edward this very evening in this library.

"I am so relieved." She stepped into his embrace and tilted her face up to meet his.

"But this complicates everything. You are not of my world, and it would be a sacrifice to ask you to marry me. Jane, I am *two hundred* years older than you."

She laughed. "When you put it like that, you do have a point. This might be taking a fascination for older men to the extreme."

"You cannot make light of everything. Would you not be sorry to leave your world and to sacrifice everything to come live with me in mine?"

She leaned into his chest, settling her face into his neck and inhaling his scent. He stroked her hair with one hand and her heart leapt in her chest. She'd never experienced such a sense of contentment and security, and that undefined feeling that *she was home.*

This is what she would miss if she returned to her world.

Janet freed her head to pull back. She gazed up into his questioning eyes. "It would not feel like a sacrifice, Edward, to stay here with you and Emma. I have grown to love you both like my family. I read my first Jane Austen book when I was a girl, and I've always felt at home in those novels, longed to be a part of that world. My time here has shown me I still have a lot to learn. But I *am* willing to learn. With your support, I could continue to develop my passions for literature and architecture, and help you with improvements to the Manor."

Sir Edward released his breath and smiled. His eyes crinkled, making him even more handsome. "You've made me so happy, Jane. But are you *absolutely* certain?" There was a gentleness to his voice. "You would not feel you were sacrificing life in your world to be with me?"

"The modern world's not all it's cracked up to be."

He laughed. "I see that you will have to assist me with some of these futuristic expressions."

"I would love to. Of course, I'm being asked to make all these decisions about my future, to express declarations of my certainty ..." She pouted and brought her face closer to his. "And yet, you haven't even kissed me yet. How can I decide before that? I could very well change my mind if everything is not up to my very lofty expectations."

He touched the tip of his nose to hers. The candle spluttered and flickered, but the smile in his eyes was unmistakable. That look alone could melt her insides.

"And yet, such a forward demand might make a man of my era quite nervous. This puts me under a great deal of pressure."

He stroked her neck and brought his lips closer to her own, holding back when she longed for him to continue.

"I fear you ladies of the future may have more experience kissing young men, and this may lead to unrealistic expectations." He whispered, as he continued to hold her gaze. "I will have to do my best to please you, Jane."

His lips brushed hers, gently at first, and then more insistently. His arms circled her, crushing her against his body. The firm muscles of his chest rested flush against her corset, but she ignored the whalebone digging into her skin, too caught up in the flood of warmth she felt throughout her entire body. The tingling sensation grew stronger than before. He ran his hands up and down her back. Her head spun and she longed to come up for air, but she feared if she broke contact with him, he might disappear into thin air. She ran her fingers through the locks of his thick hair, smiling inwardly at his groan. She'd never felt like this before. This kiss, and the promise of more to come, could keep her here indefinitely.

"Edward? What on earth are you doing?"

They broke apart from one another to turn to the shadowy figure in the doorway. Even in the dim room, the puce-colored gown was unmistakable.

"Victoria." Edward's voice was flat. He did not step away from Janet. He kept one arm firmly around her waist, pulling her body tightly to his own.

"Your guests have all been asking after you, ready for you to make your big announcement. I have been worrying myself for your welfare, searching the entire house for you." She took long strides, approaching them.

Her eyes were ablaze with the deep hatred of a woman scorned. Janet instinctively shrunk back, but Edward steadied her, holding her tight. His strong presence soothed her.

"I am sorry, Victoria." Sir Edward's voice was authoritative once again. "But I have some things to tell you. Things you will not like to hear ..."

Her eyes flashed with anger, and she pointed a finger in his face. "Do *not* interrupt me! I was worried and looking for you and I walk in to find you in the arms of this ... this ... *brazen hussy*!"

She shot a look filled with venom at Janet. Janet longed to step backwards, but managed to pull herself to her full height, concentrating on Sir Edward's strong arm around her.

"Your anger should be directed at me, Victoria. I am the one who has hurt you, and you have every right to insult me. It is I whose feelings have changed. Miss Roberts bears no blame."

"Miss Roberts bears no blame." Miss Chadwick mimicked Edward's deep voice. "Spoken like a true gentleman, Edward."

She paced back and forth. "You are a man, after all. If this woman throws herself at you, what are you expected to do? What can one expect of a woman with no background and no breeding?"

"That is *enough*, Victoria!" Sir Edward's voice thundered through the room. "I have wronged you, and I deeply regret that. But neither you nor anyone else will ever insult the woman I love."

Miss Chadwick looked as if she'd been slapped. She tried to speak, but at first no sound would issue forth. "Love? Love *her*?" She pointed one bejeweled finger at Janet's chest. "Do you know she is *nothing*, Edward? She is less than nothing. You would do better by marrying one of the dairy girls."

"Enough, Victoria."

"No! It is not enough! This ... this *harlot* comes into your house and offers you her favors—probably learned in the brothels of Boston—and you humiliate me and turn me out on the evening you are to propose to me?" Her face twisted into a horrid mask of pain. "You are no gentleman, Edward!" She picked up a small statue from the table beside her. "And you, you duplicitous American strumpet, you are *no* lady!" With one swift movement she lifted up the statue and hurled it.

"No!" Sir Edward lunged towards Victoria, but it was too late.

The statue hit Janet beside the temple with a sickening thud. Janet screamed and fell backwards, hitting her head on the mantelpiece before crumpling to the floor with a groan of pain. Edward slumped beside her, cradling her head in one hand, while trying to stop the flow of blood with the other. Bright red blood formed patterns on his crisp, white shirt. She tried to see them distinctly, but soon they began to blur.

Edward bellowed, "Fetch the doctor!" When he turned back to Janet, his eyes were moist. He brought his face closer to hers, and she tried to concentrate on those two bright, blue points above her, but even they were beginning to grow out of focus. The pain was overtaken by the tingling. It worked its way through her entire body.

"Please Jane," Edward's voice pleaded quietly above her. "Do not leave me. Do not leave me now, when we have just found one another."

A tear slipped down his face and she longed to wipe it away, but her arm would not obey. She tried to smile at him, but she feared it was a smile filled with blood.

"Jane, my darling." His voice was tender. "Find your way back to me. I shall wait for you." He choked away the tears. "I love you."

He leaned down and placed his mouth firmly against hers. She felt the comforting warmth of his lips pressed to hers. They sent a tingling sensation through her body, before everything disappeared.

Chapter 37

The sound of birds chirping filled the air. Their loud song competed with the throbbing in her head.

Janet opened her eyes to bright sunlight streaming through the windows. She squinted against the brightness, focused on the open window. A gentle breeze wafted in, strangely balmy for an October day. The tenant farmers would be harvesting in summer-like weather.

Had she slept all night?

She closed her eyes and tried to make sense of the events in the library. She winced, remembering the mad glint in Miss Chadwick's eyes as she threw a missile at Janet's head. But there was also Edward's declaration of love, recounting to him the truth about her time travel and all the relief that accompanied that revelation, and the way his kiss had the power to melt her insides. She smiled at the memory, shifting gently on the bed. A sharp corner dug into her side, and she reached down to her carry bag. Reaching in, she pulled out Edward's gift to her. Jane Austen.

Despite the pounding in her head, she opened the book to the title page. A warm glow worked its way through her body as she read his words.

Edward loved her, and she loved him. After all the false starts, all the antagonisms and difficulties, they'd finally found their way to one another. She shouldn't be wasting time recuperating in bed after the unfortunate events of the previous night. She longed to see him again, to have him pull her into his chest where she would feel warm and secure as his heart beat against her cheek.

Pushing herself up, she ignored the light-headedness. It would fade. She looked down at her clothes, still dressed in her ball gown, the large, blue sapphire fastened around her neck. Turner must have feared disturbing her after she passed out, but how odd not to have at least removed the jewelry.

Janet sat on the edge of the bed, taking deep breaths. She stretched her arms over her head, wiggling her fingers to rid her hands of the pins-and-needles sensation.

A sound from outside caused her blood to freeze. She turned her head towards the open window.

Her heartbeat slowed. She breathed slowly through her nose, concentrating. It was unmistakably the sound of an ambulance passing by. But such things did not exist. She felt a tremor in her hand, and took deep gulps of air as she slowly looked around her.

This wasn't her room at Helmsley Manor.

Two beds, an armoire. There on the bedside table was a bright, pink smartphone. *No, I must be dreaming.* This looked so much like her room in Huntington House, the room she'd left months ago. Her heart beat faster, and she willed her eyes to stay focused on a spot on the bed, but they disobeyed her command and slid upwards to the fireplace mantel, gliding across the alabaster skin, the billowing pink robes, the bright blue sky, and green leaves.

The Tiepolo.

Despite the pain, she pushed herself from the bed and took long strides across the room, to the large windows overlooking the Green. She shivered involuntarily as she looked out at the scene before her.

Power lines, teenagers in shorts and miniskirts, cars winding around the roads, a helicopter flying in the distance. Back in her world. Back where she'd thought she longed to be.

"Edward," she said out loud, her eyes welling up with tears.

His words, the kiss, the way he made her feel. All of that was over now. He was two hundred years in the past, and all she had to remember him by were his words in her book and his portrait on the wall.

Even the Tiepolo was temporary. The National Gallery would soon be taking it away, and she would have to jostle the crowds to view it, let alone ever have the chance again to touch the scratch in an attempt to travel back.

She felt the panic rising. Facing the window, she didn't hear the door open at first.

"Janet!" cried a familiar voice.

She turned to see Amrita in the doorway, dressed in jeans and a tank top. Amrita observed her strangely, her head cocked to one side.

"Where have you been? We've been worried sick about you. The police are combing the city, and it looks like you've wandered in from a costume party. What's going on?"

Janet looked down in confusion at her ball gown, at the precious jewel around her neck. What *was* going on? How could she ever hope to answer that?

"Amrita, please close the door and come here to help me out of this dress. We need to talk, and I scarcely know where to commence."

"You scarcely know where to commence? Is the corset cutting off the flow of oxygen to your brain? And where did the English accent come from?"

"Amrita. Please. I need your help. I'll talk you through unlacing me."

Amrita closed the door. Janet explained how to loosen the corset. She carried the dress and corset to her armoire, hanging them inside and pulling out faded jeans and a t-shirt. She smiled as she slipped the soft cotton over her head. "Oh, this is heaven! You simply do not realize how fortunate you are to have delightful clothes like this for afternoons of quiet leisure." She turned to look at Amrita, seeing the fear and confusion in her friend's eyes.

"Was it a head injury? Is that why you're talking so strangely?"

Janet took a deep breath. She sank down to the bed and patted the place beside her. "Amrita, you'll have to be patient with me. I know I'll sound crazy trying to explain it to you, but I need you to promise you'll make an effort to understand." Her mind raced, trying to formulate how to explain. "Can I ask first? Where did everyone think I was all these months?"

Amrita sat down beside her. "Months?" She squinted her eyes in confusion. "You've been gone *four days*. The police have been looking for you, so have the students. Your father's flight arrives tomorrow."

"My father? My father's coming to Bath?" Her voice rose alongside her blood pressure. She walked to the window once more, seeing all the people in summer clothes. Modern clothes. Turning away from the window, she said, "Are you sure it's only been four days? It's not October?"

"Janet, you'd better start explaining, because you're scaring me."

Janet crossed the room once again, feeling drained of all emotion. She took Edward's gift from her bag and handed it to Amrita. "I know this will all sound so strange, but please look at this book. It was given to me as a gift last night ... by Sir Edward, the man in the portrait on the staircase."

Amrita shook her head, a pained expression on her face. "You're out of your mind."

"I know that's what I sound like, but there must be documents we can check his handwriting against." She opened the title page and pointed to it. "It's a pristine first edition of *Pride and Prejudice*. 1813. The year I returned to in my time travel. Last night—the night I returned here—was the night he presented this book to me." She allowed her voice to drop to a whisper. "And the night he declared his love for me."

"Janet, let me talk to Professor Williams." She spoke slowly, examining Janet's face. "He can call a doctor. Head injuries are serious."

"Amrita." Janet reached out and took her hand. "Please, I'm only asking you to hear me out. If you insist I need a shrink afterwards, I'll go. But I need you to try to understand. Look at the dedication. I'm Jane."

Amrita's eyes were frightened, but she looked down and read the page. "It's beautiful—what is the verse?"

"Lord Byron, *Childe Harold*, contemporary poetry in 1813." She took a deep breath. "I met Sir Edward and his sister, Emma. I lived in their world. I was a guest in Huntington House and at Helmsley Manor."

"Janet. I can't explain the book, but maybe you found it and, with the head injury, you had vivid dreams. Maybe you really do believe everything to be true."

Janet shook her head. "I understand your skepticism. If I were you, I'd be the same. But here." She turned and pulled notebooks from her bag. "Here are my observations from the *four months* that I spent back in time." She handed them to Amrita. "They start in my modern notebook, with a ballpoint pen. Then the ink ran out and Emma gave me a journal and quill. They continue like that. Days and days of observations over months, in my own handwriting. The details are precise."

Amrita turned the pages. Janet felt the weight of the stone against her chest. She reached both hands up and held it so that Amrita could see it better. "Amrita—this jewel. Emma lent it to me for the Harvest Ball. It's genuine. I've never owned anything like this. It's been in their family for generations, and it must be worth a fortune. We can take it to a jeweler—I'm sure he'll be able to date it. As they'll be able to date the nineteenth-century ball gown in our armoire." She squeezed her friend's hand once again. "Please. You have to believe me." Her voice was quiet. "I couldn't make something like this up."

Amrita took a deep breath. Her hands trembled, but her eyes observed Janet's steadily. "I think you should start from the beginning. We know there was an accident on the Green. What happened when you woke up?"

Janet took a deep breath. A gentle breeze wafted through the window as Janet recounted her adventures to her roommate.

Janet sat in the comfortable chair in the familiar room at The Circus. The sun shone through the window as she lifted the cup of tea and took a fortifying sip. Her head still ached and she felt the occasional dizziness, but after speaking to Amrita, the police, and being visited by a doctor, she'd insisted on a short visit to Mr. Perry's. She prayed she was still in time to rescue the frescoes in Tony's mansion.

Mr. Perry examined the drawings spread across his desk. He looked up and the afternoon sunlight glinted from the glass of his spectacles. "These are extraordinary, Janet. Where did you find them?"

Her hand shook, and she placed down the teacup. "That will be trickier to explain. And I'll suggest you sit down beside me and have a cup of tea, or a shot of something stronger, before I attempt an explanation." She laced her fingers together to still her hands. "I can swear to you that an expert examination will show those papers and drawings to be from 1813, when Tony's house belonged to a Lady Whitmore. The library was spectacular. Lady Whitmore's husband and Thomas Gainsborough were old friends. Gainsborough confided in his friend that he'd tired of painting society portraits, and that he longed to concentrate solely on landscapes. The ceiling borders are believed to be Gainsborough's very first landscape commission."

Mr. Perry turned back to the sketching. "Extraordinary." He looked up. "You promise me this is all true? You can explain the full story to me later, but I need your word of honor."

She looked him straight in the eye. "I swear, Mr. Perry."

He picked up the phone. "Yes, hello. Sheldon Perry here, may I speak with Professor Jacobs? ... Yes, I'll hold ... Hello, Harry! How are you? ... Yes, fine. There's something rather urgent I need to speak to you about. ... New information about possible Gainsborough frescoes in a room we were ready to demolish ... Yes, we'll need to present it to the National Trust. ... Tomorrow's fine. I'll be by your office at nine. Thank you. 'Til tomorrow, Harry." He hung up and looked up at Janet. "Demolition is not planned until the day after tomorrow, and Professor Jacobs is a member of the National Trust, so I trust we're in time to raise doubts about the destruction of such valuable art."

He took a bottle of whiskey and two glasses from the shelf. He poured two fingers of the amber liquid into the cut crystal. "This sounds like a conversation that merits more than tea. Cheers."

"I suppose it does. Cheers, Mr. Perry." She reached into her bag and pulled out an envelope. "I was expecting this conversation. I wanted to avoid the part where you assume I'm a raving lunatic, so I brought this letter along to soften the blow."

"Miss Jane Roberts, Helmsley Manor ..." He read from the envelope before looking up, confusion marring his brow. "What is this?"

She sipped the whiskey, feeling the burning sensation as it worked its way down her throat and calmed her nerves. "Please, Mr. Perry. Just read it all the way through. It's from your relative, Dr. Perry. The one who bought this house."

Mr. Perry frowned. His confusion was evident, but he slipped the letter out of its envelope and read in silence. A few minutes later, he looked up, shaking his head. "I recognize the writing. My ancestor, Doctor Perry, was obviously in touch with a Miss Roberts, visiting Helmsley Manor. They must have met here in Bath, and they are worried about a young patient with the measles. I don't understand how you obtained this letter ..."

Janet took a deep breath. "I know it sounds like madness, Mr. Perry, but *I* am Miss Jane Roberts."

The silence in the room weighed upon her as she waited for his response.

Mr. Perry shook his head. "My dear, I know there was an accident. Head injuries are very common occurrences. Nothing to be ashamed about. Perhaps you should see a neurologist."

Janet stood and walked over to the sketching on the table. "I knew I might be coming back, and I knew if I tried to confide in you, you'd think me mad. Any analysis will prove that this paper and these lead pencils come from the early nineteenth century." She held up a sketching and tapped at the lower corner. "But the signature here at the bottom is mine." She took one of Mr. Perry's modern pens and scrawled across his notepad. "Compare the two—it is my name, but Jane instead of Janet. Apparently Janet was a name in medieval times that had fallen into disuse by the nineteenth century. It was easier to go along with the name Jane when I went back in time."

Mr. Perry walked back to the table, casting his gaze between the signature on the papers and that on the notepad.

"You have friends at the university, Mr. Perry. Have them date the paper and the lead to prove I'm right. I would be equally suspicious if I were standing in your shoes and hearing such a story, but I did go back in time. I have been missing for four days, but I spent *four months* back in 1813." She paced the room, her nervousness causing her to speak quickly. "I met your ancestor. Quiz me! Doctor Perry told me about when he bought this house, how he purchased it after he married Margaret. I know their sons Richard and Thaddeus were born here. They were young boys in 1813. Thaddeus had red curls and freckles. He was always getting into trouble. He broke his wrist falling from a tree when I was in Bath. Is that in the journal you have?"

Mr. Perry sank deep into his chair, looking pale and confused. His white curls were wilder than usual. "This doesn't make any sense."

She placed a hand on his shoulder. "I know it doesn't. I have only confided in my roommate and you. You know my father, Mr. Perry. He's arriving tomorrow. He'd never understand. He'd lock me up in some expensive, private clinic, convinced it would be for my own good. I am asking you not to reveal what I am telling you to my father. But I need two things from you." She breathed in deeply. "First, I want you to save the Gainsborough paintings. I've seen them myself, in the nineteenth-century library Tony is set on destroying. They're spectacular. That's why I sketched them."

Mr. Perry slumped listlessly in his chair. "And what is the second favor you need from me?"

"I need to see Doctor Perry's medical notebooks." She wrung her hands, avoiding Mr. Perry's gaze. "Things were ... complicated ... when I went back in time. I formed the closest friendship of my life with Miss Emma Huntington, and I want to know exactly what happens to her, and ..." Her voice dropped to a whisper. "I fell in love with Sir Edward. He declared his love for me." She looked up to see the confusion in Mr. Perry's eyes. "I know I will never return, probably never have any way to warn him, but I need to know what he died of here at Huntington House. If he was in any type of pain, if anything could have been done to prevent it. If he was happy at the end ..." She reached up to wipe away a tear. "Doctor Perry must have been his attending physician in Bath."

"Janet, if it weren't you standing before me, I'd be calling an ambulance and asking for a straightjacket. As it is, I don't know what to do. What to think." He shook his head. "But I can let you see those journals. They contain many observations about Emma and Sir Edward. If you will wait here, I'll fetch them."

Her legs shaking, Janet walked to the chair and sank down into its plush cushions. She was equally elated and terrified as she waited to read the information contained in the two-hundred-year-old journals.

Moonlight tumbled through the grand window, casting its light on Amrita and Janet as they sat on the landing.

Aside from the short visit to Mr. Perry's office, Janet spent the latter part of the day speaking to Professor Williams, the Bath police, and her fellow students. She'd repeated the lie she and Amrita had devised. She'd been hit on the head. Nameless, faceless good Samaritans had taken her home and nursed her to health. She'd regained consciousness recently and returned home. The cops had been the most skeptical, but after a doctor made a house call and reported that, despite the obvious head wound, Janet was in good health, with no other signs of trauma or physical abuse, even they backed off.

Huntington House was silent as the two women sat on the landing, with a perfect view of Emma and Sir Edward's portraits along the staircase walls.

"Do you miss him?" asked Amrita.

"I do. We spent most of our time circling one another cautiously. We only admitted our true feelings on our last day together. Just my luck to find my soul mate only to be hurled back into my own time." She shook her head. "Two *centuries* later."

"It might still work out. You never know."

"Any ideas on how?" Janet attempted a smile.

"None at all. I'm way out of my comfort zone on this one."

"Me, too."

"What did you discover from the medical journals today?"

Janet sighed. "It's worse than I thought. Emma died soon after her twentieth birthday. Edward married her off to Sir John, and, as could have been predicted, her health slowly faded away married to such a monster. She died in childbirth, alongside her son. Dr. Perry observed the birth was difficult, but not impossible for a woman in good health. She didn't have any strength left." Her voice grew hoarse. "Maybe she'd lost the will to live."

Amrita squeezed her hand. "I'm so sorry, Janet. And Sir Edward?"

"He died in the cholera epidemic of 1832. He and his estate manager did not continue with the sanitation improvements we began during my stay. His new wife, the former Miss Chadwick, cared only for redecorating the house, buying the finest gowns from Paris, and throwing the most lavish parties. She slowly squandered the sizable fortune from his estate." She swiped away a tear. "When cholera hit Helmsley Manor, Edward worked alongside the local doctor to help the tenants. Both would contract the disease. The doctor died almost instantly. Edward was stronger and was moved to Bath, where Dr. Perry hoped the curative waters would revive him."

She looked up at the portrait, at the strong and haughty Edward she knew. His eyes bored into her. His muscles strained against his britches, making him look so invincible. How could he have succumbed so quickly to disease? Disease that could so easily have been prevented with the improvements they'd been putting in place?

"It was too late. Doctor Perry could only keep him comfortable in the end. His snake of a wife was busy during the London season and couldn't even spare the time to be at his side while he lay on his deathbed. May she rot in hell." She took a deep breath. "He died in our room, looking on Apollo and Daphne. Doctor Perry reported it was the only thing that afforded him comfort in the end."

"How sad."

"His son, Edward Junior, eventually took over the estate." She indicated the portrait of a young man hanging further down the staircase. He had the same dismissive look on his face that Janet knew all too well from Miss Chadwick. "But he had his mother's character, and her profligate spending habits. It was the start of a slow decline for Helmsley Manor. The tenants fared no better. Guglielmo, the young Italian boy I told you about, and his entire family perished during the cholera epidemic. Even poor Paolo, whom I managed to rescue from the measles, was taken." She shook her head. "It seems that nothing I did made any difference whatsoever."

"You can't be so hard on yourself. What more could you have done?"

"What more indeed? Even if I'd stayed, and married Sir Edward. What then? Yes, perhaps the tenants would have been better off, without the cholera epidemic. Perhaps Emma and Mr. Bentley might have married. But I would have altered all of this." Her hands swept the length of the grand hallway. "These descendants would never have been born. Even Sir Charles Huntington, Professor Williams' friend who donated this house to the program, would never have existed." She turned to Amrita. "Do I have the right to alter history like that to save the people I love most? Is it fair to deny existence to generations of Huntingtons because I went back in time and discovered love?" She looked at the blue eyes and curly blond locks of generations of young Huntingtons lining the walls. The tears rolled unchecked down her cheeks.

Amrita leaned into her friend, slipping her arm around her shoulder. "I wish I could answer you, but I don't know. How can any of us know? We can only make decisions based on our own limited knowledge, and act on the information we believe best."

Janet nodded slowly and Amrita pulled her to her feet. Like a young child, she allowed herself to be led back to her bedroom.

Chapter 38

"Janet, you overslept."

She opened one eye to Amrita's gentle shaking.

"Your father called from the train. He'll be here in half an hour."

"My father?" She snapped up at once, wide awake. Her father had that effect on her. No time for a shower now, although she'd been ecstatic yesterday afternoon as she stood endlessly under the warm spray, oblivious to the calls for her to hurry up. What a wonderful invention. How she'd missed it these past months. Brushing her teeth with real toothpaste was another moment of pure bliss. Twigs and chalk were by no stretch of the imagination an acceptable alternative.

Janet raced to the armoire, pulling out clothes and slipping them on. She ran a comb through her tangled hair, trying to look presentable. Where was Turner when you needed her?

"Will I have time to eat something? My stomach's doing flip-flops." She entered an empty breakfast room. "Why is it so quiet?"

"Everyone's at University of Bath today for a seminar. Professor Williams asked me to stay with you today." She poured two cups of coffee. "It means I'll be here for moral support when your father arrives."

"Thanks, Amrita. I'm sorry you're missing it on my account."

"It's okay. I'd hate to leave you alone so soon. You'll have the weekend to rest up, but I hope you'll be back in classes on Monday. We've missed you."

"I'm sorry to have worried you all." She spread jam on her toast and took a bite.

"Your dad seemed really worried on the phone when we didn't know where you were."

Janet sipped her coffee. "I'm sure he'll be fine." She knew this wasn't true, but she didn't need to worry her friend. As they ate, Janet concentrated on calm thoughts.

The doorbell rang and she felt panic well up. Miss Smith's footsteps approached. Janet heard her father's booming voice as she sat, coffee cup frozen in midair.

"They've arrived." Amrita reached out and shook her shoulder. "Janet?"

"Sorry, bit of a headache," she lied. "I'm fine now." She stood as her father reached the door.

Her father filled the entire doorframe. A former college football player, his muscular frame was still intimidating decades later. He was a bundle of nervous energy, never capable of sitting or standing still for long periods. He tapped a briefcase against his leg. She knew he'd be in a foul mood after the long trip. His brown eyes were slightly bloodshot. His thick, brown hair sported new strands of grey. Otherwise, he looked exactly the same.

In all these months away, she'd never missed him, rarely thought of him. And now, his hulking form stood before her. Her palms sweated as if she were terrified onstage at the second-grade spelling bee.

"Where the hell have you been, Janet?" His eyes were hard, the tone of his voice unbending.

"Daddy, it's wonderful to see you." Janet stepped forward and placed an awkward kiss on his stubbly cheek. "Come in. Can I get you coffee? " She placed her hand on Amrita's shoulder, steadying herself. "This is my roommate, Amrita. Amrita, my father, Richard Roberts." She poured coffee. When she turned to hand her father his coffee, Malcolm materialized beside him, wearing crisp khaki pants and a perfectly ironed Oxford shirt.

"Janet, what a relief. We were so worried." Malcolm stepped forward, grasping her shoulder and kissing her on the cheek.

She stepped back, involuntarily. "Malcolm, I didn't expect to see you here."

He stepped forward and took her hand in his own. "How could I not come? I haven't slept at all since your disappearance. We've been worried sick." He tilted his head and observed her, a slow smile spreading across his face.

"Amrita, this is Malcolm Nowak, an architect in my father's firm."

Janet poured coffee, willing her hand to stop shaking. Janet gestured to the table, placing Malcolm's cup down. "You must be tired after your trip."

"A trip that appears entirely unnecessary." Her father sat across from her, a telltale scowl on his face. "Except perhaps to take you home."

"Home, Daddy? Why?" Janet quelled the panic rising within her. "I'm happy here. Why would I leave now?"

"Oh, Janet. Grow up." Her father's voice boomed from across the table. "You're twenty-four years old. You've had us all worried. And for what?"

"It wasn't my fault." Her voice sounded whiny. "Some kids hit me on the Green playing cricket. I was brought here, but I must've wandered out later. I've already explained all this to the police." She met Amrita's eyes. "An elderly couple found me when I collapsed and took me in to their cottage. It's all blurry after that, but I know they cared for me until I came to. Then I came back here." Repeating it so many times with such conviction made it almost seem true.

"And you couldn't get *any* word to us? This couple never thought to contact the police? We have to get on a plane and travel halfway around the world, and all you have to say for yourself is 'I'm sorry, Daddy'?"

His sneer became more evident and Janet shrunk back instinctively. She closed her eyes and concentrated on pleasant, calming thoughts of Helmsley Manor, of riding with Emma, teaching the schoolchildren, how her heart fluttered when Edward professed his love. Her eyes snapped open, and she took a deep breath. "No one asked you to come, Daddy. I'm sorry to have been such a burden, to have wasted your precious time." She held her father's hard gaze.

An uncomfortable silence hung in the room. Amrita squirmed in her chair. Finally, Malcolm placed a hand on her father's forearm. "Richard, I think we're tired after the flight. Why don't we go back to the hotel, take a shower, and rest." He turned his gaze on Janet. "We've been terribly worried about you. Your father hasn't slept in days. He's not himself. The important thing is that you're safe and back with us now. We have dinner reservations for eight. I'll pick you up at seven-thirty, okay?"

"That's a good idea, Malcolm. I'll be ready in the library at seven-thirty."

Janet's father stood, and everyone followed suit. "Don't be late," he growled and strode to the door without a goodbye.

Malcolm gave a little half-smile and walked around the table to stand beside Janet. "Don't mind him. He'll be fine this evening." He took her hands in his own. "You look wonderful, Janet. You have no idea what a relief it was when Professor Williams called. We were so nervous." He leaned in and kissed her on the cheek. He pulled back and searched her eyes. Not releasing her hands, Malcolm turned back to Amrita. "It's nice to finally meet you, Amrita. I've heard so much about you. Take care of our Janet, okay?"

She returned his smile.

Malcolm turned back to Janet and stroked her cheek. "See you soon."

After the front door closed, Janet sank to her seat. Amrita sat across from her and sipped her coffee in silence.

"Wow." She stared at the empty door.

Janet sighed. "You summed up my family perfectly."

"Malcolm seems really nice," Amrita's voice was encouraging.

Janet ran her index finger around the rim of her coffee cup. "He is." She breathed in deeply. "But he's no Sir Edward."

Her fingers couldn't keep up with her thoughts as Janet tapped away frantically at the keyboard. Shouts from below beckoned her to join her classmates on the Green on a sunny, June afternoon, but she couldn't be tempted away from her computer.

"Janet, take a break already," Amrita said as she bounded through the door. She walked up to the desk and placed a hand over Janet's. "I know you have dinner plans tonight, but you've been at it since breakfast. Join us. It's been raining all week, and everyone wants to be out in the sunshine."

"I can't. I've lost time with this thesis, and now I have to catch up."

Amrita turned around, looking at the closed door. She lowered her voice. "Even if you were there for months, you've only missed *four days* here. Can't it wait?"

Janet stood and rubbed her eyes. "I don't know. Am I here forever? I don't feel the tingling anymore." She paced. "Am I going back? *Can* I go back, if I want to? Edward told me he'd wait for me. But if one day is a month back then, it means he's already waited for two months. *How long* will he wait? Even if I do manage to go back, it might be too late." Her eyes welled up with tears.

"Oh, Janet. Don't cry. Can't you be happy here, if you're not able to get back? Look how you've kickstarted your thesis. You've had an opportunity none of us will ever have. You've *lived* in the period we all study, the one we all dream about visiting. Do you know how envious I am? Don't you think your knowledge would help your career?"

Janet brushed away a lone tear. "I've thought of that—to make myself feel better. It's why I'm pouring all my energy into my thesis. I can polish later, but I need to get it all down. Concentrate on the positive. Maybe it's for the best. Even if I could go back, I'd be changing the lives—even hindering the lives—of too many people. Isn't it too close to playing God?" She looked up to meet Amrita's dark gaze.

"I'm a lit student, not a philosopher. I don't know what to tell you. Before all of this happened, you liked Malcolm. Maybe you weren't in love with him yet, but he seems kind. Maybe you'll learn to love him, and you could be happy together. Couldn't you let things take their natural course and see?"

"And the dream?" Janet moved to stand before the Tiepolo. "How could I have dreamt about Edward, about this painting, before I'd ever set eyes on either of them?" She gestured to Apollo and Daphne. "Doesn't that mean something?"

"I honestly don't know. Maybe it does, but maybe it wasn't meant to be permanent. Maybe you're meant to use these experiences for something in your modern world—like a university career."

Janet walked to her bedside table and pulled out the Austen, cradling it in her hands. She opened the volume and stared at Sir Edward's dedication. "And should I just forget about this? Of all the happiness we might have had?" Her voice caught in her throat.

Amrita placed an arm around Janet's shoulder. "You may not have a choice. I don't want to see you depressed. You may have to make the best of living in the present."

The shrieks and peals of laughter wafted in from the Green. Despite the noise, Janet was certain that deep inside her body, she could hear her heart breaking.

Janet sat in a comfortable armchair before the library's window, rereading *Persuasion*. For once, she placed the characters and story on the backburner with ease, reading instead for details of nineteenth-century Bath and social customs. These were the aspects she should have concentrated on for her thesis, but the familiar stories always managed to drag her in and usurp center stage.

She turned when she heard a knock. Malcolm stood at the threshold, a smile lighting his open face. He wore a crisp blue shirt and a suit jacket, looking handsome for their dinner.

"You look nice. Shall we get going?"

"No hurry." He strode toward her and pulled up a chair. "You have this idyllic position before the Green, and it's only a short walk to the restaurant. Anyway, I wanted a few minutes alone with you before having to share you with your father." He reached out for her hand.

Janet pulled it back reflexively, busying herself with her bookmark. She gazed out the large windows. "It is beautiful, isn't it? I love to study in the library, with this view over the Green. I've grown to love this place."

"That's what I feared."

The evening summer sunshine spilled into the window, picking up the copper highlights in his brown hair and emphasizing the golden tones to his tanned face.

"What do you mean?"

He leaned in closer, his eyes searching her own. "Before your ... accident, when we'd Skype, I sensed how much this place meant to you."

He placed one hand over hers, and she fought the urge to pull it away a second time.

"I admit it scared me, thinking you might not want to come back to Boston. Might not come back to give me—give us—a chance."

She looked up from his hand covering hers, and saw the determined spark in his eye. She'd seen it her first night in Bath at the restaurant, when he told her of his feelings for her. So long ago, light years away from her life now.

"When we got the call about your accident, about how you were missing, your dad and I were terrified. I admit I feared the worst. The fear I'd lost you for good gnawed away at me." He stroked her hand. "Then we arrive in London, and get the call that you'd been found, and you're back safe at The Crescent. It was such an incredible relief. "

She looked out at the lawn, where a group of children did somersaults. Amrita had said she should try to live in the present. But she wasn't ready.

"Everything's perfect again." Malcolm brought his face closer. "You're even more beautiful than I remember. If that's even possible. There's something about this place. It suits you." With his free hand, he caressed her bare arm. "But is it wrong for me to want you back in Boston when this semester is over? I'm renovating a house in Back Bay. It could be ours if you'll come live with me. I'll change the project any way you want, I promise. I'm creating a big studio in the attic, with gorgeous views. For you. You can fill it with Jane Austen books and finish your thesis there."

His eyes pleaded with hers, and she closed her own for a moment. She thought about her first edition Jane Austen, with the words written in Sir Edward's elegant hand that caused her heart to soar. She thought of it gathering dust in the studio Malcolm would build her. Gently, she extracted her hand from his.

"Malcolm, you know how fond I am of you, and what good friends we were becoming before my accident. But this is all too sudden. I'm not able to make those decisions now. I'll come back to Boston to complete my degree, but I'm not yet sure I'll stay." She turned to him, his outline bursting into a golden glow from the bright sunlight behind him, his face shadowy. "My father's always loomed large over me and my choices, but I'm an adult. It's time I start making my own decisions."

Malcolm looked down at the floor. "I can't pretend that's what I wanted to hear. But my feelings for you won't change. I'm in love with you, Janet." He looked up, catching her surprised expression. "I wasn't going to say it, but it's killing me keeping it inside." He put a finger to her lips. "You don't have to say anything now. I told you at dinner last month. I'll wait for you to decide, but I don't want to lie to you. I don't want to have to pretend it's not how I feel." He stroked her cheek. "If you're with me, you'll make your own decisions. You know your father and I get along well. He won't tell you what to do anymore." He reached into the inside of his coat pocket and extracted a velvet box. "Don't be frightened. It's not what you think, not until you're ready. It's a 'welcome back' gift."

He opened the box to display a delicate necklace, its strands of white gold and sapphires sparkling in the summer evening sunshine. Janet caught her breath. It was exquisite, much more her style than the huge, showy nineteenth-century sapphire she'd tucked deep within her lingerie drawer upstairs. With one index finger, she reached out gingerly to touch its elegant strands.

Malcolm's face broke out in a wide grin. "I *knew* you'd like it. You don't believe me, but I know your taste perfectly. Let me put it on you."

"No!" she cried. "What I mean," she said in a softer voice, "is that it *is* beautiful and I love it. But I can't accept it."

"Yes, you can. I'm grateful you're back with us, and I wanted to show you. You're not making any promises by accepting my gift. It's a token of my friendship."

Standing behind her, he slipped the necklace around her neck, his hands resting lightly on her shoulders. He leaned in closer to secure the clasp, and she felt his warm breath on her neck. He kissed her cheek and whispered in her ear, "It looks beautiful on you, Janet."

She touched the jewelry at her throat. "Thank you."

"My pleasure." He reached out his hand. "Although I hate the idea of having to share you this evening, we shouldn't keep your father waiting."

He tucked her arm under his. Leaving The Crescent, they followed the gravel path down to the restaurant.

Chapter 39

"Janet, you've done it." Mr. Perry clasped his hands together like an excited child. "The National Trust is examining the sketches as we speak. They've already requested access to the house to examine the paintings. They're combing through archival documents from the Whitmore family, hoping to find some letters between Lord Whitmore and Thomas Gainsborough."

He reached for the brandy, pouring for two.

"The demolition is on hold while the investigation goes forward. And I'm fielding nonstop calls from art historians in London, itching to examine the ceilings for themselves. My dear, you deserve a toast."

She accepted the drink.

"To Janet Roberts, rescuer of priceless art from almost certain destruction by the barbarians at the gate."

"I'll toast to that."

"May I tell your father?"

"Please don't, Mr. Perry. You know it will lead to too many questions. I can't handle that right now."

"I suppose you're right." He held his snifter in his hand, gently twirling it. "How is it being back? Culture shock?"

"That's an understatement! I'm trying to be positive. At least I can breathe again without the corset. And I do love modern hygiene." She grew silent and looked out the window. "But you know, so many people I know say, 'We live in the best country in the world. We're so lucky. No one's as lucky as we are.' Then you travel, and you realize it's not exactly true. There are plenty of nice places, but people want to believe their reality is the best. It makes them feel better. It's not that different from how we see the past. We're always saying, 'Oh, we're so lucky to live today. Back then they didn't have this or that. How could they possibly have lived without it?' And yes, I know I was privileged to live in a grand house, but I found myself more at home with the pace, and the ideas, and the friendships, and the art of conversation two hundred years ago. I can't help but feel that's been lost too much today."

"You're a woman wise beyond her years. And is your heart surviving, too?"

"Unfortunately, a heart willing to fall in love with a man two centuries older should expect to be trampled." She sipped her brandy, a drink she'd come to associate with chats with Mr. Perry. "I look at his dedication to me and the Byron quote at least a hundred times a day. Maybe in a few months, I'll be down to fifty a day. In a year, maybe only once a month or so. I'm back in my own world, and feel even more adrift on those dark blue waves than I did before." She looked into his eyes. "I'll survive this, won't I?"

Mr. Perry clasped her hand. "Oh, my dear. You will. Take it from one who knows. The heart is an amazingly resilient organ."

In the short time she'd known him, Mr. Perry was so much more like a father to her than her own had ever been.

"You should know, you're a dead ringer for Doctor Perry. Right down to the mannerisms and the laugh. If we dressed you in nineteenth-century clothes and stood you next to your ancestor, I wouldn't be able to tell the two of you apart."

A smile spread across his face. "Amazing, isn't it? The traits that pass down from generation to generation? I've always been fascinated by his journals, always longed to meet him myself." His eyes glistened as he turned to her. "And in the end, you did it. One extraordinary girl. And my ancestor had the good sense to befriend you. Let's raise a glass to Doctor Perry."

Janet toasted to her nineteenth-century friend.

Later that evening, Janet typed furiously on her laptop. Thoughts tumbled from her brain faster than she could get them down on the screen.

"No way are you staying here all night."

"What?" The annoyance at the interruption faded when she realized it was Amrita. "Oh, sorry."

"It's Saturday night, and you're headed out with us to the pub. No protests. I've invited Malcolm to join us."

"You what?"

"You heard me. I like him. He's not nineteenth-century nobility, but he's handsome and sweet, and he has a major crush on you. He's a successful architect who reads Jane Austen in his free time. When are you going to get it through your thick skull that there aren't all that many like him out there?"

"It just ... doesn't feel right. He's back there waiting for me to return."

Amrita leaned down behind Janet and wrapped her arms around her. "Janet, honey. It's not cheating on Sir Edward if you try to be happy with someone else. You're in different centuries. I don't think he'd want to see you miserable." She walked to Janet's nightstand and picked up the glittering strands. "Now put on this beautiful necklace that a handsome, modern gentleman gave you. We're going to have fun tonight."

They sat in the same booth she'd been in before on her blind date with Reuben, a few weeks or a few months earlier, depending on how you were measuring time. Fiona, sober this time, sat with them, teasing Janet that her cousin still asked after her.

"Sic him on some other poor, unsuspecting woman," laughed Janet. "That evening belongs in the dating book of horrors."

"Amrita," said Fiona, "what are you doing next Friday night?"

"Washing my hair, most definitely."

Malcolm whispered in her ear. "Well, if that's my competition, my offer to join me in my new house is looking far more attractive. I'll have to pay Fiona to set you up with all her cousins."

Janet shook her head. "It sounds like I'll just have to find a better quality of men, preferably not related to Fiona."

"*Touché.*" He placed his hand over his heart. "Okay, guys, who wants another round? My turn." All hands went up. "Be right back."

"Wow, Janet. He's a keeper," said James. "I was sure he'd only manage to update me on the Red Sox, but he's even up on the Blue Jays."

"Thanks for your approval."

"Seriously," he said. "It's not like you're dating anyone. He's a successful architect *and* he's in good with Daddy. He told me he thinks it's great you want a career in literature, and he's obviously crazy about you. What more could you want?"

Janet sighed and looked around the table. "Is my love life, or lack of it, open to group discussion now? Back off."

"You heard the lady," said Amrita. "Give her some space."

"Who's thirsty?" Malcolm placed down the pints and everyone took their beers.

"Thanks, Malcolm," chorused the table.

"Keeper, keeper, keeper," James muttered under his breath.

Later, they returned to The Crescent. The night was warm, the stars shimmering points in the inky black sky. Janet remembered a similar evening, back in her nineteenth-century life, when she'd stood in the same spot, looking up at her room with Emma and Charles. Edward had stayed behind, but she'd felt their conversation at the Assembly Halls had been almost friendly that night.

Back then, she'd been daydreaming about her twenty-first-century life. Now she found herself at the same spot with her modern friends, doing the exact opposite. What were Emma, Charles, and Edward up to? Would she ever know? Were they still thinking of her, or was she slowly fading from their collective memory?

"Earth to Janet," said Amrita.

Janet startled. "Oh, sorry. I was just ..."

"Off in your own world. Yeah, we know. Malcolm, thanks for coming out with us tonight."

"My pleasure, Amrita. If your dad's worried about overcharging, have him call me if he wants me to look over those architect quotes for the renovation. I'll point anything out that strikes me as odd."

"Thanks, that's sweet of you." She kissed Malcolm's cheek.

"Goodnight," said Fiona.

"Hey Malcolm," said James. "You know I'm going to take you up on those tickets to Fenway when I come to Boston, don't you?"

"I'm counting on it."

When Malcolm turned to kiss Fiona, James mouthed "Keeper" to Janet, who shook her head. "Okay, let's leave these love birds alone."

The friends dispersed, leaving Janet and Malcolm alone on the Green.

"Your friends are fantastic."

"I know. They are. Most of the time, anyway." She looked up at the light in her window. "You seem to have made a good impression on them."

He placed his hands on her shoulders and gazed into her eyes. "I'm happy about that, but, truth be told, the good opinion of only one person is what counts most. And I think she's the hardest to impress."

Janet stood in silence, a light breeze tickling her face.

He must have interpreted her silence as willingness. He narrowed the space between them with a single step, his polo shirt brushing against her dress, the smell of his cologne mixing with the scent of the freshly cut grass.

Removing one arm from her shoulder, he fingered the delicate strands of her necklace. "You made me happy wearing this tonight. It suits you perfectly." His voice was a soft whisper. "Elegant, refined, and hopelessly beautiful."

He reached up to stroke the hair back from her forehead, gazing into her eyes with such longing. A longing that reminded her of Edward in the library the night of the ball. Edward striding toward her with confident steps, the glint in Edward's eyes that expressed every feeling in his heart. Edward's lips brushing her own.

She closed her eyes and took a deep breath. She fought to keep the tears from springing forth. Malcolm's comforting hand brushed her cheek. His warm breath tickled her face as his mouth came closer to hers. She felt the brush of his lips against hers, gentle at first, and then insistent. Her body crushed against his as his arms encircled her. For a moment, she lost herself in the kiss, feeling as if in a fog.

But when she opened her eyes, the night sky was clear, the stars twinkling down at her from the sky. The man kissing her wasn't Sir Edward, but Malcolm, and she didn't feel anything. His kiss didn't consume her as Edward's had, didn't make her feel her knees would give way.

Gently, she placed her hands on his shoulders, and pushed back.

The hurt and confusion in his eyes forced her to look away.

He closed the distance between them, holding her face with both hands. "Janet, what is it?" His voice was gentle. "What's wrong?"

"It's not you." She struggled with the tears welling up. Seeing the accusation in his gaze made her heart flutter. "But it's not fair to you, either. I was thinking of Edward." She wished she could retract the words the second they escaped her lips.

He stepped backwards, shaking his head. "Edward? Who's Edward?" His voice rose slightly, then he took a deep breath, and his voice was measured once again. "Are you seeing someone else?"

She shook her head and looked down. "No."

He was silent for a moment, before reaching down to place his hand under her chin and raising her face up slowly, until her eyes met his own. "But you're in love with this Edward?"

A single tear slipped down her cheek, but she did not break eye contact with Malcolm as she spoke in a clear, steady voice. "Yes. I am."

In the distance, drunken shrieks and laughter broke the silence.

He breathed in deeply. "And this is why you're telling me you need more time, why you can't offer me anything more than friendship right now."

Janet nodded.

Malcolm searched her eyes. "Then I suppose I have no choice but to be patient, until you get over this Edward and are ready to move on."

She sighed. Amrita had told her she should try, but she wasn't ready yet. And it wasn't fair to Malcolm not to be completely honest with him.

Malcolm slipped one arm around her slumped shoulders, pulling her body into his as he walked her back to the entrance of her house. He hugged her goodnight, telling her he'd return the next day to say goodbye.

Janet closed the door behind her. From the grand window, she watched with a numb heart as Malcolm walked back across the Green in the direction of his hotel.

Chapter 40

Janet woke with a jolt. The glow of the moonlight filled the room. She'd forgotten to close the curtains when she'd come up to bed last night. Turning, she saw Amrita in the bed beside hers, sound asleep.

She lay still, trying to concentrate on the dream. She'd been in Sir Edward's arms, but that in itself wasn't odd. She'd dreamed of Sir Edward every night since her return. Perhaps she visited him in his own dreams, but she wondered if that was already fading with the months passing in his world.

No, it wasn't the images that caused her to wake suddenly from her slumber. It was the tingling sensation. She hadn't felt it since her return to her modern world. She sat silently in the dark, concentrating on the pins-and-needles feeling sweeping throughout her body. It was weak, but most definitely present. "Edward, there's still hope," she whispered into the silence of the room. Could he sense her? Could he feel something, too?

Ensuring Amrita was still asleep, she opened the drawer to her bedside table and drew out the flashlight. In bare feet, she padded to the painting. In its shadowy corner, the painting did not absorb the light of the sun or the glow of the moon.

Switching on the flashlight, she shone it onto the canvas. Her light caught the green buds bursting forth from Daphne's fingers, the soft curves of her alabaster skin, the coils of her blonde hair, the billowing pink and yellow of her robes. Cautiously, she reached out to touch the scratch. Pressing her index finger to the point, she felt a jolt so strong it sent her reeling backwards. Her mouth dropped. It had never been so strong before. *Edward, Edward are you thinking of me now? I'm here. Draw me back ...*

Heart pounding, she approached the canvas. She closed her eyes and pressed her finger decisively to the gash, awaiting the jolt. It didn't come. She pressed harder and waited. Nothing.

She shone the light into Daphne's lovely face and caught the look of sadness she often saw there. *I thought we were in this together, Daphne.*

Janet stood silently for a long time, observing the painting she knew as well as her own reflection in the mirror. The tingling sensation never returned. In the end, she switched off the flashlight and crawled back onto her bed, willing Sir Edward's face to return to her in her dreams.

The next morning, Janet and Amrita came as close to an argument as they'd ever come. Janet hadn't said anything about the jolt. But Amrita rolled her eyes when she woke to find Janet hunched over the Jane Austen from Edward.

"If I see you with that bloody book again ..." Amrita shook her head. "I'm guessing you told Malcolm off yesterday when he tried to tell you how in love with you he is."

Janet flinched at the hardness in her friend's voice. "I didn't want to hurt him. I was honest with him. Is it better to pretend I'm in love with him while thinking of someone else? How honest is that?"

Amrita sat up in her bed and stretched. "Janet, what you have is one step better than lusting after Captain Wentworth or Fitzwilliam Darcy on the page. Yes, you met Edward, and I don't deny it was romantic. But you're here now. He's as real as the characters in that book. I'm afraid you're going to regret your decision, and let a wonderfully sweet guy slip through your fingers for some silly dream that won't ever come true."

"I know Malcolm's great." She closed her book and slipped it into her bedside drawer. "And he's awfully popular around here. You all seem to like him so much." She heard unattractive sarcasm creep into her voice.

"You probably would, too, if you weren't so intent on pushing him away. If you told me you weren't attracted to him, or he bored you, or he was cruel, I'd understand. But I can so clearly see the two of you together, living happily ever after in Boston. You can teach and he'll work in your family firm. You laugh together. You practically finish one another's sentences. Don't you realize how rare that is?" She walked to the door and took her towel hanging from behind it. "What could you have told him to get him to back off?"

Janet looked down. "I told him I was still in love with Edward."

"You *what*?"

Janet played with the folds in the sheet. "I didn't tell him who he was. I said he was a man I was no longer seeing, but that I was still in love with him and wasn't ready to start a new relationship." When Janet met Amrita's eyes, she saw disappointment.

"I'm going to take my shower. The weather's supposed to turn this afternoon. We're all headed over to the library this morning, then an exhibition and a film in town this afternoon. I'd ask you to join us, but I guess you'll want to be on the computer all day."

"Yeah, I will. Have fun, though. I'll want to hear about it tonight."

Amrita gave a faint nod before going out the door.

The house was quiet, and Janet had the library to herself. All day she'd been up in her room working on the computer, adding to her previously stalled thesis.

When she decided to come to the library to take a break and read *Persuasion*, she'd taken her usual seat at the window. But rain pounded down on the glass, and the fresh memories of Malcolm having confessed his love as she sat there only a few days ago caused her to seek out another spot. Up the rickety steps, hidden behind stacks and stacks of books, was a tiny desk she'd never noticed before.

Although no one was in the house to disturb her—they were probably enjoying the film by now –she liked the idea of being almost invisible, a tiny mouse in the grand library. It matched her solitary mood. She didn't feel as if she fit in anymore. Maybe she never would.

She shook her head. Self-pity was becoming too common a thread to her days. She opened up the pages of *Persuasion*, instead focusing her attention on the moment when Ann's friend, Mrs. Smith, fills Ann in on Mr. William Elliot's devious, calculating nature. Janet read of William's crippling debt and his intention to marry Ann in order to secure his inheritance. The betrayal never failed to surprise her, even after having read the book a half dozen times.

But his deviousness filled a purpose. Look how close she came to making a terrible mistake—marrying the awful William, when now she's free to marry Captain Wentworth. Her one true love.

Tears sprang to her eyes. Ever since she'd returned, anything could set her on edge. *What's wrong with me? I'm jealous about*

Ann Elliot's happiness. The thought was meant to cheer her, but the tears flowed even faster than before.

As she wiped them away, she heard the doorbell and the footsteps of the modern-day Miss Smith of Bath answering it. Voices neared the library.

"No, I have not seen Miss Roberts this afternoon," said Miss Smith in her habitual, clipped tones. "She was working in her room this morning. Perhaps she has gone out with the others."

"I should hope not." Her father's flustered, angry voice resonated off the library walls. "It's four o'clock, the time she agreed to meet us here. We're on our way to London. It's exactly like Janet. That girl's never had her head screwed on right."

Janet balked at his words. Since the age of twelve, she'd been expected to fill her mother's shoes, never enjoying a real childhood. Shopping, cooking, picking up his dry cleaning, entertaining her father's clients, reviewing his projects. And now she was the one who didn't have her head screwed on? No way was she coming down now, with her eyes red and her face tear-stained. She'd calm down and then emerge in a few minutes, maybe claim she'd fallen asleep up in the stacks.

"I've tried calling her cell, but she doesn't answer," her father continued. "Could you take a look in her room to see if she's there?"

"If you'll excuse me a moment," said Miss Smith.

"No point in racing back from Bristol if she was only going to be late," said her father.

"How did the meetings go?" asked Malcolm's voice.

She could just make out the tips of his expensive Italian shoes from her perch.

"I should have been there with you. The project's at such a delicate stage."

"I told them you had a stomach flu," said her father. "Besides, I wanted you here in case Janet called you."

"That wasn't going to happen," said Malcolm, with an exaggerated snort.

Janet frowned. What were they talking about? Approaching footsteps stopped the conversation.

"I've been to her room," said Miss Smith. "She isn't there. Perhaps she went out for a walk and got caught in this rain. Would you gentlemen care to wait here in the library? You will see her from the grand window when she returns across the Green."

"Thank you, Miss Smith," said Malcolm in a sweet voice.

The library was silent as her footsteps receded. Malcolm walked towards the door. She heard it shut. Her father settled in her favorite chair. She could observe him clearly, even if he would be unable to see her. Malcolm returned and sat in a nearby chair. Now would be the time to make her way down the staircase, claiming she'd dozed off and their voices had woken her. She patted her eyes and straightened her hair in its barrette.

"What do you mean it wasn't going to happen? Janet's call? Did you screw something up last night?"

Something about her father's sneer stopped her movement. Did he know Malcolm was going to tell her about his feelings? Surely they hadn't discussed it together?

"Let's just say her coming to live with me at the Back Bay house is far from a sure thing."

Janet held her breath. They'd discussed all of it? She knew Malcolm and her father were close, but surely Malcolm couldn't have laid out all his plans to her father without even consulting her first?

"Oh, hell. I knew it!" Her father's voice boomed across the library.

She heard Malcolm shushing him. Janet herself could never get away with that.

"Did you do everything like I told you? Did you give her the damn necklace?"

"Yeah, of course. I told her all that yada yada crap about it reminding me of her—so elegant and refined. What else? Oh, yeah, the hopelessly beautiful line you were so convinced would be the clincher."

Malcolm's voice had a rough edge to it she'd never heard before. Gone was the gentle, unfailingly polite, almost puppy-dog-sweet voice he often used with her. Her eyes grew wide and she bit her lip, afraid she might gasp and betray her presence.

"So what the hell went wrong? There must have been *something* you screwed up before that?"

"No," said Malcolm. "Everything went according to plan. I went to the pub with her friends, after I whined to that Amrita chick a few times on the phone, telling her how my life'd had no meaning when Janet was missing. I think I even told her I went back and reread all the Jane Austen books to feel closer to her." He laughed. "Can you believe that idiot bought it?"

Janet's father grunted.

Janet bit her lip. She remembered her tense conversation with Amrita that morning. He'd been playing Amrita all along, angling for her sympathy. And here *she'd* felt guilty to have hurt such a nice guy.

"The rest of them loved me, too. I thought even Janet was starting to soften. It was perfect. The moonlight, the stars. And then I kiss her and out comes this '*Oh, I'm so sorry, but I'm still in love with Edward*' crap."

Janet blanched at the high-pitched falsetto that was supposed to mimic her voice. She looked down at the cover of her book. *William Elliot is a gentleman compared to you, Malcolm!*

"Who the hell is Edward?" boomed her father's voice.

"No clue. I said I'd wait for her ... and that was that." He paced up and down. "But she'd better forget the loser—probably some starry-eyed, light-in-his-Birkenstocks lit major. And it better be soon, or the lawyer's gonna call her. And then she'll be on to us."

Janet leaned in closer, not sure she'd heard correctly.

Her father sighed. "My wife's will stipulates she'd come into the money at twenty-six, when she'll be informed. Bloody hell, I tried to convince him Janet's still weighing her career options, and the money hanging over her head would be a burden. That ... and a few costly Bermuda golf junkets made him promise to keep quiet a bit longer, but he insists she has to be told within the year. I was counting on you to have her on our side by then."

"And I was doing a good job! Then that stupid accident comes along. Who knows if it was only an excuse to run away with Edward the poet? Maybe things went wrong."

"Janet's not that devious. She never was. Takes after her mother. Always the innocent. Her mother never suspected I only married her for her money."

"You go ahead and tell yourself that." Malcolm's laugh sounded harsh. "If that were true, she wouldn't have changed her will, would she have? If she didn't suspect, she'd never have included the clause allowing Janet to take her share of the money if she didn't want to join the firm. That sure as hell doesn't sound like a naive woman who suspects nothing."

Janet felt as if she'd been punched in the gut. Her whole life explained in one overheard conversation. All the pressure to be an architect—only so her father could hang on to her mother's money. Marrying an architect was the next best thing. What was Malcolm getting out of it? Partner at least, she imagined. Maybe a cash incentive.

There was a knock at the door. "Gentlemen," said Miss Smith, "would you care to come to the breakfast room for tea?"

"Thank you, Miss Smith. It's so kind of you," said Malcolm. His voice was once again sweet and ingratiating, the voice Janet recognized from last night, or when he told her he loved her in this very room, or the first chat in which he opened up to her, sitting on The Crescent lawn on her first day in Bath. She dug her nails into her palms. Was anything he'd ever said true?

Her father rose from his chair and both men left the library, following Miss Smith into the breakfast room. Janet exhaled the breath she'd been holding. Her hands trembled and tears welled up in her eyes. She examined the cover of *Persuasion*, shaking her head. Her life was a Jane Austen novel.

She could deal with Malcolm's betrayal, but her own father? At least Ann Elliot's father was simply vain and stupid. He wasn't plotting against his daughter with William Elliot to steal her inheritance.

Her mind raced. What should she do now? The rain lashed against the windows. Her classmates hadn't yet returned. No one knew she was here. She crept down the staircase, leaving her volume on a bookshelf. Slowly, she unlatched the lock and stepped out the front door. Dashing out in the rain, she held her hands heavenward and spun around and around. The cold drops pelted her face and washed away the tears.

She strode quickly to the front door, where she stomped her feet loudly and rang the bell.

"Oh, Miss Smith!" she said with overly loud relief when the older woman answered the door. "I forgot my keys. What luck that you're home. Have my father and Malcolm arrived yet?"

"Yes. They are having tea in the breakfast room."

"Oh, I got caught in the rain." Janet looked down at her dripping clothes. "I finally decided to make a run for it. Would you tell them I'll join them momentarily, as soon as I've changed into dry clothes?"

"Of course, Miss Roberts," said Miss Smith with a curt nod.

Janet ran up the staircase, pausing before the portrait of Emma. "Hello, my friend," she whispered. "Too bad Sir John can't time travel, too. I'd have the perfect partner in crime for him."

"Well, Daddy," said Janet in the entry hall. "I'm obviously sorry to have dragged you here for nothing. And to have you so terribly worried about me. But, as you see, I'm in perfect health. And anxious to get back to my studies."

Her father grunted. "Let's hope you treat your architecture internship as seriously as your book nonsense."

"Of course. I've been specializing in nineteenth-century renovations. Getting some real hands-on experience. It's fascinating." She smiled. "Have a good trip."

He gave her a quick hug that somehow managed to maintain a cool distance. "I need to make a call. I'll let you and Malcolm say goodbye."

Of course, now I can see his acting skills on full display. Will tears well up when he takes his leave? Will he tell me he'll be counting the minutes until my return?

Malcolm turned back to ensure Janet's father was on the phone, then stepped closer to Janet, placing both hands on her waist. His eyes were soft as he observed her. "I can't pretend what you told me last night hasn't upset me."

His voice was soft and tender, and Janet found herself enjoying the show.

"You know, Malcolm." She willed her voice to sound equally tender. "I respect how open and truthful you've always been with me. How could I treat you with any less respect and honesty than you've always shown me?"

A sad smile crept across his face. His eyes glazed over.

"Are you a hunter, by any chance, Malcolm?"

"What?"

She examined the surprise on his face, wondering if it was the first honest emotion she'd seen from him since their arrival in Bath.

"Hunting. Animals." She shook her head slightly. "You've heard of it, I'm sure?"

He was slow to respond. "Yeah, I guess my father took me a few times."

She raised an eyebrow. "Your father, the poor fisherman who was hardly scraping by in Gloucester? He hunted in his leisure time?"

He frowned. "Why all the questions, Janet?"

"Oh, nothing." She smiled. "I'm only trying to get to know you better."

He took her hands. "Come back to Boston and live with me in the new house." He winked and lowered his voice. "You'll know everything about me then."

"You're tempting me, Malcolm. When you know I need time to think." She made a face she hoped looked sad. "I almost forgot! Just one minute." She touched his cheek and raced into the library, returning immediately with her dog-eared copy of *Persuasion*. "I understand from Amrita that you've been rereading all your Jane Austen recently." She smiled sheepishly. "Who's your favorite character in *Persuasion*?"

Confusion clouded his face. "Well ... I ... um, I haven't thought about it recently ... Hard to say, really ... I'd, uh, need to consider."

Janet smiled and tapped him on the chest with the volume. "How odd. You were *much* more articulate on the topic of Austen during our Bath tour." She shook her head. "You weren't brushing up on the *Spark Notes* versions back then by any chance, were you?"

Confusion flashed in his eyes. Or was it fear?

"What're you talking about?" he snapped.

"Just teasing you, silly." She laughed. "This takes place in Bath, and I think it may have become my new favorite Austen novel. Sorry, it's used, as you can see, but I want you to have it." She handed him the book. "You have a long trip back. Enjoy the read. I have the feeling you'll like it."

"Thank you." He leaned in and kissed her cheek. "This will remind me of you. I'm going to miss you so much."

"Oh, and I'll miss you, too, Malcolm. *So* much. Both you and my father."

He caressed her cheek, gazing at her with sad eyes before turning to join her father on the stairs. He opened his umbrella over both of them and they walked away from the Crescent.

Janet stood on the stoop. When they turned around, she gave a last, enthusiastic wave and a wide smile. No acting required.

Chapter 41

Amrita opened her eyes wide. "No, Janet. You must have misunderstood."

Janet sat across from her on Amrita's bed. They were both in their pyjamas. It was the first time Janet could speak with her roommate alone, and she'd recounted the entire overheard conversation. "I'm afraid not. If Malcolm weren't an architect, he could have had a brilliant acting career."

"But he was *so* convincing. I believed every word."

"So did I. At least Anne Elliot suspected something was wrong with William. Malcolm had me completely fooled."

"We're studying Austen, for crying out loud. Elliot, Wickham, Willoughby, Churchill ... " Amrita ticked them off on her fingers. "You'd think we'd be more prepared."

"Some things never change. Unfortunately." Janet pulled her hair back into a ponytail. "But I still can't understand it. He planned to move in with me, maybe even marry me. Would we have had children together? And all of it would have been a lie? How could he *do* all that, just to have more money?"

Janet turned to look at Daphne and Apollo, and her heart ached.

"But I honestly can't even blame Malcolm as much as my father. He cheated my mother, and now he's prepared to cheat his own daughter." She wiped away at a tear. "I mean, growing up I knew he never loved me, not like other parents. But now I start to wonder if he secretly hoped my disappearance meant I was dead. And that way, the money would be all his without any effort. Maybe my showing up alive ruined all his plans."

Amrita squeezed her hand. "Oh, Janet. I'm so sorry."

"There's something else." Janet cast a glance at the painting. "I was so upset this afternoon that I came up here after Malcolm and my father left. I felt the tingling again. The tingling that I've always felt before the time travel. It's the second time I've felt it. It's growing stronger."

"Do you think you can go back?" Amrita's voice dropped a notch. "Do you *want* to go back?"

"It's all I'm thinking about. I need to consider, but I can't wait too long. Four *months* have gone by in Edward and Emma's world."

Amrita looked down, tracing the flower patterns on the bedspread. "You may have to make a decision quicker than you thought. I wasn't going to tell you until tomorrow morning, when I saw how upset you were about your dad's visit. But Professor Williams told me the National Gallery will be taking away the Tiepolo on Tuesday."

Janet turned to the painting, feeling the panic well up inside. "Tuesday? Why so soon?"

"Something about a break-in at Helmsley Manor. Those paintings will be taken, too."

"Mr. Whitshaw and the intruders," muttered Janet under her breath.

"What happened to Mr. Whitshaw?"

"Nothing. It's not important. I'm going to need your help tomorrow. I have things I need to do. I'll say I have doctor's appointments and won't be in class. But I need you here with me tomorrow evening. Can you manage?"

"If you need me, yes. What are you going to do?"

Janet looked at the painting, at the sad luminous glow of Daphne's face. "I don't know yet. But I need to decide quickly."

The next morning, Janet paced, checking her watch as the sunlight streamed through the cracks in the curtains. She'd showered and dressed before the sun even rose, her troubled mind devising options.

Her watch read 7:30. Still early, but she'd no time to spare. Taking her cellphone, she stepped into the hallway.

"Oh, Mr. Perry, it's Janet. I apologize for disturbing you so early. I remember you told me your brother's a solicitor. I'm in urgent need of legal advice. Could you get me an appointment with him today?"

Later that evening, Janet packed her bag. The tingling had grown stronger throughout the day, the pins and needles almost unbearable when she stood too close to the Tiepolo. In her bag she placed Edward's book, the necklace, medicines, deodorant, a toothbrush and toothpaste. She smiled, knowing they wouldn't last long, but some material comfort in the first weeks would be welcome. She'd toyed with the idea of the Western Civilization textbook she'd been devouring in the past days, but decided unintentionally changing the course of history could be too dangerous.

The guilt of altering lives already disturbed her. She tried not to dwell on it. If it wasn't meant to be, this simply wouldn't work. There was no reason to stay and regret her choice for the rest of her life. This is what she'd told herself all day. But the truth was, as the day progressed, the butterflies in her stomach multiplied tenfold.

She walked over to the painting and touched the scratch. A shock ran through her arm, causing her to wince in pain. But she didn't let go until she couldn't stand it anymore. She staggered backwards, dropping on the bed, panting.

Amrita slipped into the room at ten that night, as they'd planned. The rest of their classmates were out for a drink to celebrate a birthday. Amrita joined them and then faked a stomachache.

When she entered, her eyes conveyed her fear. "Janet, I've been thinking about this all day. Are you sure?"

"I'm scared. I'll admit that, but I've never been more sure about anything in my life. I've never felt more myself as I do with Edward and Emma back in the nineteenth century."

"What if you change your mind? Once the painting's gone, how can you come back?"

"I don't know. I don't even know if it'll work *this* time, but I have to try." She walked to her bedside table and took out an envelope. "I've written a note, saying I'm upset about things I've learned about my father and Malcolm and my inheritance, and making it clear that I'm going away, and have no wish to be followed. I'm an adult. If I don't wish to be found, the police will not launch an investigation." She breathed in deeply. "I've also spoken with a lawyer, and left similar instructions with him. We've made arrangements for my inheritance. I'll trust you to say my goodbyes to everyone, and to tell them how much I'll miss them.

Amrita's eyes filled with tears. "We'll never see one another again, will we?"

"Not in person, Amrita. But I'm counting on you." She slipped a USB key into her hand.

"What's this?"

"Work on my thesis. I still want to complete it and publish it—with your help."

"What?" The confusion was clear in her eyes.

"We'll complete it together—both our names on the thesis, but it will launch the academic career of only one of us." She squeezed her friend's hand. "You must promise me you'll do it."

"Do what, Janet?" Her lip trembled.

"I've figured it all out. Four months is 120 days. That's ten *years* in Edward and Emma's world. In four months' time— at the end of October—you must go to Helmsley Manor. I'm leaving you this letter to give to Mr. Whitshaw, saying I discovered something and I'd like to take a look at the commemorative foundation stone of the Helmsley Manor School."

Amrita looked confused. "We were there together. *What* Helmsley Manor School?"

"Trust me on this. You'll find everything you need to complete a thesis on social customs of the time. If you combine the work I've already done, the materials you will find there, and your brilliant insight into family relations in nineteenth-century England, we'll have one hell of a groundbreaking publication. In the farewell note, I even said I left my USB key for you to work with my research since I'm leaving academia. What do you say? Please agree, Amrita. I need you ..."

Amrita was silent for a long time. "I'd rather be publishing with you, revising together, maybe visiting one another at our universities and speaking together at conferences."

"I'd love that, too, but it'll be hard to manage two hundred years apart."

"So you're sure." Her voice was quiet.

"Yes," Janet whispered, keeping her eyes fixed on Amrita's gaze.

Amrita took a deep breath. "Okay, then. I'll probably regret saying this, but how does it work?"

Janet walked to her bed and reached underneath, pulling out a baseball bat. "I took this from James' room. The first time I travelled back I was hit in the head with a cricket ball, the second by a statue Miss Chadwick threw at me." She handed Amrita the bat. "The way I figure it, I have to touch the scratch, then you give me a quick whack in the head. Judging from the tingling, it should be quick."

Amrita let the bat fall to the floor. "Are you out of your bloody mind? I'm not clubbing you on the head!"

"Please, Amrita." She tried to keep her voice calm. "If the situation were reversed, I'd feel the same. But it's the only way. Judging from the last two times, the tingling gets stronger, I touch the painting's scratch, and then I get a blow to the head, which apparently sends me back."

"And if I hurt you?" Tears welled up in Amrita's eyes.

"I've seen you play cricket. You're awful. Why do you think I chose you and not James?" She smiled, but saw the tears roll down Amrita's cheeks in response. She gathered her friend into a hug. "It's okay. It doesn't have to be hard. One swift hit. Miss Chadwick seemed to enjoy it."

Amrita laughed through her tears. "Okay, I can do this." She stepped back and took a deep breath. "Are you ready?"

"One minute!" Janet picked up her bag from her bed, placing the strap over her head and resting it on her shoulder. She walked slowly to the painting, looked up at Daphne and stroked the scratch with her index finger. The tingling spread through her. She took a deep breath and faced Amrita. "You're a great friend, Amrita. Don't forget—the end of October."

A single tear slipped down Amrita's cheek. "I hope you're happy, Janet." Pulling back the bat, she took a deep breath, then swung her arms, gathering speed.

Janet closed her eyes and felt the sharp thud against the back of her skull. Her eyes snapped open as she hurtled forward against the mantelpiece.

Chapter 42

Janet's skull ached and she felt dizzy, but this time she hadn't lost consciousness. She rubbed the back of her head. Amrita's batting skills were better than she'd bargained on.

Her eyes flickered around the dark room. She was no longer in Huntington House. She struggled to breathe. The dark bookshelves, the moonlight shining in the high windows, the orange glow in the fireplace. Her gaze slipped upward. Yes, there it was. Her old friend. The Tiepolo.

She blinked, afraid her mind was playing tricks on her. But when she opened her eyes, the room was exactly the same. Helmsley Manor. Most definitely the library of Helmsley Manor. Her breaths came faster. She'd hoped the tingling sensation, the painting, and a blow to the head needed to be combined for the time travel, but a part of her had been unconvinced. And yet, here she was.

She heard a movement and stood very still. In the armchair, a shadowy form was faintly illuminated by the flickering of the fire. She dug her nails into her palms. Could it be?

Silently, she crept towards the chair. Hope filled her heart with each step. But what if she hadn't returned to the same time? Fifty years earlier or later could change everything.

She took a step forward. From this angle, she could observe, while still shrouded in the room's inky shadows. The clouds covered the moon, but her eyes soon adjusted to the darkness. Her heart beat faster as she made out the outline of a face in the light of the fireplace.

Edward stared into the flames, his face so still and pensive. He did not sense her presence. Was she visible? To come all this way and be invisible would be too much to bear.

Gathering her courage, she took one long step until she was at an angle between the chair and the fireplace. Edward turned towards her, but his face registered no pleasure. The silence in the room was deafening as they observed one another.

Edward straightened in his chair. "I fear you are a figment of my imagination. I have waited for you so long. Night after night, I sat in this library. You never came."

Janet longed to race to him, but held back. "I am here now, Edward. Time does not pass the same way in my world as it does in yours. Am I too late?" Tears shored up behind her eyes, ready to spill over if his words smothered her hopes.

He gazed out the window, where the moon had broken out from the clouds. Slowly, he turned. His expression softened. "Jane, come here. Let me touch you to ensure you are real. Each evening I sat before our painting, hoping you would return to me."

"I have."

She closed the distance between them and placed a hand against his warm cheek. Over five months had passed as he waited for her to return. She sank down into his lap, resting her face against his chest, listening to the steady beat of his heart. A living, breathing human being. No longer a mere portrait of a long-ago resident on the wall of Huntington House, but the flesh and blood man she loved.

He wrapped his arms around her, rocking her gently and kissing her tousled hair.

This is where I belong.

"Jane," he laughed and gently pushed her back, allowing his eyes to linger over her body. "What are you wearing?"

Janet looked down at her clothes. "Ah, a modern sundress. Corsetless, of course. That instrument of torture was abandoned by women long before my time."

He traced her lips with his index finger. "I like these future sundresses, as you call them. It highlights your figure perfectly—perhaps *too* perfectly. And all that display of shoulders and bare legs. I will have to insist you only wear these clothes when we are alone together, or you will set tongues wagging." He winked. "I have dreamt of this moment so many times. I had given up hope that it would come true." His voice trailed off in a whisper. "But have you thought things through fully? Are you certain you wish to stay with me in this world? Will your family not miss you?"

Janet looked up at Apollo and Daphne. "It was my last chance to return, Edward. The painting—your painting—is being gifted to London's National Gallery. The painting is the door between our two worlds." She stroked his cheek. "Only one uncertainty bothers me. The first time I travelled, I arrived in Huntington House, yet the painting wasn't in Bath. Every other time, my journey has ended where the painting is. "

He was quiet a moment. "But the Tiepolo *was* in Bath when you arrived that first time. I was worried about some rot to the frame, and had it restored. I brought it to Bath for that work, and the painting was indeed at Huntington House, in a secret vault. None of the servants even knew about it."

"Then that explains it. It was the one thing I couldn't resolve." She placed her hand in his, feeling its warmth. "You know I had to convince my friend to clobber me on the head to return to you?"

Edward winced. "When I think about Miss Chadwick's fury when she threw the statue. You disappeared in my arms, Jane.

It was terrible. Victoria fled from the room, so only I witnessed it. After her act of violence, I was no longer honor bound to her. Still, that knowledge brought me no relief when I was so anxious for your welfare. Following your explanations, I at least knew that you had returned to your time, but whether you were alive or dead after such a blow to the head, I did not know. That doubt has haunted me each day. " He furrowed his brow. "And now you inflicted such pain on yourself? For me?"

"You're worth it, Edward." She curled into his chest, feeling its solidity. His warm hands stroked her back. "I cannot lie and say I won't miss my modern life, or my friends, but it was easy to say goodbye to my family. My mother died when I was young. I loved her and miss her every day. All these years, I've worked to maintain a relationship with my father, believing only that he had difficulty expressing his love outwardly." She wished to stop, but knew she must speak the words aloud. "But the truth is, he never loved either of us. He married my mother for her money, and he kept me close to control my inheritance. It was purely a business deal."

Edward gently pushed her back, searching her face. When the tears began to flow down her cheeks, he wiped them away.

"You learned this when you were back?" His voice was gentle, his eyes full of pain.

Janet nodded. "I overheard a conversation. And now everything makes sense."

He stroked her hair back from her face. "All I want to do is make you happy, Jane. But I am afraid you might have run away from something, perhaps in a moment of weakness. It would be selfish of me to keep you here if you cannot be happy with your decision. Are you sure you have fully considered everything? Are you certain you want to stay? Want to stay with me?"

Janet looked into those serious blue eyes, the eyes she'd dreamt about before she'd even known him, the ones she'd been terrified she'd never see again when she returned to modern Bath.

"Edward, I've never been more certain about anything in my life. I lived in your Bath home on my return, passed your portrait on the hallway each day—yours and Emma's—and missed you desperately. The news about my father only banished any guilt I may have felt in reaching my decision otherwise."

He caressed her bare shoulder. She was dressed for June when it was a cold March night. The fire crackled before them and the golden glow illuminated his face.

"I do not wish you to be bored in a life much quieter than what you are accustomed to in your world. I have been thinking about your words. About how much the world has changed for women in the future. If you would like, you can continue your work with the school—and I'll need your architect's eye on work on the manor and the improvements on the cottages."

She reached her hand behind his head, running her fingers through his thick hair. "It will be very, very important for me to improve the sanitation of the cottages. I do not wish to speak with you about the future. I think it is better you not know, but I will say that Helmsley Manor needs to avoid problems that will break out in crowded, unsanitary living quarters. We must set aside the funds and the time to improve the tenant homes. This must be a priority. Please trust me on this."

He smiled. "I will trust you on this and on everything, my sweet Jane. For you have made me the happiest man of all time by returning to me."

He pulled her gently towards him. Her lips neared his, and she longed to feel the pressure of his kiss, but one last doubt nagged her. She reached her hands to his shoulders and pushed back.

The pain on his face caused her to flinch.

"What is it, Jane?" His voice was soft. "What have I done?"

She placed her index finger over his lips. "One last point, Edward. It is Emma. She absolutely must *not* marry Sir John. I insist on this point. You *must* find a way for her to be with Charles. This is non-negotiable."

He removed her finger from his lips, and shook his head. "We are not yet married, and you are already berating me? What am I getting myself into?" His face broke into a wide grin. "I have already arranged everything, and spoken to Charles' aunt. They will reside here until he comes into his inheritance. His aunt was hesitant at first but now agrees it is an excellent match. And the wedding is to be in two weeks' time."

Janet clapped her hands together. "Two weeks' time! How exciting! Oh, Emma must be so overwhelmed with all the planning. She will need me." She slipped down from his lap.

He pulled her back. "*I* need you, Jane. If you agree, I believe Emma could be easily persuaded to change her plans to accommodate a double wedding at Helmsley Manor." He brought his face closer. "That is, if you will consent to be my wife."

The blood coursed through her body. She and Edward, husband and wife. Changing history. The thing she'd most feared. Yet she'd returned for this.

She placed a hand gently on his cheek. "Edward, my love. As I already told you, I asked my roommate to clobber me over the head with a baseball bat in order to return and be with you. My answer is unhesitatingly yes."

The glint in his eyes stopped her heart for a moment. There was no trace of the proud, haughty Sir Edward she knew from the portrait. Only tenderness and love shone from deep within those blue eyes. His lips brushed against hers, his kiss growing insistent and all-consuming. Her heart raced. Her body tingled, but this was no sign of imminent time travel. For the first time in her life, Janet knew without a doubt this was exactly where she was meant to be.

She tightened her embrace, rubbing her hands across his shoulders, learning the feel of the real-life man—muscles and skin rather than careful brushstrokes—under her fingertips. When he moved to kiss her neck, she gasped for air. Dizzy with emotion, she opened one eye and met Daphne's gaze. For a split second, she thought she saw a smile on the wood nymph's face. She winked at the beautiful, alabaster face. *Thank you, Daphne.*

She grasped Edward's face with her hands, tilting his eyes to meet hers. She observed the handsome face that had infuriated and excited her in equal measures. The face she looked forward to seeing each day.

Meeting his kiss, she allowed herself to drown in it, as she had the first time she'd dreamed about him on her very first day in Bath. His arms wrapped around her, pulling her tightly to him. She felt certain her heart would burst.

The tingling washed over her body, and she lived the moment, as if she'd been born to the period.

Epilogue

The October air was crisp as she stepped out of the rental car. She breathed in, feeling the cool, fresh air penetrate deep into her lungs. A crow squawked from above and she followed it with her gaze, following its path as it soared across the burnished oranges, reds, and golden shades of the autumn leaves.

Locking the car door, her black boots crunched over the gravel path on her way to the manor house. She stopped short at the entrance. She'd last been here on a sunny May day, but it looked so different in the diffused light of autumn. Even the stone appeared altered in the cooler light.

Amrita sighed. On her last visit, she'd been here with Janet.

Taking a deep breath, she gathered her courage. Last night, she'd slept poorly, uncertain if she could truly go through with this. But hadn't she promised her friend?

She'd shared the contents of Janet's letter with Mr. Whitshaw, who'd sounded as excited as a schoolboy. He opened the door almost immediately when she rang.

"Miss Amrita, a pleasure." He shook her hand. "Please come in. I have tea waiting in the library."

She stepped into the grand foyer, looking around her once again at the curving, mahogany staircase and glistening floors. *This is the world Janet inhabits now. Can she sense me?*

She followed Mr. Whitshaw into the library, where she sat in a plush chair before the fireplace. The Tiepolo, now in the National Gallery, used to hang in that spot. Were Janet and Sir Edward sitting before it now? She could never get her head around this fluidity of time. Sitting in the home where Janet was also living, two hundred years earlier, left her hopelessly confused. She gratefully accepted the tea.

He settled into the chair opposite her. There was a glint in his eye. "I know you are anxious for me to accompany you to the Manor School. Since you read me the letter over the phone, I've been tempted to take a peek myself, but I've practiced restraint awaiting your arrival."

"Thank you. I know what an unusual request this is."

Mr. Whitshaw shook his head. "I am becoming accustomed to unusual requests." He held out a plate to her. "Biscuit?"

She took one and settled back into her chair, eager to hear what Mr. Whitshaw wished to recount.

"After we spoke on Friday," he slid to the edge of his chair, "I received a call from Janet's Bath solicitor, a Mr. Perry."

"Mr. Perry? Janet used to work for Mr. Perry, an architect."

"Yes. His brother is a solicitor. Janet spoke with him before leaving your program. Apparently, her father and his business partner were attempting to control her inheritance. Perhaps it would be more accurate to say they were attempting to steal her inheritance." He shook his head. "She signed legal documents that when she came into her legal inheritance—left to her by her mother—she wished to donate the money to Helmsley Manor, to create a museum here with the work Sir Edward Huntington collected ..."

Amrita gasped. Her cup clattered in its saucer.

"Yes, I know. Exciting, isn't it? But that's not all." He placed down his tea cup and rubbed his hands together. "The *very same day*, I received a call from a solicitor in London. It seems Lady Jane Huntington, the wife of Sir Edward, set aside valuable jewels and substantial assets. She stipulated they should be placed in a vault until such a date, which, by a strange twist of fate, was also last Friday." His voice rose with excitement.

Amrita's stomach fluttered. Her throat became dry. "Lady Jane had the solicitor keep the instructions for *two hundred years*?"

Mr. Whitshaw chuckled. "Unusual, isn't it? It was passed from solicitor to solicitor through generations, until the date when they were charged to contact whomever was caring for the home. Coincidentally, the *very same date* that Miss Roberts requested that her solicitor contact me." He leaned in closer. "Tell me, Miss Amrita. Do you believe in fate? Do you believe—please don't think me mad—do you believe people can have connections across centuries?"

Amrita took a deep breath. "Very much so, Mr. Whitshaw."

"Both Lady Jane and Janet were extremely insistent on one crucial point: that the Tiepolo should return home. There will be discussions with the National Gallery, of course, but I am hopeful the painting will soon hang in its place of honor." He indicated the fireplace. "The rest of the artwork will remain. Sir Edward and Lady Jane even had additional pieces in the vault all these years, purchases from their honeymoon trip to Venice."

"Their honeymoon trip to Venice?" Her high-pitched voice sounded foreign to her ears. Everything was so odd. This was far too much to process. If she weren't driving, Amrita would have welcomed a strong whiskey.

Mr. Whitshaw's knee bounced up and down, like an excited child describing an adventure. "There will be money for needed repair work, and Helmsley Manor and its art collection will return to its past splendor and be open to paying visitors. At long last." He sighed. "But I am keeping you from your own discovery. Let me fetch the keys, and we will go together to the schoolhouse."

The deep gulps of autumn air calmed Amrita's nerves. She delighted in the crunch of leaves under her boots as they followed the gravel paths to the tenants' cottages. She needed to clear her head. Since Janet's last disappearance, she'd often startled at the bizarre nature of her situation. Did anything truly await her at the school?

Her breathing grew labored as they wove around the cottages. The cottages were different from how she remembered them on their visit last May. Larger, with more windows, and wider spaces between them. How had she simply not noticed this earlier?

"And here's the Helmsley Manor School," Mr. Whitshaw said, indicating a small but neat building. "I'm sure you remember it from your visit."

Amrita felt a sharp pain behind her eyes. No, she'd most definitely never been here, but she nodded slightly.

Mr. Whitshaw took a set of keys from his pocket and walked up the three steps to the schoolroom door. Opening it, he ushered Amrita into a simple but bright classroom, with old-fashioned desks with holes for inkwells.

"This school was actually in use up until World War II. Helmsley Manor fared much better than the surrounding manors, and remained a working farm until then. The tenants' homes are such excellent examples of progressive planning for the time. But the land beyond has all been bought by property developers." Someone approached the door. "Ah, Julian, come in, come in. Our neighborhood mason."

A slight man tipped his cap and placed a toolbox down on a desk. As he opened it and removed tools, Mr. Whitshaw ushered Amrita back outside. "And here is your foundation stone."

Amrita moved closer. She knelt down before the stone, brushing away the dead leaves and high grass to see the engraving. *Helmsley Manor School is dedicated to the manor children and its talented architect, Miss Jane Roberts, on this day of 28 August 1813.*

"Janet," she whispered, her heart racing.

"Pardon, Miss Amrita?"

She took deep breaths to steady herself. "Nothing, Mr. Whitshaw. I was reading the words aloud."

"Yet another coincidence. Our modern benefactress and Lady Huntington had such similar names. Miss Jane Roberts was Lady Huntington's maiden name."

"So I see. That is a coincidence."

Things were so much stranger than she could have imagined. Only Mr. Perry knew anything about this. She'd be visiting his studio this evening, grateful for another person with whom she could talk things over. Her sanity depended on it.

The mason emerged from the school entrance with a hammer and chisel. "This is the foundation stone you want removed?" He indicated the spot.

Mr. Whitshaw nodded, and the mason sunk down to the ground. The chipping sound rang through the silence of the countryside.

Mr. Whitshaw stepped closer to Amrita. "I must admit, I am not expecting this to yield anything. But the discovery Janet claims to have made was too tempting. Who can resist a mystery?"

They watched the mason's progress with growing interest. With a crowbar-like instrument, he hooked the stone and slowly eased it out of its position. Amrita held her breath.

The mason examined the block and issued a low whistle. He tapped the top and smiled. "This almost fooled me for a moment. This is just a thin slab of stone." He looked up at them. "Look, you can slide it out." He revealed a hollowed stone. "Well, I'll be ..."

Amrita and Mr. Whitshaw moved in closer. Amrita felt tingles of excitement race through her body. Could Janet have truly kept her promise?

Their heads close together, they peered into the hollowed foundation stone. "Miss Amrita, it is your discovery. Please do the honors."

Amrita reached towards the stone, to the waxed cloth that lay within. Her trembling fingers clasped the bundle and extracted it from its hiding spot. Her heart beat frantically and she walked over to the school steps and sat down to provide herself support. Slowly, she unwrapped the layers of thick cloth, allowing them to fall to the leaf-scattered ground, until she reached five leather-bound journals. Her breath caught in her throat.

"Oh, my dear." Mr. Whitshaw raised his hands to his mouth. "I can scarcely contain my excitement. What does it say?"

Amrita swallowed with difficulty before gingerly opening the cover. "*The diary of Lady Jane Huntington, 1814-1824*." She met the surprised looks of Mr. Whitshaw and the mason. She turned once again to the journals and glanced quickly through the pages. "They're legible," she said with a sigh of relief. "Brittle paper, but no water damage."

There was silence as all three of them examined the journals. The wind whipped through the trees, and the creaking of the branches filled the silence.

"Well, my dear," said Mr. Whitshaw. "It seems that Janet's information was correct. You must read them and see what they contain. Would you like to read by the fire in the library?"

Amrita turned her face, glancing into the little schoolhouse that Janet built, where she might even have been teaching classes in her own time as she, Mr. Whitshaw, and the mason simultaneously discussed their find. "Would you mind if I stay in the schoolhouse a while? To take a look? Then I'll come to the library before I return."

"Of course. It's a fine day."

"I should gather my tools. You can call me tomorrow and I can return to secure the foundation stone back in its place," said the mason. Amrita shook his hand and thanked him. Mr. Whitshaw left her the keys and asked her to lock up when she was finished, before the two men walked to the manor house together.

Amrita took deep breaths and went to the teacher's desk, slowly sinking into the rigid wooden chair. Sunlight streamed through the window, warming her shoulders and hair. Her fingers still trembled as she placed the diaries down on the desk. As she lifted the first to examine its pages, an envelope slipped out and fluttered to the desk.

Amrita gasped. Her name was scrawled prominently across the envelope. After glancing around the room, she turned back to the envelope and gently slit it open. Her heart beat faster as she slid the letter out to see familiar handwriting.

Dear Amrita,

I hardly know where to begin. I am writing you only a few months after leaving you in your—my old—world. Yet here, ten years have passed. I am thirty-four years old, with four beautiful children and a fifth on the way. Can you believe it? I'd never even thought about having children back in our world. It seemed so far in the future, and now I will soon be the mother of five.

I never imagined I would say this to anyone, but I will be eternally grateful to you for clobbering me over the head.

My life here is a happy one. I was right to return, for Sir Edward and I are something I've never believed in: soul mates. I cannot imagine life without him. He is the ideal husband, and father, and brother, and friend, and companion. All those aspects of him I would have missed had I remained in my world.

With my father and Malcolm, I knew only selfishness and deception. Edward has taught me what true love is, and I long to pass these own lessons on to our children. Emma has become a sister to me, and we spend much time with Emma, Charles and their children. They live on the neighboring manor. Charles' aunt left the property to him in her will. Married to Charles, Emma has flourished, and her art abilities have far surpassed mine. She paints, and has completed a lovely portrait of our family. Charles and Emma now send the children of their tenant farmers to Helmsley Manor School, learning alongside our own children. As word spreads, other progressive landowners have asked about our school. They think of replicating their own, which fills my heart with joy.

My first student, the young Italian, Guglielmo, is now a strapping man of twenty. Edward and I have sent him to Italy, to his native Tuscany, to study agricultural production, and he returned to teach Edward and the farmers. He assists Edward on the manor, and Edward is convinced he will one day be foreman of Helmsley Manor lands, should he wish to be. Edward is now speaking with former colleagues at Oxford to have Guglielmo admitted for his studies.

Edward and I have worked side-by-side improving the tenant homes and introducing bathhouses. The cholera is going to spread across England in less than a decade, and we must be prepared. I have spoken to our neighbors about our improvements. Edward tells me he can see them longing to flee when they notice me approach, ready to corner them at the local balls and church events. But my persistence has paid off; many of the neighboring manors have improved their housing and sanitation, and seen an overall improvement in the health and welfare of their workers. I pray we will be safe from the worst of the outbreak.

Our neighbors know about my love of architecture, and they often seek out my advice on projects. Edward supports me fully. He is proud to have a wife whose opinion is sought on domains usually reserved for men. He is always the first to examine my work, and continues to be my biggest supporter. Our oldest son, Alexander, sits beside me at my drafting table. He has an eye for architecture and a thirst to learn. I teach him, and I wonder if he will choose this course of study.

My life is narrower in some respects. Aside from a honeymoon trip to Italy, and occasional journeys to London—and twice to Paris—(oh là là! Nineteenth-century Paris! I so wish I could share that experience with you), we are mostly in the vicinity of Helmsey Manor and Bath. Yes, my dear friend, we have been inhabiting the same room at Huntington House. Have you sensed me? I have tried hard to channel you and our classmates—but I do not feel the tingling any longer. Perhaps I no longer desire it.

For although my nineteenth-century life has a smaller scope, it suits me better. It is more rich and layered, more intellectually stimulating, filled with genuine love and friendship, and fewer distractions. I do not suppose that all would feel the same, and I am certain that others would lament the loss of modern technology and progress. But I realize only now that I never truly felt rooted before, never felt I truly belonged. Yet here I am content. I am home.

And you, my dear Amrita? I hope you are enjoying the Austen seminar I was unable to complete with you. I do hope these journals will add to your research. I thank you for your willingness to 'co-author' a thesis with me—and felt my co-authorship would make a good cover for any close questions about how you discovered the journals—but I do hope you will reuse my primary sources for your own future publications. I know your interest in family dynamics in the 1800s, and I have done my best to record customs, traditions, and popular thinking on the topic in the hopes it might be useful to you. I do not doubt you will be a brilliant scholar and professor, and will add much to modern-day knowledge about life in the nineteenth century. It warms my heart to know that interest in the lives we all lead now will be studied by you and your students, two hundred years later.

For the past is not merely faded words on brittle, yellowed paper. I know that now.

Judge us kindly, for we live based on the knowledge available to us during our lifetime, just as I hope scholars will judge all of you kindly two hundred years hence.

My dearest friend, my husband is urging me to hurry. We are to visit Emma, Charles and their family, and I long for an afternoon of chatting with dear family and friends, with our children playing hide-and-seek in their grand manor home. Who knew I was such an eager homebody? But with my dear husband at my side, surrounded by my family and friends, there is nowhere else I long to be.

I wish you every happiness in the world, Amrita, a long life filled with career success, health, family, dear friends, and, eventually, a loving and supportive partner on your journey. I think of you often, and consider myself lucky to have become your friend.

With much love,
Jane(t)

Amrita startled at the sound of a crow. She took a deep breath and looked out of the window, admiring the bright sunlight filtering through. With a smile, she slipped the letter into the inside pocket of her jacket. She opened the journal to its first entry.

27 March 1814

I have returned to Helmsley Manor after a long journey, following the unfortunate incident at the Harvest Ball last October. Edward surprised me with his proposal, and now I am hard at work with my dear friend Emma—about to become my sister—as we plan our double wedding at Helmsley Manor. How much work there is to do planning the ceremony with the household staff. But every day is a joy, and I have never seen Emma happier.

Edward, Emma, Charles and I spend each evening together in the library, reading Byron and Keats and Austen and Radcliff, and enjoying one another's company.

I cannot help but marvel at my good fortune, in having safely returned from my long journey, all thanks to a dear friend who sent me firmly on my path. For I know I have returned to exactly where I belong, and that certainty fills my heart with hope and optimism for the years that, God willing, await me.

Amrita looked once more out the window, at the trees swaying in the light breeze. She smiled at the thought of being immortalized in a nineteenth-century journal. Turning back to the familiar writing, Amrita continued reading.

The roaring fire warmed her, for the wind had grown biting as the day wore on and the sun slipped low in the late afternoon sky. Amrita gratefully accepted the tea Mr. Whitshaw offered, sipping it and feeling the steam tickle her cheeks. She cupped the porcelain in her hands to warm her fingers. Her heart beat erratically, still stunned by all the revelations.

Mr. Whitshaw settled in the armchair next to hers. "Was your discovery what you'd hoped for?" His eyes sparkled.

"Ever so much more than I'd hoped for. I've only read a small part of the diaries, but they're a treasure trove of information. Hardly anything escaped Lady Jane's notice: education, childrearing, social customs, health and sanitation, immigration, the workings of a grand manor, the lives of the tenant farmers, politics, art and literature. And, of course, architecture." She took a deep breath. "I hardly know where to begin."

"It sounds like a pleasant conundrum." He sipped his tea. "The burden of having *too much* information in a discovered journal. Almost as if she left them for a future scholar to stumble upon ..."

Her heart thumped in her chest. She knew these would be heady days, with little sleep and long stretches of caffeine-fueled writing binges. "There was one thing that was odd. She mentions a vault underneath the library, with a secret staircase hidden behind the Tiepolo. I assumed it was some kind of Gothic-novel-inspired tale."

Mr. Whitshaw's teacup slipped from his fingers, crashing to the floor. The rose-patterned ceramic shattered and tea pooled dangerously close to his feet.

Amrita jumped up, gathering napkins from the tea tray and mopping up the spill. "Mr. Whitshaw, are you alright?"

"Leave that." His voice had an uncharacteristic harsh edge to it. "Please find the page. What *exactly* does it say?"

`The urgency in his eyes startled Amrita, and she left the sopping napkins covering the spill and returned to her seat. Taking the first journal from her bag, she flipped through the pages. "Yes, here it is. It's odd, because otherwise, she's describing a trip they took to Bath, and their stay at Huntington House. At the end of the entry is a hastily scribbled line. Here. 'Do not overlook the library vault, whose secret passageway begins beneath the Tiepolo.'" She looked up and shook her head. "What is that supposed to mean? A note to herself? Maybe something she read in Radcliffe?"

Mr. Whitshaw ran his fingers through his hair, causing it to stand up on end more defiantly than before. "I know this will sound strange, but I believe this is a message to us." He jumped up and began fumbling through an incongruous, modern filing cabinet Amrita had not noticed earlier. "It must be here ..."

"What must be there?"

"Ah!" A yell of triumph echoed throughout the library. "Thank goodness." He strode back to his seat, oblivious as he sloshed through the spilled tea and crunched the broken porcelain of his tea up beneath his shoes. "The letter from the solicitor. The instructions from Lady Jane Huntington."
"The instructions about the return of the artwork and her desire to open this as a museum?"

"Yes, yes," said Mr. Whitshaw impatiently. "But there was one curious line. Almost as if it were in code. Ah, here it is. 'Look to Tiepolo's Daphne. If dark blue waves were to carry her eastward, observe the spot the wave's crest would reach. Search for the secret handle that will unlock the vault.'"

Amrita caught her breath. "You received that from the solicitor?"

"Yes. He did not know what to make of it either. There were no additional instructions, and I did not understand the reference to the dark blue waves."

"Byron," whispered Amrita.

"Pardon?"

Amrita took a deep breath. "Byron's *Childe Harold's Pilgrimage*. The dark blue waves of the Mediterranean that carried Byron to adventures in distant lands. Tell me, what are the average height of waves in the open sea?" She strode to the mantelpiece, studying the wall above it.

"I ... uh ... I'm not quite sure. Maybe moderate waves reach one to two meters?"

"And which direction is north in this house?" said Amrita, observing the spot where the Tiepolo once hung.

"Beyond the mantelpiece is due north. What are you getting at?"

Amrita spun on her heel and looked into his eyes. "Do you have a ladder, Mr. Whitshaw?"

He looked at her with an expression of utter confusion.

Amrita took a deep breath. "I'm guessing here, but I think these are deliberate clues. I know the painting well from Huntington House. If the painting were hanging here, Daphne would be right in this segment of the canvas." She indicated a spot with her hand. "The dark blue waves carrying Daphne eastward would move in this direction. " She swept her hand upward to the right. "I want to look up a meter or two above this height, along the wall."

Mr. Whitshaw stood in silence, stroking his chin. "Yes, of course. A ladder," he mumbled, as if breaking out of a trance. "One moment."

"This is insane," said Amrita out loud in the empty library. "We'll take a look, and then I'll head home."

When Mr. Whitshaw returned with the ladder, he set it up where Amrita had indicated. "Shall I?"

"It's fine. I can go, as long as you hold the ladder." Gingerly, she crept up the rungs, careful not to look down. Amrita was scared of heights, but her mounting excitement helped her to ignore the panic she often felt when looking down. She reached the top and looked straight ahead at the wall as her right hand rubbed the length of the stone. The ancient fireplace was solid and smooth. She didn't know exactly what she was looking for, and her hand slid over the stone without noticing anything beyond the ordinary.

"Did you find anything?"

"No." She stretched her hand as high as it would go. She felt a groove in the stone. "Wait. I think something feels different here." She rubbed her fingers against the groove until she felt cool metal beneath her fingertips. Even up on the high ladder, it was well hidden. "Mr. Whitshaw," Her voice shook with excitement, "it's a metal lever."

"Oh my." He clapped his hands together. "Are you sure, my dear?"

Amrita took a deep breath. "There's only one way to find out." She pulled with all her strength, but the lever did not budge. "Do you think it still works after all these years? Might it have rusted?"

"Here? Protected in the library? I don't think so. Try again!"

Amrita grasped the metal once more and pulled as hard as she could. This time, she felt the metal give way. "It's moving!" She felt the ladder jolt slightly and scrambled down the rungs. Her heart pounded, thinking about the fall she'd narrowly missed. But when she reached the bottom rung, she noticed a slight crack in the hearth wall. "It can't be!"

"What?"

"Don't you see it? The wall moved." She hastily pushed the ladder aside. Grasping the edge of the stone, she pushed the opening wider. The entire fireplace wall groaned as it opened, a clever facade. Her eyes opened wide as she turned back to Mr. Whitshaw. "It's a secret passageway!"

"My heavens. The messages were correct."

They both peered down to the staircase at the shadows that yawned beyond.

"It will be pitch black. I'll fetch lights."

Mr. Whitshaw was gone in the blink of an eye, and Amrita stood transfixed. "Janet," she whispered into the gaping darkness. "What are you up to?"

He returned with an oil lamp and a flashlight. "Come on."

"Down there? In the dark?"

"Where else? Aren't you curious?"

"Yeah, but I'm also scared of rats." She took a deep breath. "Ugh, okay."

They crept down the stone staircase. At the bottom, they stood on a solid stone floor. The only light entering was from the secret doorway they'd opened. Shining their light on the walls, they saw it was a circular vault, windowless and with no other entry point. Amrita brought her glow of light lower and gasped as she saw the objects stacked along the floor and against the walls. Forgetting her fear of rats, she stepped over to one and unwrapped the cloths shrouding it.

"Mr. Whitshaw. It's a painting!"

He stopped closer with his oil lamp, casting a circle of light on the canvas. "Not just any painting. I think it's a Gainsborough." He began to unwrap another. "We'll have to get experts in, but I think this is another Tieopolo."

Even in the darkness of the room, Amrita could see the tears spilling from his eyes.

"Help me," he whispered. "Help me to carry these upstairs where we can examine them better in the light."

Forty minutes later, both Amrita and Mr. Whitshaw sat in the library, staring in stunned silence at the thirty paintings that lay scattered across the room, propped haphazardly against chairs and bookshelves. The library was a riot of colorful oil paints and intricate, golden frames.

Mr. Whitshaw looked dazed. "Each and every one by a famous artist. Tiepolo, Tiziano, El Greco, Gainsborough, Tintoretto, Giorgone, Turner, Poussin ... a Caravaggio, for crying out loud! Paintings thought to be lost forever, and they've been here all along. In a secret vault." His voice was an emotional whisper. "Do you know what this means, Amrita?"

"That Helmsley Manor will have an impressive art gallery of the highest level."

"Only a year ago, we worried about Helmsley Manor's fate—that it might have to be turned into a hotel or luxury apartments. Now, with this discovery, and the money Janet has left to us, we have an operating budget, a sizeable gallery, money for needed repairs. Helmsley Manor will be filled with visitors once again. As the Huntingtons would have wanted."

"Thanks to Janet and Lady Jane," whispered Amrita. She stood and moved to the enormous canvas that stood beside the fireplace. "This is the only painting by an artist who is not of world-renown, yet it is my favorite. There is something in the journals that leads me to believe it may have been painted by Lady Jane's sister-in-law, Emma Bentley. Sir Edward's sister."

She registered Mr. Whitshaw's surprise, then looked once again into the eyes of Lady Jane, surrounded by her family. She smiled as she gazed upon Janet's beautiful face, regal and elegant, peering out at her. She wore an Empire-waisted white muslin gown, with a light blue, fitted pelisse studded with crystals. Her hair was piled high on her head, falling in soft curls around her face. Tiny flowers were woven into the intricate strands. Her face glowed with happiness, a sparkle animated her eyes. Beside her stood Sir Edward, tall, and proud and handsome, an arm resting gently, almost possessively, on her elbow. He wore breeches and a fitted blue coat, and although his look was serious, Amrita could detect a tenderness in it, too. He was a different man from the one who hung on the stairwell in Huntington Manor. He and his wife looked perfect together. Gathered around them were their children, blond-haired Alexander and Elizabeth. Little Robert, with his dark curls, a spray of freckles across his nose and a mischievous look in his eyes, clung to Janet's skirts, and baby Amrita rested in Janet's arms, one chubby hand pressed to her chest. The sunlight shone down upon them and Amrita could almost feel its warmth, beckoning her into the canvas and among the lives of this happy family.

Mr. Whitshaw crossed the room to stand beside her. "You're certain the baby is named Amrita, like you? You read it correctly in the journals? How unusual to have given a child an Indian name at the time."

Amrita smiled. "I gather Lady Jane was an unusual woman."

"I believe you're right. Are you certain you can't stay? There are so many rooms. I can make one up for you. The art historians are arriving tomorrow from the University of Bath. I'm sure you'll want to be here to have them confirm our suspicions about the paintings."

Amrita turned from the painting to face him. "I'll return tomorrow with Mr. Perry. He promised to drive me back. He's so excited to hear about the journal and to see the paintings tomorrow."

"Of course, my dear. In the excitement about the paintings, I'd almost forgotten. You'll want to review the journal entries."

"Yes, I will." *Maybe it will help me make sense of this odd day. And I need to talk things over with Mr. Perry. He's waiting for me at The Circus. I need to talk to someone who knows the whole story.*

"I will walk you out to the car, my dear." His cellphone rang and he looked down at the screen. "This is the head of the art history department. I'll have to take it. Will you wait one moment?"

Amrita nodded absently and Mr. Whitshaw left the room. Amrita turned her full attention back to the portrait of Janet and her nineteenth-century family. Surely those who knew Janet and saw the portrait would wonder, but they would probably only enthuse about the amazing similarity. After all, it wasn't logical. Even to her.

She gazed into her old friend's eyes. "I'm happy for you."

The rosy face stared back at her from the flat canvas. As she examined the familiar contours of Lady Jane's face, Amrita felt a strange sensation, a slight dizziness, and a pins-and-needles feeling that spread across her arms and legs. She heard the keys of a distant piano, *Voi che sapete*. She closed her eyes to steady herself, but when she opened them, the painting was an indistinguishable palette of peaches, and pinks, and blues, and greens. Her vision grew blurry as the tingling grew stronger.

"Amrita, my dear. Are you unwell?"

She turned to the voice at the doorway. Mr. Whitshaw stood there, a look of concern marring his gentle face. She took a deep breath. The tingling disappeared as quickly as it had come.

"I'm fine, I'm fine." She willed her voice to sound normal. "Only daydreaming. I think I need to get home and rest after an emotional day."

He smiled and beckoned to her. Amrita walked towards him, turning one last time to observe the painting before she reached the threshold. Janet's smile seemed to bid her a temporary farewell as Amrita left Helmsley Manor.

Acknowledgements

As any writer understands, I am eternally grateful to all those who have helped me – in ways small and large – as I was writing this novel.

I workshopped this novel through Critique Circle and benefited from reviews, comments and suggestions for improvement from so many incredible critique partners. Some joined for a few chapters, others provided valuable critiques and advice throughout the entire process. Special thanks to Grace Tierney, NJ Layouni, Ashlinn Craven and Chantelle Rhondeau who weighed in throughout the entire novel and whose suggestions greatly improved this work.

To the wonderful Women's Fiction Writers Association – for their support, webinars, craft classes, online writing spaces and welcoming, talented authors.

To my editor, Valerie Valentine. This is the second novel we've worked on together and I am so grateful for your help in improving my work, and for your thoughtful readers' notes. Thank you, too, for your much appreciated enthusiasm for my story (and for Jane Austen!) Special thanks to Roxana Coumans for her excellent (and rapid) proofreading services.

This is also the second time I work on cover design and book formatting with the über talented Joanne Morgante and Roberto Magini of Maxtudio. Thanks for always effortlessly transforming my art-challenged visions into stunning graphic reality. Grazie!

To all the closet Jane Austen fans out there. Whether it's in trains, planes, buses or chatting during breaks at business meetings, when mention is made of enjoying nineteenth-century English literature, conversation inevitably turns to mutual admiration for Jane Austen. These conversations are always such a pleasure.

And, most importantly, to my readers. Thank you so much for reading my stories and supporting my work. Like all authors, reviews mean a lot to me. If you enjoy this novel, I would be deeply grateful if you would take the time to review on platforms like Goodreads, Amazon and Kobo. Reviews help other readers to discover my work, and I'm extremely appreciative for all your feedback. Reviews do not need to be long – even a couple of lines is incredibly helpful! Thank you!

Finally, last but certainly not least, undying thanks to Francesco, Alessandro and Nicolò, for your constant support.

About the author

KIMBERLY SULLIVAN grew up in the suburbs of Boston and in Saratoga Springs, New York, although she now calls the Harlem neighborhood of New York City home when she's back in the US. She studied political science and history at Cornell University and earned her MBA, with a concentration in strategy and marketing, from Bocconi University in Milan.

Afflicted with a severe case of Wanderlust, she worked in journalism and government in the US, Czech Republic and Austria, before settling down in Rome, where she works in international development, and writes fiction any chance she gets.

She is a member of the Women's Fiction Writers Association and The Historical Novel Society. She has published several short stories and two novels: *Three Coins* and *Dark Blue Waves*.

After years spent living in Italy with her Italian husband and sons, she's fluent in speaking with her hands, and she loves setting her stories in her beautiful, adoptive country.

kimberlysullivanauthor.com
Twitter: @kimberlyinrome
Instagram: kimberlyinrome

Printed in Great Britain
by Amazon